INTO
THE RIFT

Also by Clay Harmon

The Rift Walker Series
Flames of Mira

INTO
THE RIFT

CLAY HARMON

SOLARIS

First published 2024 by Solaris
an imprint of Rebellion Publishing Ltd,
Riverside House, Osney Mead,
Oxford, OX2 0ES, UK

www.solarisbooks.com

ISBN: 978-1-78618-864-9

10 9 8 7 6 5 4 3 2 1

A CIP catalogue record for this book is available from the
British Library.

Designed & typeset by Rebellion Publishing

Printed in Denmark

To Dad. I can't imagine who I would have become without you, and I never want to.

RA-THUZAN
REYKYA NIGHTWATER'S EDITION 5

BELONGS TO GETH
(REPLACE WITH 6TH EDITION ASAP)

✗ Capital   🌋 Inactive Volcano

‑‑‑ The Granite Road   🌋 Active Volcano

THE FIREMAW

WATER E

[UNEXPLORED REGION]

HOW TO CHANGE???

THE BLACK DEPTHS

KARATOA

YSSAL EAK

AD S

ASSHOLES

YAROKLY

NO MAN'S LAND. NO COUNTRY WANTS TO CLAIM LAND ANYWHERE NEAR BLACK DEPTHS

THE FAR EASTERN BRINK

SOM'ABAST

RAVADA

XERIV

SULIAN DAW

THE BURNING MOUNTAINS

SUGAR MUSHROOMS! SHIRRALLAH WILL LOVE!

COFFEE TO DIE FOR! ANNIVERSARY GIFT FOR SHIRALLAH?

ARE THEY REALLY BURNING? ANOTHER EXPLANATION?

CALLO

RONA

RUMORS OF NEW TYPE OF ELEMENTAL WORTH LOOKING INTO?

CLAIMS OF LIVING ABOVE GROUND. AFTER WORK WITH DARKWATER - INFILTRATE RONAN CULTURE, LEARN SECRETS

T TECTONIC PLATES. ALWAYS COLLAPSING R CARTOGRAPHERS AY THROUGH

THE EVENTS OF FLAMES OF MIRA

Manservant JAKAR ET HOSSA enforces the rule of Magnate SORRELO ADRIANN in the subterranean city of Augustin, hunting down members of the reformer movement who threaten Sorrelo's rule. In secret, Jakar is one of Mira's most powerful elementals, bound to six elements when most elementals are only bound to one, but his power comes at a price. He is bound to Sorrelo Adriann by magic that will kill him if he disobeys any of Sorrelo's commands, and his elemental powers will fade if he does not stay close to his master.

Soon, the inevitable happens—Sorrelo Adriann is overthrown and Jakar is forced to flee into the planet's crust alongside Sorrelo and his two children, EMIL and SARA ADRIANN, as well as the master smith of the Foundry, MATEO.

The Adrianns cannot make a plea to the man who rules above Sorrelo and Mira's five other territories, an immortal man known simply as the SOVEREIGN, to help them retake Augustin. The Sovereign has retreated from the public eye over the years to prepare his son, the child prince BILAL, to transition as Mira's new Sovereign, and appears to have temporarily lost interest in governing his own country. The

Adrianns can't request help from the Sovereign's invincible primordia, either—elementals who enforce the Sovereign's rule—as each one is more mentally unstable than the last. They choose to head for the neighboring territory of Callo, where Sorrelo's brother, LUCAS ADRIANN, serves as righthand man to Callo's magnate. With Callo's army, they might have a chance to reclaim the Augustin throne.

After a confrontation with Master Smith Mateo, Jakar reluctantly admits the truth of where he came from—he was turned into an elemental in his native country of Som Abast by a cult called the Ebonrock. The Ebonrock kidnap children and turn them into powerful elementals to help them find the lost gods they worship, the Great Ones, but two years ago, the Adrianns stole him from Som Abast.

On the trip to find Sorrelo's brother, tragedy strikes—Sorrelo is killed, and Jakar is now freed from the magic that had bound him to his former master. The power has passed down to Sorrelo's children, but none of them know how to wield the magic, and Jakar is faced with a choice: escape before they can learn how to force his obedience or stay and help them retake Augustin. He has grown to care dearly for Sorrelo's children—Emil, especially, who has been nothing but kind to him and whom Jakar believes would rule Augustin as a kind and just leader. Jakar chooses to stay so that he can help Emil bring permanent peace to Augustin.

Sara Adriann solves the puzzle behind the magic that binds Jakar to the Adrianns. A flesh sacrifice is required to complete the binding, and so she carves into her flesh the command word that Sorrelo once used to command Jakar, the word *Ig*. Jakar is now bound to Sara, but he is unable to tell Emil, as Sara has commanded him into secrecy.

Emil decides they must find his and Sara's youngest sibling, EFADORA ADRIANN, who is living abroad in the territory of Manasus, and so the group splits up. Emil and Mateo head to Manasus to find Efadora while Jakar and Sara continue on their trek to Lucas Adriann in Callo. Jakar soon realizes that his fears of serving under Sara are unfounded—she is strong yet sympathetic, and she shows little interest in using the magic that binds him to her commands. Jakar finds himself developing feelings for her.

Efadora Adriann, who lives as a ward to the magnate of Manasus, learns that bounty hunters are looking for her family. Her friends in the local gang betray her to cash in on the bounty, but Emil and Mateo arrive in time to stop them. Efadora, now heartbroken, swears off ever having friends again.

Meanwhile, Jakar and Sara are faced with betrayals of their own. Lucas Adriann expresses no interest in helping his family retake Augustin, as he knows Jakar is secretly one of Mira's most powerful elementals and wants to harness that power for his own. Jakar and Sara kill Lucas as well as Callo's magnate during their escape, and soon they are without a plan or hope of retaking Augustin.

Jakar refuses to give up hope, as he is starting to fall in love with Sara and doesn't want to see the Adrianns fail. Sara recruits the help of a longtime smuggling friend, a vile man named RODI KANNA, who has vast connections among the sellswords of the territory, and with his help, Sara proposes to several bands of mercenaries to form an army and help her retake Augustin. With nothing to pay them with, she proposes they take their fill from the Granite Road instead, Mira's primary trade route, on their march to Augustin. Jakar opposes the plan, knowing a mercenary army won't restrain themselves—many innocent people will die on the Granite Road if the army is allowed to march south.

Jakar now faces the choice to help the Adrianns retake Augustin or stop Sara's army. He attempts to sabotage the plan by assassinating Rodi, but Sara stops him, using the magic that binds them together for the first time since binding Jakar to her. By cowing Jakar, she reveals his elemental power to the mercenary army, too, and emboldened by the knowledge that Sara has an enslaved elemental to help them, the army eagerly takes to the Granite Road. During the march, Sara avoids Jakar, only lingering around long enough to ensure Jakar's elemental powers don't fade. Their relationship continues to deteriorate as people along the Granite Road start to die.

Emil, Mateo, and Efadora, who have been waiting for word from Sara, receive a secret message from Jakar pleading for them to stop her. Efadora and Emil remain in denial over their sister's actions, but go after the mercenary army, hoping to catch Sara before she reaches Augustin. On the road they encounter two of the Sovereign's deranged primordia, and the group barely escapes with their lives. Efadora learns that all six of Mira's primordia are bound to the Sovereign by the same magic that binds Jakar to the Adrianns.

On the Granite Road, Jakar's predictions come true. Sara is unable to stop her own army from killing more and more innocents, and Jakar continues sabotaging Sara's efforts. Sara, in a moment of rage, puts Rodi in charge of Jakar, magically commanding Jakar to listen to Rodi as if the commands came from her. Rodi takes his revenge by forcing Jakar to do the unthinkable. The mercenary army watches as Jakar executes every single person in the town of Cragreach.

When the mercenary army reaches Augustin, Jakar is a shadow of who he once was, traumatized by Cragreach. With help from the smiths of the Foundry, Sara overthrows those who deposed her family and becoming Augustin's interim magnate. Unable to cope with the pain he has caused, Jakar resolves to end his life, but a young smith named ESTER convinces him to try one last time to stop Sara. Rumors of Cragreach have finally reached the Foundry, and Mateo has entered the city in secret to lead his smiths once more. Jakar realizes that if Mateo is in Augustin then Emil is, too, and he becomes desperate to reunite with the one person he cares about most in the world, put an end to Sara's rule, and dispel the mercenary army that now prowls the city streets.

Mateo and the smiths, abhorred that they helped a mercenary army guilty of war crimes, are intent to stop them at all costs, and Sara commands Jakar to kill Mateo. Jakar refuses to obey the magic binding him to Sara, and the magic starts to torture him to death. Efadora and Emil realize Sara has completed the binding ritual that lets her command Jakar and see their sister for the monster she really is. Emil tries to stop Sara before her magic kills Jakar, and in the ensuing fight, Rodi kills Emil. Efadora, enraged that Sara would allow her mercenaries to kill their brother, is captured by her sister.

A tenuous peace falls over the city as the audencia—a council of judges who lead Augustin alongside the ruling magnate—demand retribution for what occurred on the Granite Road. Jakar and Rodi are put on trial, and Rodi tells Sara that if she allows him to be punished, the mercenary army will burn the city to the ground. The audencia calls for Jakar's head, not knowing that Sara and Rodi were the ones who had been pulling his strings all along, and Sara is tasked with executing Jakar.

When Sara stabs Jakar with her family's rhidium-lined Meteor Blade, it isn't Jakar who is destroyed but the magic binding them together. Jakar takes the blade and kills Rodi with it, starting a war in the city streets. He, alongside the smith Ester and her brother DAMEK, encounter the primordia NEKTARIOS, who has finally arrived in Augustin to cow the city into order and enforce the Sovereign's rule. Nektarios plans to find the Adriann family and kill them, starting with Efadora, and Jakar attacks him before Nektarios has a chance to hunt Efadora down. Despite the primordias' reputation for being unvincible, Jakar puzzles out their secret weakness, using clues he gathered during his years growing up with the cult that raised him. He paralyzes Nektarios using electricity and he, alongside Ester and Damek, manage the impossible. They kill a primordia for the first time since the Sovereign began his reign two-hundred years ago.

Jakar destroys the mercenary army, and with Sara deposed, Jakar and Efadora flee Augustin so they never have to see the woman who betrayed them both ever again. Jakar heads for Som Abast, hoping to find the elemental children he was raised with. Efadora asks him to let her come along, and Jakar agrees, unwilling to admit that he needs an Adriann at his side if he wants to retain his elemental powers and use them to stop the Ebonrock. Efadora doesn't tell him that she's figured out part of the magic that binds him to her family—that Ig is the word she must use to give him a command—but she doesn't yet know that a flesh sacrifice is required to complete the ritual. She has no interest in commanding Jakar, though. Where she once wanted to be ruthless and clever like Sara, she has now resolved to be better than that. To ignore the dark tendencies that come so easy to the Adriann family and be kind and strong like her brother Emil.

Unbeknownst to them, Sara, who awaits trial in Augustin, is found by the primordia Aronidus, who is intent on finding the Ebonrock cult so that he might finally break the magic that has forced him and the other primordia to serve the Sovereign for centuries.

Now Jakar and Efadora head for the distant country of Som Abast, intent on saving Jakar's childhood friends from the Ebonrock cult, who force their slaves to toil in the Black Depths in search of the lost gods they worship, ancient beings known only as the Great Ones…

PART 1

Chapter 1—Jakar

I scrabbled at the wall of rubble, praying to Fheldspra or Fedsprig or whichever deity felt like listening that the tunnel to my homeland wasn't blocked off, but with every rock I removed, there was another waiting behind it.

"We should've known this might happen," Efadora said.

I didn't answer, returning to my fox Dionys so I could rummage through the saddlebag on his flank and rip out the map we'd purchased in Berta. Efadora added, "This is pretty bad, isn't it?"

Tunnels collapsed all the time in Mira, but there was no circumventing the Rift—a boundary that separated the country of Mira from the rest of the world, and one we needed to cross if I wanted us to reach Som Abast, my city of birth. My path to revenge, to kill the cultists who raised me, wasn't quite so straight anymore. "There's a town south of here that might know of a new route," I said as I ran my finger along the map. "Port Lora."

"I know that name," Efadora said. "It's a trading post. Father always complained about how Augustin imports would go missing there. People go missing too, I've heard."

A trading post on the edge of the Rift would likely know of a way through. "If we go there, should we be worried?"

"If I was a tax collector? Sure. They're the ones with targets painted on their backs. People who seem too put together, too. *And* those who aren't put together enough to defend themselves." She looked me up and down, and I could see what she was thinking. The bandages covering my burned arms didn't make for a good case. "I'm sure we can manage to blend in. Maybe."

I leaned against Dionys and took to examining the map for anywhere that could promise a way through the Rift that wasn't Port Lora. Efadora came to my side to help, and an awkward silence filled the gap as we studied the map. It had been several weeks since we'd left Augustin together and almost a month with just the two of us, but we still hadn't figured out companionable silences. Or I hadn't, at least. Too much baggage between her family and me, not to mention I didn't have much in common with an aristocratic teenager.

I folded the map and stuffed it in the saddlebag. "Port Lora's where we have to go. Map says there's a tunnel leading there about ten miles back."

Efadora groaned and buried her face in the neck of her mount, Citra. The fox reached back and nibbled the bottom of her shirt. "Too many setbacks," she said, her voice muffled. "We won't have enough food to go all the way to Sulian Daw. We don't have any money, either."

"We'll figure it out." Sometimes it took months to locate a new route through the Rift, but if that's how long it took, then that's how long it took. I'd find the people who'd enslaved Quin and the others I grew up with, even if it took years. I gave Efadora a sidelong glance and wondered how long she was willing to stick around. She insisted she had no home to return to, that she wanted to see more of the world by my side, but surely she would tire of my company eventually. I wasn't exactly a pleasant person to be around. Not since the events her sister had put me through.

Efadora mounted Citra and glared at the wall of rubble like she was trying to blast her way through with her resentment, and guilt ate at the pit of my stomach. She didn't know the real reason I'd brought her along—that if we parted ways, my

18

elemental powers would fade. As a flesh bound, I had to remain in the presence of an Adriann if I wanted to continue using my powers, thanks to Sorrelo forever binding me to his children upon his passing. She thought I'd allowed her to come out of lingering loyalty to her brother, or because I trusted her. The former was true, but the latter... well, if she ever learned how to make the necessary sacrifice to complete my flesh binding and tie the two of us together, she would be able to control me with a Word. Trust would never be possible with that hanging over my head.

Footsteps crunched through moss coating the floor of the small cavern, and five men and women appeared from an alcove I hadn't noticed, one hidden in shadow. "Hello, friends," the lead man said. The flame of his torch reflected off the flash of his smile. Two more people appeared in the tunnel behind us and cut off our escape.

"You'd think all these bandits would've learned better by now," Efadora muttered.

"Any chance you'll let us go?" I called out to the lead man. "It's been a long journey and I'm tired."

The leader stopped a dozen feet short of us, and the woman flanking him squinted. "You a cripple or something?" she asked me.

I lifted my dirty, bandage-coated arms in front of me. "No. A leper. Caught the Salin Chill a few weeks ago and my dick fell off. Highly contagious."

Every male bandit stared at my crotch in horror. "He's bluffing," the leader said, but stepped back and nudged his female companion forward. "You first."

Efadora jumped off her mount and pulled me away from Dionys and Citra. She'd turn into a ball of fury if anything happened to our foxes. We moved to a better lit part of the cavern, between an amber geode and a bush with bulbs that glowed like lightning, putting us directly between the group of five and the two flanking us. I pulled my knife out of the sheath strapped across my chest and the sword from my scabbard. Shooting pain pulsed through the knuckles in my right hand, and my left wrist ached—both wounds from the battle of Augustin. Only luck had prevented my bones from rebreaking, traveling as hard as we had, but my injuries were certainly taking their time to heal, too, even after two months. I needed rest. I needed a week or two on the mend. But I was stubborn.

The woman stalked toward us as her friends fanned out. I dropped my weapons to my side, opening myself up when she came within striking range, and she took the opportunity, a glimmer of confusion in her eyes. She should've listened to that voice in her head. I dodged the steel as I felt the wavelengths of iron cut through the air, and the blade passed within inches of my cheek as my knife followed up on her back swing. My weapon pierced boiled leather, going deeper until it found the soft flesh of the woman's side.

Efadora reached for the ground. She let loose an ear-piercing whistle as she flung a handful of dirt at the closest man's face, and the bandit snarled in pain as he clawed at his eyes. She threw herself at him and sank her knife into his stomach, then ducked as he tried to grab her. He collapsed on the ground and didn't get back up. The others rushed us, but Efadora and I were already back to back, our month-long journey across Mira's territories having etched this song and dance into our bodies. We didn't know how to talk to each other, but we could do *this*. The leader swiped at me, but I parried, and he let out a frustrated yell as he tried to smash me in the head with the flaming torch in his other hand, but I caught it in my knife's guard, showering sparks onto my hair and bandages. I sliced upward and he tried to step away, but the tip of my sword cut into the inside of his arm.

The two men behind me who had been advancing on Efadora started screaming. Efadora still had a lot to learn with the sword, so found advantages in other ways—she must've thrown the fluorosulfuric acid bombs I'd cooked up for her last week. Efadora's footsteps echoed behind me as she ran at them, then there was the *ting* of metal on metal and the low gurgle of her blade sinking into their fleshy parts.

"Kill those pricks," the leader hissed at the remaining two as he retreated with a hand pressed against the cut on his inner arm, blood leaking through his fingers. They came at me with desperate energy, and I sidestepped one swing while blocking the other with the sword. Pain radiated through my knuckles and aggravated the burns under my bandages, and I almost failed to move away from my opponent's follow-up thrust. For a moment I thought one of them would land a hit on me, but a rock Efadora had thrown flew past my head, which bounced off one of the bandit's shoulders and gave me enough time to leave a deep gash in their neck. I felt the iron of the other bandit's blade arc toward me, and I blocked without looking, letting instinct guide me. My blade was hilt-deep in his side before he had another chance to strike.

I went on my guard at once, expecting the leader to come for us, but he was gone. The *slap* of his boots echoed across the cavern. "Citra!" Efadora yelled. The leader had mounted Efadora's fox, which yelped as the man dug his heels into her flanks. Efadora was already halfway to them before Citra bolted, but she wasn't fast enough. She'd jumped onto Dionys before I could do anything.

Both foxes and their riders disappeared down the tunnel, and I dropped my sword and ran after them, knife in hand. The old wound in my chest—the one from the meteor blade when Sara had tried to execute me—burned and the bones in my arms ached as I jogged through the winding tunnels. A man screamed in the distance. I reached a straight path and found the leader swinging his sword wildly to ward off Efadora as the stump of his other wrist drew lines on the ground, his chopped-off hand lying in the dirt. Past them, Citra and Dionys watched warily, Citra's mane slicked red.

"Efadora," I called out.

The bandit leader turned at the sound of my voice and the former princepa darted forward. "Fucker," she hissed, tackling him to the ground, her knife quickly finding the meat of his throat. He gurgled, pawing at the wound until he stilled, then she stabbed him three more times for good measure.

"He's dead," I said, frowning at the anger coursing through her.

"Yeah," she said, out of breath, and rolled off him. "I'm tired of these wolves climbing out of their dirty holes."

"I agree… it is getting old." I studied the bandit leader's blood staining Efadora's neck and earlobe, and couldn't help but think back on old memories. She had Emil's temper. Her brother had once stormed out of the inn on Dagir's Pass steaming with the blood of his enemies, the top of his ear missing and a world of hate in his eyes. It was a sobering thought.

The Adrianns had inherited bad blood from their father. I had to remind myself that it didn't define them, though, that Efadora strove to do right by the people she cared about, despite her temperament.

I only hoped she cared about the right people.

We made our way back to the cavern and the rest of the bodies, hoping to find things to sell. Those struck by Efadora's acid bombs smelled like chemicals and rancid flesh, the skin on their faces red and shiny. Neither they nor the other bodies had anything more than pocket lint and a few spare coins from a currency I didn't recognize.

"Look," Efadora said as she investigated the alcove the bandits had come out of. "There's a tunnel here."

We climbed onto our foxes and rode into the side tunnel, which was much deeper than I expected, and I struck flint to torch until light flared in the darkness. This tunnel wasn't on our map, which was a testament to just how shoddy maps could be if they weren't penned by a cartographer, and it made me think of Carina. I missed her and Meike's company dearly. Carina had done so well with Efadora, helping the girl cultivate an interest in cartography while providing a great distraction from the loss of Emil, and I'd found Meike's silent company and calm observations soothing. The two of them were probably in Manasus by now, apprising Magnate Bardera of the situation in Augustin. Based on what Meike had told me, Magnate Bardera was already seizing key mines from Radavich now that they were without a magnate after I'd killed their last one, and Bardera would likely find a way to take advantage of Augustin's problems next.

The situation in Mira would only grow worse over the coming months, but that was a problem for someone else. I had already washed my hands of Mira, the same as Efadora.

Darkness gave way to pyremoss, which crawled along the ceiling and filled the tunnel with warm light, and in the ambient glow I caught sight of a crate sticking out of a recess. The faint sound of rustling cloth and creaking leather reached us. The former princepa and I regarded each other, then dismounted and moved forward carefully, weapons drawn.

We found a young man somewhere between Efadora and Emil's age standing among a scattering of bedrolls and boxes, his short sword between us and him. He was slight, with hair cut close to his scalp. "Hello," he said, and offered a smile. The smile didn't seem forced, as though he was greeting us as old friends.

"Decided to sit this fight out?" I asked.

"I don't fight. I just watch the camp." He studied our blades. "You killed them, didn't you?"

"Good guess," Efadora said, taking a step forward, but the man put a hand up.

"Wait," he said quickly. "If you're here, it means you're headed to Port Lora. Let me take you there."

"I think we'll manage fine without you," I said.

"Whatever map you're using, it probably doesn't tell you that this tunnel will take you straight there. You won't have to backtrack. I promise." The young man swallowed hard. "You must be hungry too. My brother and his wife run a *bougera* in town. He'll give you all the free food you want."

The offer sent pangs through my stomach. It had been ages since I'd sunk my teeth into baked food. "What do you think?" I asked Efadora. Already a sour feeling was eating away at my insides from those bandits we'd killed, and I knew I would be in for a rough time later when I lay down to sleep. For months insomnia had dogged me, ever since I was forced to kill those innocent people on the Granite Road, and killing bandits, even in self-defense, took its toll. But I would kill more if it was necessary. Anything to find and save the other children I grew up with.

That said, I'd had my fill of death on this passing, and even though this kid was a bandit I wasn't sure if he deserved it. But if we let him go, it risked him finding more of his kind so he could hunt us down in revenge.

"It's a pretty gracious offer," Efadora said to the boy, "considering we killed your friends. I'd hate to escort you all the way to Port Lora only to knife you because you decided to double-cross us."

His seemingly genuine smile returned. "No double-cross. I swear. I'll even give you some advice as a gesture of goodwill. You're better off going back the way you came than finding a new way through the Rift, if that's where you're going. The collapse only happened a few weeks back, so it'll be a heap of time before the cartographers find a new way through. Happens every year or two. Just make sure my brother has a chance to fill your bags with enough meat pies to get you home on full stomachs."

"We're not turning around," I said. Resting in Port Lora had sounded fine and well, but not if it delayed us for months instead of weeks. Maybe my elemental power could guide us through, or perhaps it would just get us killed. Crossing the Rift involved countless mazes stretching dozens of miles.

Efadora and I took everything of value from the camp that could fit in our saddlebags, then the former princepa tied the boy's hands together before I helped him onto her fox. "I'm young, but I've killed more people than you've met in your life," she said as she rode behind him, her knife pressed to his back. "Don't push me."

"Port Lora's a port, if you didn't know. I've met a lot of people."

The boy cried out, and he shied away from her, rolling his shoulder where she had poked him. "Maybe I'm getting bored from all this traveling and I'll kill you for fun," she said.

The boy muttered in a language I didn't know before saying, "I'm sorry. I'll just stop talking."

As I watched her hold Citra's reins in one hand while she kept her knife near the boy's kidney with the other, a bad taste formed in my mouth. Her cavalier attitude toward our captive was too reminiscent of my years serving under her father, Sorrelo Adriann. Sorrelo would sometimes taunt me or look at me in disgust if I showed signs of disobeying. What would happen if Efadora ever learned how to use my flesh binding and I decided to disagree with her? It was an absurd thought for multiple reasons—for one, she had no way of knowing about the flesh sacrifice she would have to make that would allow her to control me with a Word, but I hadn't expected Sara to figure it out, either. And more importantly, Efadora wasn't the type. She hadn't once shown herself to be so cruel to me. But once upon a time I had laughed at the idea of Sara Adriann sinking so low, and it had ruined my life as a result.

Or maybe I was just oversensitive. I wasn't sure if I'd ever be able to look at Efadora without her family's sins hanging over her head. Maybe my scars were too many to let me see clearly.

The former princepa and I had traveled alone together for weeks now, but we still hadn't talked about Sara. Or about Emil. Or about most of the terrible things we'd left behind in Augustin.

Chasms still yawned between us.

"Quit squirming," Efadora said to the boy.

"This would be a lot easier if my hands were free."

"Just do what I say, or I start playing tic-tac-toe on your back, all right?"

"Efadora?" I said. "Let's take it easy."

She looked at me as if I'd spoken another language. "Huh?"

I thought about pushing the matter, but undermining Efadora in front of our captive didn't sound like a good idea, especially if we were going to let him go. Maybe revenge *was* on his mind, and he would see us as an easier target if he saw us arguing. I bit down on my lip and focused on the path ahead. "Never mind."

Chapter 2—Efadora

"WE ALMOST THERE?" I asked Torlo, punctuating the question by tapping his side with the flat of my blade as a reminder that he should keep himself honest.

"Quarter mile, tops," the bandit said.

Torlo seemed way too relaxed for someone whose friends had just been killed, which made my hackles rise—he was either overconfident, or he knew something. I didn't love the idea of leading a local at knifepoint into a town full of strangers, and it didn't help that we were in the eastern reaches of Byssa, at the edge of Mira, where opinions of Mirans liked to fester. Father once told me that the countries east of the Rift hated the Sovereign, and that the people of Mira got some of the flak as a result, and enough foreigners passed through the border here that their opinions rubbed off on the local Mirans. We were still in Mira, technically, but hailing from Augustin would only count against us now.

If we were smart, we'd throw Torlo down a ravine and slip into Port Lora with no one any the wiser, but for some reason, Jakar didn't want to kill the bandit.

"Probably for the best you killed them," Torlo said. "They hurt a lot of good people, I'm sure."

"And I'm sure you had *no* idea," I said. "If you think badmouthing your friends is going to impress us, you're wrong."

"I'm just thinking out loud," Torlo said, and let out a tired breath. "The boys weren't big on killing, then Kasonian took over and if there was ever anyone who'd get blood on their teeth, it was him. I only started running with them a week ago."

"You know what? I'm really sick of talking about bandits." Torlo represented everything I hated—ten thousand others just like him had burned half of Augustin's capital for a quick coin, all working under Sara's wing, and one of them had killed the kindest person I'd known. My brother was dead because of people like Torlo. Sure, Torlo hadn't joined any of the fighting, but Sara hadn't done much fighting either when her horde murdered their way through Augustin and killed Emil. Her support was what made it all possible, though. If you were complicit, you were dead.

Once again, I shoved away thoughts of my sister. Someone who thought themselves wise once said that time healed all wounds, but that wasn't true. If I ever saw Sara again, I would end her.

The tunnel turned onto a ridge overlooking a massive cavern. "Here we are," Torlo said.

Wooden bridges linked together dozens of tall, uneven pillars sprinkled throughout the cavern, rising out of a floor several dozen feet down. I leaned over my saddle and saw glossy black water rippling far below, covering the whole of the cavern floor, reflecting the light of a ceiling aflame with millions of roosting fireflies. The wooden bridges before us zigzagged to the cavern's center where a squat pillar supported the city of Port Lora. The place crawled with buildings and people like a mound of fire ants, and a set of spiral stairs led from the city to a series of docks floating on the waters below. We stepped onto the first bridge, its rockwood planks sturdy enough to support a whole caravan.

"The lake used to sit about ten feet under these bridges," Torlo said. "The quake changed all that. Nearly ruptured my eardrums when the channels drained."

We passed traders and convoys leaving town, most of whom gave Torlo and me an odd look, and I tried to keep my knife hidden. Leather creaked as I leaned to get a good look at the pulley system moving goods from the city to the docks—they reminded me of Augustin, but these ones seemed frailer, the docks on the water haphazardly built. "If this place is a port, who do they trade with?" I asked.

"These channels skirt the Rift for a hundred miles, and you've got ports north of here that go all the way to the edge of the Dead Bogs. Then you've got ports to the south where the Skorpian Sea starts. Port Lora does most of its trade with Xeriv, Karatoa, and some other countries east of the Rift. Or did. Always a rough transition when Mira's cut off from the east."

"There was always only one way through the Rift?" Jakar asked.

"Before the last quake? Sure was. It's a rare thing to find a tunnel unbroken from one side to the other. Quakes collapse old tunnels and reveal new ones, so maybe we'll get lucky and find more'n one way through the Rift this time around. Either way, it'll take time."

Again, I could feel the eyes of the locals raking us over. "Are the guards going to give us trouble?" I asked.

Torlo snorted. "Nah. The guards don't care who passes through here. Our mayordomo even had a good long laugh when she got word all the way from Saracosta that we were supposed to start writing down the comings and goings of newcomers in our logbooks—you know, after Augustin's capital almost burned down and all that. Or so I heard. The people here prefer to move about unseen and the guards know it. You'll make it in without a problem."

What about making it out? "Thanks for the reassurance."

He adjusted his wrists, now red from the rope. "Happy to help."

The guard post on the edge of the plateau stood empty, and every single person beyond moved like they were late for an appointment. The swarm made me appreciate Citra all the more—if I were forced to walk through this chaos being as short as I was, I'd be stepping on toes out of frustration within minutes.

"Smell that?" Torlo asked after he stopped us in front of a shop in a quieter part of town. "I promised you food, now prepare to be blown out of the water."

We slid off our mounts and tied them off at the hitching post. Torlo angled his bound hands toward me, and I hesitated. It had to come to this eventually, I supposed, and he'd behaved extraordinarily well considering we'd killed his friends. He rubbed his wrists after I sliced the rope, hitting me with the warmest of smiles. "C'mon," he said.

The inside of the bakery transported me back to when I was eight years old again visiting my favorite padanaria with Mother, the aroma of spice and meat intermingling with the smell of sugar and flour, setting my mouth a-tingle. A couple worked behind the counter, the man kneading dough and the woman carrying an armful of tindermoss. "Hi, Juromal," Torlo said. "If you gave these two as many meat pies as they can carry, you'd be doing me a *real* big favor."

Juromal stopped his kneading. "Are you high?"

"Your brother promised it to us," I said.

"Why would he do that?"

"They saved my life," Torlo said, forcing a smile and avoiding eye contact with his brother.

"His gang tried to murder us and take our stuff," I said. "We saved his life because we decided not to take it."

Juromal looked at Torlo, slack-jawed, before bringing his attention to us. Scarlet red filled his cheeks. "I'm so, so sorry," he said. "My brother was taught better than that. Of course we'll give you what he promised."

Juromal, in his barely contained fury, packed up the food, apparently ready to do to his younger brother what we had only threatened. I had to hand it to Torlo—I'd entered Port Lora half-expecting an ambush by more of his accomplices, but he had kept his word.

"Again, I'm sorry." Juromal handed us two food-stuffed bags bursting at the seams. He had cleared out a third of his stock, and despite everything, I couldn't help but feel bad. We desperately needed the supplies, though. "Torlo has behavioral issues. Often hangs around people who are no good for him."

"We all know people who weren't good for us," Jakar said. "It's all right."

"We can't pick our family," I added. "Getting a bad one in the bunch is inevitable."

Juromal nodded, nonplussed. We headed outside, and the yelling started before the door hit the frame. "Now we find a way through the Rift," Jakar said. "Food won't be an issue now."

We led Citra and Dionys through town, taking turns going into businesses or asking passersby if they knew about a new passage east. The results were depressing. Cartographers and scouting parties had headed into the Rift as soon as the last route collapsed, but they had either given up or never returned. The economies of multiple cities, along with the entire country of Xeriv on the other side, rode on this discovery, though, so there was no shortage of volunteers looking for a big pay day selling a way through.

"I'm sorry for this," Jakar said.

"For what?" I asked.

"In case you ever thought you'd bitten off more than you can chew."

I laughed. "I asked if I could come. Besides, name one thing in the territories that's worth me sticking around for."

For a second I panicked, thinking he would say Sara. "There's Manasus," he said. "You've got Meike and Carina and Magnate Bardera. I'm sure you made other friends there while you were living with the nobility."

I hadn't told him about my "friends" in my old gang and

their idea of friendship, or about Carmen and how I had gotten her dad killed. There was a lot I hadn't told Jakar, I realized. The reason I'd come on this trip was because it had been a fast pass away from Sara, as I'm sure she would have come for me if I'd gone with Meike and Carina to Manasus, and I had every intention of never seeing her again. I didn't have the energy to admit this to Jakar, though. Fortunately for me, he didn't seem ready to talk about her, either. "Sure, the trip's hard," I said. "It even sucks most of the time. But I'm seeing so much of the world I never would've otherwise. Makes me feel more important than any princepa who spends their passings laughing at masques while getting their food served to them. If we have to wait around in Port Lora, then so be it. I'd be doing the same in Manasus, except there I wouldn't be doing anything with my life other than waiting around to die."

The concern on his face softened. "So long as you want to be here."

We went to the southeastern area of Port Lora—the last place we hadn't checked. I watched the swing of his ponytail as he led the way, thinking about another reason I had tagged along. About how spending time with him sometimes felt like I was with Emil. It sounded like something he'd appreciate hearing, but the idea of sharing it made my mouth all cottony. Emil was the only one in the family who knew how to talk about these things.

"Look at this," Jakar said as he ripped a piece of parchment from a pole. "'Guard work needed for expedition into the Rift. Visit Darkwater Trading Co. for more details.'"

"Think I can get hired on for guard work?"

"You're a little young, but we can try."

I grabbed his hand and lifted it to showcase the grimy bandages covering his arms. "You think you have a better shot?" I asked, and let go. "I've heard of Darkwater. Some of the nobiletza in Augustin own competing interests in Byssa that were being put out of business by Darkwater Trading Company. I think the company's pretty big in Xeriv."

We found Darkwater's modest shop on the edge of town with a sign hanging above the entrance along with the company sigil painted on the door, an octopus grasping two thorny vines hard enough to draw blood. Inside, a scruffy, plump man sat at a desk, the windows behind him overlooking the water and showing the amber glow of the minerals on the cavern's wall far in the distance.

"We're here about the flier," Jakar said. "We're two very capable people who'd make great caravan guards."

The man stopped scribbling in his logbook and gave Jakar the once-over, pausing on his bandages. "I'm sure."

"I'm just a little tender from some old burns. I can wield a blade just fine."

The man went back to his scribbling. "That flier's old. The caravan to Ravada leaves tomorrow and we already hired who we need."

"Ravada?" I asked. Ravada was the capital of Xeriv, just on the other side of the Rift. "I thought it was just an expedition to find a way through."

"That's how we advertised it, yes. Some of the companies here would play dirty for a map through the Rift, so we had to keep ours on the hush-hush." The man sounded bored and was apparently unconcerned with telling us his secrets.

"You're the only ones who know a way through?"

The man showed his yellowed teeth. "Yes. This is our first caravan through, but make no mistake, our route is as good as gold."

Jakar and I exchanged a glance. "We'd like to barter passage," Jakar said.

The man set his pen down. "We don't usually offer that kind of service."

"Usually," I said. "That means you're open to negotiation."

He studied us above steepled hands. "Twelve grams of dymium is the price."

"We don't know how much that is. Do you take standards?"

"You're going to Ravada, which means you pay with

Xerivian currency. Fortunately, we do currency exchanges here, and twelve grams would come out to…" He pondered for a moment. "A hundred in Miran standards."

I could barely contain my excitement. A hundred standards was a steal. "Sounds perfect," I said quickly.

"Let me clarify when I say 'a hundred.' That is one hundred *pounds* in standards. We deal in weight with deals this large, but I believe one hundred pounds would equate to about nine thousand, six hundred standard coins, or near enough."

I suppressed an angry laugh. "What if we brought our own mounts and food? Can we get a discount?"

"No. That's the price."

Jakar frowned to himself, and I wondered if he was doing the same calculations I was. We could sell Citra and Dionys and the rest of our belongings, but that would only get us a fraction of the way.

"There is another arrangement that can be made," the man said. "Are you familiar with serf contracts?"

So this had been the offer all along. We'd made a mistake by revealing our hand too early and showing how badly we wanted to cross the Rift. Jakar's eyes had a faraway look, and it wasn't hard to guess what he was thinking. He used to pretend he was a serf working for my father as a cover story to hide the secret of his flesh binding.

"Yes, we know what they are," Jakar said. "What are the terms on the debt?"

"I would have to reference company policy, but if you would like a rough estimate, twelve grams would take about eight months to work off."

"Can my sister and I discuss this outside?"

Jakar's discomfort shouldn't have come as a surprise, I told myself. I followed him out the door. "I get it if you don't want to do this," I started. "But whatever gets us through the Rift, you know?"

"I wanted to see if you felt uncomfortable about signing a serf contract, actually."

"Oh. I mean, I'm traveling with one of the strongest elementals in Mira, so I figured we'd, you know, extricate ourselves once we got to Ravada. Ravada's huge, from what I hear. Plenty of chances to lose ourselves in a crowd."

Jakar touched one of his bandages. A self-conscious gesture. "If Darkwater is big like you say, they probably have deep pockets to pay for more than enough swords to protect their interests. And I'm still fragile."

He looked himself over. He'd once told me his fight with Nektarios, the Sovereign's primordia, had resulted in a broken hand and shoulder as well as a sprained wrist, not to mention there was the wound in his chest where Sara had stabbed him during his trial. And the burns. It had been nearly two months since we'd fled Augustin's capital, but he still had a way to go until he was back to his old self. "Fighting a company's worth of hired guards might be difficult when we reach Xeriv," he said.

"Then we stay here?" I asked.

The question seemed to bother him more than the serf contract. "We don't know how long it will take someone else to find a way through the Rift. We don't know if Darkwater will start selling maps or if they'll keep it a secret so they can monopolize what might be the only way through. What we do know is that we can be on the other side in a dozen passings if we sign that contract."

"So we go."

He gave an unhappy nod.

"We'll escape Darkwater once we're through the Rift, not a problem," I said. "I'll carry the slack if you can't handle getting us away on your own. I'm getting pretty clever with a blade thanks to you."

"Right," he said, but the brittleness in his expression showed how he really felt.

Chapter 3—Jakar

EFADORA BURIED HER face in Citra's neck one last time and took a deep whiff. "I'll miss you, *mi ven*."

Citra gave her one last lick on the face before the buyer led him and Dionys toward a stable full of stout-faced salamanders and other foxes. "So where does that put us?" the former princepa asked.

"At about seven months and four passings of serfdom instead of eight months and twelve passings."

"It's sulf-spit they won't let us bring our foxes. Seems like now we'll be more of an inconvenience to them."

"They probably don't want us riding off." I was more annoyed they wouldn't allow us to bring any of our belongings, including the alchemical weapons I had concocted for Efadora, but at least we had bartered with Darkwater to let us keep Juromal's meat pies and the roll of fresh bandages I'd bought for my burns.

We moved into the bottleneck at the top of the stairs leading to the docks below, the thick of people a little unnerving as the catwalks and stairs creaked and the floorboards bowed as we descended. The stairs spiraled down the circumference of the massive pillar Port Lora sat upon, and I noticed the scars on the pillar's sides where support structures must have been ripped from the rock when the channel drained. The harbor at the bottom smelled of fresh rockwood, and roosts of fireflies shivered and hummed where someone had slathered firefly paste onto the rock. At the end of the dock, Darkwater laborers hurried to strap boxes to a collection of small vessels that would ferry us to the far side of the channel.

We found the passenger vessel, a twelve-man rowboat, as well as the only occupant on it who wasn't a guard. Torlo looked up from his lap. "Oh, hello."

"Did you follow us?" Efadora asked.

The bandit smiled warmly. "Course not. I'm smart enough to know you'd never want to see me again, but I'm a Darkwater employee now."

I took a seat beside the young man and Efadora followed suit. "Darkwater told us they weren't hiring," I said.

"I signed on to do a few months' work for passage through the Rift. Did you know they're going all the way to Xeriv? If those maps are on point, they'll be the biggest company both sides of the Rift pretty quick."

"You signed a serf contract?" I asked.

He nodded, oblivious to the fact he'd made the biggest mistake of his life.

"Did you read the fine print?" I asked. "The section on debt accrual was longer than every other section combined. If they do anything for you outside of what's defined in the contract, they'll charge you for it and extend your service." I leaned closer so the guards wouldn't hear. "Slavery's illegal in Mira, but not to the east. The Sovereign has no influence as soon as we pass through the Rift. Darkwater will make you a slave in everything but name."

Torlo frowned for the first time since we'd met him.

"Your brother seems like the kind of person who'd skin you alive for signing a serf contract," Efadora said.

Her words seemed to steal the life from him. "He doesn't want to see me anymore."

The ensuing silence was awkward. A range of emotions played across Torlo's face, which he tried to hide. After a moment, he said, "Sounds like we're all in the same boat." He laughed. "Why'd you sign those contracts if they're such a terrible idea?"

"Booked a villa in Ravada for a vacation before the quake, and my brother didn't want to cancel and lose out on the deposit," Efadora said.

To Torlo's credit, he didn't press on the obvious lie.

The boats glided across the still waters of the channel, weaving between pillars until we reached the shore where a line of carts waited. More guards, laborers, and traders moved around them, six of the seven carts already filled with securely fastened boxes. Our boat ground against mud, and I climbed out, moving warily around the strange-looking animals hooked up to the front of each cart. They were shoulder height and walked on four limbs, with thin fur and dense muscle. Their faces were unsettlingly humanoid.

"Cliff chimps," Torlo chimed in, noticing my confusion. "Gangs of them swing along the fungi and stalactites over the Skorpian Sea."

The chimps' feet gripped the uneven rock with five toes and opposable thumbs. The closest one bared its teeth at me, and I stepped away to examine the wheels on the carts. They were made of rubber—a material I hadn't seen since Sulian Daw—and were honeycombed, allowing them to flex under the weight of the boxes. The setup made it clear this journey would be a hard one, which wasn't such a terrible thing on its own, but the seat at the front of each cart was big enough for only one person, and each was taken by a trader. "Are we supposed to ride on the boxes?" I asked.

Someone let out a throaty laugh, and I turned to find a guard riding an exceptionally large stone fox. He was a Tulchi man with a long, auburn beard, a streak of white through it. "You won't be riding shit-all. You'll get knocked off within a hundred feet if you try riding the boxes. Three'a you will be walking."

"Seriously?" Efadora asked. "We could've been riding on Citra and Dionys."

"Here are the rules," the guard said. "My name is Arhan, and my word is the religion we practice around here. You go where I tell you. Unless I say otherwise, you stay with the caravans at all times. If a guard or I ask for your help, you jump to. We set up camp at passing's end, you shut up until we break camp. Best get as much sleep as you can, 'cause if you can't keep up, you get left behind. Got it?"

"All right," Torlo and I said at the same time Efadora said, "Sure."

"What's that on your backs? Serfs forfeit their belongings upon signing."

"I talked with the man in the office," I said. "He said we could keep what we have."

"I was never told that." He let out a sharp whistle, catching the attention of the nearest guard. "Take their bags."

Efadora and I took a step closer to each other. "Go talk to your boss," she said. "What's ours is ours." Her words were milder than what I'd come to expect, and there wasn't the usual fire in her voice. She understood the futility of the situation.

"Don't you worry, young one," Arhan said. "We have a schedule to stick to, so we'll sort this out later. My men will safeguard your belongings in the meantime. You'll thank me for it. Promise."

A guard slipped the bags of food off our shoulders and disappeared further into the caravan. "There's one last matter to take care of," Arhan said. "We need to get the three of you marked. You'll be happy you did it now—best to get it out of the way before the trip's taken its toll."

Efadora gave me an uneasy look, and a guard appeared out of the chaos of the caravan holding an iron that glowed dark red. "A branding iron?" I asked.

"It'll protect you. Criminals, traffickers, and everything in between won't give you a second glance once they know you're Darkwater property."

"We weren't told about this," I said. I was outraged, but more for Efadora's sake than my own. I didn't like seeing her in pain.

"I know what you're thinking," the man said. "But it really isn't as painful as it sounds. We don't heat the iron up so much. The burn won't be too deep. It'll feel like hardly more than a sting. So, who's first?"

"I'll do it," Efadora said. There was determination in her eyes as she looked at me like this was just another hurdle in the journey. She wanted to prove herself, I realized. I wanted to argue, to find some way out of permanently marking our bodies, but what was there to say? There was no getting past this.

"On your knees, then," Arhan said.

Efadora knelt on the rock and tilted her head forward while the guard brought the iron down on the back of her neck. She let out a hiss then choked in a breath as the metal sizzled against her skin, the knuckles of her fists almost bone white. She didn't complain, but her trembling gave her away. The mark that was left behind was a crescent shape pointing up like a bowl, and with branching arms—the legs of an octopus without the head.

I helped her to her feet. I considered asking if she was all right but she wouldn't have liked that. I'd been the same way as a teenager, wanting to prove myself strong. Torlo went next—he let out a cry and nearly bucked away from the iron, then was left on his hands and knees to gather himself while the guard departed to reheat the iron. He brought a shaking hand to the back of his neck, but resisted the urge to touch the wound. I helped him up next. "You did good," I said, and squeezed his hand reassuringly.

Once the guard returned, the iron more orange than red, I knelt down. A bright, piercing pain touched the back of my neck, and once it was gone, I stood, facing Arhan as he continued to watch the spectacle. He said nothing, only held my gaze, as if waiting for something.

"Is there anything else?" I asked.

Arhan rode off without a word while laborers shouted at one another to finish strapping the last of the boxes to the carts. "I don't like this," Efadora said.

"No turning back now, I don't think."

The laborers jumped on the ferries and pushed off, headed back to Port Lora. The thirteen guards took positions throughout the caravan with Arhan at the front, who shouted a command in a language I didn't recognize. The cliff chimps snorted and grunted, pulling the carts into motion. Efadora and I grabbed onto the side of the nearest cart for support, and Torlo did the same with the one in front of us.

The tunnels smelled of wet vegetation and fresh leaves and were covered in glowing patches of bio-luminescent vegetation, from white to green to purple to even red-like pyremoss. With every dip or rise of the tunnel that was extreme enough for a tire to lose traction, the cliff chimps' muscles would bulge, and they would growl as they maintained control of their carts. These passages had likely been soaking underwater for millennia, and while they'd had some time to dry, the ground was still slick, and the sharp rocks poked me through the soles of my boots.

"Are you all right?" Efadora asked, breathing lightly.

I realized I had let out a whimper. "I'm fine." Using the cart for support had stoked a small fire in the wound Sara had given me—every time I caught myself when I lost footing, molten sparks stabbed me in the sternum and the bones in my wrist ached.

There would be a week of traveling like this to Ravada.

I needed a distraction. I thought of Emil's helpful words to keep me going, his self-conscious laughs, the set of his brow when his determination became unbreakable, and how he would look at me when he thought I wouldn't notice. When that wasn't enough, I focused on darker motivations—on my revenge, brought about by years of forced labor and torture under the cultists who'd raised me, the Ebonrock. And when that wasn't enough, I tried to glimpse that drunken euphoria I'd felt upon realizing my binding to Sara Adriann had been severed, the memory sweet despite the agony of her attempted execution that went with it.

Knowing flesh bindings could be broken had unlocked something inside me. Anxious energy filled me if I thought too much about the children I grew up with—of Quin and the others—and how they were enslaved in the Black Depths, toiling away until the work killed them. I could save them. I didn't know how, but it was possible.

As I huffed it through the twisting, turning tunnels, I sank into the same trance I'd used when performing mindless labor for the Ebonrock, and when the guards called for a halt along the first expanse of dry tunnel since the start of the trip, I realized hours had passed.

Efadora bent over and vomited on the rock, spewing out food that we probably should not have stuffed our faces with before surrendering ourselves to Darkwater. She wiped her mouth and wavered on her feet.

"I'll find you water," I said.

I went for a guard to ask for a waterskin. While Efadora swigged and washed out her mouth, I approached the owner of the cart we had walked beside, who was prying barnacles and coral from his tires with metal tongs. "Would you mind letting my sister ride on the back of your cart?" I asked.

He shook his head and shrugged. I almost argued until he said something in a different language, and I realized he didn't speak Miran. I mimed sitting on the cart. He shook his head adamantly and gave a quick wave of dismissal, then hurried away.

"Already forgotten what I said?" Arhan asked. I hadn't noticed him standing behind me, accompanied by one of his guards.

"My sister's having a hard time climbing over some of these rocks," I said. "She's small enough to wedge herself between some of the crates without falling out."

"I'm all right," Efadora said, joining us along with Torlo. She and Torlo were passing the waterskin between them.

"You're welcome to ride a chimp," Arhan said to the former princepa.

"I'm guessing for a price."

"Smarter than you look, sweetheart. Yes, for a price."

Efadora took a swig, swishing it around, then spat it close enough to Arhan's feet that a splash of water darkened the leather of his boots. "No, thank you, saior."

The sergeant walked off without another word, his guard in tow. "That's probably the last person you want to antagonize," I said.

"I think my patience for mediocre men is starting to thin out. I read the contract through. We're property of Darkwater, so he can't hurt us."

"Girls your age don't talk like that much, you know that?" Torlo asked. There was a glimmer in his eyes.

"My age? I'm almost as old as you. What are you, seventeen? I'm sixteen."

I wanted to point out that a year made a world of difference to a teenager, but Efadora had always wanted to get her childhood over with as soon as possible. "I thought you were fifteen," I said.

"Turned sixteen three passings after we left Meike and Carina."

Torlo continued to stare at Efadora, obvious enough with his feelings that it almost hurt to watch. Apparently, he'd forgotten how she had treated him not a passing earlier. I tried to think of what Emil would have done to boys who came sniffing around his little sister. Maybe it was for the best I left the matter alone. It was inappropriate for me to play a role I wasn't fit for.

The rest of the passing went a little easier. We left the damp and slippery tunnels behind and trekked through drier passages lit with every color of the spectrum. We passed through cavernous biomes full of strange creatures that had probably gone a thousand generations without human contact, and we moved slowly through alien jungles feeding off steaming, volcanic geysers, every guard ready to cut apart anything that so much as looked at us sideways.

Arhan called for a halt in a grotto with a crystalline pool to draw water from, and where both tunnels moving into and out of it could be easily defended. Efadora and I set our bedrolls next to a glowing, ruby red geode. Torlo walked up to us with a bedroll tucked under his arm. "Is it all right if I bunk with you two?"

I didn't mind, so I let Efadora answer. "Yeah, I guess," she said.

I hunted down one of the guards and asked where our packs of food were. "Sergeant put them over there," the woman said, pointing to the guards' supply cart. I found the packs crammed in the back, but when I opened them, all I found were jars of aloe and several rolls of bandages smelling like meat pies.

Arhan was sitting in front of a fire cooking sausages in a pan, and every guard who wasn't on watch sat with him. "Our food is gone," I said.

The sergeant's smile was sickly sweet. "It's been a long passing. Can't be expected to keep tabs on your shit when I've got a caravan to lead."

"Is that dinner for you and your subordinates?" I asked, nodding toward the pan of sausages.

"Looks like it, doesn't it?"

"Hmm. Not much food there. Did you already fill up on meat pies?"

The leather in Arhan's gloves creaked. "Amazing. This might be the first time I've been accused of stealing." He turned, looking at each guard in the circle. "Some of you have worked under me for a good while. Am I the type of leader to steal from another man's mouth?"

"No," some of them chorused, more offended than Arhan looked.

"There's an issue with what you're saying, is all," I said. "You tasked one of your guards with our packs when we left Port Lora, but when I talked to the guards on watch, they said that you'd personally moved them to the cart where I found them."

Some guards averted their eyes to the fire. Others frowned at the sergeant, puzzled. It was clear some of the men and women working under Arhan were loyal to him and had likely helped the sergeant eat my food, but the rest hadn't known any better. My words had also embarrassed Arhan. Angry colors crawled up his neck. "To think some pissant serf decided to come round here and question me," he said. "Nobody took your meat pies, and how dare you question my integrity in front of my subordinates."

It took a lot of willpower not to roll my eyes. There was a saying in my home city of Som Abast, that it took three moments of challenge to find the measure of a man, but for Arhan it had taken only one. It was clear he valued the appearance of integrity over actually having any.

He grabbed for something behind the rock he'd been sitting on, and when he straightened, his arm was swinging. I failed to duck, and his whip wrapped over my shoulder, snapping across my back. The whip's end left an explosion of fire on my lower back and sent me to one knee.

"Maybe you've failed to understand the dynamic of our relationship," the sergeant said, faltering at my lack of reaction. He and his subordinates glanced at each other, probably wondering why I wasn't screaming by now. He cleared his throat and continued, "It's my duty to protect Darkwater's interests, but not if those interests are faulty. You must be defective in the head if you think you can call me something I'm not in front of my men."

I squeezed my eyes closed, shutting out the pain radiating through my back, and focused on not letting anger get the better of me. The last thing I wanted was to start a fight and get Efadora and myself stranded in the Rift. I picked myself up, gave the sergeant a humorless smile, and found the caravan watching us. I relaxed my jaw enough to say, "Apologies for accusing you of being petty enough to steal our food to spite me and my sister. It won't happen again."

Confusion crept onto Arhan's face—that certainly wasn't what I had accused him of, and I was staring him down, fists clenched after a blow that would have left most others whimpering in the dirt for the next ten minutes. Traders whispered to one another, pointing at me. Arhan dragged the whip back and started looping it together, but didn't move to strike me again. "I'm sure it won't."

I backed away, trying to ignore everyone's eyes, and Arhan tossed the whip next to his rock and went back to cooking the sausages. Even from this distance, I could smell them burning.

Chapter 4—Ester

ESTER GRIPPED THE chains attached to the thirty-foot-long metal beam, pulling hard enough for her to start wondering if her arms might make a sudden departure from their sockets. Twenty men and women strained against ropes to keep the beam in place as it hung against the lip of Augustin's fourth level, and Arc Smith Artur scampered along the top of it as they worked to fasten the beam to where the ridge had crumbled from the falling ice sheath.

"A little higher, Ester," he called out. Ester dug into her metal working, searching for that delicate balance between applying enough power and causing a hernia, and she took two slow steps back. Her helpers let out all manner of animal noises as they adjusted to keep the beam in its new position, and Arc Smith Artur drove each stake into the beam with a single strike of his hammer. After he'd traveled the length of the beam, he hopped off, and Ester let slack into the chains wrapped around her waist until they clattered to the ground. She was rewarded with the sound of the beam groaning as it settled in place, and the others dropped their ropes, rubbing their backs and catching their breath.

The arc smith listed instructions to a cadre of woodworkers who prepped buckets of concrete to pour into the framework.

"It's starting to come together," Ester said when he finally joined her. "Augustin almost looks like a city again."

"But does it feel like a city?" He pointed to a boy and his mother who had been watching the construction. "He doesn't seem to think so."

The boy was crying. He and his mother stood at a street entrance, the mother trying to lead her son onto the ridge, but he had put his roots down. Ester moved to join them. "Is he all right?" she asked.

"Fine," the mother said. "Just scared. Thinks another ice sheath will fall."

Artur knelt before the boy and used his scarred palms to envelop his little hand. "It's all right, small one. The last ice sheath only fell because the Iron Sorrow made it fall. He's gone now. Gone far, far away."

The appearance of this boy sure seemed rather timely for the arc smith. Artur was on a mission to prove to Ester that the Iron Sorrow was a blight, but he couldn't accept that it was a lost cause for her. Jakar was a good person, and nothing could shake her conviction on the matter. She wondered how long Artur had ignored the boy crying at the street entrance, too, at least until he had a chance to use it as a lesson about Jakar's corruption.

"Where'd Iron Sorrow go?" the boy asked, wiping his nose with a sleeve.

"Banished. He'll never come to Augustin again. The smiths will never let *Dor Di Fero* hurt you. I promise."

Ester let out a disgusted sound and all three turned to her. "Apologies. Dust in the air from all the construction," she said. "For what it's worth, the Iron Sorrow left because he wanted to. If he ever returned, he would never dream of hurting you."

More tears welled up in the boy's eyes, and Ester cringed as she watched the dam break. Artur pursed his lips, shaking his head at her, and rubbed the boy's upper arm in comfort. "As smiths, sometimes we need to enlist outside help to complete very important tasks. Would you be interested in that?"

The boy gave a small nod and swallowed, overwhelmed by the offer. Artur continued, "There are many shops and businesses in the city that have been struggling to get up and running again. Their biggest supporters are the people in Augustin who shop at their stores. My mission for you is to be brave and to help your mother with her shopping. Do you think you can do that?"

"Aye, saior." He smiled through his tears. Soon he was the one pulling his mother across the ridge, guiding her through the flurry of workers.

"I know the Iron Sorrow wasn't banished," Artur said to Ester, "but telling this to children serves no purpose other than to cause them to live every passing in fear."

"Maybe if half the Foundry wasn't preaching that Jakar serves the Great Ones, children wouldn't be so afraid of him."

They rejoined the construction workers, and Artur asked, "Are you denying what the Iron Sorrow did?"

"Of course not, and you know it. The point is that he was forced to commit evil by the former princepa."

"No one is truly forced to do anything."

"He was."

"That opinion is naive, Apprentice Ester. There are always sacrifices to be made to avoid bringing evil into the world. Even if the person must sacrifice themselves."

Not much could get to Ester, but his casual suggestion that Jakar should have killed himself was an exception. She dug her nails into her palms and considered telling him that talking Jakar off the edge of the river and helping him defeat Nektarios two months earlier had been one of the most fulfilling moments of her life. She also almost asked why Artur hadn't done a little sacrificing himself and been the one to chain himself to the metal beam, as it was obvious he feared the beam falling into the chasm and dragging him with it. But she kept her mouth shut. He was her mentor, technically, even if she wasn't too sure what he was teaching.

"Arc Smith Artur and Apprentice Ester," a voice called out.

Smith Helcia approached them. "A moment of your time, if you please."

"Yes?" Artur asked.

"The master smith wishes to speak with Ester about an important matter. I'm here to finish her work while she heads to the Foundry."

"What's it about?"

"That's between her and the master smith."

"You understand the nature of mentorships within the Foundry, yes? I know what she knows."

Smith Helcia offered a short bow in deference, gluing her gaze to the ground. "I don't know what they're meant to discuss. I'm sorry, saior."

It seemed petty to take joy in Artur's ruffled feathers, but Ester had been pious enough this passing. "I'll see you later," she said with a smile, then headed for the nearest ramp.

Fires from a thousand torches glittered on the small lake that had formed on the sinkhole's floor. Even several weeks later the shattered ice sheath was still melting, the blue mountain feeding water into the lava that sent a constant cloud of steam billowing along the east side of the chasm. It was a blessing to the barrows, as it supplied much needed warmth to the commoners living on the upper levels, even prompting some of the poor to call it a parting gift from the legendary Jakar. Screw what Artur had said—the city felt more alive than ever. Everyone was working together to bring Augustin back to its former glory.

No, Augustin would be even better than before. The audencia could elect a wet towel as the new magnate and they'd have a better track record than their recent string of rulers. Indecision had evidently paralyzed them after what had happened with Sara Adriann and Olevic Pike's coup. It was said, though, that they would reach a decision soon.

Ester spotted the back of the master smith's shaggy-haired head in the bowels of the Foundry. The man was overseeing the construction of metal girders in the Deep Forge, watching while several smiths slid a completed girder into a narrow chute leading to the capital's main tunnel. "Hello, Master Smith," she said to Mateo. "You wanted to see me?"

His nod was sluggish. "Yes. Thanks for coming."

She couldn't help but notice all the bruises, scraps and scabs covering his arms. "It's probably not my place, but when is the last time you've gotten some rest? All this work is making you clumsy. I wouldn't want you falling into a forge by accident."

"I've tried to catch some shut eye, but every time I lie down, my mind starts going down the list of all the work we still need to do."

"You have fifty brothers and sisters and many thousands of Augustins willing to take your shift for you. The city repairs won't stop to wait for you if you took off for a few hours." It felt strange admonishing the master smith, but he needed to hear it before he hurt himself.

"The brain understands what you're saying, but the heart keeps making other plans." He gave a tired wave. "Follow me."

They plunged into the depths of the Foundry until they reached an older area, where veins of ancient pyremoss along the walls were as bright as lava and where low rankers like Ester were very much encouraged to avoid. The master smith stopped in front of a sturdy metal door that he set his hand on. It rumbled and clicked, unlocking, and he opened it to reveal a small room with nothing but a rug on the floor. "You're no longer part of the reconstruction project. I'll be sending you outside the city to look into a matter that's rather sensitive."

"You're sending me home to Tulchi, aren't you?"

He cocked his head. "Why would you think that?"

"We both know why, Master Smith. The arc smiths and the senior arc smiths think I'm some gnat buzzing around who won't shut up about Jakar. I'm creating a rift between the older and newer members."

"Brothers and sisters fight sometimes. It's not your fault."

"It might not be my fault, but you wouldn't know that talking to some of the smiths. I've been fighting a losing battle ever since I got here. I shouldn't have been honest about my upbringing." Ever since Arc Smith Artur had "reported" her offhanded comments about her cultist parents and her brother Myrilan's fixation with the Sovereign, among other things, Ester had been treated like a permanent visitor to Augustin instead of family. When she had talked about her past it hadn't occurred to her the truth would alarm anyone— the smiths back in her home territory of Tulchi had had no problem accepting a few skeletons in the closet. This had been her introduction to how fundamentalist the attitudes were in Augustin.

"I know things have been hard for you," Mateo said. "You should be receiving the full support of your brothers and sisters, especially considering what you and Damek went through. If it helps, my feelings about Jakar don't resemble the beliefs of the other longtime members."

"I know," she said, keeping her eyes to the ground. She wanted to tell him his feelings about Jakar didn't do much good when he constantly kept them to himself, but that wasn't fair to him. Radical notions, like Jakar not being a demonic stain sent from the Black Depths, took time for the senior members to accept.

"Important conversations are happening behind closed doors," he said. "Progress is being made. In the meantime, feel comfort in knowing you're loved here, even if it's what some of the older smiths would consider tough love. I'll renounce my faith before I let anyone send you home because of a few outdated beliefs."

"Why am I here, then?"

He reacted like she had asked about his dead mother. Or the late princep, Emil. "The senior arc smiths and I are sending you on a mission to recover the stolen contents of this room." The exhaustion behind his words deepened.

She examined the room again. "Someone broke into the Foundry?"

"They did. And they took our rhidium."

The back of her neck prickled. "Someone stole the rhidium? All of it?"

He rubbed the tip of his sandal across a section of the floor where grime collected in sharp angles. "We had thirteen crates here. Five hundred and forty-six vials. Altogether, they weighed just shy of two hundred and fifty pounds. Someone broke into this room and carried it off. They likely had accomplices."

"Was it a smith?"

He frowned, but she couldn't help that this had been the first place her mind had gone. He pulled up the rug to reveal a trapdoor underneath. "Help me with this."

Behind the trapdoor was a tunnel. Mateo said, "Months ago when Olevic Pike usurped Sorrelo Adriann and took over Augustin, he had this tunnel collapsed so no one could use it to move around the city unchecked. Someone dug it out these last several weeks. We're not sure when the rhidium was stolen, but we think it was recently. Perhaps within the last few passings."

"I know you don't want to hear this, but the trapdoor has a lock only a smith can open. Are you certain it wasn't one of us?"

"As certain as I can be. Only the senior arc smiths and I know about this trapdoor. I think the thieves got through because the last smith to use it forgot to lock the thing. That smith was me. I used it to help the Adriann children and Jakar escape during the Listener's coup."

"Ah." The master smith's love affair with insomnia suddenly made more sense. "Are any of the other trade schools missing their rhidium?"

"We haven't asked yet, but it's hard to inquire about such things without news of our break-in getting out. But as far as I know, we're the only institution that keeps our rhidium stores in the capital. Chances are we were the only ones hit."

"Why would someone steal our rhidium?"

"I think you know the answer to that. Because of the power it can promise. As a metal worker, Emil Adriann was one of the deadliest swordsmen in Mira at just nineteen years old, and now we run the risk of five hundred and forty-six others just like him running around Mira, participating in the growing conflicts between the territories."

"Undergoing the rhidium trials is suicidal for anyone outside the Foundry, though. Faith and ceremony are the foundation of a smith's transition to an iron worker, and whoever stole the rhidium will have neither of those. Without Fheldspra's guiding hand during the trial, it is hopeless. What these thieves have done is idiotic."

A heavy thought appeared behind Mateo's eyes. He studied her for several seconds, and that thought made his expression draw down in shame. "Faith and ceremony are important, but not required. If whoever stole the rhidium knows how to properly administer it, they'll be able to ensure that a significant portion of those who take it survive."

"But consuming a piece of blade someone forged with their own hands here in the Foundry is still essential. It creates a union between Fheldspra's fire and the iron worker's soul."

"They don't need Foundry-forged steel. They don't need steel at all. They just need the base component iron. 'Iron working' isn't just an appellation."

It was a strange thing for Ester to hear this information about one of the Foundry's longest living traditions. That the sacred ritual was a lie. It bothered her to the point where she was tempted to tell him he was full of guano. How could the highest-ranking member of the Foundry not understand his own religion?

"Why do we tell our brothers and sisters the rituals are important, then?" she asked.

"They *are* important."

"Then why don't we tell them how it really works?"

"Because it doesn't matter, in the end. The how of it is like a nesting doll—we learn the mechanisms behind a phenomenon only to wonder about the secrets behind those mechanisms. Down and down you go until it ultimately it is a matter of faith. You must choose where you put that faith. No matter how my knowledge of the world might change, I choose to believe that Fheldspra is ultimately responsible."

She understood the logic, but the road to wrong answers was often paved with sound logic. "Explain it," she said.

"Which part?"

"The entire binding process. Chances are whoever stole the rhidium knows smith ritual isn't needed to become an iron worker, and if I have to hunt them down, I risk finding out anyway. Imagine how I'd feel if I'd learned the truth while interrogating a group of criminals and the kind of resentment toward my faith that would cause. I'd be lying if I said I didn't feel some resentment now. If there was ever a time I needed guidance, Master Smith, it's now."

He pursed his lips, but nodded, and proceeded to tell her in full just how faithless the rhidium trials were.

"This is bad," Ester said when he finished. "Really bad. Where does that tunnel lead?"

"The thieves dug here from the Guild of the Glass. The senior arc smiths are speaking with the guild right now, but no one there seems to know anything. Most of the guild members are faithless, so I'm hoping your growing nonconformist reputation will resonate with anyone who might know something. Discretion is paramount, however, so be careful with how you divulge information when you ask questions."

She chewed on the words. "Again, no offense, Master Smith, but I don't buy that the reason you're putting me on this is because I'm some sort of maverick the faithless might relate to. The senior arc smiths would never agree to me heading this investigation, given my rank and my family. Is there another reason?"

A new emotion crossed Mateo's face, one she had never seen on the master smith before. Cold fear. "Whoever stole the rhidium knows we'll turn the city upside down to find it, which means they likely took it into the crust. And I need you out of the city. The audencia received word yesterday that the

Sovereign is coming here personally to get an account of what happened on the Granite Road and how the city managed to let itself be ransacked."

Oh. "Did the Sovereign mention anything about investigating his missing primordia?" The last time she had laid eyes on Nektarios, official representative of the Sovereign and one of the seven most powerful people in the territories, she was helping Mateo dump his body in the river. She'd suggested they cut the corpse into pieces so no one would wonder why they were dragging a body-shaped bag across the city, but doing so had been like trying to cut through rock with a kitchen knife. She had been sure at the time they'd disposed of it without witnesses, though that confidence was quickly eroding.

"No mention of Nektarios," he said, "but we can't assume anything. Maybe he doesn't want anyone knowing the man is missing and is keeping his search discreet."

"What's going to happen if the Sovereign finds out a smith helped kill him?"

"I don't know. The Sovereign's been... less cruel toward the Foundry, despite our feelings toward him, for reasons I don't understand. We can't rely on that grace if he finds out you, Damek, and Jakar killed Nektarios. It's why I need you and your brother out of the capital."

"We should be preparing to fight. I should be here."

"No, we should not. Fighting is what put us in this position in the first place. Let me worry about the Sovereign while you focus on finding our rhidium."

Maybe she was being paranoid, but if the Sovereign was aware of Nektarios's fate, she doubted the country's ruler would be happy with just killing her, Damek, and Jakar as payment. The Sovereign was an existential threat to everyone in the territories. She didn't care how impossible it sounded— the man had committed genocide to maintain order in Mira, and there were breadcrumbs in the history books proving it. The end of the conflict over the Ivy Passage between Radavich and Tulchi seventy-five years ago that Jakar told her about.

The other conflicts she'd learned about more recently, like the Salt Riots in Manasus one hundred and twenty-five years ago. The Flowstone Skirmishes between Saracosta and Augustin seventy years before that. The Merchant Wars at the start of the Sovereign's reign. There were others, she was sure. The trouble was getting anyone to believe in genocide when there was no clear evidence of it.

They needed iron workers to take up arms, and soon. They needed to expand the order. It was time for the Foundry to militarize.

But that would be impossible if she didn't find the rhidium.

Chapter 5—Ester

THE SECRET TUNNEL brought them to the Guild of the Glass, into a storage room lined with telescopes Ester had seen guild members take to the upper levels to look at the stars, the firelight reflecting off lenses and turning the glass into orange disks. A padlock lay in shards beside the door where the senior arc smiths must have broken through to get a head start on the investigation. She caught stern voices echoing in the halls beyond.

Senior Arc Smiths Panqao, Celestana, and Porcia crowded around a short, overweight man, their heavy smiths' robes making them look like a trio of specters looming over the man they were interrogating. "There must be some sort of leasing or rental arrangement," Panqao said. "You expect us to believe you don't keep track of guild members who borrow such expensive-looking telescopes?"

"Every member of the guild is a professional," the man said as Ester and Mateo joined them, trying and failing to keep a cap on his annoyance. "We never encounter issues with our telescopes being 'misplaced,' so why would we keep a ledger?"

Ester glanced at the room they had emerged from. From the sound of it, the senior arc smiths were assuming a guild member who'd entered that room to borrow a telescope must have been the one to break into the door hiding the tunnel. "I mean, yes, a member might break or misplace a telescope," the short man said, "but they report it immediately and perform the repairs themselves. Telescopes are one of the simpler contraptions we design in the guild." Several glass monocles hung from chains on the front of his coat, swinging with each exasperated word. "Besides, the question is moot. Anyone, not just those looking to use our telescopes, can walk into our storage room and access the door to the tunnel."

"I don't see guards outside the guild, so that means anyone in the city could have entered your halls and broken into those tunnels?"

"Yes. In theory. The late Magnate Sorrelo swore me to secrecy that I would never discuss that door's purpose, and I've been faithful to his promise since the start. I've had guild members ask about it, but it was idle curiosity at best."

"That's enough, Senior Arc Smiths," Mateo said. "Guild Master Azelo, if you'll allow us to have full leave of your halls, we'll try not to bother anyone."

"You still won't tell me what this is about?" Azelo asked.

"Apologies, saior. My hands are tied."

Azelo scurried off. Senior Arc Smith Porcia, who usually wore an expression severe enough to be carved from obsidian, rubbed at her face like she was barely holding onto her composure. "Apologies, Master Smith," she said. "We found dirt tracked out of the tunnel and nothing else. We're looking into whether the thief is a member of the Guild of the Glass, but as you heard, this place is far from secure. It could be anyone at this point."

"Regardless of who stole it, they're going to try to smuggle it out of the capital," Ester said. "Did anyone talk to the guards at the city entrance?"

The specters turned on her. "It'd be insulting if you think we didn't," Celestana said. "We spoke with them over two hours ago. Hundreds of carts have left the city in the last passing alone, and there aren't records of any rhidium in their logbooks. If the rhidium was smuggled out, they hid it well."

"Did any of the guild members notice anyone suspicious hanging around the halls?"

"Yes, *Apprentice* Ester," Panqao said. "A guild member named Xander gave basic descriptions of three non-members he noticed walking the halls the other passing, but hasn't been helpful beyond that."

"I want to talk to him."

Instead of answering, Panqao looked to Mateo. "I know you don't mean it, but this is insulting. You're putting the fate of hundreds of future smiths in the hands of someone without tempered faith. Augustin isn't her home. She isn't a practiced bounty hunter. She's undermining your teachings. This will ruin us."

All the warmth left Mateo's face. "We talked about this. This is about more than just the rhidium. You'll accept my decision, or you'll be spending time slaking in the caves."

Watching the master smith threaten a council member with solitary confinement was almost too awkward for Ester to get pleasure out of. Almost. Mateo turned to her. "Please go ahead. And be careful with your questions."

After some asking around, Ester learned that Xander was working in one of several workshops within the guild's sandstone halls. She came to a room where a dozen men and women bent over long tables fitting together pieces of glass and metal for projects at different stages of production. Some worked miniature forges with molten glass at the ends of their blowpipes, others treated finished pieces in pools of strange liquid, and a few worked with containers of powders and liquids she couldn't even begin to identify. Fingers of incense floated through the air from candle holders, probably meant to combat the faint chemical smell.

"Xander?" she called out.

A sturdy man with wavy black hair, spectacles, and thick legs for climbing perked up. "Yes?" He'd been working on a discolored lantern.

"My name is Ester. Can we talk?"

She led the man outside, stopped, then brought him to the far end of the hallway just in case. "I heard you saw some strangers lurking around the halls recently," she said.

"Sure did." Xander described the man and two women—black hair, milky skin, stout like most Augustins—which truly was useless information. Ester tried to keep the disappointment off her face. When he'd finished, he asked, "What's this about? I asked your smith friends, but they're not the most forthcoming bunch."

"I'm sorry, saior, but it's sensitive."

"It's about that door in the storage room, isn't it? I caught a glimpse of the other side when your friends were questioning me. It's a tunnel, right? Does it lead to the Foundry?"

It had only been a few hours and word was probably already getting out about the secret tunnel. Her gut reaction, which came from a knee-jerk need to obey Mateo and the senior arc smiths, told her to deny everything. But what was the point? The rhidium was already gone. There wasn't much else that people could steal from them, and the Foundry would likely re-collapse the tunnel and seal the trapdoor. She was getting more than a little sick of the smiths' obsession with secrecy, too. Everything she'd been told about the rhidium trials was a lie. What they'd said about Jakar was a lie.

"You're right," she said. "It is a tunnel, and yes, it leads to the Foundry. The people you saw used it to steal from the smiths."

"Oh." He went quiet. "Isn't stealing supposed to be sacrilegious?"

"The Sky Scrolls teach that stealing is a cold thing. It corrodes Fheldspra's warmth. You work for what you own and share the excess."

"I suppose I can get behind that message. So what they took was important?"

She hesitated but nodded. "Very."

"Do you mind if I see the tunnel? I might be able to help."

There was no telling how hot the water would be if Panqao

and the others found out, but Ester figured Mateo was already kicking her out of Augustin, and at this point, a bad idea was better than no idea at all. "All right. Technically I'm not allowed to, so we'll have to be quick."

"Let me grab my lamp first."

There was no sign of the senior arc smiths on their way to the storage room. Xander moved a foot into the tunnel and knelt in the dirt, then struck a match to light his lamp, yellow light mixing with the red glow of pyremoss in the tunnel. He pinched some dirt off the ground and rubbed it between his fingers. "I asked the guild master months ago about this door because I always noticed bits of dirt trailing out of it, but he always told me to mind my own business. Still, I couldn't help but wonder. People around here are bred to ask questions, so honestly, I'm not at all surprised your secret tunnel was found out." He grabbed the side of the lamp and pulled a shutter, the yellow light turning green. He pulled again and it changed to blue, which transformed into a purple hue as it met the pyremoss's light.

Pinpoints of sparkling light covered the tunnel's ground and walls, like mica in granite.

"What is that?" Ester asked.

"People accept bioluminescent plants are a fact of life in Mira, but not many ask themselves why these plants glow. It comes from microorganisms that form symbiotic relationships with their host plants. So you have some types of organisms in flora like lightcaps, pyremoss, and the fungus inside certain geodes that take energy from their surroundings to generate their own light, and then there are other organisms that don't glow on their own, but light up with refraction."

"Refraction?"

"A beam of light will hit the plant and the plant bounces the light off like a mirror. So sometimes it's a matter of using the right light." He reentered the storage room with his lantern of blue to reveal a trail of diamonds leading to the exit. "Your thieves left more than just dirt behind."

Four figures entered the blue light—Mateo with the three senior arc smiths in tow. They froze when they saw Ester and Xander in front of the open door.

"Oh, Ester," Porcia said.

"Before you yell at me," Ester said quickly, "Xander found a lead."

She nudged Xander to move, hoping that if they kept their momentum going, they could stay ahead of the smiths' outrage. Xander squeezed past the council, where the sparkling trail headed toward the guild's main entrance, and they passed through the sandstone pillars onto the third level ridge. They picked their way through scaffolding, nobility, and the well-to-do commoners who lived on this level, Xander holding his lantern close to the ground so he could see the trail in the wash of light on the ridge. The trail thinned. Soon they were picking out specks of light every several feet.

They entered a corridor, descended a stairwell beside a pawn shop to the first level, and found themselves in a back alley where the trail stopped at the door of a rug seller. Ester offered the senior arc smiths an excited look, but Porcia was the only one to return it.

Tightly rolled rugs stood inside bins lining the walls of the shop, and a man with thinning hair and a gray beard was leaning on the back counter reading a book. "Welcome—" he said, looking up, but the greeting died when he saw his reckoning in the form of five very angry smiths standing before him. Xander snuffed out the flame in the lantern.

"I think you know why we're here," Mateo said.

Some of the fear left the rug seller's face. "*Nãu*, actually." He set the book down and straightened. "Not interested in listening to a bunch of *cabescoras* accuse me of any wrongdoing, either."

Cabescora roughly translated to "slaghead," and was one of the oldest slurs for smiths out there, coming from a time when the Foundry was still planting its roots in the territories. It still held its power, though, if the loss of color in the senior arc smiths' faces was any indication. Ester's childhood had weathered her from such insults. "Kind of strange you'd think we were here to accuse you of something when we've barely said a word," she said.

The rug seller's expression fell. "Hard not to come to that conclusion, considering the hateful looks all'a you are giving me."

"Celestana," Mateo said coolly. "Please retrieve the city guard. Tell them they need to arrest this man and close his shop down immediately."

"On what grounds?" the rug seller half yelled. "Y'have no evidence I'm involved in whatever you're likely trying to frame me for."

"Thieves who stole from the Foundry left a trail that led here."

"So? I'm sure whoever you're looking for hid in here before continuing on their merry way. Not like I'm working my shop every moment of every passing."

Celestana exited and left a tense silence in her wake. Ester recognized the truth of the matter—they would have a hard time extracting information from this man, as no new Listener had been appointed to head criminal interrogations and the audencia were up to their necks in civil disputes and restructuring the royal secession. The city would be slow to prosecute him. Mateo could try calling in a favor, but his relationship with the audencia was stretched thin since the Foundry's involvement in helping Sara Adriann's mercenary army invade and take over Augustin. Detaining the rug seller until the audencia saw his case could ruin his business and coerce him to talk, but the rhidium would be long gone by the time he cracked.

"Where is your trader's cart?" Ester asked.

"Excuse me?"

"These are some nice rugs. I bet people from all over the territories buy them. I'm sure you own a cart for exporting or even importing some of the rarer thread, but I didn't see it in the stall next to your shop. Where is it?"

The stupefied look on the rug seller's face told Ester all she needed to know. The man could deny owning a cart, but all they would have to do was visit the second level and ask for his registration card. The city gates would have the cart logged if it left the city, too. "It—it's gone," he said.

"Let me guess," Porcia said. "You just noticed it was stolen and you were on your way to report it when we showed up."

The shopkeeper didn't answer, just stared like a lobster in a pot. "Help us," Mateo said. "We'll find out you were involved and then you'll be executed. Does death by ash or ice sound like a future you want? Cooperating at this point is the only way the audencia will spare your life."

Celestana returned with two guardsmen, and one of them came to the master smith's side. "Under what charges are we arresting this man?" the guard asked.

"Theft."

"What did he steal?"

"The Foundry will sort that out with your lieutenant. Just trust me, saior."

The guards glanced at each other. Their hesitation would have perplexed Ester a year ago, before everything, but she couldn't blame them now. There was a chance they had fought a smith or two during Sara Adriann's invasion of the capital.

The guards threw the rug seller in shackles and led him out the door, and Panqao rummaged through the mycelium cabinets behind the counter while Porcia investigated the back office. "It was smuggled out of the city, without a doubt," Mateo said. "All towns in the crust are now required to log any trade goods that pass through, so we have a promising lead."

"At least until they find out we're following them, or they get extra paranoid," Ester said. "They might switch carts or find side tunnels to avoid the towns."

Mateo turned to Xander. "You've been an incredible help. I'd like to find some way to repay you for your service."

The guild member nodded with a pleased look. "I'll pay the

Foundry a visit to hear what you have in mind." He gave Ester a quick wave, mouthed *good luck*, and left.

The senior arc smiths didn't waste time. "You've done a terrible thing," Panqao said, setting his palms flat on the counter. "If there was ever an organization that would share our secrets, it would be the Guild of the Glass. They are the most faithless of the trade schools."

"And so what if people find out the rhidium is missing?" Ester asked. "If the public knew how it really works, then sure, I could see anyone with a taste for moving up in the world going after the thieves. But they don't."

Those words dragged Celestana and Porcia out of the back office. Panqao opened his mouth, but seemed unsure how to respond. "She knows," Mateo said. "I told her how the rhidium trials work when I brought her in to help."

"I'm sorry, Master Smith, but was it smart telling this to someone who can't even keep her mouth shut around a member of the Guild of the Glass? The guild was likely involved in the theft, for Fhel's sake. Imagine if all of Mira knew the secrets to binding with rhidium. Thousands would die to get their hands on that kind of power. The faithless would pillage the Foundry and the Star Mines, and it would destroy us in the process."

"I made the right choice asking for her help. We have a lead now thanks to her. I think I made the right choice telling her the truth, too."

"I don't know how much more faith I can give," Panqao said. His lower lip trembled. "The Iron Sorrow butchered an entire town on the Granite Road. Good, honest people who did nothing wrong. And then there are the survivors of the Battle of Augustin I've had to contend with. Do you know how many sobbing mothers and fathers and sons and daughters I've counseled? I don't sleep anymore, Master Smith. When I do manage it, it is only nightmares. This was only made possible because of the Iron Sorrow, and Ester defends him without abandon. Now you plan to make her our only hope for finding the rhidium, and already there's a guild member who seems smart enough to piece together what we've lost and is likely telling everyone he knows as we speak? It's too much."

Exhaustion pulled at Mateo's face harder than ever. "What are you saying?"

"I can no longer be part of this order if it's the kind of place that allows Apprentice Ester to exist within its ranks."

Ester wanted to tell the senior arc smith to enjoy his new life outside the Foundry, that someone as old as he was didn't know how to adapt to new, progressive ideas, and to continue having him would only put the Foundry in danger. But all she could focus on were the tears falling from his eyes. The closer she inspected his hard wrinkles and sunken eyes, the more haunted they looked.

She felt sick to her stomach. Instead of chasing peace, all she wanted was to keep opening the Foundry and the rest of Mira up to more tragedy by forcing them to fight.

The master smith eyed Panqao. Porcia's brows had drawn together in surprise while Celestana seemed relieved someone had finally put to words what everyone else was thinking. Nobody spoke until Mateo turned to Ester. "Go home. Pack your things and let Damek know both of you will be leaving the capital as soon as possible."

Chapter 6—Efadora

BY THE FOURTH passing I knew Arhan needed to be reminded of what it was like to bleed.

Normally a quick killing would've been enough, but my tastes had evolved. Some people just needed to live in suffering instead of being sent off to the next life. All it took was a very short conversation and a coerced ride on Arhan's stone fox to realize he needed to be knocked down a peg in the worst way possible.

We had been stopped in a cavern where the chimps and stone foxes drank from a pond below a waterfall pouring from a chute that offered a window to the stars. It was the first time in weeks I'd caught a glimpse of the sky, but the chute had to be at least a quarter-mile thick, and I didn't need to be reminded of all that unstable rock above our heads.

Jakar, Torlo, and I rested by the water—Torlo examined the cuts on his legs, Jakar changed the bandages for his burns, and I tried my hardest not to vomit what little water I'd managed to keep down. My head pulsed like a struck gong. Then the guards shouted, signaling the traders to start rounding up their chimps and reattaching the harnesses. "You should rent out a chimp to ride," Jakar said to me. "Ignore your pain, but you can't stop yourself from passing out." He leaned closer, glancing at Torlo to see if the boy was listening. "Our debt will be irrelevant once we reach Ravada and escape Darkwater anyway."

I would've given a no on principle if he'd suggested this a few passings ago, after Arhan whipped him. Jakar hadn't given the caravan leader the satisfaction of reacting, and I wanted to show Arhan weak links didn't exist in our little group. However, the last hour I'd been walking in a trance, my vision going in and out, and I was pretty sure I would hit the ground cold at some point this next stretch. This part of the trip came down to survival, and pride didn't mix well with that particular instinct.

"All right," I said.

The traders made final checks on the fastenings to their cargo while Jakar and Torlo limped to their places beside the carts, and I went searching for Arhan. He was meeting with four of his guards, talking and laughing, and the noise died down when I approached them.

"I want to rent one of the chimps to ride," I said.

Arhan's eyes practically glowed. "But you were so uninterested the last time I offered."

"What can I say? I warmed up to the idea. It's still within my rights to purchase a ride with serf debt, yeah?"

"Of course, of course." He turned to his companions. "This is an important lesson if you want to be leaders, gentlemen. It doesn't matter how well you get along with those under your charge. When the chips are down, you help them. Got it?"

"Aye," they said enthusiastically. I couldn't tell if it was my lightheadedness or their admiration that made me want to throw up more.

"Good." He let out a sharp whistle and the caravan creaked into motion. "Now take your positions."

The guards hopped on their foxes and trotted away, and I started for the caravan. "Do I just, like, jump on one of them?" I asked over my shoulder.

"Wait," he said. "We're not done talking."

I didn't have much energy to run after the line of carts, the first of which had disappeared behind a bend in the tunnel. "What?" I asked, rubbing my eyes. "The caravan's getting away."

"You're a hateful little thing, aren't you?" he said. "You knowingly signed a serf contract, yet you and your brother act like shits every chance you get. Respecting your owners is rule one as a serf."

"Actually, rule one is 'I hereby declare I am of sound mind and body to review the contents of the contract herein.'"

He offered his sickly-sweet smile and mounted his fox. "Yeah, I suppose you're right." He pressed his heels in and the mount broke into a trot. "Good luck."

"Wait," I said. "Where are you going?"

"Got a caravan to lead, sweetheart. Catch up while you can. Hopefully, I'll see you with us still when we make camp at passing's end."

"What do you want from me?" I called out, my voice so hoarse it cracked.

The caravan had disappeared by now, the light from the lanterns fading. Arhan turned the fox around and returned. "No more disrespecting me in front of my men," he said. "They look up to me, and I don't need some spiteful twelve-year-old trying to ruin that. You'll talk to your brother and make sure he acts like a good serf, too. And if you ever find yourself in conversation with one of my guards, you'll be sure to sing my praises. There's a promotion waiting for me in Ravada that depends on how well this caravan goes, and I'll leave your body in a hole before I let you jeopardize that. Deal?"

It took effort to keep the disgust off my face. Here was a man trying to keep me from undermining his precious reputation, just what Jakar had warned me about. Did his guards really respect him, or did they see a weak man with a fragile ego? I'm sure he fooled most of them. Leaders often did.

Sara had acted the same way, always clinging to her reputation, to her legacy. The realization made me bristle.

"Deal," I said.

He pulled me onto the fox, and I tried to ignore his breath on the nape of my neck and his arms pressed against my sides as he held the reins. The stone fox caught up to the caravan, and Jakar frowned at the way I was nestled between the sergeant's arms. I could almost picture the dumb smugness on Arhan's face. We reached the front, and he helped me onto the back of one of the two cliff chimps pulling the lead cart. I straddled the animal's neck, which, for some odd reason, gave me déjà vu of being a little girl on Father's shoulders. "Here," Arhan said, handing me a waterskin. "This is yours. Gulp it all down so you're watered the next time you have to walk. Anything else you need?"

I glanced at two nearby guards, who were listening. "No, thank you, saior," I said, trying to keep my teeth from clenching. "This is already more than I expected."

Arhan nodded in approval and stalked off to do his rounds along the caravan. Yeah, that promotion of his wasn't happening. Killing him would be too easy, and I would make him suffer until he saw that treating serfs like garbage would only bring him pain. I would show his toadies his true colors, the last of which would be red.

Like an old muscle being reworked for the first time, I was jolted by the realization of how long it'd been since I'd hungered for a bit of cruelty. It had been the name of the game among the gangs of Manasus, had become my entire world during the battle of Augustin, but had disappeared during my travels with Jakar. Defending ourselves from highwaymen meant killing, but there was a brutal zen to it. It needed little forethought. In fact, it taught me something I'd suspected about myself for a long time—that I could kill casually and feel nothing. What I wanted to do to Arhan was more than eliminating a threat, though.

An image came to me, one of Jakar as he suppressed disapproval. He'd looked at me this way a few times, often in reaction to my more cold-blooded comments. He'd never been very good at keeping his feelings off his face. Not unless it was pain.

I swallowed the guilt back. Arhan was rotten, and that rot needed to be put on display for everyone who thought him worth following. Hopefully before we reached Xeriv.

The only person in the caravan traveling in front of me was a willowy figure riding a stone fox while holding a glowing white crystal above a map draped over his mount's neck. It was the caravan's cartographer, the one guiding us through this endless maze. "Do you know someone named Carina?" I asked.

He looked over his shoulder. "*Madaf, ga*?"

"Oh. Sorry."

"Don't be. I speak Miran." He spoke without the hint of an accent. "You caught me in the middle of a thought. Why would I know someone named Carina?"

"She's a cartographer who trained in Manasus. Are you from Yarokly? That's the country she's from."

"It's as though every Miran I encounter thinks every foreigner comes from the same place. No, I'm from Karatoa. North of Yarokly. Not too far from Manasus, actually, if they weren't separated by the Black Caldera. I live in Xeriv's capital but got stranded on this side of the Rift after the quake. Trying to get back home, like most of the people in this caravan."

"Ah. Sorry, by the way. I didn't mean to offend. It's just been a while since I've talked to a cartographer."

He brought his attention back to his map. "I know you didn't."

Conversation clearly didn't interest him, but seeing him brought about an intense longing to see Carina again. *Faults above*, I actually missed Mira. I missed Carina and Meike and Magnate Bardera. I missed Emil. "What's your field of study?" I asked.

He folded the map, slid it in his pack, and slowed his mount so we rode side by side. "What's your name?"

"Efadora."

"Pleasure. I'm Geth. My field of study is the Black Caldera, actually. Imagine being the person who finds a way through it. It would forever change the east and west, since trade could completely circumvent the Rift on its north side. The cash I'm making on this trip is seed money for that expedition."

Magnate Bardera once told me Manasus's north and east borders were defined by a very clear line of certain death. "Not sure how traveling close to a mega volcano is much of an improvement from the Rift."

"The tunnels are full of poisonous gas, but its last eruption was more than a thousand years ago."

"Barde—*someone* told me the shock waves destroyed cities over a hundred miles away. So there goes all the trading posts on your route. It's been a thousand years, sure, but that just means the next time it erupts, it'll be sooner rather than later."

He shook his head. "The Black Caldera scares many, which means a lot of people have no idea the volcano is dormant now. I'll be the one to show them. Texts from the Sihraan Empire tell of a path through the area, so I promise you it exists."

"My friend Carina told me Sihraan texts tend to jerk people around. One set of ruins tells you one thing and another tells you the opposite. The Sihraan Empire was the Great Contradiction."

He tilted his head. "Yes, some cartographers follow that school of thought. The texts I've been working from were detailed enough to be worth looking into, though. C'mon, kid, we just met and you're already calling my field of study sulf-spit. Ease up."

"Sorry." I decided that I liked this man. I added, "Carina also told me the Archive's been around since before the territories existed. You'd think you guys would've learned everything about the world by now."

He laughed, the rich sound echoing across the silent caravan. "A cartographer's senses only extend so far. There could be something hiding a short walk below us and no one would ever find it. Besides, cartographers weren't always focused on mapmaking. We used to be a pretty religious bunch."

"What would the Archives even worship?"

"The Sihraans, believe it or not. It was a core tenet among cartographers to repopulate the Sihraan's ruins after the people of the Empire disappeared. Then it evolved into just trying to find the ruins and log them. Then we became Miran mapmakers, until we reached a point where we wanted to map out other countries, so we expanded east. If you don't believe me, look at some of the vows that Archive initiatives make before becoming cartographers. To 'become one with the Sihraans' and all that."

"So do you moonlight as a religious fanatic when you're not studying the Black Caldera?"

He stiffened. "Of course not."

The comment was meant to get a laugh—I would've settled for a smile, even—but Geth rode off until he was just outside conversational distance. It seemed like an overreaction, but how would I know? Emil once told me I had a knack for saying the wrong things with the right intentions.

WE STOPPED FOR camp in a grotto where the guards combed the nearly fifty feet expanse of jungle to check for dangerous wildlife. I slid off the chimp, which let out a sad hoot and nudged my leg with a knuckle as I walked away. I hunted down Jakar and Torlo and found them near a wall, Jakar and a middle-aged woman kneeling over Torlo who lay on his back, eyes closed, the soles of his feet raw and bloody.

"That looks... painful," I said.

"His shoes fell apart," Jakar said, rubbing at the place on his chest where Sara had stabbed him. Bags hung heavy under his eyes, too. Apparently all three of us were in various stages of falling apart.

"By Taz'cal's strength did this boy keep pace as long as he

did," the trader said, "but he won't be walking next bell." She fished out two pouches from her personal bag on her cart and handed them to Jakar, who scooped out a fingerful of the dark paste inside. "It's made from dehydrated blackberries and boiled stalag acorns," the trader said. "Give it to your friend. The other pouch has yarrow extract to keep the wounds on his feet from getting infected. It won't do a thing to heal it, so you'll have to figure something else out if he has any hope of walking anytime soon."

"Thank you," Jakar said. "My old teachers from when I was a kid used yarrow extract to treat my cuts and scrapes. Are you from Sulian Daw?"

That's when I noticed that Jakar's accent was a faint shadow of the trader's.

"I am," she said. The woman had a stony hue to her skin, too. She spoke in Sulian, slowly and awkwardly, and Jakar answered. She continued in Miran. "I'm from a small city called Kenah, not far from Som Abast, but I haven't been there since I was a little girl. I'm Xerivian in all but blood."

"I'm Jakar. That's Efadora and this is Torlo. My sister and I are trying to get to Sulian Daw."

"I'm Namira. You signed a serf contract to get through the Rift? Does your neck hurt from carrying all those rocks around in your head? You would've saved time by waiting for a new trade route to be established and booking passage the normal way."

"What's done is done. At the moment I'm only concerned about how invested the sergeant is in getting my sister, Torlo, and me to Xeriv."

"Apologies. *Dren isc prysiet.* Hard truths are oft ill given in harder times. I can tell the grunts are taking inspiration from our sergeant's lack of compassion, so slowing the caravan down for you three will be out of the question. They won't let anyone ride on the back of the cart, either." She wiped her face and let out an exasperated sound. "I'll need a case of wine and a long vacation before I lease my cart to Darkwater again."

As if sensing I had reneged on my promise to lick his boots, Arhan rode our way, scoping the line of traders breaking down their carts for passing's end. "Torlo needs to purchase a ride on one of the chimps," I said to him.

"Offer's only good for you," he said. When he saw Torlo's feet, he cringed and turned his head. "He's too heavy."

"What about shoes?"

"Do you think Darkwater is in the shoe business, sweetheart?" He continued to avoid looking in Torlo's general direction. "You serfs can trade shoes amongst yourselves. That's the only way Meatfeet is getting a pair." He noticed the pouches in Jakar's hands. "I see you purchased some extra rations with serf debt."

"Actually," Namira said, squaring up to the guard leader who loomed over her on his mount. "That was a gift from me, or is that a problem? Harassing contractors isn't within your purview, I'll remind you."

The sweetness in Arhan's smile soured. "The contract you signed stated that you would, in fact, follow my orders."

She barked out a laugh. "Yes, to comply with any order that ensures the safety of the caravan. I don't see any danger around here. Do you?"

Arhan made a face and nudged his fox down the line.

"I'm sorry I can't be of more help," Namira said after he left. "I'd offer to let Torlo ride on my lap, but the tunnels will buck him off within the hour." She watched his blood soaking into the dirt, opened her mouth to speak, then thought better of it and walked off.

An hour later I sat on my bedroll, nibbling on the rice and half a potato in my stone cup. Torlo stared at the stalactites illuminated by green moss, his eyes glazed, and I wondered if he'd be dead in the next passing. No, he'd wait around in a glowing grotto like this one until the panic set in, then he'd flee into the pitch darkness and die of dehydration within a week. Or become something's meal a lot sooner. Powdered bark currently caked his feet—it was benthic willow that Geth had been gracious enough to hand over, which was meant to dull the pain—but it'd rub off as soon as he stood. I'd asked around about shoes, and the guards had ridiculed me while the traders gave profuse, useless apologies.

The distant look in Torlo's eyes bothered me. Someone with such a brainlessly warm demeanor wasn't supposed to look so sad.

I forced my attention away from him and onto Jakar. "How are you holding up?"

"Great," he said. He coughed out the word like he'd been holding his breath.

"You can tell me," I said, lowering my voice. Fair enough he'd want to hide his pain from Arhan, but I was different. Or at least I hoped I was. "How hurt are you?"

"I've been hurt the whole time." A bead of sweat slid down his temple. "I should've taken it easy after Augustin. We've been traveling too hard. My hand and my shoulder weren't so bad when we reached the eastern reaches, but catching myself every time I'm about to fall on my face is undoing a lot of that."

I scooted over until I was sitting right next to him, then said even lower, "I saw the map Geth's using to guide us. It's a key, so he's the only one who's supposed to be able to read it, but you're bound of silicon, right? So you can read it too?"

He nodded.

"Let's steal it. We'll kill Arhan and the other guards, then we'll take the caravan over and go at our own pace. If Geth or the traders don't like it, then too bad. They help us or get left behind."

His concern deepened. "I can barely hold a sword at the moment. If there were two or three guards, maybe, but I'll just get us killed, or Geth will make a run for it and then we'll be stuck here."

I squeezed at my fingers, thinking. Sometimes I forgot Jakar was just a man, a person who could be pushed past his limit. I'd spent too much time before the battle of Augustin building him up in my head as the person who had cut his way through the Granite Road for Sara, the weapon who'd earned the nickname *Dor Di Fero*. The Iron Sorrow. I couldn't think of him like that anymore. He could be hurt or killed if too much was asked of him, and I was worried that even though he was aware of his injuries, he'd push himself past his breaking point if I let him. Or forced him to by doing something stupid. And Fhelfire, my plan *was* stupid, I supposed.

Then there was Torlo. Torlo wasn't my friend—in fact, he still irritated me—so if he had to be left behind because he wasn't strong enough to carry on, maybe that was just how it had to be. I scarfed down the last of my food and wrapped myself tight in my blanket, then turned away to face the wall. The end came for all of us eventually, and now it had come for Torlo.

After an hour of staring at the inside of my eyelids and debating furiously with myself, I threw off my blanket in frustration and scanned the camp. Jakar was shifting around, but that was normal for him, even when he was dead asleep. I still hadn't worked up the courage to ask him about his nightmares. They'd been a staple of his ever since we'd skipped town out of Augustin, and I knew they had something to do with what Sara had made him do. I also knew the people we had to kill on the way here hadn't helped, but I didn't know what the alternative was. I used to think that people who couldn't take a life when it was necessary were weak, but now I wasn't so sure. Jakar had killed more than anyone and it had taken something from him I wasn't sure he could get back. I spotted two guards sitting on rocks on one side of the camp with a third at the opposite end, but everyone else was asleep. I kept out of sight and slunk off, keeping my head low.

The rest of the guards slept in a line, alternating head to toe, their sword belts lying at their sides. Embers from their fire cast them in a low light, and I left the shadow of the closest cart to approach the nearest guard. The two on watch sat with their backs to me, talking in low voices. I moved to my hands and knees and crawled to the nearest sleeping man, then watched him breathe in and out, in and out. I wondered how easy it would be to sneak up to Arhan and bury a blade in his jugular. My fingers danced toward the sleeping man's sword belt and I slid his knife from its leather sheath, waiting for his breathing to hitch. It didn't. I felt the edge but found it too dull, then slowly pushed his knife back where it belonged.

I moved to the next man. He didn't breathe deep and even the way some did, making it easy to tell if they were fast asleep—he was so quiet that he could have been faking it for all I knew. But if he was, he wouldn't have been letting me pull his weapon out of his belt as I was doing. I watched his eyelids until I had the knife in my hands. I felt the edge. It would have to do.

Moving from cart to cart, I kept myself out of the sight lines of those on watch while staying as quiet as possible, passing traders fast asleep under their carts. I stopped at one belonging to a squat easterner I'd noticed using a spool of twine to secure some of the smaller boxes, found the spool and cut off a ten-foot piece, then continued onward.

At the last cart, I hid behind the back wheel and checked for the rear watchman, who sat fifteen feet away against a wall. He was partly facing my direction, but he wasn't moving. People on watch tended to get a little bored and restless, but this one was rock still. The longer I stared, the surer I was that he was sleeping. I moved to the tread of the wheel and worked the blade into the rubber, cutting off a piece roughly the length of Torlo's feet.

Fhelfire, this was stupid. I was partially shrouded in darkness, but if the man opened his eyes he'd have to be braindead not to instantly connect my figure with the only kid traveling with the caravan. They'd string me up with the twine I'd stolen. All to help Torlo. It was best I go wrap myself in my blanket again and forget I'd ever thought up this idiotic idea.

The work was slow as I kept my eye on the sleeping guard, but soon I had cut two shallow depressions into the wheel and held the slices of rubber in my hand. The damage wasn't obvious—someone would have to be looking for it to see it, and it was the rearmost wheel in the last cart of the caravan. The cart owner might experience a bumpy ride, but he'd probably blame the terrain.

I examined the blade longingly. If I didn't return it, the guard would notice it as soon as he woke, and knowing Arhan, the sergeant would scour the caravan until it was found. One guess where he'd look first. I snuck back to the gaggle of sleeping guards and returned the knife, then headed to my bedroll.

A handful of hours later, Torlo woke up to the camp rising and me applying a liberal coat of benthic willow to his feet. "What're you doing?" he croaked, groaning as he sat up.

"Birth Passing present," I said as I tied the first slipper on, making sure the twine wouldn't cut into his skin.

"My Birth Passing isn't for eight months."

"Early present. Or late. You pick."

When I finished, he pulled himself up and tested the shoes, limping around. "They're soft. What are they made of?"

"Rubber fixed to pieces of wisteria root that I glued together with some resin. Don't ask where I got the rubber, and don't tell anyone about it, either. Hopefully, Arhan or his goons don't take too close of a look."

He fiddled with the knots. "Gonna have a bad time trying to get these off."

"Find a way. You'll need to clean your feet every passing's end so your cuts can breathe and don't get infected."

He nodded, staring at the pathetic-looking shoes. I'm sure he was smart enough to guess where the rubber had come from. When he looked up, water glittered in his eyes. "This is the nicest thing anyone has ever done for me."

"Stop. You sound like a child."

I stalked off, a sickness coursing through my stomach as I thought about the expression on his face. Nobody had ever looked at me like that before. *Why* had nobody ever looked at me like that before?

Into the Rift

It was a fluke. He was a bandit, and he would've killed me the first passing we met if our situations had been reversed. That's what strangers did. That's what friends did. I had Sara's teachings and my time in Manasus with the Titanite gang to prove it.

Chapter 7—Ester

RED CATERPILLAR SCARS riddled the stump of Damek's arm where he'd once had hundreds of stitches, the old wound seasoned with echinacea powder to prevent infection and garnished with a hint of unprocessed Ash leaf for the pain. Ester gave it a final once-over before covering it with new bandages.

"They can't send anyone else?" Damek asked.

"It doesn't matter who they send. We still have to leave."

He watched her, dejected, while she stuffed clothes in his rucksack. He was in one of his black moods—he'd refuse to help, forcing her to do everything until it was done or the arguing started. Ester kept her mouth shut, though. She was the one who'd convinced him to leave Tulchi in the first place, and barely a year later she was asking him to go back. And to go without her.

"What are Mom and Dad and Myrilan going to say when they find out I'm only half the person I was when we left?" he asked.

He resorted to 'half talk' so often now that Ester couldn't do anything other than ignore it. "Myrilan is long gone working for the treasury," she said. "Mom and Dad are going to love seeing you."

After a moment, he smiled. "They'd shit gravel if I told them a primordia was the one who took my arm... right before we killed him."

"Hey now, don't go taking all the credit once you start spreading the word. I want songs written about me, too."

"Fine. Your name's easier to rhyme with, anyway."

Her grin faded. "But seriously, keep it to yourself. Myrilan can never know."

"Obviously. I shouldn't even be going home. I should be traveling with you."

"Senior Arc Smith Celestana forbade it." She kept her eyes on his pack. *He'll only slow you down*, the senior arc smith had said. Ester was now at a point with the Foundry that she'd consider disobeying someone like Celestana, but this trip would likely have a dead body or two by its end, and she'd rather her brother not be one of them.

Once again, she struggled to hide her gloom, but Damek was too busy grumbling as he tried to lace his boots. Her entire perspective on the Foundry had shifted in a direction she still didn't fully understand. What else were they lying about? Mateo would shame her if he knew how often she fantasized about the rest of the council getting on with their pilgrimages to the Star Mines and disappearing forever. It was every smith's destiny to work the Star Mines once their hair was grayed and even though Panqao's was still salt and pepper he planned to leave for the mines within the week. There he would mine rhidium in the bowels of the land, close to Fheldspra's heart where he would seek *aufkung*, or spiritual enlightenment, until the day he died. Once Ester found the missing rhidium and returned to Augustin, she could push for change within the Foundry without ever having to worry about Panqao interfering again.

For the last time, she and Damek exited the little hole-in-the-wall they had shared together this past year, passing wind-whipped torches and the rough, cracked corridors of the fourth level to descend into the warmth of the trade district. Mateo waited for them inside an old epoxy shop—the one Magnate

Sorrelo and Jakar had dragged Bolivar Adriann out of so many months ago. The place smelled of old, tacky resin and burnt moss, the shop having been abandoned since before the Burning of Augustin. Xander was waiting alongside the master smith, hands folded in front of him as he examined one of the old stirring cauldrons.

Mateo nodded to Damek. "You look much improved." He turned his attention to Ester. "I met with the senior arc smiths and we decided it would be for the best that Xander accompany you on your trip. We think you'll find him useful."

"I thought bringing people into the fold was a cardinal sin among the senior arc smiths," Ester said, a little too bitterly; they wanted to send Xander with her but not Damek? She glanced at her brother, the pain in his eyes from this development clear.

"I'm sorry, saiora," Xander said awkwardly. "It's my fault. Mateo asked how he could reward me and I insisted he let me help. I've been due for a research trip into the crust and figured I'd get by just as well in your company, considering I would have you for protection."

"So I'll have to worry about watching someone else's back while I'm tracking down the rhidium?" Ester asked. Xander's lack of reaction upon mention of the rhidium meant the master smith had already briefed him, which meant there really was no turning back.

"I really do think he can help," Mateo said. "Going alone probably isn't for the best."

It wasn't fair. Ester wanted Damek at her side, not some guild member she hardly knew. What could she do, though? Damek blinked hard at the ground, but he didn't complain.

"Fine," she said. "We need to talk before we go. Xander will wait out front."

The glass maker didn't argue, leaving without a word, and Ester could barely wait for the door to shut. "Tell me what the Foundry's learned about electricity so we can take advantage of the weakness Jakar found when he killed Nektarios."

Mateo ran a slow hand along a stone tray full of different colored stones used for constructing mosaics. "Jakar told me he thought the chronographers of the Tempurium might use electricity in their binding ritual with salt, but they've been less than helpful with my inquiries, as usual. Not that I expected anything more. The trade schools have never been willing to reveal their secrets and I don't see that changing. Outside that, I've put out some feelers on how electricity can be weaponized. Strictly for educational reasons. I still have no intention of allowing the Foundry to fight."

"Sure, sure. What did you find out?"

"I've only heard whispers. Rumors of people salvaging apparatuses from Sihraan ruins that strike harder than any doline eel could manage. I've heard of a group on the outskirts of the Manasus capital claiming they can 'make magnets bite.' That lead's a little thinner. Other than that, not much else."

"If we find what we're looking for, are we going to follow through with building weapons? For educational reasons, of course."

The master smith gnawed on his bottom lip while he studied her, probably not very keen on her demanding tone, but she was past being polite. This conversation was the only thing left she had control over, and she would make it count. "I know it's disappointing to hear," he began, "but I've never been more careful with an investigation in my life. If the Sovereign found out we were looking into how to create weapons that could incapacitate his sycophants, he wouldn't see us as a nuisance. He would put an end to us. There's no telling how many of his agents are roaming the territories since Sara Adriann and her mercenary army happened, so I have to move carefully with this."

It wasn't what Ester wanted to hear, but what was new? "All right. Thank you for the update."

"Of course." He rubbed his arm absentmindedly—a surprisingly self-conscious gesture. He seemed embarrassed. "A lot has changed these last several months. Sometimes

I think about how much I've changed. I want you to know you're partly responsible for this. I'm incredibly proud of you, Apprentice Ester."

The words caught her off-guard, and something deep inside her lifted. Suddenly she didn't want to do this anymore—she wanted to stay and help Mateo deal with the Sovereign and whatever nonsense he brought with him. She didn't want to leave this man who was obviously on the verge of collapsing at any moment. "I... thank you." She pulled him into a hug. Her family and the Foundry were the only people she knew who expressed physical affection—a tragedy, she realized, because physical touch seemed so very necessary for human connection—and she was about to abandon both. "It means the world to me. Please promise you'll sleep."

He stepped back, his eyes crinkling. "For you? Very well."

SHE, DAMEK, AND Xander left the capital in travelers' bat-hide leathers, along with foxes and fake travel papers supplied by the Foundry. Mateo had learned the rug seller's cart passed through the city gates three passings ago with a full load of rugs, a man named Breach riding the helm. They rode for Sanskra, the first town outside the capital and one the thieves would've had to pass through on their way through the crust. Damek's traveling companion was waiting for him there as well, someone the Foundry had hired to accompany him to Tulchi.

Damek kept grunting in frustration, rolling his shoulder to readjust the satchel's strap across his body every other minute, his balance shaky as he held the fox's reins with one hand. "I wonder how many times over I can drink myself into oblivion in some backwater town if I sell my fox," he said.

"A bit of practice is the only thing keeping you from doing what anyone else can," Ester said. "You'll recalibrate."

"I need my arm. I can't do this without one."

Thinking about all the things he couldn't do was all Damek

cared about anymore. She understood why he struggled—
she'd spent so *much* of her time understanding—but she
had no idea what to say to help him through it. No matter
her words, they were always the wrong ones. She considered
starting the hundredth version of the same argument they'd
had for weeks—that he was capable of so much more, if only
he set his mind to it—but kept her mouth shut. Maybe it
wasn't right for her to tell him what he could or couldn't do
when she had no firsthand experience in what he was going
through.

"My first girlfriend was born with a hand that didn't like to
listen," Xander said. "She's a demon on foxback now. Last I
heard she became a courier. With a bit of practice I'm sure you
could ride your fox with the best of them."

Damek tugged at his satchel strap. "Is that why you two
broke up? Because of her deformity?"

"Not at all," Xander said awkwardly. "I wanted to make
my mark on the world when I was a teenager. Delusions of
grandeur and whatnot. So no, it had nothing to do with that.
For some reason I thought love couldn't fit into the equation
of all the things I wanted to do and all the places I wanted to
see. But as it turned out, all my decisions ever did was take me
away from the people I cared for."

Youth and idealism, the perfect mix for tunnel vision. Ester
remembered her string of obsessions growing up, ending
with her entry into the Foundry. Sure, dedicating her life to
smithhood had taken her away from her parents, but she
couldn't complain. At least Damek got to tag along and
remain a part of her life. It had also helped the two of them
escape those dark, drippy chambers her parents dragged them
to where they would meet with hooded cultists to worship at
the shrine of Terias, Aspect of the Wilds. All those busts and
carvings of terapedes, maw foxes, and flesh-eating plants still
disgusted Ester if she thought too much on them. The idea
that she'd almost been indoctrinated into a cult disgusted
her, too. Any kid in the territories with a healthy respect for

self-preservation was taught that fire was the best protection from the horrors of the crust, and there, Mom and Dad were kneeling at the claws of those that would tear them apart in an instant.

"You're sure you didn't leave that girl behind because you'd have to take care of her?" Damek asked.

Ester turned to her brother, startled by the rude comment, and Xander let out a snort of outrage. "Absolutely not," he said. The guild member glared at the scattering of travelers trotting along the road farther down the tunnel, stewing, but Damek was too oblivious as he fiddled with the ten little things that bothered him while he rode. Ester realized her brother hadn't realized he was being mean to Xander because he was only thinking of his current situation—of how Ester was leaving *him* behind—and that realization hurt.

Light blazed on the plateau in the middle of the lake where Sanskra stood. With the extra paperwork required for all trade and travel, it took half of forever to get through the line backed up all the way to the entrance tunnel. When they reached the front, the guards didn't give their forged travel papers more than a cursory glance.

"I'd like a moment of your time, saior," Ester said to the man at the barricades holding the logbook.

He leaned over to check the dozens of people waiting behind her. "Don't have one to spare."

"Please. I'm tracking someone wanted by the Foundry."

"You a bounty hunter?"

"I'm a smith, actually. I was wondering if I could look through your logbook and check for a certain cart that passed through here about three passings ago."

He looked her up and down, incredulity forming in the creases of his face. "Where are your robes?"

"This isn't a trip I want to advertise."

"Do you have a writ from the audencia authorizing access to our logbooks?"

"No. This is all off-record."

The guard spent a moment balancing on the fence, then Ester saw him start to tip the wrong way. If this had been months ago, he wouldn't have batted an eye before handing the logbook over to a smith. Even one without robes. Trust in one's neighbor had died the passing a mercenary army decided to march on the Granite Road.

"Orders are orders," he said. "Would love to help you, but I really can't."

"That's a lovely engagement band," Xander said. "When's the wedding?"

The guard glanced at the secular steel ring on his finger. "Not till next year."

"So I'm to guess you've yet to purchase a wedding band for the lucky person in question?"

"Still a ways out before we shop for anything like that."

Xander slipped off one of his rings. He glanced at the other guards—they were neck deep in dealing with the crowd—then handed it over. The ring was translucent, but when the guard held it up, light played on fiery ribbons of color, like lava flowing through a glass tube. "Early wedding present," Xander said. "Sorry I won't be able to make it to the ceremony."

The guard's breath caught. "This is guild glass?"

"Aye. Made it myself."

The guard turned the ring over and over, thinking. "All right, all right," he said, and pocketed the ring. He reached under his table and grabbed another logbook wrapped in twine. "What you're looking for would be in here. Be quick."

We took the book to the water's edge just inside town, under an eave with glowing white moss curling over the edge of the roof. "There," I said after a few minutes. "Our thief, Breach, is headed toward Telos." Telos was Augustin's easternmost town with a population of hardly more than a couple hundred. Four passings' ride by foxback. "He'll have his back to the Tear, which means we can corner him."

"What if he lied to the guards and is headed somewhere else?" Damek asked.

"There'll be a Telos destination stamp in the cart's registration log, so good luck explaining that to the guards in any town sitting in the wrong direction," Xander said. "Breach probably knows this, too. These new regulations out of Saracosta saved us, I think."

"Thank the Sovereign," Ester said, and clapped Xander on the back, knocking his spectacles off his nose. "And thanks for what you did."

He adjusted his spectacles and gave a pleased smile, and all of Ester's resentments toward him evaporated. How could she have let Panqao's disillusionment eat at her so much after everything Xander had done?

Damek stirred. "I never would've thought to do something like that. You're in good company." His expression dropped as he stared at the obsidian pendant hanging from her neck that he'd gotten for her the passing she was accepted into the Foundry.

Ester couldn't think of anything to say. This wasn't the Damek she knew. She missed her brother.

They stopped at an inn called The Caterpillar. The place seemed to be in the middle of celebrating their grand reopening, with its floors and ceiling sporting new beams of rockwood planks, freshly stained, and the air smelling of dirt that a flood of patrons had tracked in on their boots. A fire roared in the hearth where laborers, likely on their break, joked and laughed into their cups. A middle-aged woman sat at the end of the bar with a clipboard in hand. "Senna?" Ester asked.

"Yes, saiora. Lia?"

Ester nodded at the fake name and gestured toward her brother. "This is Lidorno."

"Good, good. I'll take good care of you," the woman said to Damek. "Worked with many soldiers in my time. We'll be in Tulchi before you know it."

Damek's smile was wooden. "Pleasure, saiora."

The traveling nurse provided small talk for the next several minutes. To the woman's credit, she didn't give Damek's wound undue attention aside from asking about his current healing and pain regimens, but she didn't pretend the wound didn't exist, either. It was as though she knew exactly what to do and say at every moment. At first Damek couldn't stop with his sardonic remarks, but by the end he had resorted to the self-deprecating humor he'd developed in the recent weeks, which meant a good mood and easier smiles.

Ester had a lot to learn from this woman. Sometimes she thought she knew how to handle this new Damek, and other times she felt way out of her depth. As much as she resented Senior Arc Smith Panqao, she had to hand it to him for having his apprentice hire the right person to travel with Damek.

"Gonna turn in to get some shut eye now," Senna said. "Meet here at passing's eve?"

Damek nodded. When Senna left and it was the three of them again, Ester handed her bag of standards and bits to Xander. "Mind grabbing us some mole-rat jerky next door?"

"Can do," he said.

Once he left and Ester was left alone with her brother, she turned to Damek, who continued to nurse his horn of wine. "So you like her?" she asked.

Damek shrugged. "Tell me of a travel companion who didn't get on your nerves at one point or another and I'll buy you a drink. But yeah, she's promising."

"Do you have your caravan ticket?"

"Assuming you weren't lying those five times you told me it was in the front pocket of my satchel?"

"Right." A long moment passed between them. "You should know I don't like this either. It's not right that we have to part ways like this."

"Well, we have to, so no use dwelling on it. I see why the Foundry chose him over me."

She swallowed. How could she argue with him? Xander was capable, but that had nothing to do with Damek's injuries. "I'll make it up to you."

"This is probably the worst time to be promising that. I don't even know when we'll see each other again."

"After I find the rhidium. I'll return it to the Foundry then head straight to Tulchi. Maybe I'll wrap this up quick enough to catch up before you get there."

The ball in his throat bobbed. "Don't promise that. Do what you have to first and convince the smiths to stand against the Sovereign. If I ever had a reason to give up my other arm, it'd be to do to the other primordia what we did to Nektarios."

Ester looked around, but the tavern noise was too loud for anyone to have heard. She hated thinking about it, but Damek was right. Pushing the Foundry into action was more important than a family reunion. The primordias' casual cruelty and the Sovereign's secret genocides needed to stop, yet there were so many places for her dreams to go wrong. The arc smiths and senior arc smiths could dig their heels in if she pushed too hard. What if she never found the rhidium?

There was another possibility to consider. Maybe everything she hoped the Foundry could achieve would come to pass after all. Maybe it would all go right only for her to find out they weren't strong enough to take on the Sovereign anyway. Maybe her reward for success would be to watch the Sovereign crush her and everyone she loved with ease.

Chapter 8—Jakar

A QUAKE HIT the caravan on our fifth passing through the Rift.

The ground began to move at the same time a deep rumble filled the cavern, like an avalanche roaring in the distance, but in every direction. The caravan jolted to a halt, filling with panicked voices that were barely audible over the rumbling, and I lost my grip on the cart as the ground jerked up. I fell onto my back and knocked the wind out of myself. I lay there wheezing, forced to wait it out while swinging torches on the carts played bizarre shadows on the walls. Was it time to die? Death had stopped scaring me on the passing my flesh binding nearly killed me in Augustin's Foundry, but a frantic energy filled me anyway. There was still so much to do, so many people to save.

The rumbling stilled. Everyone else was sitting, lying on the ground, or in the seats of their carts, staring at the ceiling, waiting to see if the Rift was playing some cruel joke on us before it crushed us all. The silence stretched into minutes.

Efadora appeared at the top of my view, upside down, and she helped me to my feet. "What's wrong?" she asked. "You look like you ate month-old meat."

I tried to swallow the nausea that had swelled into me

during the quake, and after a few moments it started to fade. "Motion sickness."

She left to check on Torlo, who was already brushing himself off, and I wondered why I'd lied to her. The nausea had started when opening my Eye during the quake to search for elements I was bound to. I'd been looking for fault lines that could cause the tunnel to collapse and kill us, but instead of seeing glittering trace elements, like a sky full of stars, the elements had been awash with white fire. Then the nausea came.

"We almost out of this flame-forsaken Rift?" a Xerivian trader shouted in a thick accent.

"Next passing," Arhan yelled back. "Double and triple check your carts. Secure whatever shook loose. Your contracts are voided if the products aren't delivered in full."

The caravan rolled into motion, and I rubbed at my chest. Getting knocked off my feet had brought about a new level of pain to my wounds, and now I couldn't stop my breaths from coming out sharp through clenched teeth. Weeks of hard travel had only allowed my chest to half-heal, but now the stab wound felt as though it had happened just yesterday. This wasn't a mind-over-matter situation anymore. I needed medical attention.

The following hours were a painful blur, rivaling one of my worst days at the Ebonrock compound. Arhan's voice penetrated the fog in my brain—it was a command to set up camp—and it was as if his voice had become magic, turning my muscles to jelly. I fell to my knees. Someone was striking flint to the tinder inside my torso, over and over, drumming to the sound of my heart, and a pair of hands grabbed me. Their owner was talking. The hands managed to help me hobble to a wall out of the way of everyone.

"I knew you were full of guano," a voice said. It sounded like Efadora. "You need to tell me whenever you're hurt, all right?"

"Just dehydrated, is all."

She knelt in front of me, her outline fuzzy. "I know dehydration and this ain't it."

I started coughing, my chest seizing in wracking, horrible pain that left me sliding on my side into the dirt. Spit and phlegm left dark, bloody stains on the ground.

"Oh, fhelfire," Efadora whispered. She pulled me until I was sitting up, then she helped me lift my shirt over my head, drawing in a breath through her teeth. Angry purple veins covered my chest, sprouting like roots from the old wound in my solar plexus. I could feel the blood needling under my skin, like a thousand sparks igniting and being quenched by my blood, over and over again.

"I'm dying," I said stupidly.

We looked at each other for a long moment. Different thoughts seemed to cycle through her head, most of which involved fear, and it became clear she didn't want me to die. She, an Adriann. I wasn't sure why that was significant or surprising. We'd been traveling together all this time, getting along well enough. Still, there was a weight to seeing her acknowledge the feeling.

"Jakar?" Torlo asked, limping over to us.

I wiped the spit from the side of my mouth and crossed an arm over my chest, but there was no hiding it. "I need a doctor."

He nodded as though I'd made a simple request for a waterskin, then limped away, almost stumbling. He was struggling in his sorry state, too, but I had faith in his strength. At least one of us would make it to Xeriv.

"This isn't normal," Efadora said. She touched my wound as gently as possible then waited, and I nodded in permission. "I'm the last person to know about diseases of the crust, but I think I would've heard about a symptom like this before."

A couple traders stood off to the side, eyeballing us and conversing in their native tongue. Then Geth was standing over us, his arms crossed. "Out of the three of you, I didn't expect the Sulian here to get the worst of it."

"Thank you for the helpful input," Efadora said, annoyed. "Any chance you know what's wrong with him?"

"Well, we've traveled through dozens of ecosystems we barely understand. He was probably bit by something that wanted to say hello."

Torlo rounded the cart with Namira and a guard in tow. "Here," he said. "Someone needs to help him, quick."

"And what am I supposed to do?" the guard asked.

"Namira said you two had a conversation about poultices and herbs. You're trying to finance schooling so you can apply to the Menders' Halls, yeah? Can't you help him?"

"He's a serf, though."

The few guards possessing consciences had resorted to saying this when they couldn't summon the word *no*. Torlo smiled like the man had told an innocent joke, but the expression wasn't mocking. "We know the real reason. Come now. Namira said you're no fan of how the sergeant's been handling this run. Jakar is Darkwater property, anyway, which you're supposed to be protecting."

The guard squinted at my chest. "That really does look awful." He came to my side, adjusting the sheath to his blade so he could kneel. "Reminds me of poisoning, but looks to be from a cut, not a bite." He noticed my shoulder. "What's that?"

From his angle he could see the scarring that peeked out from behind the top of my shoulder, and I pushed my back flush against the wall. "Nothing. Just an old scar."

"Throwing a party over here?" a voice called out. "Best be waiting until we cross into Xeriv to celebrate. Still plenty of danger to be had." Arhan joined us. "What are you doing, Vikozo?"

The guard stood and about-faced. "Attending to the serf, Sergeant. He's sick."

"Sometimes you have to know when to cut losses. Aren't you on first watch? You should be at the north side of camp."

"But Sergeant, I don't think we should be writing the serf off so quickly. We don't even know what's wrong with him. You've barely spared him a second glance."

Arhan shook his head, lips pursed. He let out the sharp, three-toned whistle I recognized, and soon the men and women under his command were collecting behind him. "To be a good leader is to know when to make the hard choice," the sergeant said to them. "It is to accept that those under your charge won't always like you. These are sacrifices you'll need to make if you want to get the job done." He unclipped the whip from his belt. "Vikozo, take your chest guard off. Undershirt, too."

The color drained from the guard's face. "Sir?"

The sergeant stared at him until he did as he was told.

Arhan whipped the man six times in front of everyone. Vikozo was sobbing after the second and groveling in the dirt by the last. Many of the traders shifted uncomfortably, some even spoke among themselves in quiet shock, but they weren't foolish enough to try to stop Arhan. There would have been only one outcome if they'd tried. I watched the spectacle in my peripheral—I knew enough about that sort of work to guess at every little detail with my eyes closed—and concentrated on the other guards instead. They looked on with hard eyes, gazes crystallizing with each crack of the whip. It was hard to tell which of them would turn to stone and which would shatter in outrage on some passing farther down the road. A few struggled with the spectacle, but they did as well as they could to mask their disapproval lest they wind up kneeling beside Vikozo. When would Arhan's behavior become too much?

Vikozo refused to look in our direction as two guards helped him to his feet and brought him to their side of the camp. "Arhan really is something," Efadora said in a low voice.

"They'll spin whatever you're thinking of doing to make him look brave or the victim," I said, and coughed. "Don't waste your energy."

I saw in her eyes the Adriann need to balance the world around her. That look of hers was worsening with each passing, that red-hot desire to right her personal wrong.

The former princepa reexamined my wound and her anger dissipated. "We have less than a passing to go. Can you make it?"

I shook my head. "If we're that close, maybe I can find my way if I go at my own pace."

"Right." She seemed smart enough to realize I was only placating her, that to be left behind in the absolute darkness that dogged our caravan would be a death sentence. She eyed the cartographer who had lingered to talk to Namira. It was obvious what she was thinking. The map.

Namira parted ways with Geth and approached us. "Listen," the woman said in a voice only loud enough for Efadora and me to hear. "I know I'll regret this, but I can get you through this last stretch. Come find me in a few hours." She seemed to regret the words as soon as she'd said them, but she left without another word. Geth was observing us from a short distance away, a curious look on his face. How loyal was he to Arhan?

We made our beds, and I filled Torlo in on Namira's vague offer—the last thing I wanted was for him to inadvertently raise suspicion. He and Efadora waited up with me, and once everyone was asleep, I snuck off through the shadows and crawled under Namira's cart, where she lay wide awake. Distant torchlight glistened in the whites of her eyes, keeping company with the regret those eyes contained. "You tell anyone about this, I'll kill you," she said. She pushed against the underside of her cart and a panel swung down. "It's a tight squeeze," she said. "About as tight as it gets. Don't break anything."

I climbed into the compartment, gasping as I did so—there was less than a foot gap between the cart's false bottom and the real bottom, and the compartment was half-filled with unlabeled packages. I couldn't even turn around. "I can't get you out until we're in Darkwater's warehouse," she said, her voice muffled past my feet, "but at least you won't be dead. Or maybe I'm getting ahead of myself. We'll find you a doctor as soon as possible. Also, don't make any noise or I'm leaving you in there."

The panel clicked into position followed by the snap of a lock. I considered opening my Eye to see if I could guess what the woman was smuggling, but rewarding my curiosity with overwhelming nausea didn't seem all that worth it.

I didn't realize I'd dozed off until voices were rousing the camp. "Where is he?" Efadora asked from the other side of the panel my head was squished against.

"Right here," the trader said, followed by a gentle knocking. "Keep it to yourself."

Arhan's voice couldn't have followed up sooner. "Where's your brother?" he asked.

"This might surprise you, but he had the impression he might die," Efadora said. "He snuck ahead."

"If that were true, whoever was on watch would've arrested him."

"They probably missed him. You're the one who trained them, right?"

A few seconds of silence followed, then a whistle. "Check the caravan for any hiding serfs," the sergeant called out to the guards.

Chapter 9—Efadora

THE GUARDS SEARCHED the caravan while Torlo, Namira, and I kept it cool off to the side. They started with Namira's cart, and I watched with my heart in my throat while they searched the crevasses between the crates stacked on the back. It quickly became clear there was no space for a person to jam themselves between the boxes, though, which was the same story for the other carts. Arhan berated his subordinates, but he couldn't punish anyone because it was impossible to know who Jakar had supposedly snuck past.

Arhan eventually made the call for the caravan to get a move on.

Watching the back of Namira's cart while I walked, I started wondering if we'd get to Xeriv only to find Jakar dead, and I swallowed back the way that thought pulled at the base of my chest. No, Jakar and death were oil and water, and he'd been through much worse thanks to my family. If Jakar was incapacitated until after we reached Xeriv, maybe it was best for me to escape Darkwater before we reached civilization. That way, I could come back for Jakar later and hope Namira took care of him in the meantime.

"Sergeant?" I called out when Arhan trotted by. "I want

to rent out a ride one more time." It was time to conserve strength for my getaway.

His sourness from earlier had never left, making his smile sickly sweet. He was probably thinking of how he could be a vindictive twat one last time before we left the Rift. "Of course." He offered a gloved hand, but I shook my head. "I can do it," I said.

"Take it," he hissed.

I guessed I had no choice. "I know you're up to something," he whispered in my ear after pulling me onto his fox. "Your brother went ahead? Crock'a shit."

"You were going to abandon him. Can you blame him for going?"

"So why'd you look so nervous when we were searching the caravan?" He reached under my shirt and pinched my side, twisting hard.

"*Fi cosa*," I said, and threw my elbow back. It glanced off his arm guard. I tried to wriggle off the fox, but he held me in place and pinched harder, stealing my breath away.

"You're going to be my pet project now, you know that?" he whispered. "I'm scheduled to escort a caravan to Callo next month, and I'm gonna request Darkwater let me bring you along. You'll be my number one fan by its end."

His breath was hot on my neck and smelled of rotten jerky. My eyes filled with tears, and I focused all of my concentration on not crying out. He let go. I tried to come up with a retort as we reached the lead cart, but all I could think about was my fear, of my white-hot need to get away from this man, to the point I almost leapt on the chimp when we reached it.

Riding the chimp while heat crept into my face, I rubbed at my side and thought of the dread that had risen inside me, how sick the idea of him laying a hand on my body had made me, the pain of it notwithstanding. The fact he considered it his right to touch me was worse than the pinch itself.

Soon I was fantasizing about all the different ways I could make the light leave Arhan's eyes. Jakar would have to understand that Sulian Daw had to wait until I'd killed this shit stain of a caravan leader.

The next few hours passed in a blur—I ran a number of plans through my head, but none of them looked particularly promising. I'd need to steal a fox if I were to have any hope of outrunning the guards. The only person without a heavily armed fox was Geth, but he barely spent time with the caravan anymore. He was constantly riding up ahead, avoiding my gaze and ignoring my calls when I tried to ask how close we were.

The path opened up to a cavern so large that the ceiling and walls arced into the darkness, firefly roosts collecting along the ceiling so far away their light didn't do a thing to help us. Patches of giant white mushrooms lined the path and the air smelled of freshly churned dirt, like the mole-rat farms outside Augustin. "Stop!" someone yelled, but it was Geth shouting, not Arhan. The sergeant raced to the front, where Geth waited at the edge of the lanterns' light. "What's wrong?" he asked.

"Cave-in," Geth said.

"Trapped?"

"No. We just have a Sihraan city in the way now."

The caravan inched forward until it stopped a short distance from the newly created ridge. All of us collected along its edge, where the reflection of our torches glistened against the tips of buildings, plazas, and aqueducts. Over a thousand feet of cavern floor had collapsed onto the ruins that had been hiding beneath it. Namira dug into her bag and threw a handful of something that pattered like rice against the rooftops below. Fireflies roosting above us—these ones yellow instead of red like back home—swarmed, zooming toward the city and clinging to anywhere Namira's feed had come to rest. The trader flung another handful.

"How we gonna do this?" a guard asked.

Geth pointed at the blackness toward the invisible far ridge. "The tunnel out will be on the opposite wall. We can't be more than a few miles from Ravada. We can ditch the carts and walk the rest of the way."

A dozen traders spoke up at the same time until Arhan's voice cut through them all. "Quiet. We'll sort this out soon enough. If we have to leave the carts here, then so be it. We've got the manpower to leave behind a watch. But first we gotta worry about our first problem, which is whether we can get to Xeriv at all. We'll head to Ravada so Darkwater can bring back supplies to construct a bridge. All of you wait here while the cartographer and I scout ahead." He searched the group and his eyes landed on me. "You're coming along too."

"I'm going as well," Namira said.

Arhan laughed.

"I'm sure Darkwater's contractors would appreciate that at least one person with a more personal interest in these carts tag along with the scouting party," she said. The traders who spoke Miran voiced their agreement.

"Ya know what? That's not such a bad idea. You'll become plenty useful, I'm sure."

I leaned over the ridge while Arhan, Geth, and a guard named Cravas—Arhan's preferred bootlicker—grabbed some rope. How hard would it be to scale the far wall if I broke away from the group? They fastened some rope to the lead cart and the five of us were provided gloves for rappelling. Arhan went first, followed by the rest of us, and Cravas brought up the rear. I had only the faint illumination of the feasting fireflies to show me where to land thirty feet down. My feet hit the roof of an ancient, squat building that was covered in moss-filled fractures. "Down," Arhan ordered while I was still gaining my bearings, and we descended a spiral stairwell leading to the street below. Arhan tailed me, one hand on the hilt of his blade while he carried his torch with the other. So he wasn't completely stupid.

"Amazing," Geth said. "This has to be the easternmost known ruin by at least a hundred miles. And it's pristine." He turned full circle. "Could've told me the Sihraans left this place a year ago and I'd have believed you."

I already disliked this place. A place this big shouldn't have been this still. Even in the more remote parts of Mira—the ones safe enough to travel, at least—the walls were alive with ecosystems brimming under the surface. But this place was frozen in time. Sterile.

Once I'd overcome my initial creeps, I noticed this place was nothing like the ruins back home. Sihraan ruins in Mira usually consisted of a handful of collapsed buildings or an alcove worn down to its edges. The more preserved cities were big enough for ruin folk to populate and harass outsiders, but those ruins were small potatoes compared to this place. These ruins smelled wet and new, simmering with something I couldn't define. The echoes of our footsteps bounced through the white marble streets so loudly, it was as if there were dozens of us strolling just behind every corner. When one of us talked, phantoms whispered from dark crevasses.

"Pretty amazing place to leave behind," I said to Geth. "Must've had a hell of a reason." I caught movement in the corner of my eye and whipped around, but it was just my shadow.

"Prevailing theory is a plague. Maybe we'll find answers here."

"All I'm hearing are great reasons not to be here," Namira said.

"There'd be bodies if it was a plague," Arhan said, his voice edged with nervousness.

Geth stuck his head through a dark entryway. "Bones at the least. In the hundreds of years cartographers have explored Sihraan ruins, not a single body's been found. That lends to the Six Civ theory, which says the Sihraans weren't one empire but several, and when each civilization did whatever it was they needed to do, they packed up and left. That fits with the Great Contradiction, about how evidence of their art, education, science, and culture has little consistency. All they share are geothermal—"

"How's about we keep focusing?" Cravas said. "Remember the sergeant's orders." He looked to Arhan for approval, but the sergeant didn't notice.

Geth bristled. "You're going to do just fine in Darkwater, you know that?"

Cravas seemed incapable of figuring out he'd just been insulted, but he kept his mouth shut anyway.

Geth ran his hand along stained pipes the color of old moss fused to the walls and floors of the city. They looked like the irrigation and plumbing systems in Augustin, but the longer I studied them, the less sure I was that they were for carrying water. What else could these pipes be for, though? Arhan took us to the far end of the city where the wall yawned before us, and we stopped at a gaping hole where the floor met the wall. It was about fifteen feet in diameter, perfectly circular, the blackness inside impenetrable.

"What the hell is that?" Namira asked.

The walls inside the hole were a uniform, inky black. Volcanic rock, maybe? The light of Arhan's torch danced inside the rim, revealing its forty-five-degree descent. "There are chutes like these in Mira's bigger ruins," Geth said. "One theory is that they were sacrificial pits, but nobody's bothered to explore them all the way to the bottom. They're miles long and impossible to scale. One slip and…" He let out a long whistle. "I haven't seen anything like this before, though."

He rubbed at etched designs that grew out of the hole like fungus; they consisted of dozens of whorls and recursive lines that seemed to eat at themselves. Staring at them for too long made me feel funny. I ran a finger along the inside of the chute and found it close to the texture of sandpaper. Talk about a tough way to go.

I couldn't help but glance at Arhan.

"What're you doing?" Cravas asked as Geth pulled out a piece of paper and some chalk. "Sergeant's word is to look for a way out."

"Relax," Geth said, and pressed the parchment to the pattern rimming the sacrificial hole, then rubbed the chalk against it. "Stop trying to score points with the sergeant one last time before we reach Xeriv."

"You may not be a Darkwater employee, but you should still be respectin' me and the others enough not to give us lip."

"I figured you could use some extra lip since yours seems to be stuck to the sergeant's pants buttons."

The guard grabbed a fistful of Geth's shirt and pulled. Geth fell back, but jumped up and swung. His fist cracked Cravas's cheek with a meaty *thwack*, and Cravas stumbled, almost tripping over his own feet. He recovered and pulled out his sword, but Geth was already running.

"Above and below," Arhan growled. "Be gentle with him," he yelled at Cravas as the guard pursued Geth. Despite his words, he unsheathed his own blade, then followed his bootlicker down the street. I eyed the opposite direction longingly, but Arhan was carrying the rucksack of climbing gear. Namira and I shared a look and took off after the group.

A block away, the light of Arhan's torch was swallowed by the door to a marbled, cylindrical building. My boots rang against a grate when I stepped inside—a mess of metal and piping lay underneath the grated floor, and a twenty-foot-tall contraption sat in the center of the room that sprouted a hundred more pipes which disappeared into the ceiling. Geth stood with his back to the contraption, blade up and ready to stick Cravas or Arhan, both of whom were just out of sword's reach.

"How about we all just count to ten?" Geth said, breathing lightly. "You deserved that, Cravas. Arhan, you can't deny me my natural instinct to defend myself, okay?"

Arhan sheathed his weapon. "Cravas," he said, and his lackey did the same, letting out a frustrated snort uncannily similar to a boar's. Arhan motioned to the exit. "All's forgiven. Let's get back on track."

Geth looked over his shoulder. "While we're here..."

"You're standing on shaky ground, cartographer. You're blurring the line between disobedience and open opposition to Darkwater's interests. One of those gives me power to punish a hired hand."

Geth answered by pulling a lever on the contraption. The metal rattled, vibrating and clicking, and the sound moved up the mess of pipes until the whole room filled with faint, *ting*ing music.

"What did you do?" the sergeant asked, his anger edged with fear. "What is that?"

A low light winked into existence, coming from grimy bulbs that circled the room. "Faults above," Geth said, and erupted in giddy laughter. "The Hydraulics Thesis wasn't a crock after all."

The street outside came alive, casting light on marble surfaces, changing the city from something ghostly to something almost glowing and alive. "This is peak geothermal engineering," Geth said. He played with more buttons and levers on the machine. A high-pitched pressurized sound, like water hitting lava, blasted the air. The light brightened, and two bulbs popped, showering glass that fell through the grates and sent a corner of the room into shadow. Metal screeched against metal and a doorway opened, revealing a chamber on the other side. Geth gasped like a boy on his birth passing. "Can you believe that little room will take you up and down? Or that's what Huchon Folque theorized."

"Up… or down?" Arhan asked. I couldn't tell if he wanted to hightail it out of here or keep asking questions. He had to see the value in this place. The longer Geth held his attention the more time I had to think about my predicament—it'd be a lot harder to escape Arhan after we left the ruins, but if I escaped now, I couldn't leave without scaling the wall. I needed Arhan's rucksack.

"That chamber might take you a hundred feet up or a hundred feet down, or even a thousand feet down. Who knows? They were smarter than anyone else alive."

Geth's face was full of dumb fascination. Cravas's anger had finally faded, and now he wore a look of mild intrigue, peering up at the ceiling to watch the pipes shiver. Arhan's interest changed into something darker. Namira stepped away, grabbing my arm.

"Efadora," she whispered.

Arhan took a step toward us, his hand resting on the hilt of his blade in a way that was supposed to look casual, but his eyes said otherwise. "Can't believe it," Cravas said. "This place could give Fedsprig a run for his money, the way it's lighting up. Darkwater'll treat us like kings soon as they find out." He barked out a laugh. "Maybe I'll get your job, Sergeant, and you'll be leading your own platoon. How'd you like that, yeah?"

Arhan didn't answer, his eyes examining each member of the room, calculating. "'Great things await when man and mountain meet.'"

"Wha...?"

Steel slid against leather, then Arhan's blade sank into the guard's side. "W-Why?" Cravas hissed, drooping to the floor. Arhan frowned at his subordinate, watching blood drip through the grate and splash on the pipes below, sizzling. Cravas stilled.

"He asked a good question," I said. "I mean, I get why, but he looked up to you. Figured that'd make you hesitate for at least a second."

The sergeant wiped his blade on Cravas's vest. "Others like him'll come. In the meantime, Darkwater'll give me in a year what I was hoping to get in ten, all thanks to the technology in this city."

"These ruins are mine," Geth said, murder in his eyes. "I brought us here. They're going to the Archives."

"Shut your mouth. All of this was an accident. Maybe we can sort out how we'll divvy it up between Darkwater and you mapmakers, but first we have to reach Ravada."

"I know exactly how much he's going to give you," I said to Geth, and gestured toward Cravas. "Does Arhan seem like someone who plans to share?"

Namira pulled me onto the street, and Arhan followed, Geth tailing a healthy distance behind. The working glass bulbs glowed white, and jets of steam whined and groaned from places where metal had rusted and broken. Several city blocks had come to life, rumbling like they were full of people.

"I'm next," Namira said matter-of-factly. "Arhan needs the cartographer, but I'm just one more person who can lay claim here. He'll stick me as soon as I let him."

"It's the punishment you deserve," Arhan said, slowly advancing. "I told you to leave the serfs alone. You don't respect authority."

"You get the respect you deserve," I said, and let out a bitter laugh. "At least now we know how you act when your bootlickers aren't watching."

I faltered when screaming echoed through the street, coming from everywhere and nowhere. It took a second to pinpoint the source. It was the caravan.

Chapter 10—Ester

ESTER AND XANDER camped by firelight at the edge of an abyss, Ester slathering preserve over sourdough while her companion gawked at the brush strokes of red and green in the sky. Nebulae, Xander called them. They were at the border of Augustin, and of Mira, really, near the northern end of the Tear. Ester thought back to a particularly dogmatic member of the Foundry who'd once sworn on his future grave that Fheldspra had used the First Forged Blade to gouge the land from the surface all the way to the core. Anxiety sat like a rock in her chest every time she glanced at the bottomless depths, then at the trail leading alongside it. The man named Breach and the other rhidium thieves were either desperate or stupid to take their prize this way. Judging by how the trail could barely support a group walking single file, she figured maybe they were both.

"Let's eat and wrap up quick as we can," she said. "That path isn't going to get any wider."

"Let's not rush," the guild member said. He fiddled with a long gadget of interlocking pieces of metal and glass on his lap, his wool blanket littered with tools and spare parts. "A breather will make sure we don't lose our wits when we need them most. Besides, we know they're on foot now. They won't be moving too quick lugging around all those vials."

"Assuming they haven't fallen all the way to the core already." She was naive to think the thieves would have stayed inside the territory. She'd found the rug cart abandoned in a side tunnel just outside Telos, and after some investigating around town and a heavy dose of Xander's charm, some folks had shared the location of a well-trodden smuggler's path leading out of Augustin, which went all the way to Byssa. But why go there? They'd been traveling more than a week pushing along Augustin's northeast at this point, and the longer this trip went on, the heavier that rock in Ester's chest became. The Sovereign would have come and gone from Augustin by now. Fheldspra's mercy forsaken, there could already be primordia sniffing their trail.

"What do you think of my work-in-progress?" Xander asked, brandishing his weapon with a strained smile, as if attempting to help her think of something else. He'd been frowning at the look on her face.

"Looks like scrap metal," she said, and tried to smile back.

"More or less. But it's a weapon too. Can't do much else with it other than chuck it at your opponent's head, but once it's done, it'll be a regular terror. Funny things like walls and barriers won't get in its way, assuming the science is right."

"Will it be ready when we catch Breach?"

"No, no," he said quickly. "Honestly, I don't even know if it'll work. I still need to find the right power source for it, assuming I get the design right."

"Ah." She went back to nibbling on her toast, or trying to, with what little appetite she had.

Xander didn't seem to want to give up on distracting her from her gloom. "Some secular circles outside the Foundry love to discuss rhidium's origin. Did you know that? The guild's convinced falling stars brought it here, that it might be a piece of Ceti herself. Seems strange. Your Foundry dismisses this theory out of hand and say rhidium is a divine gift from

Fheldspra, and yet the place you mine your rhidium from is called the Star Mines."

Ester glanced at Ceti's cold, twinkling light. "'Star' in the old tongue is estre, which also means heart. It's what I was named after. The smiths say that rhidium is the heart of Fheldspra and that's how we become connected to Him during our trial."

"Didn't you tell me your parents were cultists? Odd that they'd name their daughter after Fheldspra's heart."

"They named me after Heart of the Wild, which is a thorny root you find in Deep Mira. My parents think that Heart of the Wild comes from the heart of the deity they worship, Terias."

The silence stretched out until she thought maybe Xander had lost interest. "Interesting how beliefs across the world share so many similarities," he said, pushing a piece of metal into his gadget. "That none of them are exactly right and the truth sits somewhere in the middle. It makes you wonder if all these beliefs are branches of something much older. No offense."

"None taken."

The guild member scooped up his tools and stuffed them in his pack, then gingerly wrapped his experiment in his blanket. Ester watched him, trying not to let his comments bother her more than she let on. In no world would Terias and Fheldspra have come from the same place.

She'd been wrong about her religion before, though.

They set out on the narrow path, leading their mounts by their bridles. The foxes acted more relaxed about the whole affair, enough for Ester's mount to chirp and nip at her, causing her a miniature heart attack every time they started to grow rowdy. Fortunately, somebody had planted pyremoss in a long, continuous patch above their heads, which meant she didn't have to sacrifice one hand to holding a torch. Instead, she focused on which thing she would need to grab in the likely event she fell to her death.

"Eyes and ears open," she said. "I've heard of bats as large as wagons that roam the Tear."

"No worries," Xander said. "The bats around here are vegetarians. It's the ones in the Tear's southern region you have to worry about. Those are the blood suckers. They make meals out of cartel members looking to harvest the Ash plant."

As soon as the words left his mouth, a rhythmic *thwump*ing filled the air. It sounded like several pairs of wings, and the depth of the sound made Ester picture beasts as big as her nightmares yawning just outside the light. The foxes let out small barks, their feet tapping the ground, but the beating faded into the distance.

"See?" Xander said.

"Right."

The path moved up, down, widened, and even thinned at a few heart-stopping points, but the trek wasn't hard on the body. There were alcoves along the way where they rested, until Xander mentioned the bats loved to scrabble at the vegetation growing inside. "You haven't talked about your family since we left Sanskra," Xander said as we walked. "Don't you have another brother? Myrilan, right?"

"I haven't really asked about your past yet, either," she said to change the subject. "Come to think of it, you know a lot more about me than I do about you."

He took the hint. "Is that right? I hadn't realized."

He was avoiding the subject. Ester sympathized, but the man knew information that could put the Foundry in a very vulnerable position, not to mention he'd witnessed some very personal moments between her and Damek, so she didn't feel quite so bad about pressing. "Where's your family?" she asked.

"Dead."

"Oh. I guess that's what I get for asking. I feel like an ass."

"It was a harmless question." He took a second to continue. "They died and some friends of theirs took me in. Odla and Garin. After I did some growing, I started taking odd jobs here and there, traveled, then joined the guild. Not much more to my story beyond that."

"There's not much to any story if you're vague enough. I bet I'd find it interesting if you added more details."

He didn't answer, but this time she pressed no further. She'd wondered why a nonbeliever wanted to help the Foundry (other than to force her into offering him free protection while he performed his research in the crust), and she concluded he was a man running from something. She knew a little about what that was like. Maybe once they recovered the rhidium, she'd try to get to know him better. She wanted to figure out what it was about him she found intriguing.

Voices bounced off the chasm walls, and a group appeared over a rise farther along the path, headed their way. "Black winds," she said. There was no way for the groups to get around each other.

"Ho," she called out to the line of people.

"Hello, saiora," said the leader, his accent from the old tongue mild. He had a square, grizzled jaw and a scabbed-over cut on his forehead. "Unfortunate, this, I'd say."

"How far along is the path behind you?" she asked.

"'Bout five miles out from Byssa. One'n a half till there's a place where we might be able to squeeze by."

The man had several companions trailing him, which would make backtracking for them more difficult. "There's an alcove about a thousand feet behind us," she said. "We'll back up to there and let you by. How's that sound?"

"Much obliged," the man said. Ester's fox dipped and moved its head to see behind itself as Ester forced it to backpedal, uneasiness rippling through its body. Xander's efforts with his fox were just as awkward.

"Where you two coming from?" the leader asked.

"The Augustin capital. Yourselves?" I asked.

"Naxion. Small town not far from here, just inside Byssa's border. Headed to the Augustin capital ourselves, actually."

"On what business?"

"Complicated. Apologies, saiora. Would rather say our business is our own and leave it at that."

"Fair enough." She missed the days before Olevic Pike and Sara Adriann, when passersby on the road weren't always traveling with one hand on their weapon or one foot out the door. Augustins used to be open and warm—part of what attracted her to the territory—but she supposed that was just another dying Foundry tenet. The path behind them rose a little, and she caught a better glimpse of the men behind their leader. They wore undershirts with no coats, with red trim embroidered along the collars and cuffs. "You're all native to Augustin, aren't you?"

"Saiora?" There was an edge of concern in the leader's voice.

"I'm a smith from Augustin. I work with the commoners every day. Sometimes you can just tell."

She knew a lot more about them than she let on—they were part of the Augustin corps, wearing the same standard issue undershirts she'd cleaned and packed into Damek's wardrobe dozens of times in recent weeks. If she had to guess, they were deserters. Had likely trashed their overcoats so they wouldn't be identified. But if that was true, why head back to the capital?

They reached the alcove. Xander nudged his fox into the crevice, and as Ester's mount started backing into the ten-foot-deep cubby, the leader made a gesture with his hand. A signal. She didn't know what it meant, but the hard look in his eyes gave her a damn good hint. She slid her blade from its sheath and pointed it at the leader's nose.

"What are you doing?" Xander asked.

"I want our friends here to make their intentions clear before I back myself into this death trap."

"Dunno what you're talking about, saiora," the leader said in a low voice. His voice was monotone. Dead.

"Why'd your friends just squeeze past their foxes like they're ready to help you corner us? Are you scared I might report you? I know you're all from the corps."

The deadness in his face trembled. Cracks of emotion formed, and they were full of rage. "I don't answer your questions. You'll answer mine. For weeks we've wondered why you and your kind helped them. Those demons who burned our homes and slaughtered our families. Why you helped the Exile."

The Exile. Was that another nickname for Jakar? "The Foundry didn't have a choice," she said. "We're sworn to serve the magnates, and we didn't know at the time what happened on the Granite Road."

"But you found out eventually. Ain't no secret the master smith supported the Exile and claimed his innocence during his trial with the audencia. Now he's lurking in the territories' shadows 'cause of you."

She choked back her disbelief, her words lost to her. Everything was a mess in Augustin, but how could she even begin to explain Jakar's situation? She'd failed plenty of times while speaking to the commoners and knew that people like this man, who knew nothing about Jakar, would always see it as black and white instead of chaotic gray.

"So you want to kill me because I'm a smith?" she asked. "Because of what the Foundry did?"

"We're headed back to Augustin's capital to turn ourselves in. Been living for weeks sick with our choices. We just want it to end." He sniffed, wiping his nose. "Most I ever been afraid in my life was when we fought the brothers and sisters of the Foundry. You know that? We was terrified to hurt the people who was supposed to care for me and my soul. But you fought us anyway. Hurt us bad."

The pyremoss's light stained his tears red. A sickness burned Ester's insides as she watched him, thinking about how right he was. The Foundry's goal was to take care of the people they served, to be the fire and warmth in the darkness. But not the passing when Sara Adriann came knocking on the backdoor of the city. Was this the unavoidable cost of war? That they had to hurt their neighbors as badly as they hurt their enemies, even if it was unintentional?

Her blade hovered a foot from the man's neck, but he didn't move to draw his weapon. Instead, swords slid from sheaths behind him. She glanced over her shoulder and saw Xander with a glass beaker in one hand and a knife in the other—cut branches lay at his feet, and he had stoppered the beaker, which was filled with crushed leaves floating in liquid. He shook it hard. "Excuse me," he said, nudging her to the side, and chucked the beaker at the leader's legs. It broke, splashing dirty liquid onto the men's feet, and they struggled not to flinch or slip as broken glass bounced off the ledge.

"The fuck was that?" one of them said.

Chirps filled the air. It sounded similar to an excited cave fox, but an octave lower, and Xander pulled Ester into the alcove, squishing them into the warm fur of her fox. "What's happening?" she asked. Xander's fox, stuck deep inside the crevice, let out a scared yelp, and a deep *thwump*ing reverberated through the air, coming from wings so numerous that the air started vibrating. The leader of the deserters stepped toward us, but a black, furry body as big as a small house materialized from the darkness and smashed into the cliff side, knocking him off his feet.

Ester's world became beating wings and swarming bodies of dark fur. The deserters yelled and their foxes screamed in terror. Everything was chaos. Claws scratched at the rock as the bats tried to squeeze against the crevice, pushing her into Xander and her fox over and over again, more than once a bony arm smashing against her torso and head, hard enough to leave bruises. Painful minute after painful minute passed.

The bats flew away, and everything became silent. Ester lit a torch and found the pyremoss along the ridge ripped to shreds with gouges covering the cliff face. The others were gone. "What did you do?" she asked.

"Just a little chemical reaction with the help of some of the figs here and a little guild concoction we call Gravel." He held up a vial of gray powder. "It's great for scrubbing our equipment while we're out and about in the crust, but it leaves a nasty burn when you mix it with water. So I made myself a stink bomb. Good job distracting them, by the way. I had a hell of a time cutting into those figs. They don't ripen for another month."

Once again Xander had saved the mission, yet the emptiness wouldn't stop sucking at Ester's chest as she stared into the abyss while he calmed down the foxes. The reasonable part of her knew this was how it had to end, yet the feeling only worsened. She'd been forsaken in the deserters' eyes. To them, the Foundry was the reason a mercenary army was able to ravage Augustin's capital and kill thousands.

And they were right.

Chapter 11—Jakar

I WRIGGLED IN the cramped space, trying to force feeling back into my legs and keep the claustrophobia at bay by taking long, rhythmic breaths. I'd made a mistake realizing how similar my hiding spot was to the wooden cage the Ebonrock stuck me inside after my flesh binding. Now every fiber of my being wanted to reject this place like spoiled food. It was almost funny—on the Granite Road, I'd pictured myself in that cage so I could escape those I'd killed in Cragreach, but now all it did was terrify me. Maybe this new aversion to cages was a good sign.

Arhan, Efadora, and the others had been gone a while now. Maybe I could sneak out and pretend I'd managed to catch up to the caravan. It was a weak excuse, but for now all I cared about was escaping this prison.

After a few shoulder pops and knee scrapes, I turned myself around and found the trapdoor. I used my metal working to undo the locking mechanism on the other side until the door squeaked downward, then I wormed my way out and collapsed on the rock in a painful heap.

Resting in the hiding spot had helped, but it was impossible to say how long my second wind would last. I still wasn't sure

I'd survive whatever had poisoned me. I hid behind one of the wheels, counting everyone milling around the caravan. Most of them were near the ridge to the ancient ruins I'd overheard them discussing. I'd have to sneak past them and look for the tunnel to Ravada that Geth had mentioned, hopefully finding Efadora along the way.

"I knew it!" someone shouted from the back of the caravan. "I'm gonna skin whatever two-timing leech fucked with my cart." A trader stomped his way to the rest of the group. "Someone shaved the rubber off one of my wheels. I knew I wasn't crazy. Who's gonna reimburse me? Darkwater?"

Torlo shied away from the group, shifting his feet to somehow make them look smaller. Past him, white light illuminated the far ridge, coming from inside the city. No, part of the city itself was glowing. Everyone else was too busy mesmerized by the spectacle to care about the frantic trader. Almost everyone, at least. "What's that on your feet, serf?" one of the guards asked in a brusque, Yaroklan accent.

Torlo gave one of his many smiles, but this one was hollowed out. "Nothing. Why?"

"No, no, definitely something." The guard shoved Torlo to the ground. "See? That's what I thought. Rubber."

A pair of guards dragged Torlo to his feet. "That serf is Darkwater property," the cart owner said, "which means Darkwater is going to pay me back."

"Sorry, *kozakha*. Can't make no promises about repayment. Arhan's orders—a crime of this nature is a capital offense. Take comfort in knowing justice will be dealt."

I scrambled past the wheel as two guards held Torlo by the arms and a third unsheathed his sword. "No!" I said, reaching out. The sword was thrown from the guard's hands and clattered to the rock, and the man frowned at it before picking it up. My chest seized in wracking coughs, and when I pulled my hand away from my mouth, specks of blood dotted my palm.

"Where the depths did you come from?" the guard said.

"You were supposed to be for the worms by now, *se sa*."

I opened my mouth to give the story I'd carefully concocted, but vomit came out instead. I wavered, trying to get hold of my nausea, and the guards watched with mild disgust. "I don't make the rules," the armed guard said, advancing on Torlo, who tried to struggle free. "I'm of the same mind as the sergeant. He'll be happy to have this thief out of his hair. I'll make it painless."

I pushed again with all my elemental might, trying to do something, anything, from this distance. The weapon shot out of the guard's hand, a glinting metal blur, and sliced into another guard standing next to the ridge. The struck man screamed, stumbling backward until he fell, and the sword's owner cried out, holding his wrist. Nauseating pain overwhelmed me. I crumpled to the ground, trying to keep what little was left in my stomach inside, and more people shouted, rushing to help. Both guards restraining Torlo let the serf go and checked the ledge for the missing guard. "What was that?" someone asked.

Torlo took off, headed for the rope that the scouts must have used to descend into the city. A guard went after him, but the kid was already gone, the rope shaking as he descended as if his life depended on it. Which it did. I could tell the others still had no idea what had happened. I stumbled toward the fox standing apart from the rest of the mounts—Geth's fox—and pulled off the pack and his spare half-sword. "Stay back or you're next," I said through gritted teeth, my head spinning, and headed for the rope. Everyone's attention was on me now, but it was hard to tell who believed me and who didn't.

"Whoever lets him escape is getting flayed," a guard said.

I pushed against their weapons enough for them to notice and for fear to cross their eyes. The nauseating pain spread further, and I knew they could kill me if they attacked. I tried with all my might to keep the agony off my face, the sweat sliding over my cheekbones, and I reached the rope, awkwardly climbing over the edge while holding the sword in my other hand. The drop was more than thirty feet. I took a deep breath, then cut the rope. It snapped. My stomach lurched until it was doing cartwheels, and right before I hit the rooftop I pushed with my power. I hit the stone only hard enough to send painful vibrations up my feet.

The guards shouted at me from above, but at least I'd bought myself time while they looked for another rope. Torlo was gone, but in that moment I was more interested in reining the sickness in. There was a light show going on at the far end of the city that sang with faint clanging and screeching. That had to be where Efadora was.

I moved through the shadows of the city streets, making a wide arc instead of heading directly for the light show. I couldn't move very fast without the dizziness sending me stumbling, and I didn't want to risk a run-in with Arhan. I hid inside a building entrance to take a break and let my vision clear. A dim glow had pervaded this part of the city—the buildings were made of marble and the streets of white stone, with copper tubes threading their walls, green and broken from centuries of disuse. Inside the building, rubbish littered a floor scarred with black marks, marks caused by heat. I squinted. The rubbish looked like a pile of weapons. I crossed the floor and picked one up—I only called it a weapon because it was clear a projectile was meant to feed in from the pack sitting on top. It reminded me of a crossbow, except the thing was made of metal. I pushed a lever and out popped a projectile from the ammo pack—a smooth length of metal the size of my thumb. It wasn't sharp. It looked like it was supposed to travel between two of the foot-long rails that comprised the weapon's length. The weapon had a trigger like a crossbow, so I pulled it.

The rails clicked and the projectile slammed out of the weapon, smashing into the far wall in an explosion of dust and rock. "Above and below," I muttered, and I jerked my forearm back when it touched one of the rails, which now glowed a faint orange, the heat leaving smoldering marks on my bandages. Echoes of the collision still bounced around the building and a marble dust cloud hung in the air.

I carefully examined the molten-hot rails. The weapon wouldn't hold up after a handful of shots, but what it lacked in durability it made up for in power. Fighting had happened in this ancient place, I realized. That seemed like an important thing to know.

I grabbed a fresh rail weapon and hurried out the door. Maybe I didn't need my power to save Efadora after all.

Chapter 12—Efadora

THE STREETS CALLED to us behind Namira and me, but fleeing wouldn't do much good about getting that rucksack slung over Arhan's shoulder. "Help us," I said to Geth. If the cartographer attacked him from the rear, I could rush Arhan and risk a scratch or two to bring him down.

The sergeant angled himself so he could keep us and Geth in his field of view. "You a fighter?" he asked.

Geth didn't answer, but he didn't advance, either.

"That's what I thought," the sergeant said. "You attack and I'll kill you, or you attack and I'll fend you off, then my men will cut you to pieces when they get here."

"Assuming they're still alive," I said.

"What's that supposed to mean?"

"You didn't hear that scream on the ridge?" I had no doubt in my mind Jakar had something to do with it, but the thought wasn't exactly a comfort. He was still hurt. The guards must've discovered him.

"A girl like you is a know-nothing," Arhan said. "Acting like she always has tricks up her sleeve. Hah."

He jumped forward as he laughed, moving so fast that Namira and I barely had time to make a break for it. We got tangled in each other and I tripped. My first instinct was to search the ground for a rock, for anything, but then Namira pulled me up and away. I couldn't see him, but I could hear Arhan's boots tapping after us. A hand grabbed a fistful of my hair and threw me at the ground. My head bounced off stone and a white light flashed across my vision. Namira was scrambling, her footsteps echoing away. A pulsing ache filled my head, and I squeezed my eyes shut, allowing myself two heartbeats to ground myself, then I struggled to my feet. Arhan and Namira were gone, but I caught a glimpse of Geth turning a corner. I was pretty rattled but otherwise okay.

I came to a doorway with stairs descending into some kind of basement, where Arhan's angry shouts bounced their way up to me. At the bottom was a corridor with metal doors lining both sides. The far side was a dead end, and Namira had her back to the wall with Arhan several strides away and Geth right behind him. Another standoff.

Namira's wide eyes fell on me, then flicked to the open door closest to her, then back to me. A red light flickered from a bulb above the door, and I noticed a pipe leading away from it, which joined others that snaked their way toward me. They ended at a console built into a nearby wall, a console that looked like the one in the power room Geth had used, but smaller. It had eight levers. There were eight doors.

Arhan's rucksack lay discarded next to the console. All I had to do was pick it up and run.

"Don't be an idiot," Arhan said. He was talking to Geth. "Help me."

"It's a tough call," Geth said. "I can side with the cart owner trying to make an honest living, or I can side with the company trying to take what belongs to me and the Archives."

"Shit what you want! Shit what I want! You can find your way to Ravada no problem, yeah? Then go. I'll find my way there in due time. Take your head start and make your official claim on this place. We both know the city'll look favorably on whoever makes first claim. All you have to do is walk away."

His voice quivered. The man was afraid. Terrified, in fact. A struggle would be a toss-up in tight quarters—Geth's short blade could move faster than Arhan's full-length sword if the sergeant went for Namira first, and if Arhan attacked Geth, he was smart enough to know Namira would come at him with the desperation of someone whose life was on the line.

"Is that right?" Geth said. "I just walk away?"

"Yeah. Good luck and good fortune to you."

Fhelfire, the man was actually considering it. Namira didn't wait for his answer, though. She jumped for the doorway and Arhan jumped after her. I grabbed at the lever with a symbol etched in the pommel that matched the door she fled through, and metal screeched against metal.

The door closed slowly—plenty of time for Arhan to go in after Namira. But the sergeant moved with the staccato footsteps of someone afraid that Geth's blade might bite him in the back. He disappeared, then I heard Namira grunt in rage, which evolved into a screech. She reappeared, slipping through the closing doors and releasing a curtain of blood from her upper arm. The doors shut, followed by a howl of agony. Arhan's wails faded like he was being carried off.

"Genius," Geth said. He hadn't moved the whole time. He peered at the blinking light above the door, which had gone from red to blue. "It's a transportation unit that moves people sideways through the city."

"Now is a good time to shut up," I said, and hurried over to Namira, who clutched at her arm while blood flowed over her fingers. "Are you all right?"

"I'm well enough," the trader said, eying Geth with a murderous rage. "I'd be a lot worse off if I'd given him five more seconds to think on the sergeant's offer, though."

Geth's wistful look faded, replaced by a small smile, as though she'd said the most ridiculous thing in the world. "Hearing that man's pain was as satisfying as I could've imagined. Don't think I'm not happy about it."

I didn't fail to notice how he had sidestepped the accusation.

"Whatever," I said. "Can you take us to Ravada or not? If Arhan's just getting carried off to another part of the city, he'll be hunting us down again eventually."

Geth studied Namira, but his focus wasn't on her wound. It was on all of her. I realized he was thinking about the kind of claims she might make on these ruins.

"My map's back at the caravan," he said a few moments later.

"You didn't bring it with you?" I asked.

"It's not a problem. I know where to go from here. Let's put this place behind us."

Chapter 13—Jakar

I RAN INTO Efadora, Namira, and Geth where the creaking pipes and grimy lights ended and the darkness of the city started, within line of sight of the ridge where the exit tunnel waited far above our heads. Relief flooded my aching chest. "Where's Arhan?" I asked.

"You're alive," Efadora blurted, then clamped a hand over her mouth and cringed at the words echoing down the street. She pulled her hand away. "The bootlicker with Arhan is dead and the sergeant is taking an involuntary tour of the city. What's that?"

I brandished the rail weapon. "A Sihraan secret."

Geth held out a hand. "You have my pack and sword? The map's in my pack. I'll need it if you have any interest in getting to Ravada."

I undid the buckle to the belt with the sheath and handed it over. "Wait," Efadora said to Geth. "I thought you said you didn't need the map to find your way."

Geth ignored her, holding his hand out. It was enough to pique my curiosity. I didn't usually like antagonizing people who didn't deserve it, but my patience was stretched thin and I was tired of surprises. I opened his bag and rummaged through it, but didn't see anything out of the ordinary. Just rations, ink and quills, a few rolled-up changes of clothes, a few sticks of pyroglycerin, and the map. I pulled it out.

"Won't do you much good," Geth said. "It's just a key. It isn't transcribed for public use yet."

The map had a line that twisted and turned from one corner of the parchment to the other, and was covered with numerical values and arrows pointing to different points along the line. Each number corresponded to a quartz deposit with a unique silicon composition. Among the densely cluttered numbers, I spotted a line branching off at the end. It showed two paths along the final stretch of the journey that led into the country of Xeriv. I opened my Eye, searching for nearby quartz. There wasn't much—the city was mostly marble—and the elements shone bright enough that it almost seared my mind. Nausea seeped in, but simply observing the elements didn't affect me nearly as much as manipulating them. I quickly found what I was looking for.

"There were two ways out of the Rift, and you led us down the long way. The one that stranded the caravan," I said.

"What?" Namira asked. Blood slid down her arm from a red-stained cloth tied around her arm, but the pain didn't do much to detract from her anger.

"This map shows a fork at the end with two ways into Xeriv. The other one looks like it would've cut down our journey by a full passing."

"You don't look like a cartographer," Geth said coolly.

"Maybe you should focus on telling us why you took us this way instead."

The looks of three people on the verge of murder seemed enough motivation for Geth to talk. "A friend gave me this map because she knew of my interest in Sihraan ruins. This way still gets us to Xeriv, the path's just a bit more complicated. Look at it any way you want, but I was still fulfilling my duties."

"You stranded the entire caravan just to satisfy your curiosity?" Namira asked. "If anything happens to my cart, you'll pay for my troubles or you'll be dead."

I slid the map into Geth's bag and slung the pack over my shoulder. He didn't argue.

"You're all alive," a voice said. Torlo limped toward us, the smile on his face as wide as a chasm. "Some guards are several blocks off from us, sniffing about. Can we get out?"

We reached the wall under the ridge, where dozens of feet of smooth-faced rock separated us from freedom. I swallowed hard. "I can get us out of here," I said. "Just… there's a chance I might faint." I looked around, but there wasn't anything soft lying around to break my fall. "Here goes nothing."

I planted a palm on the rock at waist height, took a deep breath, and curled my fingers. I dug into the stone and sent compression sparks dancing over the tops of my knuckles and heat radiating into my palm. Someone gasped, but I ignored it and molded the depression in the rock into a foothold, then repeated the process a couple feet higher. Pain and nausea spread through my body like a wave. I reached up and created a third handhold while sliding my foot into the first.

The climb was slow and miserable. The upside was that the rock in this cavern gave way more easily than anything I'd molded before—instead of like hard putty, it fell to my will like soggy rice. My vision swam until I had to squeeze my eyes shut and focus on the sensation of my hands digging into the rock. Warm, rancid vomit fell down the front of my shirt. When had I vomited? I'd stopped moving, I realized, clinging to the rock face for who knows how long. Time was stretching and compressing like the rock under my grip. I shook my head hard, trying to shake the disorientation loose, and kept moving. Three-quarters of the way up, lightning lanced through my gut and I nearly lost my grip.

With each foot I ascended, more sparks were added to the cloud filling my torso. I stifled a sob when my hand found the lip of the ridge and I climbed over. I barely cleared the ledge before collapsing on my back, and I turned my head to vomit again. Creeping dread distracted me from the sickness.

I was intimately familiar with the pain arcing through my

stomach. It had plagued me six times in my life, on those passings I had ingested rhidium and spent hours lying on those awful stone slabs to endure my Imbibings. The pain, sickness, and disorientation weren't as intense as before, but I would remember that agony for the rest of my life.

Why was I really sick? What was happening to me?

Geth grunted his way over the ridge, followed by Namira, Torlo, and Efadora. I managed to sit up, my back pressed against the tunnel wall while the others caught their breath.

"That climb sure is hell on the forearms," Geth said, massaging his fingers. "Oh, and to address a more important matter. What the fuck are you?"

I gave a pained shrug.

"I'd call you katsu if those existed."

"I don't know what that is."

"It's the Ronan word for maker. Katsu were the architects of the world, according to their myths. So what's your story?"

"I'm just an elemental, like you."

Geth snorted. "You're *just* a liar, you mean."

Efadora placed the back of her hand against my forehead, her touch cool and soothing. "You look terrible. Can you make it to Ravada?"

"Let's find out," I coughed out.

She and Torlo helped me to my feet. We had a good view of the caravan, and I could see the traders on the opposite ridge pointing at us. The lights from the city would have illuminated our ascent, but hopefully the guards roaming the city hadn't thought to look up.

"Keep me steady," I said, and shakily moved to the edge and peered over, positioning myself above the trail of handholds. I slammed my heel down and a deep crack reverberated into the open space. A five-foot wide section of rock, leading all the way to the cavern floor, cleaved away from the wall, tipping toward the city until the thin, thirty-foot tall pillar smashed into the nearest building and let out a deafening crash.

I would've collapsed if Efadora and Torlo didn't catch me.

Cleaving so much rock would have been impossible without a heat source, but my power had been acting funny lately. I was stronger.

Stronger, as if I'd undergone another Imbibing.

"Let's get our head-start," I tried to say, but it came out as a half-groan, half-mumble. They got the picture, though. Efadora and Torlo almost had to drag me into the tunnel.

Chapter 14—Ester

ESTER EYED THE town of Naxion as it sat on a plateau of rock sticking out from a cliff face on the opposite side of the cavern. A long fall separated her and Xander from the town, with dozens of pillars, some as wide as a house and others as slim as a coffee table, dotting the chasm and linked by planks of rockwood. The foxes barely noticed the drop as the two of them navigated the planks, and Ester tried—and failed—not to look down. A path on the cliff side was one thing, but crossing lengths of timber while on the back of a large animal was something else entirely. Apparently half of Byssa was like this. Travel was ingrained in Bys culture more than any other territory in Mira, and Ester wondered if it had to do with getting away from their home territory as a self-preservation tactic.

To her horror, she realized the planks weren't even nailed to the rock. One of them shifted as her fox stepped off it, making her heart skip a few beats. "Do the locals have steel spines or do they just believe in survival of the fittest?" she asked.

"Naxion's an easy place to defend, don't you think?" Xander asked. His attention was focused on the town, his head rigid. "You've got about a hundred choke points. Or you just kick off a plank or two and wave from the other side."

"Is that even necessary this far out?"

"Towns like Naxion are afraid of the ruin folk. Ruin folk would never bother them, but it is what it is. If you wanted to practice your manners, now's the time. The Bys hate outsiders who are sloppy with their words."

They left the last of the planks, and the foxes crossed the plateau toward the palisades surrounding the edge of town. Stone obelisks lined the road, with cracks in the stone that were filled with glistening green and white opal. "More defenses?" Ester asked.

"Cult monuments, I think. People in these parts are a little more open to those affiliations. Obelisks have something to do with the goddess Brexa, far as I know."

At the town entrance, the human defense consisted of one man sitting at a desk wolfing down a plate of noodles. "My friend and I are looking for someone," Ester said. "A few of them, most likely. We traveled all the way from the Augustin capital and would really appreciate it if you could let us look at your logbook."

She waited for the inevitable argument; to push against the man's incredulity and suspicion. The guard set his fork down to pull out his logbook, then dropped the loosely bound set of papers in front of them. "Go ahead. No skin off my teeth."

Ester shared a look with Xander before eying the first page. "There's nothing here."

"Shit outta luck then, I suppose." He slurped another mouthful of noodles.

"Isn't every incorporated town supposed to keep tabs on who passes through now, by order of the Sovereign?"

His fork paused, noodles sliding off the tines. "You a loyalist?"

She shook her head. Apparently, the people around here snubbed Miran sentiments even more than the Foundry. She would've felt a kinship with the man, except now they'd lost a lead on their thieves. "I'm just a little annoyed I might lose the people I've spent more than a week tracking because you can't do your job."

"Feel free to turn round and slither back into whatever crevice you spawned from, then."

She gave him a flat look, but he was already back to slurping his noodles. "Have you seen a small group of people carrying crates into town? It would've been within the last passing or two," she asked.

"*Net.*"

"Let's just take a look around," Xander said in a low voice. "I'm not surprised if the thieves slipped past this man."

They entered the town, and Ester immediately felt dozens of prying eyes. The locals looked to be finishing up work for the passing, either headed home or to the nearest tavern, covered in dust and sweat. Were they looking at her Tulchi-auburn hair, or were they just naturally suspicious? Maybe someone knew about the stolen rhidium after all, or maybe they simply thought she was ruin folk in need of a poke to the kidneys. The town was a half-circle built against the rock, with two dozen buildings and a handful of tunnels that likely led to some farm or water source. Open sky yawned above them, and even though they were several hundred feet from the surface, a constant, faint screaming of wind echoed through the air. Everything about this place whispered to Ester that she wasn't welcome.

The inn was a nice contrast—the inside was gray stone and gleaming rosewood with a roaring hearth in the corner. Smatterings of locals and off-duty guardsmen laughed and drank by the fire, and to their credit only half of them gave Ester the stink eye when she entered.

"Someone around here must know something," she said while they sat at a table. She took a pull from her cup of ghost mango mead. "You see how they're looking at us. It can't be just because they think we're ruin folk."

"Perhaps." Xander wiped mead from the beard he'd been cultivating since they'd left Augustin. "But I wouldn't be surprised if that's all it is. I don't think you realize how hated ruin folk are in the crust. There are a lot of misconceptions surrounding them, from them either being subhuman to savages who sacrifice careless travelers to their dark gods."

"They kill cartographers on sight, so I doubt they're friendly."

"They're just afraid. They want nothing to do with Mira or the Sovereign because of the horror stories they grew up hearing. Ruin folk have long memories, untainted by the Miran government's meddling."

Could the ruin folk know the truth about the Sovereign's genocides? "Tell me about these horror stories."

"They have names for the Sovereign. One of them—can't quite pronounce it in the old tongue—means 'the Great Cannibal' in Miran. Some call him the Vampire. They say he drinks the souls of his enemies, and that's how he doubled the length of his life. Most of the nobiletza living in Saracosta support him because they hope currying his favor will win them longer lives."

Ester ran her thumb along the rim of her stone cup, thinking of Myrilan. "My brother's an amateur historian. The Sovereign was all he cared about growing up. It's funny knowing how he talks about all the good the Sovereign has done when nicknames like 'the Great Cannibal' exist. You know why the territory rulers are called magnates? Because before Mira was established, certain trading companies became so powerful, they ran entire cities and enslaved people en masse. Then the Sovereign came along with his sycophants and brought order to the territories after the Merchant Wars. He became ruler, started regulating everything, then abolished slavery. He built routes like the Granite Road, which helped towns in the crust flourish and the economy to improve. He established a common currency, created the University and the Seedheart Lodge in Saracosta, both of which innovated medicine and evolved into the Menders' Halls. There are a hundred other changes his government made to the infrastructure too. To thousands of people the Sovereign became someone worth dying for. I know Myrilan would."

Xander took a long drink, watching her from over the top of his cup. "Are you sure it's just your brother who loves the Sovereign?"

She scoffed. "Obviously." The word came out louder than she intended.

The man was unruffled. "Apologies. That was uncalled for. It's all right to acknowledge the good someone has done even when you stand against them. There's courage in that."

"To say I disagree with the Sovereign is an understatement," she said. "As a smith, I'll never support him. Sometimes I just struggle with the fact I have a brother who works for the Miran treasury. It's caused tension among my brothers and sisters in Augustin."

"I'm sure Myrilan has some redeeming qualities," Xander offered.

Bless Xander's heart for always trying to make her feel better. She ruminated on the words she'd just shared with him, of her acknowledgement that the Sovereign had done good for the country, and realized she never would have admitted this to anyone other than her closest confidantes. Xander had a way of conversing that she craved—he challenged her without passing judgment, and it allowed her to be honest in a way that helped sort her thoughts out. She'd spent so long bottling up her feelings that she hadn't realized how much they'd been eating at her until letting them out. The side of Xander's mouth turned up, and Ester realized she'd been looking him in the eyes for far too long.

"Myrilan did have some good in him, I guess," she said.

"Like what?"

"He feels deeply. A little too deeply, maybe. It made him sensitive to other people."

"There's not enough empathy in this world. It's a rare and valuable trait."

"You're right. But growing up, kids were always cruel to Myrilan when they saw how sensitive he was." A pang of guilt over disparaging Myrilan stirred inside her as she thought back to all those times she and Damek were forced to scare off Myrilan's bullies. Myrilan had been a desperately lonely boy—he'd worn his feelings on his sleeves, so of course he'd attracted the wrong type of people. He'd been a passionate person. A kind person. Maybe it was something he hadn't lost.

"Thank you," she said. "Talking this through helps."

"Funny how the act of saying something out loud makes one feel better," he said. "It gives shape to something that feels nebulous and insurmountable. Pain is easier to manage when you can define it."

She nodded, noticing his gaze flicker to her hand where it rested on the table. Was he thinking of touching it, or was she imagining it? She downed the last of her drink, refusing to entertain the thought, and eyed the guardsmen in the corner. "Might as well get this started."

Before he could respond, she left her chair and crossed the room. She nodded to the four guardsmen, her smile as she stood over them perhaps a tad too forced, judging by the way they stared at her after pausing their card game. "I'm looking for information," she said.

Two of them whispered to each other and giggled, then downed their shot glasses, and the third sized her up. "Interesting place to be looking."

"Some thieves stole something very precious to me and my family. I figured as guardsmen you might keep track of anyone who looks out of place."

"Aside from you?"

She sighed. She missed her smiths. Even though some of the old guard drove her half-crazy—even though the senior arc smiths wanted her gone—the order helped their neighbors without question. She would've helped this man if he asked for it.

"I haven't," the fourth man said. There was a hint of kindness in his gaze, and Ester realized just how upset she probably looked. This search was taking everything from her. "Visitors stick out like a sore thumb 'round here," he continued. "Only people worth mentioning are the ruin folk we traded with a few weeks back."

Ester nodded in appreciation, failing to hide her disappointment.

"Cleaned us out," he said, "Legitimately, of course, with hard coin. Ruin folk're born and bred to take, though, so wouldn't surprise me if they snatched whatever it is you lost."

"What do you mean they cleaned you out?"

"Of course we didn't know they were ruin folk at the time. If we did, the blacksmith woulda told them to jump in a ravine. They bought out all our weapons and armor. Likely to use our own swords and shields against us."

The back of Ester's neck prickled. Someone with vast quantities of rhidium would need a supply of steel for the trials. "How would I find the ruin folk?"

He coughed out some of his drink in laughter, but Ester kept her gaze level. "You serious?" he asked. "You don't find them. They find you."

"Let's pretend I wanted to make it very easy for them to find me. Where would I go?"

"Er, well, there're some steps and a tunnel a few miles northeast'a town. Leads to some old traders' trails that we used before the Sovereign built all them roads. Can't miss the sign. Folk live outta some old ruins called Mulec'Yrathrik." The word was rough coming out. "No one's been able to find the place, though. Poke around down there and their blades'll find you."

"Bovo," the first man said. "Trying to get the girl killed?"

Bovo shrugged. "She's within her rights. Who am I to get between an outsider and their grave?"

Ester nodded in thanks and returned to Xander. "Looks like we're hunting ruin folk now."

"Hunting?"

"The locals were telling me about some ruin folk who bought all the town's weapons and armor a few weeks back. Not much of a stretch to think that the people who stole our rhidium had their friends find as much steel as they could."

"Sounds as good a plan as any, but remember what I said about the ruin folk. They're a misunderstood people. If we're gonna meet them, we should keep it diplomatic."

"*I'm* going to meet them. You're staying here. You've been exceedingly helpful so far, but this next part of the journey isn't for performing your research."

He finished his mango mead and stood. "Ready when you are."

She eyed that funny little turn of the mouth and the amusement in his spectacled eyes, and a lightness stirred in her chest. She was hoping he'd say that. It was funny how at the start of this trip she would have done what she could to keep him home, but now she couldn't imagine doing this without him. It made where they were headed next that much more worrisome, though. He didn't know how to fight, and if that was ever relevant, it was now. "You're all right with some trouble?"

"I'll take trouble here over that mess in the Tear. At least now we'll be expecting it."

"If it comes to a worst-case scenario, you'll stay behind me, yeah?"

"Don't worry. I'll be cheering from the back line."

Chapter 15—Efadora

OUR GROUP CHOKED on dust and squeezed through a hole Geth had blasted into existence with his pyroglycerin, then followed a narrow passage that led us to a ridge overlooking a wide tunnel of people below. They were walking to and from what looked like the entrance of a city, many of whom had paused to look up at us and the explosion. Ravada. "Thank the Aspects," Namira said, cradling her cut arm. "I never thought I'd be so happy to see strangers."

Jakar crumpled to the ground, bringing Torlo and me with him.

"Up you go," Torlo said, and I helped him get Jakar on his feet. Angry veins had snaked their way above Jakar's shirt collar, and the whites of his bloodshot eyes were stained purple.

"Mind taking over?" I asked Geth. He hesitated, but took my place and wrapped Jakar's arm over his shoulder. "We're finding a doctor first and foremost," I said to the cartographer, then took the rail weapon from Namira. "That's not a suggestion."

I took us down the first of the switchbacks that led to the road. Jakar had stopped stumbling—his feet now dragged through the dirt. "Are you going to make it?" I asked him.

His eyes roamed the ceiling and the walls, as if he were seeing monsters that weren't there, and I tried not to panic. "You'll be all right," I whispered to both of us.

On the main road, people wore robes the color of flowers and cream, with gemstones laced through their hair, both cloth and minerals pristine and gleaming. Our dusty, sweaty, bleeding group shoved its way past them, eliciting a fair share of annoyed cries. A few of them tried to ask questions in Xerivian—to ask about the explosion or if Jakar needed help, based on the way they eyed the billowing smoke and Jakar's unconscious form—but Namira offered curt replies and kept moving. Hopefully, these people didn't linger long enough to tip off Arhan and his bootlickers. The tunnel led us to a city-sized cavern where Ravada, Xeriv's capital, waited.

I'd grown up thinking Radavich and Saracosta had big cities, but those places didn't hold a candle to here. The first thing my attention gravitated toward was the snow on the slope of the far wall. It was falling from some hidden hole in the ceiling. A massive lavafall on Ravada's left side illuminated forts, manors, and a citadel, the light adding to the glow of thousands of torches scattered throughout the city. Ravada twinkled with every color of the spectrum, and I noticed how many gemstones were interspersed among the architecture. A river cut its way from one end of the cavern to the other. To my right, two-story clay villas and colorful mosaic walkways shouted mid-level affluence. Bingo. "That way," I said. "I bet the doctors there are rich enough to have what Jakar needs but poor enough not to laugh us out the door."

"Good doctors cost good money," Geth said.

"I wonder how much their lives are worth to them, then."

The cartographer was unimpressed by my threat, which I had to admit was pretty empty. "Namira, could you spot us some money?" I asked.

"I'm a little low on funds at the moment," she said. "In the hole, technically. That was supposed to change once I finished this Darkwater gig." The look she gave Geth dripped with acid.

"Geth? It's the least you can do."

"I'm in the same boat as Namira."

"Imagine that," Namira said. "Asshole."

"I know a place we can take him," Geth continued. "He's not much, but he's trustworthy, and trust is about as valuable as any legitimate doctor."

"I beg to differ," I said.

"You wouldn't if you knew how many eyes Darkwater can pay for around here."

"He's right," Namira said. The words sounded as though they'd gone bad in her mouth. "You're runaway serfs now. That's a heavy crime here in Xeriv."

I touched a finger to the half-healed brand on the back of my neck. "Let's go, then," I said, trying to keep my voice level as I watched Jakar's eyelids flutter and droplets of sweat slide down his temples.

Torlo and Geth helped Jakar to the streets below. The snow hill on the city's far side irritated my eyes—it was bright enough to fill the whole cavern with ambient light, tinted from the lavafall and the torchlight. We reached the streets and Jakar slumped, eyes closing, causing the group of three to slide to the ground.

"I'll take him," Torlo said. He gingerly picked Jakar up, draping the man's body over his shoulders, and his skinny body started to buckle. "It's all in the technique," he said when he saw the look on my face, then grinned with pride. He took a step forward, hissed in pain, and collapsed. I jumped forward, cradling Jakar's head to keep it from smacking against the stone.

"My feet," Torlo said. "Ow, ow, ow!"

The boy picked himself up, took a careful step, then fell into a heavy limp. "Can you help?" I asked Namira. "I have an idea." The woman nodded without question, and we moved to the far end of the street past the onlookers, who were interested enough to see what was going on but not interested enough to help.

"Distract him," I said, pointing at a street vendor selling candied fruit from a booth on a sidewalk, and Namira jumped to the task. The vendor sat on a stool, bored while he awaited his next customer, and perked up when Namira approached. She spoke to him in Xerivian, moving frantically close and peeling back the cloth wrapped around her arm. He cringed and gave a half-hearted answer. I circled to the other side of his booth and entered the side alley where the vendor's pull cart sat with a handful of bags. I pulled the bags out, then set the rail weapon inside before checking on Namira, finding her doing an exceedingly effective job at disturbing the trader and keeping his eyes off me. I wheeled the pull cart away. I circled the block and returned to where Jakar lay on the sidewalk with Torlo, who was heavily favoring one foot, and Geth. "Put him in this," I said, checking the shadows for any Darkwater employees, though I wasn't sure what to look for.

Torlo and Geth loaded Jakar into the cart, then the four of us headed down the street through the press of people, past the fruit vendor where Namira still talked, laughing and patting him playfully on the chest. She slid her bandage in place and broke off to follow.

Geth led us near the hill of snow to a neighborhood full of one-room houses made of brick and sheets of metal for roofs, and I noticed how old clothes and looks of mild desperation went hand in hand with the people crowding the streets. "Here," Geth said, turning down a muddy side alley where beads of water clung to every surface and a backdraft of chilly air pushed past us. He stopped near the end and whipped aside the blanket hanging up as a door. He said something in Xerivian to the occupant inside. A tall, broad-shouldered man appeared, took in our sorry little group, and said something to Geth. Geth answered and the man shook his head. He picked Jakar up and carried him inside.

The man dumped Jakar onto an old mattress in the back corner of the shack. "Is he all right?" I asked as the man knelt.

"Be patient," he said in a heavy accent. He removed Jakar's

shirt, sucking in a breath, and after a moment that lasted half of forever, he said, "No good, no good. Where to begin? Cold compresses, perhaps. That would help with the fever and slow blood flow. I will make him comfortable at least."

"Make him comfortable?"

"The best gift to be given to some."

My stomach dropped. This wasn't how Jakar was supposed to go.

A cry of pain came from the couch by the door. Namira sat next to Torlo with the boy's foot on her lap, and she was slowly peeling the rubber from his feet with her good hand. "It's fused to your wounds," she said. "I have to take this off now before it heals too much." She pulled again, and Torlo bit down on his shirt collar. Rubber separated from skin, and after a dozen seconds of trying not to squirm, Torlo asked, "Is it done?"

"I've got about an eighth of it off."

"*Prad!*" Torlo cursed.

"Wait," I said. "Where's Geth?"

Nobody had an answer.

I wondered what could have compelled Geth to disappear, now of all moments, and I didn't like the answer. "Excuse me, saior," I said to the Xerivian as he wiped sweat from Jakar's hairline with a washcloth. "Where's the local Cartographer Archives?"

"You should stay here, yes. For your friend."

Jakar's sickly, frail body splayed on that dirty mattress was difficult to look at, but I told myself that escaping such a sight wasn't why I needed to leave. Geth needed to make a formal claim on the Sihraan ruins, but Darkwater would as well, just as soon as Arhan showed up. Maybe Geth figured that selling out a few escaped serfs could work as a negotiation tactic with Darkwater and had decided to dump us in a place where we could easily be found.

"Please just tell me where the Archives are," I said.

The man scribbled directions onto a corner of old parchment paper. I raced down the muddy alley, shoving my way into the foot traffic on the street beyond, and raced toward the Archives. I passed a restaurant with tables on a front patio and grabbed a knife off a table, the yells of angry patrons chasing me quickly fading. Next I stole a dirty rag from a clothier's booth and ripped it into strips, then tied the knife against my forearm, covering it with the sleeve of my shirt. Geth would die before he could sell us out. I wouldn't let Jakar wake up shackled to some serf bunk in Darkwater… and if he didn't wake up, I needed to solve this problem without him.

The Cartographer Archives sat next to a plaza with shrubs of every color and gurgling fountains, the two-story building extending backward several hundred feet, dwarfing every cartographer hall I'd encountered in Mira. Xeriv didn't have a Sovereign who'd gone on a book-burning rampage a couple centuries earlier, so the size made sense. Administrators in decorative cave-diving leathers worked the front, but they hardly looked in my direction as I plunged into the hallways.

I skidded across the polished stone when I caught Geth's voice coming out of an office up ahead. It sounded like he was speaking to two colleagues and was in the middle of paraphrasing our little foray in the Rift. He spoke Miran, but someone else was speaking a strange language, likely Xerivian, while the third person acted as a translator for the two. Based on Geth's words, it sounded as if his colleagues were planning to file a claim as soon as possible with the city, but they were worried. Darkwater had their grubby fingers on all sorts of positions of influence, could push and pull the city until its government bent to their will. If they wanted to claim the Sihraan ruins for themselves even though they weren't the first to file, they could make it happen. Geth stormed out, and I barely had time to turn around and hide my face. He was too irate to notice me, headed in the opposite direction.

I followed him into a library lit with glowing yellow quartz veins that ran through the polished stone floors and ceiling, where he disappeared into one of the rows of books. I crouched behind a desk near the entrance, fiddling with the knife under my sleeve. Ten minutes later he reappeared and sat at a table, then opened his book and stared hard at the text with enough heat to almost burn a hole in it.

"Must be a good book," I said.

He jumped, his gaze shifting to the exit. I sat in the chair opposite him. "Shouldn't you be taking care of your friend?" he asked.

"Not much I can do. Figured I'd check on you instead."

I tried to read the text—a symbol was scrawled on the front that prodded old memories—but he moved his forearm over the pages. "What do you want?" he asked.

If I killed him, it wouldn't be hard to flee before I drew too much attention. The building was mostly empty. I'd have to go for his neck, though, to stop the screaming. The neck would mean a lot of blood, so I'd have to avoid as much splatter as I could. What if it took more than one stroke?

Geth's chair scraped against stone. He pushed away and jumped to his feet, and a blade no longer than his finger appeared in his hand. "I think you should leave."

I looked down. The knife had poked through the fabric of my sleeve. I pulled it out. "Now seems like a good time for you to sell us out to Darkwater to get a stake on those ruins. I won't let that happen."

"Don't be ridiculous."

I circled the table. He backed away, but I rushed to put myself between him and the exit. "I've talked to con artists before," I said. "They always tell me I'm crazy. You know that? Or they'll ask why I don't trust them. That's always a question a liar asks. It's usually around that point in the conversation when I force the truth out."

"Yes, I'm sure. A girl your age must have worlds of experience."

Geth didn't know that nobiletza understood manipulation and gaslighting before learning their ABCs, and my time running around with the gangs of Manasus had finely tuned my sense for betrayal. "Are you seriously trying to tell me you're not hiding something?"

"I'm not turning you in," he growled. "Darkwater will skin me alive as soon as Arhan tells them what I did to their caravan. Besides, I have more interesting questions I need answers to."

"About the ruins?"

"No."

"So more interesting than the place you screwed over a whole company to find?"

He didn't answer, and once again I considered how strange it was to be reading at a time like this. Another glance at his book and it all clicked. Father had owned multiple books with the same symbol on the front cover, which he'd stashed in his private selection. A selection he had stored alongside precious gems, heirlooms, and some paintings of his children and Mother. It was a stash he would kill over. "That book's on elemental power, isn't it? You're interested in Jakar."

He considered my words, then gave a halfhearted nod. "His power is the kind that's meant to be kept secret. I'm sure an escaped serf like him wouldn't appreciate me knowing just how valuable he is."

"He's not going to kill you just because you know what he can do. He's not like that." I tapped the flat of the blade against my thigh, thinking. I couldn't decide if trusting Geth was worth the risk. "If you're that interested in Jakar, then you want to keep him alive too."

"Absolutely. Depths if I know how, but Shirallah will do what he can. I pulled some strings with the Archives and they're looking into spotting me money so someone with more know-how can look Jakar over. It won't be much, but maybe we can learn if he'll live or die."

I set my knife on the table and backed away. "All right. I believe you. What about Jakar's powers are you interested in?"

He shifted his weight from one foot to the other, as if trying to figure out if disarming me was a trick. "I'm reading up on the katsu. They could do what Jakar did, but exponentially more powerful. Cartographers believe they're responsible for all the manmade tunnels everywhere, even ones we're discovering that couldn't have had human contact for thousands of years. It's a long shot, but you can't fault me for wondering where your friend comes from."

Jakar's trying to figure that out himself, actually. I eyed the shelves of books. There were thousands, tens of thousands of books, even. We were closer to Jakar's homeland than any Archive west of the Rift, and this place had records that went much further back, which meant possible answers involving the people who'd raised him. Maybe even secrets about the flesh binding and ways to break it that didn't involve me trying to murder him.

"Let's make a deal," I said. "Give me access to your books and I'll help you find a way to fight Darkwater for access to those ruins."

"No offense, but I know an empty promise when I hear it. What's a kid like you going to do?"

"I'm good at making trouble." I itched at the chance to fight Darkwater again, as it would mean another chance at Arhan. He would die a slow death, one way or another.

"No offense, but I'm not convinced. Sorry, kid."

Above and below, my life would have been so much easier if I was an adult. I was tired of being underestimated. I tried another tactic. "If you want to learn more about Jakar, it'll mean dealing with me. So let me see your books and it'll make me happy. Our interests are aligned, so I don't see the big deal."

He rubbed the grizzle on his jaw. Perhaps he was weighing the trouble of helping a runaway serf, but he had to know Jakar and I were a package deal. Jakar would tell Geth nothing if I asked it of him.

"I'll find a way to help you with Darkwater," I added. "You have nothing to lose."

"Fine. Help yourself to the library, and in turn you'll tell me what you find. Not sure what you'll do about Darkwater, but if you want to risk a serf collar, that's on you."

"High risk, high reward."

He offered his hand, and I took it, giving it two hard shakes.

Chapter 16—Ester

THE FIRST RULE Ester had learned as a kid, along with everyone else in Mira, was never to explore the crust without a map. Yet here she was, eating her way into the inky blackness with nothing but a torch and Xander's lantern to guide the way. "Any chance your magic lantern can tell us where to go?" she asked.

"A device that can guide us into Sihraan ruins is a bit beyond my capabilities."

"Look," she noted, pointing at worn wheel grooves and boot marks scuffed into the ground. "This must be the old traders' trails." She pulled her sword out, just in case, and felt for the presence of nearby iron. None so far.

"Is it a good idea to do this with weapons drawn? Ruin folk might give an eye for an eye if they think you're aiming to kill."

"I won't take chances. Not now." In truth, while she wouldn't dream of disarming herself when there were so many unknowns ahead, it was Xander's presence that kept her paranoid of looming threats. She regretted bringing him along. There was nothing for him to contribute and he was risking his life for nothing. How could she hope to guard him when she could barely see five feet ahead of her? She couldn't send him back now, though. She tried to remind herself that this was what he wanted, that maybe he *could* be the voice of reason if their run-in with the ruin folk called for it, but all she could think about now was losing him to a blade in the darkness.

The path took them gently but steadily downward, and Ester noticed the lack of bioluminescence. Someone must have scraped it all off. Another sign they were headed the right way. The tunnel widened, and just beyond the firelight were all sorts of pockmarks in the walls and alcoves. Perfect places to hide. Ester's sword hand prickled and her power caught a glimmer of steel at the very edge of her senses. She brought a hand up and stopped, and Xander paused behind her. Weapons, belt buckles, and the metal fastenings of boots floated ahead, hanging off what appeared to be two people waiting in the shadows. They were crouched and facing Ester's direction, waiting.

The light from Xander's lantern flipped and danced on the walls before the sound of breaking glass echoed through the tunnel. Ester tried to bring her sword hand up, but a set of arms wrapped around her torso, pinning her arms to her sides and sending her torch clattering over the rock.

"Fuck off!" she screamed. She tried to smash the back of her head into the face of the man restraining her, but found only air. Her heel came down hard on a boot and elicited a cry. Cloth swished over her head at the same time someone tried to grab her sword hand, and she twisted hard, feeling steel separate flesh.

A group of them were trying to restrain her—they smashed the sword out of her grip and got her feet off the ground. She thrashed but couldn't shake them. The disorientation worsened, and her thoughts turned fuzzy. The dampness inside the bag was more than just hot, condensed breath and spit, she realized, as she caught a whiff of the acrid smell of chemicals. Then she was out.

* * *

SHE CAME TO with a spongy tongue, the sensation of cool rock pressed against her cheek, and intense thirst. Her throat felt as though she had inhaled a pile of dust. She sat up, wiped the grit from her lips and the side of her face, and scanned the room, which was lit in the center by a three-foot-tall crystal glowing pale blue. Someone had tied her hands and feet. A box made of metal sat next to the doorway, rusted to oblivion, and her surroundings were carved from yellow and brown stone. No, it was marble with centuries of stains. She didn't know much about Sihraan ruins, but it was safe to say that's exactly where she was.

"Hello?" she croaked. She spat out the last of the dirt in her mouth.

The door creaked open and a woman poked her head in. "*Es'sa?*"

"Can I get some water?"

The woman disappeared without another word. Ester scooted to the metal box and stuck her hand into a rusted-out hole, trying to saw through the bonds, but the metal crumbled to dust. What was the box even for? It was connected to the floor and she could see wires and debris on the bottom, but she ultimately chalked it up to another Sihraan mystery. She struggled to her feet and hopped to the crystal instead. She tried cutting at the rope's threads with the point at the top, but still no luck.

If they wanted her dead, she'd be dead. Still, she didn't have high hopes for survival, if the words of those guards in Naxion could be trusted. And what if the ruin folk had nothing to do with the stolen rhidium and she'd gotten herself captured for no reason? Nervous worry filled her when she thought of Xander. He wasn't a threat, but if it was information the ruin folk wanted from either of them, they didn't need two people to get it.

She should've made him stay in town. If he was hurt, or

worse, it would be all her fault. They'd spent every waking hour together since leaving Augustin, and it wasn't until he'd been taken away from her did she realize the emptiness he was capable of leaving behind. The hole in her chest that had plagued her for weeks grew ten times bigger. If she ever found out the ruin folk hurt Xander, she would gladly pay it back in kind.

The door opened, and Xander entered the room carrying a glass of water.

They stared at each other for several long moments. He grimaced. There wasn't fear or worry on his face, and he wasn't bound by restraints. Ester noticed the blood-stained bandage wrapped around his leg. He'd walked in with a slight limp, too, and now favored his right foot. He looked to the ground in shame.

"You're the one who grabbed me from behind," Ester heard herself say.

He nodded and offered the glass of water. She stared at it.

"I spent the last two hours rehearsing this conversation, but now that I'm here, I forgot what I wanted to say." He sounded different now. He had a Bys accent.

"I'm… sorry you're having such a hard time." The end of the sentence came out as more of a wheeze, and she broke out in a fit of coughing, leaning against the glowing crystal.

Xander set the water in front of her and stepped away. When she recovered, she considered kicking the glass of water at him, feeling the need to refuse anything he had to offer. Trying to kick with her bound feet didn't sound like the smartest idea in the world, though. She swallowed her anger and hopped forward. She stumbled to her knees, wincing, and spent a few seconds reining herself in, trying not to show the near-overwhelming urge to cry. She was truly alone. Her reward for sending her brother and closest confidante off and letting a stranger into her life had been a knife wound deeper than anything she'd felt before.

She pressed her back against the crystal and sat, downed a

few gulps of water, and said, "I guess it'd be stupid to ask if you were working with the rhidium thieves since the start."

He had a face full of guilt. "No, it's not stupid. Not stupid at all. I manipulated you and the Foundry. What I did was terrible."

"If it was so terrible, why do it?"

"Because we need the rhidium. My friends and I are about to put ourselves in a lot of danger and we need whatever edge we can find. The rhidium would serve a better purpose with us instead of sitting in some forgotten storage room. We lied and cheated our way into getting it, but my plan can make all the difference. I just didn't realize how much harder it would become when I was doing it to a friend."

My plan, he'd said. She considered the Bys accent, and her next thought made her sick. "This is the part where you tell me your real name isn't Xander," she said.

He looked at the floor. "I was figuring I would wait until later to tell you... but yes. Stealing from the Foundry came with a huge risk, which meant the name tied to that stolen rug cart would become an enemy of all smiths. I made my friend assume my identity when he drove the cart. This was my plan, so I should shoulder the responsibility."

Ester took in the man named Breach, the person she'd been hunting all along, and the loneliness she felt earlier rotted out, leaving only a hollowness behind. "You could have gotten away clean if you hadn't helped us find a lead on the cart back in Augustin. Why put a smith on your own trail?"

"We know the risks of working with rhidium. We need an expert who can help us. You can make sure the process is as safe as possible."

Sitting in this room, riddled with bruises, so hopelessly tied up that Ester couldn't hop more than a few steps without falling on her butt, had been part of the plan orchestrated by Xander—no, Breach. The humiliation of having been played so thoroughly filled her up, making her cheeks heat, and the idea of hurting him didn't sound so bad all of a sudden.

"How?"

"How what?"

"I…" she trailed off. *How could you do this to me?* was the question she'd almost asked. She didn't want to know the answer, didn't want to find out that the feelings she'd started to nurture for him hadn't been reciprocated. And why would they be? She'd done well to hide them, didn't want them to complicate her mission to recover the rhidium.

She started again. "So now you're going to convince me to help you? A bit of an oversight putting that into your plan, don't you think?"

"Stealing the rhidium was a long shot from start to finish, and it was never an integral part of our plan. It was the icing on the cake. There have been many rumors about the smiths wanting to fight the Sovereign, so asking for your help didn't seem impossible."

Ester's heart started beating faster and faster, to the point she could almost feel it rattling in her chest. Her breathing shortened. There was a lot of talk outside the Foundry about the smiths betraying the Sovereign? She thought those conversations had been hidden among the arc smiths and senior arc smiths, far from the public's ear. As far as everyone knew, the Foundry was doing everything in its power to extricate itself from politics, given Master Smith Mateo's very vocal proclamations.

Was it her fault that word had got out about some of the smiths wanting to stand against the Sovereign? What if the Sovereign had heard those rumors while he was there?

"Are you all right?" Breach asked.

She drank the rest of the water and squeezed her eyes shut. "I just need a minute."

She lost some of the sensation in her hands and started trembling even though the room was warm. After a few minutes, the panic attack began to subside. "You need to let me go," she said slowly, trying to keep the tremors out of her voice. "I need to get back to Augustin."

His face turned one shade lighter and his mouth parted in worry. "Ester, I'm not going to hurt you. Don't be scared."

"Scared? You think I'm scared of you or your friends? If word is getting around that the Foundry might betray the Sovereign, then all of my brothers and sisters are in danger. What do you think the Sovereign will do if he hears the wrong rumor? Or the worst one? You have to let me go."

He frowned but didn't answer.

"What are you going to do?" she asked. "Are you going to blackmail me? I show you how to become elemental and you'll let me go?"

Again, he didn't answer.

Another person entered the room. Someone who was stout, broad of chest, and with a very unpleasant demeanor. "Will she help?" he asked in the old tongue.

"I don't know," Breach answered, speaking the language slowly and awkwardly, "but take care. She might understand you."

They looked at Ester and she nodded. The newcomer approached her and stopped just beyond kicking distance, kneeling on one knee. "Breach told us you're interested in fighting the Sovereign," he said, continuing in the old tongue. "If you help turn some of our fighters into metal workers, you will get what you want."

His utterance of such a sacred title made Ester wish he'd stood a little closer. "That's a power you earn," she said, speaking in Miran. "Look at the primordia if you're wondering what it looks like when someone wields that kind of power before they've earned it. I don't know you and I don't know the people you want me to help. The only people who will be using that rhidium are trainees inducted as apprentices in the Foundry."

"We will see."

"Yeah, we'll see you using the rhidium without my help. You'll have to watch people I presume are very important to you die painful deaths."

His lip twitched and the fist resting on his knee tightened. "Then I guess we don't need you." He stood and left, leaving her alone with Breach again.

"Your plan was terrible if it was predicated on me helping you," Ester said. "The fact your boss wants to kill me when I've done nothing wrong only proves why I shouldn't help you."

Breach rubbed his brow. "Don't worry about Neale. He was just trying to intimidate you. He wants my plan to succeed, but he hasn't seen it as necessary since the start."

The logical part of Ester couldn't help but acknowledge how bad Breach was at this part of his plan. He could've threatened her all he wanted, even if he didn't plan to follow through with killing her. He knew how badly she wanted to leave, so he could have leaned hard into the blackmail angle. There was even a chance she would've relented. Instead, there was pain in his eyes, as if he were the one being held hostage.

"What are your friends planning to do?" she asked.

"Fighting the Sovereign is out of the question. We could take on his standing army since most tunnels render numbers useless, but his primordia would rip right through our front lines. Or they could make their own tunnels so the Sovereign's army could flank us. What we have to do is undermine his authority. Have those loyal to him lose faith until no one supports him and he'll have no choice but to step down."

"It's a bit of a stretch if you think he'll step down because nobody likes him. A lot of people already don't like him."

"He's surrounded by people-pleasers and sycophants, so maybe his view on reality is skewed." He came to her side, knelt, and set a hand on her shoulder. "Please, Ester. Fights like these aren't a series of well thought out plans that systematically tear the leadership down one block at a time. It's mostly just bumbling your way along until you find the strategy that works best while making mistakes that get people killed who don't deserve it. It's ugly and terrifying and awful, but we can make it less so with your help. To be frank, none of my friends ever thought my plan would work, but I know the Foundry wants what we want."

For a moment, Ester fell into those desperate eyes and felt her head tilt toward his hand. But only for a moment. "No," she said, shrugging his hand away. "I'd be betraying every one of my brothers and sisters if I shared the Foundry's secrets without their permission. And besides, you lied to me, Xa... Breach. There's nothing you could say that I would believe."

He moved away, filling the room with sullen silence. Then he left and the lock clicked into place behind him.

BREACH AND NEALE returned several hours later, a rockwood knife hanging from Neale's grip.

He let the blade hover an inch from Ester's nose. "You will stay here," he said in the old tongue. "We will create metal workers with the rhidium. Help us if you wish, or don't. It makes no difference."

"That's not what we agreed on," Breach said.

Ester's anger and exhaustion left no more room for fear. "I'm not staying," she said as she looked past the rockwood blade and glared into Neale's eyes. "My brothers and sisters are in danger. I'm going back to Augustin."

"How can I trust you to keep our secrets? We've done well to keep places like this hidden from the world above."

"You've never been my enemy. Only the Sovereign and anyone who would threaten my friends and family. You *will* be my enemy if you keep me hostage."

"Very well. We are keeping the rhidium, though."

That was quick. It seemed the plan all along had been to let her go. "I'm not leaving empty handed," she said. "The rhidium is Foundry property."

"I don't care. We need it more than you."

"Like I said. I'm not leaving empty handed."

The leather of the knife's handle creaked from Neale's grip as he glared back, brows furrowed. "Perhaps I will take your hands, then, so your argument is moot."

Breach gently pulled Neale away. "Don't threaten her. You can't blame her for anything she's done or said, and her request is reasonable. We'll give her some of the rhidium and keep most of it for ourselves." He looked to Ester. "Does that work?"

Ester struggled to answer with anything other than an angry retort. She settled with eying him until he broke her gaze, and the small satisfaction she experienced as a result was enough for her to say in a civil tone, "I suppose I don't have a choice. Now let me go."

Breach took the knife and cut the rope linking her ankles together, then the bindings on her wrists. The rope fell to the floor, and Neale quickly retrieved the knife so he could stand several feet away with his arms crossed, positioned as if she might attack them, but Ester just stared at Breach. If it had been earlier, maybe she would have bruised a cheek or two of his and broken a nose, but her exhaustion was too deep, in more ways than just physical. She never wanted to see him again.

"I told Neale and the others that there's no chance of you finding your way back here with a gang of smiths to get revenge."

"And?"

"And they believed me. But you might want to reassure Neale that you won't come back to take back the rest of the rhidium."

She turned to Neale, who still hadn't relaxed. "I'll have more important things to worry about than tracking down the rhidium a second time," she lied. In truth, it would be up to Mateo whether or not to let the matter rest. She suspected she would be marching back here with a coterie of her brothers and sisters in due time.

Neale led them out the door. The building she'd been held hostage in sat on a short ridge overlooking a cavern covered in crumbling stone, dilapidated structures, and swamp

Clay Harmon

water. People moved throughout the ruins, where makeshift structures and jerry-rigged walkways overlaid the ancient, yellowed stone. There had to be thousands living here. Even so, only about a quarter of the ruins looked inhabited. "That's a lot of people," she said.

"The ruin folk will do whatever they can to keep their numbers hidden," Breach said. "Cartographers are warned again and again not to tread this deep into the territories, but they never listen. I can't understand their obsession. Some things are meant to be left alone."

Neale left and returned a short while later with a heavily stuffed bag. Inside were her vials of rhidium wrapped in cloth.

"I know the Star Mines only resupply the territories once every ten years, but that pack gives you time to come up with a solution," Breach said. "If you can tolerate the Archives and the Tempurium and all the different trade schools playing with rhidium without your supervision, you can deal with us doing the same."

She had no interest in arguing. She just wanted to get back to Augustin. She needed to be away from Breach.

He pulled some parchment out of his back pocket. "Here's a map to Naxion. You should take the long way back to Augustin's capital, too. Go north until you hit the Granite Road, then head home that way. You know, in case the Sovereign really did try to follow us."

She resisted the urge to smile bitterly at the idea that Breach had given her directions back to this place. The more she thought about it, the more confident she was that she would see him again in the future, ready to take back what belonged to the Foundry.

The thought was quickly replaced by her anxiety over the Sovereign's visit to Augustin. "Primordia have a hard time with electric shocks," she said. Angry as she was with Breach, it didn't change the fact that the ruin folk planned to fight their common enemy. She could set aside her aversion to him for at least a moment. "It won't incapacitate them for long, and you probably won't kill them anyway, but it's better than nothing. The master smith mentioned rumors of salvage in some Sihraan ruins that can produce electricity."

He turned his head, pensive. "Occasionally some of the ruin folk venture into the unexplored parts of the city and someone will injure themselves touching some old metal. I'll be sure to look into it. Thank you."

She nodded. Unsure of what else to say, she turned and hiked for the pathway leading to the exit tunnel at the top of the cavern, and glanced back to see Breach staring. Again, an overpowering feeling of betrayal threatened to take over, but then she felt guilty for the anger. What was wrong with her?

Breach could've taken a long swim in a short lake for all Ester was concerned. She had recovered some of the rhidium and accomplished her mission to the best of her ability, and had done so no worse for the wear. This was a moment to celebrate. Her feelings about particular ex-companions no longer mattered because the Foundry was what was important, and it would always stay that way.

Anxiety, like a taut wire, dogged her as she entered the tunnels and left Mulec'Yrathrik in the dust. She hoped Mateo and the others were safe.

Part 2

Chapter 17—Jakar

I OPENED MY eyes to ruddy yellow light and the smell of wet moss, damp blankets twisted into ropes over my legs, and my body feeling like someone had tossed it down a hole. I struggled into a sitting position with a grunt.

"Hello?" I croaked. I was in a one-room shack, by myself. I waited, watching the cool drafts of air sneak past the swinging blanket serving as a door, but nobody came. I forced myself out of bed and fell on my face.

I pushed myself up, and that's when I noticed the bandages were gone from my arms. The skin was now thick, rippled, and hairless, and I could barely feel my fingers pushing against them. My burns from Augustin had finally healed. How long had I been out for? I was in a sleeping area in the back corner of the one-room shack, and there was a kitchen in another corner, with a living area at the front and a woodstove beside it that was doing a poor job of keeping the place warm. I rushed to the water pump sitting above a pail full of dishes left to soak, and I pumped at it desperately, gulping at the cold water that came out. A handful of seconds later I noticed I was pumping icy, rancid grime into my mouth. I heaved, vomiting into the pail of dishes and onto the floor.

Syrupy thoughts leaked into my brain. I remembered the tunnels to Xeriv, then stumbling through city streets, surrounded by flashes of colorful clothing and glittering gemstones. Then nothing. Where was Efadora? Was she safe?

I stumbled through the blanket-door into an alley, where the breeze ran over my sweaty skin, brisk as frost. My bare feet squished through cold mud, and I reached the street at the end of the alley, stepping onto the firm dusty stone of the sidewalk, the air smelling of dirt, spices, sweat, and the occasional whiff of sewage. The street was packed with people, carts, and strange, quadrupedal animals, and passersby pushed past me, speaking a language I didn't understand, the pack animals grunting with exertion. It was foolish to consider venturing out in a city I didn't know, since I knew better than to presume Darkwater had forgotten about me. But whose home had I woken up in? Was I safe there? I took note of the stack of barrels to my left, the bags of rice to my right, then let the tide of people take me.

Soon I veered off the sidewalk, and a merchant yelled at me as his animal—which was a donkey of sorts with milky eyes and bulging muscles—jostled me. I nearly fell, but waved in apology and kept moving. Everything around me was organized chaos. How could I possibly find Efadora in all of this? The alley I had exited was one of dozens, and corrugated metal offered an overhang that protected people from the flurries of snow that drifted down from the mountain of ice near the cavern's wall. Water dripped from the cavern ceiling, hitting me with fat droplets, and I forced myself back onto the sidewalk and under the overhang where the cram of people was twice as dense. I kept waiting to see the ghostly pallor of a Miran or the ash-gray complexion of a Sulian, hoping to ask someone, anyone, for information, but everyone around me had skin of sandstone and wore strange clothes. Maybe leaving the shack had been a bad idea.

Several intersections down, a massive warehouse sat on the opposite street corner with a chipped wooden sign swaying on a signpost. Above the signpost was a sigil of an octopus grasping two thorny vines.

Hanlovaja Kanija Darkwater
Zavanie! Dauka! Linh!
Darkwater Trading Co.
Storage! Shipping! Leasing!

The warehouse took up an entire city block. Doors lined the wall facing a side street, all of them open with dozens of workers straining to load and unload carts. Frail-looking men and women wore metal shackles on their necks while stern faces watched them, oiled leather whips hanging from the overseers' belts.

Someone grabbed my shoulder and turned me around. Three men stared me down, all wearing moth-eaten coats adorned in official-looking patches, the leader babbling to me in his native tongue. They looked like private security.

"I'm sorry," I said, raising my hands. "You have the wrong person."

The lead man tried to usher me across the street, but I didn't budge. He tried again, this time with a good shove, and my feet scraped over the curb as I caught myself. I panicked. My fist smashed into the man's face and he fell into his friends. When he recovered, he and his friends unsheathed knives from their belts, and bystanders pushed to get out of the way, some of them surprised, others not so much. The lead man's neck and cheeks were flushed, angry red.

"Please don't do this," I said.

They attacked.

I swiped at the air. They grunted and gasped as their blades flew from their grips, and one of the weapons shrieked as it scraped against stone and buried itself to the hilt in the street. Another bounced in the air and rattled onto a rooftop, and the last flew half a block away and landed in the back of a cart. My attackers froze, and others on the street corner tried to give us a wider berth. The Darkwater overseers beside the warehouse watched the spectacle with curious expressions.

I took off running, my feet slapping against the grimy stone.

I was leaving grooves in the rock, I realized, and it took conscious effort to cut myself off from my power. I coughed and wheezed and smacked into person after person, leaving shouts and curses in my wake. For a wild second I thought I was lost until I saw the stack of barrels and the pile of rice lining the entrance to the side alley. I turned into it. A man stood at the opposite end, and he waved frantically as I barreled toward him. "Jakar!" he said in a heavy accent.

I slipped in the mud and my body gave out. I slammed into him, but he was so large that one step back was all he needed to catch me. "Come," he said, and slung my arm over his shoulder, helping me through the curtains. He let me crumple on the couch. "Ah, yes, you would wake when I take the risk of traversing a market visit."

"What is this?" I asked, my chest whining as I struggled to catch my breath. "Where am I?"

"I am Shirallah." His voice was deep and scratched from tobacco. "I thought I was... ah, what is the word? Your Aperika. Death Carer. But perhaps I should self-offer more credit at my medicine skills. I am friend."

A linen blanket was draped over the couch, covered in blocky caricatures of the pack animals I'd seen on the street, and I grabbed it to drape over my legs for warmth. Baskets woven with a strange local plant the color of bone lined the walls, full of Shirallah's belongings, and the air smelled rancid. "I'm sorry," I said, eying the gift I'd left on the kitchen floor.

He laughed. "You do not drink the unboiled water of the Nephrite River. I will get you something to stomach."

"Do you know Efadora? I need to see her."

"Of course, of course. She will be along. Being that you have been unconscious for two weeks continuous, sam bador, she was not the type to stick around. Also, she has been keeping herself busy instead of looking upon you in such a state."

"Two weeks?"

"Yes, yes. We did not think you would make it, to be truthful. An elder from Saving's Grace of Chalu'uht came by this most recent passing to perform Fell's Spark. Last rites."

Could I really blame them for giving me up for dead? I lifted the ratted brown tunic someone must have slipped over me and found the usual scars, but no purple veins. Shirallah grunted. "I shall be damned. We brought in a mender to give you the once and twice over, but they had not the faintest clue what was wrong. Would you know perhaps, friend? Geth believes it was a bite from the wrong sort of insect during your travels."

"A bite makes sense," I said mildly. I thought back to the confrontation in front of Darkwater's warehouse and how my elemental power had manifested much, much stronger than before.

I had my suspicions about what had happened. I had bonded to a seventh element. What that element was and how I'd undergone a binding without consuming rhidium, I had no idea.

Someone rushed through the curtains. It was Geth, and he froze when he saw me. "You're alive."

I unclenched my hands and told myself to relax. I was too jumpy. He peered outside, then moved the blanket back in place. "I'm guessing it's just a coincidence that a guard two blocks down just asked if I saw any crazed, fleeing Sulian men recently. Right?"

"It is my fault," Shirallah said. "Jakar returned to the living at a time when I stepped out. He is not at fault for wandering."

I described the confrontation to them, and Geth snorted. "That wasn't Darkwater security. "If they were, they would have knocked you out cold and thrown you in chains before you knew they were there. Scammers, most likely. They impersonate debt collectors and let you know they're taking you to the Balog Brotherhood or some other gang that'll flay you for owed debt, unless you sweeten them up with a small fee."

"People fall for that?"

"Visitors know Ravada's reputation. Last thing some traveler wants is a misunderstanding with the local gangs."

"Should we be concerned about the guards?"

He shrugged, and a knowing grin spread across his face. "If they come around and poke their noses where they shouldn't, I'm sure you can deal with them without issue."

Shirallah glared at him, but Geth didn't notice or care. The eagerness in his voice was clear—he wanted another glimpse of what he'd seen at the ruins. What were the chances he would encourage a guard to come sniffing around here? It sounded like something a person who'd strand a caravan in the Rift to satisfy his curiosity would do. I kept the curtains in my peripherals, just in case.

Shirallah moved to a bag sitting on the table and pulled out cuts of meat wrapped in paper, along with a clean pot from beneath the counter. He set them beside a cutting board with clumps of dough dusted with flour. "You are trembling," he said to me, rolling the first clump. "It is time for your stomach to be filled. Your stomach will be sensitive, yes, so I will prepare a soup that will go down easy."

Geth collapsed on the edge of the couch next to the wood stove with a satisfied sigh and massaged one of his thighs. "It's been a busy week for busy souls, Jakar. You came to at a good time. We're getting our slice of revenge on Darkwater soon. Now you can help us."

It was a struggle for me to stay calm. "Where's Efadora?" I asked.

"Good question. I thought she would be back by now. She can tell you all about what we have planned."

I tried to stand, but my legs shook and I collapsed on the couch. "She's a wanted serf. What about Namira or Torlo? Where are they?"

"You worry too much. I haven't seen them either, but they've been getting around just fine. Efadora is nineteen, Jakar. That's fully grown around these parts. She can't be chaperoned for the rest of her life."

"She doesn't know this place and she doesn't speak the language. And she lied to you. She's sixteen."

"Oh." He frowned, but the expression disappeared quickly. "I'm sure she's fine."

I tried to pull myself up again, but collapsed a second time. Shirallah pursed his lips and started chopping the meat and vegetables as fast as he could. "You shall have your strength again soon, yes, yes," he said.

Chapter 18—Efadora

LEANING OVER THE side of the warehouse's roof, forty feet in the air while blood rushed to my head, wasn't an ideal place to position myself while trying to peek inside a grimy window. The roof's overhang created a foot-long gap between me and the glass, and a wedged foot between broken roof tiles was what separated me from my work and becoming a broken, bloody mess on the street below. I tried to rub at the glass with the palm of my hand, but it had to have been half a century since someone had cleaned the thing. The grime held on good.

"Fire and ice," I grunted, pulling out my dagger. This was taking too long. I swung the dagger's butt at the window's base, shattering glass, and I paused, but the work of the hundred-plus serfs on the warehouse floor swallowed up the sound. I reached through the hole, unlatched the lock, and swung the window inward, then I sat on the roof's edge and gripped the stone, letting myself slide off until I hung by my fingers. No space below me, I told myself. Just me and the window in front of me.

Namira had blanched at the plan, going on and on about the dangers of climbing on the roof of a business where falling off the side could have been the best-case scenario, but a few carefully chosen words about it being our only way to get revenge on Darkwater had shut her up quick. I swung my body, feeling my grip on the smooth stone shift, and landed on the window frame. The frame was thinner than I thought, and I tumbled forward, my stomach trying to rise into my esophagus as the warehouse floor yawned beneath me. I fell five feet and hit the nearest rafter with my stomach. I clung to the beam for several seconds to catch my breath and wait for the overseers to start shouting. Nope, they were just yelling at the serfs. I had a bat's eye view of the shelves, crates, and empty carts covering the floor, and of the armed guards patrolling the catwalks a third of the way up, half-watching the chaos below. None of them looked up. Not yet, at least.

I crept from rafter to rafter to the corner of the warehouse, where below, a series of doors sat. Behind those doors, the rest of Darkwater waited, and so did Arhan. "Hurry up," I muttered as a guard took his time patrolling away from the catwalk below me. I straddled the rafter's cross section and dug the toe of my shoe into the rockwood of the vertical beam, and the metal spike on my boot bit into wood. I tested my weight by taking my other foot off the rafter. My hold was firm. I drove the spike on my other foot into the vertical beam and started descending.

I was small enough to hide behind the beam as I reached the catwalks' eye level. The storage shelves this far into the warehouse seemed to be for long-term storage and where fewer workers treaded. I touched ground, peered around the beam to check for any guards headed my way, and tested the nearest door. Unlocked.

A hallway stood on the other side, and as I shut the door behind me, I heard the sound of clacking footsteps from beyond the corner ahead. I dodged into the nearest room—a supply closet—and waited until the person passed and exited into the warehouse.

In theory, the only person in this building who could recognize me was Arhan since the rest of his bootlickers from the caravan had been reassigned to guard the ruins. Darkwater had managed to carve a path for their caravan to reach Ravada and had spent the last two weeks working hard to widen and fortify that path. Hopefully, they were distracted enough to let a runaway serf sneak into their building and get her revenge. I'd found a few Darkwater posters spread throughout town with a rough sketch of me and Jakar, and the burn on the back of my neck which currently sat beneath a hefty layer of makeup could always give me up if I wasn't careful, but easterners had a hard time telling Augustins apart and I had to admit there was nothing remarkable about my features. The fact I was a sixteen-year-old who'd warranted a wanted poster, however, made anonymity a little harder. But that's what the dagger in my belt was for.

The side door I was looking for wasn't far. I opened it to find Namira waiting on the opposite side of the street trying to act casual. I waved her over, trying equally hard not to look desperate, and she tried not to look guilty as she approached me. "You got in," she said when I shut the door behind her.

"Yep. Which way to Arhan?"

"I thought we were finding my contract first."

"Show me where the officers' barracks are, then we'll break off."

"No deal. We get the contract, then we go for Arhan."

"Or we do both at the same time. Just show me where to go and I'll do the rest. It's better we separate anyway in case we're caught."

Namira's nostrils flared, but she squinted down the hall. "Let me know next time, before we're in the beast's belly, that you want to improvise, yes?"

Darkwater still had her cart, and the city was being a thorn in her side about letting her reclaim it. First, she had to show proof she'd even signed an agreement with Darkwater, which she'd tried to explain was still with her cart. She led me through the cool amber glow of quartz sconces and over tattered rugs and stone, each hallway as similar as the last.

The occasional pack of people hurried past us, but they paid us no heed. Somehow, the fact they didn't give two rats' asses about us made this plan seem even crazier. Nobody who worked here expected to see someone so deep in the bowels of their building unless they belonged here, apparently. Namira glanced over her shoulder, as if sensing my growing nerves, but I swallowed them down, hoping my expression would console the cracks starting to form in her own. Faults above, this was idiotic.

A guard rounded the corner, leading a line of workers with bowed heads and metal collars around their necks. Lucky for Jakar and me that Darkwater hadn't had any spare collars handy in Port Lora when we signed our last-minute contracts to cross the Rift, though I'm sure Jakar could have used his iron working to unlock them once we escaped into the ruins. Still, the sight of those collars made my heart flutter. That was the life waiting for me, and that possibility currently sat on a razor's edge, threatening to tip the longer I stayed in this building. This was the first time in a long time Jakar wasn't around to save me, I realized.

"Are you okay?" Namira asked.

I had stopped walking. "Yes," I said, even though I couldn't move.

"Do we need to turn around?"

I shook my head, took a deep breath, and did something I hadn't tried in a long while. To emulate Sara's confidence. She once told me that fear of failure was often the culprit of failure. I needed to commit to the plunge.

The hallway opened up to a room with racks of guard outfits and two doorways in the far corners. "This is the guard's fittery," Namira said. "Right door leads to the barracks."

I nodded. According to the guard whose palms Geth had greased, Arhan went to bed early and woke up early. "All right. I'll give you a five-minute head start, then I'll slip in and out."

I turned to go, but she put a hand on my shoulder. "Wait. Maybe… I don't know. I have a bad feeling. Is this worth it?"

"Of course it's worth it."

"Risking your freedom for a bit of revenge?"

I shrugged her hand off. "See you at Shirallah's."

Again, I tried to pull away, but she stopped me. There was panic in her eyes. "Please. I lied to you. I thought maybe I could convince you to leave after we grabbed the contract. You'll get caught."

I was significantly less pleasant about removing her hand this time. "Why do you care? We don't know each other."

It was like I had slapped her instead of pulling her hand off. Clearly the words hurt her, but I didn't understand how. She needed me to break her in and I needed her to find Arhan. A mutually beneficial friendship. She didn't understand that someone like Arhan needed to be put down before his ambition devoured everyone around him. The man was just like Sara, and I knew firsthand what kind of damage his personality could cause. I would be the one to put a stop to him, and I planned to enjoy that moment.

"Go," I said.

Her eyes flitted past my shoulder and fear cut through her gaze, the sound of a closing door following. Arhan stood half-frozen, having just entered the fittery with a young guard in tow. His companion had a fresh face and a dumb look—just the way Arhan liked them. "You," the sergeant—now captain—said.

My small blade was already out, followed by Namira's. Arhan's companion took a step backward, but Arhan held him in place. "Rikten, no," Arhan said. "Being good at your job means knowing when to stand your ground. You can't let a child and this poor excuse of a trader intimidate you."

"You're the one who walks around the barracks with a dirk at your waist," I said. "I can understand why you'd be scared. I'd be scared of me, too."

I advanced, Namira following, and Arhan pulled out his dirk. Rikten wrested himself from the older guard's grip, and Namira and I moved until we were several feet away. The fittery was hardly bigger than a living area, full of piles of dirty uniforms and empty scabbards. "Pretty lucky you'd have that weapon on you, even in a place like this where you're supposed to be safe," I said. "Is it because you dream about me creeping in and slitting your throat?"

The skin around Arhan's eyes and nose quivered with anger. "I'm supposed to apprehend you, but Darkwater's gonna accept your death just fine. I'm a captain now. I handed them Rathmgar on a platter. I bet they'd turn the other way if they knew I'd made the end of you nice and miserable."

I smiled. He really did carry that weapon around because of me. The realization was intoxicating and empowering—my first taste of revenge. I wanted more. "I've been improving my knife work for this moment. I learned all the right cuts."

Fear flickered across his face, then it was gone. I'd forgotten how much I savored these moments, when my target knew exactly how much they'd underestimated me, knew what I was capable of.

"Just let us go," Rikten said in an accent I couldn't place. He was caught in the middle of three sharp points with nothing to fend us off with, and it made him rigid as a board. A flicker of regret passed through me but I did well to set it aside. "Darkwater'll pay what you want," he continued. "I'll pay what you want."

"Just do it and be done with it," Namira whispered, checking the hall behind us.

Rikten grabbed a balled-up shirt and Arhan raised his dirk. The dirk was half a hand longer than my dagger, and Arhan had a longer reach, but I was prepared. I slid out one of the throwing knives I'd hidden in my belt under my shirt.

I threw it at the same time Arhan clutched Rikten's sleeve.

Arhan pulled, and my knife bounced off Rikten's shoulder, leaving a deep gouge in his neck. The younger guard let out a soft gasp—he'd been trying to throw the shirt as Arhan yanked him—and the shirt snagged on Namira's blade. Arhan shoved Rikten at me. The younger guard hit me as he tried to staunch his wound, his mouth an o, and I stumbled back. Namira tried to shrug the shirt off, but her blade had penetrated the fabric and it only made a slight tearing sound while it clung on. She didn't seem to realize in her panic that she could just stab at Arhan and the shirt wouldn't have made a difference. Arhan backhanded her wrist and sent the dagger clattering to the floor.

The guard had his arms around Namira, dirk pointed at her throat before I could stop him. Rikten gurgled on the floor next to me, looking up at me until the light faded. His blood coated the front of my leathers and I could taste it on my lips.

"How many times are you gonna try to kill me before you lose everything?" Arhan asked, his cheeks flushed.

"You're dead already," I said. "Accept it." I tried to sneer the words, but all I could see, all I could think about, was the terror in Namira's eyes. "I'm sorry," I said.

She said nothing, only begged with her eyes for me to save her.

In a flash I realized I'd overestimated myself. Again. We should have never come here. I should have picked a better moment to take Arhan down. I had failed Namira.

I ran.

I barreled past people, but none of them tried to stop me. Not until I encountered an overseer with a lone serf did someone try to block my path. He stepped in my way, uncertainty in his eyes when he saw the lack of a serf collar on my neck, but I twisted my body as I crashed past him. He got a hold of me, but my dagger left a red line blossoming on his forearm. He let go with a cry. I launched myself through a side door and onto the busy street.

I didn't stop until I was ten blocks away. My lungs screamed at me, and I tried to catch my breath as I stood in a plaza before a small castle of white brick, red trim, and hexagonal towers. The home of some ancient family, now a Xerivian landmark. A brook trickled through the plaza and couples followed the walkways arm-in-arm. They looked on with little more than idle curiosity at the panting teenager in their midst... at someone who had just narrowly escaped slavery and gotten her companion killed.

Namira had to still be alive. Arhan hated me, not her, and she wasn't a serf. It would be a lot harder to explain her death away.

What would Torlo say about this? We'd kept him out of the loop because he would've insisted on helping, and this was a two-person job. He helped Namira mercilessly the way he helped me. She meant a lot to him.

The knot in my throat grew, making it hard to breathe.

I left the plaza and headed for the Helm of Taz'cal, the distant flurries of snow near the top of the small mountain so violent I could see them from here. The tip of the Helm was supposedly exposed to the surface, invisible because of the angles, and I imagined Jakar causing an avalanche that destroyed Darkwater's warehouse while keeping the other buildings safe. He would have known what to do.

As I neared the Ravada slums, which sang with *pinging* water droplets on metal roofs and hummed with thousands of whispers, conversations, shouts, and the slapping of sandals and boots against mud and stone, my nerves grew. I hated these walks to Shirallah's. Would this be the time I found out Jakar had passed on? Half the time my anxiety became so bad I had to turn around, resorting to pacing through the neighborhood until I found my courage. Namira distracted me from this fear, though.

I pushed through the heavy curtain that served as Shirallah's door, glanced at the couch, and was distantly aware of my mouth falling open.

I jumped at Jakar, who had been carefully spooning soup into his mouth, and I wrapped my arms around him. "Mhphrm," he said, returning the hug while he struggled to swallow his food. "I was just about to go looking for you."

"You're better," I said, pulling away.

"That's not saying much. I'm still fragile."

As I took in his tired eyes, something broke inside me. My eyes warmed, threatening to fill with tears, and I left the couch to give the other side of the shack a close examination while I reined myself in. Fhelfire, I was going to cry over almost losing Jakar when I'd just thrown Namira's life away. Guilt did its job of pushing the tears down. Someone like me didn't deserve to cry.

I faced Jakar again, who looked none the wiser. Geth, who sat on a chair by the woodstove and watched with a more perceptive eye, did me a favor by not commenting. Why did seeing Jakar alive and well upset me so much? I was more independent than anyone my age had a right to be. But there was alone, and then there was *alone*, alone.

"Where have you been?" Jakar asked through the miserable hunger on his face, and slurped another spoonful down.

"About that." It took some time, but eventually I found my words and told him about my failed plan.

"That's what you were up to?" Geth kicked his feet on the table and crossed his arms, letting out a low whistle. "Such a stupid plan that I can't help but be impressed by its boldness."

Shirallah, who now sat on the other side of the woodstove, on top of a basket bowing under his weight, knocked Geth's feet off the table. "That is not the correct response, *maj kach*. It is time we must learn how to correctly save Miscala Namira sooner rather than later."

"Why?" Jakar asked me.

Such a simple question cut deeper than I expected. I opened my mouth, ready to explain exactly the kind of person Arhan was and why it was so important he needed to be removed from this life, but I realized how reckless I would have sounded when my plan had failed so badly and I had gotten Namira captured.

"They'll interrogate her," Jakar said. "Does she know where Shirallah's home is?"

I shared a look with Geth and Shirallah. "She could find her way here with her eyes closed," I said.

Shirallah grabbed an empty pack and started throwing things inside. "We will pack what we can carry and move on. Geth, will you please gather the food? Store it in this bag, *kalas*."

Jakar tried to help while Geth, Shirallah, and I packed, but his legs and arms trembled. As I picked up my only change of clothes, I glanced at Shirallah, wondering how much of his property he'd just forfeited to Darkwater.

I'd really fucked this up.

It was time to double down and make sure we saved Namira. Finding her meant another chance at killing Arhan, and once that was done with, Jakar and I could leave Ravada in the dust along with the rest of Xeriv. After that, it would be pointless for Darkwater to harass Shirallah. We'd all live happily once more.

This time I'd make sure Arhan begged for death before I gave it to him.

Chapter 19—Ester

ESTER COULDN'T QUITE put her finger on how Sanskra felt different. She entered the town's north entrance, her fox padding around bright and sweaty faces hustling to load and unload the mega-caravans that had become commonplace in the territories. The place looked virtually the same—fresh rockwood buildings gleamed with fresher paint, and the faceless statue of Fheldspra, made of black rock and infused with glowing fire opal, stood watch in the town center. Yet the air felt different on Ester's skin. Tasted and smelled different. Mistier, with the faint aroma of granite, as if a chamber had recently flooded. She chalked it up to Travel Syndrome, which had a tendency to make everything that was once familiar feel strange.

She stopped in front of The Crab and Standard and tied her fox to the hitching post outside, then entered the general store, the pack of rhidium strapped to her back. She went to the small cafe in the back, which served fresh ridge crab and lobster sandwiches, and approached the young man behind the counter.

"Looking a bit thin in the face," the man said, wiping fish oil off his hands with a rag. "Sandwiches here can fill in those lines if you'd like to put an order in, saiora."

"Tongs and hammers," Ester said.

The man gave her the once-over—she was used to incredulity over her metal working status these days—but he nodded in acknowledgment of the code word and led her to the supply closet. "Could you make me a crab salad sandwich to go?" she asked. "I'll be out in a minute."

"Of course."

Ester shut the door to the closet behind her, lifted the rug, and set her hand on the door to the Foundry cache built into the floor until it clicked open. She carefully unpacked the rhidium vials and set them inside. Almost two hundred of them, safe and sound. The senior arc smiths would probably ridicule her for the unnecessary precaution, but at least her paranoia would be put at ease. She'd learned a hard lesson in who to trust.

She handed the man at the counter four bits and a quart, and he offered a sandwich wrapped in wax paper. "Any news of the Sovereign's visit?" she asked.

"Left the capital about three weeks back."

"Which passing?"

"On Suffing, Half Moon down."

She did the math in her head. "So he stayed in the capital for a week and a half?"

"About that, yeah."

"Thanks for the information."

He touched his right temple—a gesture of deference to Foundry members—and Ester smiled. It was good to be home. "I'll be back by the end of the passing," she said.

She rode her fox toward the capital, watching the traders, hired swords, and food vendors roam the roads outside the city gates and shout at each other like it was just another passing. Maybe she really was being too paranoid. The Sovereign had given the Foundry their space for two hundred years, so why break his streak now? She patted her fox's neck and scratched the back of his ear. "Sorry for running you so hard."

She climbed the wide steps of the Foundry and passed

through its pillars, taking in the wealthy traders and nobility browsing the counters. Everything was exactly the same as she'd left it. Smiths worked the forges, squeezed the bellows, and quenched hot metal in water basins, or carried boxes of scrap metal around, just as they always had. She frowned. She didn't recognize anyone working the front room.

"Sister," she said to a passing smith. The woman stopped and tilted her head quizzically, waiting. When she didn't offer a return greeting, preferring instead to stand there with cold politeness, Ester continued, "Are you new here?"

"Yes."

"I'm Ester. I'm a fellow smith."

The woman stared. Ester waited for something like a name, or anything, really, but the woman didn't show an ounce of interest in talking. Perhaps Ester was expecting too much from a recent transfer, or maybe the woman knew who she was and had the same bone to pick as some of the others.

"I need to speak with the master smith," Ester said. "Or one of the senior arc smiths. Where can I find them?"

"Back chapel."

Again, the woman stood silently, and it became clear she was waiting to be dismissed even though Ester was just an apprentice. "Uh, thanks," Ester said. "I'll see you around."

The woman walked off, and in her wake Ester caught the whiff of a coppery odor. She committed the woman's face to memory and decided to give her a fairer shake when she had the time. Knowing some of the smiths here, this new smith's eccentricities would only work against her.

Uneasiness threaded its way deeper into Ester's body the further she moved into the Foundry's fiery halls. Of the twenty-plus faces she'd caught sight of since arriving, she hadn't recognized a single one. They frowned at Ester or acted like she was invisible. She found four people standing in a semi-circle in the back chapel, in front of the dais where the fifth stood over them. They paused mid-conversation to look at her.

"Hi," Ester said slowly. "I'm looking for Mateo."

"Who?" the man at the podium asked.

She scoffed. "The master smith. Who else? I'll take any of the senior arc smiths if I have to. It's important."

The man stepped down from the podium and pushed through the semi-circle, and the rest of the smiths turned to silently watch. He was a slight man, lightly freckled, with a narrow nose and a welcoming face. "Welcome. I am the master smith of Augustin. Call me Hartlan. Are you a transfer?"

A cold droplet of sweat that had been forming at the base of Ester's neck during her trek through the Foundry slid down her back. "Yes. I just arrived at the capital."

"I see. I apologize, but these last few weeks have been very hectic. News of your arrival must have gotten lost in the shuffle."

She forced a smile. "I was told to report to Senior Arc Smith Porcia or Celestana, or to Master Smith Mateo. Where are they?"

"The former master smith and the senior arc council were relieved of their duties. They and the rest of the smiths were transferred to the Foundry in Saracosta."

"You're joking, surely?"

Hartlan's companions folded their arms simultaneously while Hartlan's face hardened. "Their reassignment was the Sovereign's decision," he said coolly. "I hope you will think twice before criticizing it, and I hope you'll find us acceptable replacements."

Ester glanced past Hartlan. None of his companions had the sharp bone structure of Saracostans or Manasans, the stout features of Augustins, the auburn hair or narrow noses of Tulchians, nor the willowy height or mud-brown hair of the average Bys. It was impossible to place them.

"Of course I find you acceptable," she said.

"Good. What is your name?"

"Apprentice Jesmon. I transferred from one of the towns hit by the mercenary army. Beledor."

"I see. You will need to be assigned to an arc smith first thing so your training can be continued. Assist the forges until I find someone suitable for you." He offered a hand. "And welcome to Augustin."

Smiths always embraced each other to signal the end of important conversations. Ester didn't point it out, though. She took his hand, and she shook it, a coppery aroma assaulting her once more. His gaze flicked toward her mouth. "Something wrong?" he asked.

He must've noticed her nostrils twitching. "Never. I'm looking forward to getting to know everyone here."

She backed out of the chamber, and the group seemed to let out a collective breath before turning to each other and resuming their conversation.

Reaching the front of the Foundry was like that first step Ester had taken out of the Tear. She swallowed hard, trying to rein in the dread creeping through her, until a smith walked by and noticed her distress. She forced a smile and kept walking.

It wasn't until a few hours later when she was eating in the meal hall, where a handful of smiths ate and kept to themselves, did she remember telling one of the smiths her real name. What if the woman mentioned the encounter to the new master smith? Were Hartlan and his new clan working for the Sovereign?

A theory was growing like a tumor in her mind—one she couldn't dislodge no matter how hard she tried or how unpleasant it felt. What if the Sovereign had replaced her brothers and sisters with people he'd flesh bound? By doing so he could control the Foundry and quash any possibility of the smiths rising against him. Princepa Efadora had admitted to seeing binding scars on a primordia she and her brother had confronted in the crust, so the Sovereign was capable of creating flesh bindings, which meant he could simply replace any traitor with someone faithful to him. The only part she didn't understand was why he wouldn't use flesh magic on her brothers and sisters and leave them here instead of taking them to Saracosta.

What if everyone around her served the Sovereign, and not by choice?

Her instincts told her to run—to hide in the city or leave it entirely—but she needed information on the Sovereign's visit and to know if Mateo and the others were hurt.

She studied the smiths hunched over their food in the eating hall. None of them had shown interest in her, but they hadn't shown interest in each other, either. During the four hours she'd spent working the bellows in the front room, not once did anyone make small talk. It was either "Increase the heat" or "Hold this bucket" or some other command. She'd spent weeks wallowing in homesickness and this was what she'd come home to.

After finishing her meal, she headed for the front, prepared to explain why she needed to leave. The Foundry felt more like a prison than anything now. Everyone was too busy or didn't care to spare a second glance, though. She passed through the line of customers and entered the heavy traffic outside, and on the trade district's ridge in the entertainment section, she found laborers staining a newly built tetaro, the workers half-hidden under the play stage. She asked if she could help, and they handed her a can and a brush.

"I just arrived at the capital," she said after several minutes of staining the rockwood. "I heard the Sovereign paid a visit. Did anything of note come from his stay here?"

A man with a bushy mustache wiped the sweat from his forehead and stretched his back. "Was calm, far as visits from Saracosta go. Sovereign had some of his primordia along, but they didn't stir the pot or nothing. Was a good visit, all round."

"Would you mind walking me through it, from what you know?"

"Dunno much. Whole audencia lined up in the trade district to receive the Sovereign's entourage when he arrived. Sovereign had his son Bilal along, too. Two of them and a couple primordia toured the city to survey the damage. Even stopped to watch the crew here painting a tribune on the third level. Spent most of the first passing that way."

"What about the next passing?"

"Closed session with the audencia, I think. Stayed with the Foundry after that."

"What do you mean, he stayed with the Foundry?"

He set his brush in his can, wiped his forehead one more time, and set his hands on his hips. "You're a smith. How don't you know?"

"I just arrived here, like I said."

He looked her up and down as though he wanted to argue, but thought better of it and continued, "The Sovereign and his son holed up in the Foundry for the rest of their trip. The public wasn't even allowed to enter to worship. Don't ask me what for, though. Best ask your *ermo a'erma*."

The other painters had stopped to eavesdrop. "Anyone know anything else?" Ester asked.

"Smith Reeda... I miss her so much," one of the workers said. "Talked to her lots after the mercs killed *me molis*. I didn't even have a chance to say goodbye."

Had the Sovereign forced the capital's smiths to return home with him to Saracosta so he could keep an eye on them? Ester set her can and brush down and bowed her head. "Thank you for letting me help, saiors."

"Course," one of them said. "Don't be a stranger. Fheldspra knows it's been hard enough with the new brethren."

ESTER ROAMED THE city until she found a lone smith loading some slag into a cart from one of the non-Foundry blacksmiths on the fourth level—slag bought by the Foundry for re-smelting. "I don't think we've met," she said.

He shook his head and lifted the handles to get his pull cart off the ground, but Ester's boot pinned the handle down. "How're you liking Augustin's capital so far?"

He stepped away from the cart and gave her a curious, but mostly empty, look. "It is good. It is a nice city. Very devout."

"Absolutely. Everyone's really come together since the Burning. It's almost like we're back to normal again."

"It is not normal. A taint lingers."

Ester had banked on the man saying *something* weird, she just didn't expect it so soon. "What do you mean?"

"Once we atone, Augustin will be clean."

"We, as in the smiths?"

He nodded.

"We atone through work," she said. "It's why we forge tools for the community. I can think of others in the territories with more to atone for than us."

"No."

"What about the primordia?"

Rage flashed across his face, so fast it was more flinch than facial expression. "Do not speak that way."

Loyalist or not, no smith held respect for the primordia. Not only did they wield the power of the Great Ones, but they were awful, violent human beings. "How long have you been a member of the Foundry?" she asked.

"A while."

"What was it like working in the Foundry in the country's capital? Did the Sovereign ever attend services?"

"He… did not. But he held our order in the highest regard."

"Was he a friend of Master Smith Hartlan?"

"He… he was a friend to us all."

A sweat had broken out on the man's temple, and he stared at a point above Ester's head. "What made you want to join the Foundry?" she asked.

"I…" He didn't speak for several seconds. "I had a niece. Serilia. I adopted her after her parents passed. She was mauled in one of the crags but was saved by a passing smith. I knew then I wanted to join the Foundry."

Ester frowned. Serilia. She knew that name. "Did you grow up in the city or in the crust? Where's your niece now?"

He put his head in his hands, the tips of his fingers turning white as they pressed into his skull. A shuddering whine came out of his throat, and he smacked himself in the skull once, as hard as he could. Ester froze. She looked around, but nobody was in this stretch of corridor to have witnessed such behavior.

The man was suffering from flesh magic, she realized.

The smith twitched once, twice, then his hands slowly fell to his sides and he picked up the handles to the cart. It was as though Ester didn't exist as he pulled the cart toward the ridge. She watched him disappear beyond the curve of the corridor.

Chapter 20—Jakar

"TELL ME IF this sounds accurate," I said. "You think if we hide where Darkwater will most expect us to go, it will actually be the place they least expect?" I unfolded one of the cots the cartographers had provided us with and set it closest to the door. "That's the only reason I can see for hiding in the Archives."

"Cartographers have a nasty habit of creating friction with our clients," Geth said as he laid a blanket on a cot. "So all I have to do is say the word and my associates will cover for us, no questions asked. The depths know I've had to help a few of them out of a tight spot myself. Besides, I don't think Darkwater will expect you to make nice and work with me after what happened with the caravan."

I lit a torch and set it in a sconce so I could examine the geometric mazes covering the walls of this modest back room. The maze was littered with blocky depictions of beasts and ruins, and I realized it was a stylized map, though of what, I had no idea. "So how are we saving Namira?" Efadora asked.

"Traps and guards will be numerous," Shirallah said. "It would be foolish to attempt a forced visit within that warehouse, yes, yes."

"All right, then we stake out the place and wait for them to move her."

"They're not going to move her," Geth said.

"Arhan will have to leave at some point. We'll grab him and interrogate him. He'll tell us how to save Namira, and then we'll kill him."

Efadora, I realized, reminded me of Sara when speaking of righting a wrong. Sara would emphasize certain words while she talked, as if she was excited to get to the end of each sentence, and her hands would move in sharp, short movements. Just a coincidence, I told myself.

"We made it to Ravada and we escaped Darkwater," I said. "We should be riding hard for Som Abast, not staying here, Efadora."

"You don't want to save Namira?"

"She willingly took a terrible risk and paid the price. You're lucky to be alive. I'm sorry for sounding crass, but we need to keep going to Som Abast."

"I'm not leaving until we do this."

I gave her a long look. "Taking down the cultists who raised me, and saving my friends are too important."

"And Namira is *my* friend. I'm not going until we help her."

This was not how it was supposed to go. Saving Namira would waste time I was worried we didn't have—or perhaps I was being paranoid? Either way, the path to Som Abast was now clear; I needed to convince Efadora to go and she was acting frustratingly stubborn. "This isn't just about Namira. We're risking everything by staying here. I feel good enough to keep us safe now, but I'm not interested in putting it to the test and taking more lives."

"I already gave my answer. I'm not leaving Namira behind. What happened to her is my fault."

I knew Efadora well enough to recognize that I wouldn't be able to convince her to abandon this plan. I could either help her or leave her behind—the choice was obvious. "All right. But before I agree to help, answer me this. Are we trying to save Namira, or are we trying to kill Arhan?"

"Both, obviously. Don't you want to punish him for what he did in the Rift?"

Torlo smiled sadly. "If killing him's what you're after, I'll help, but if you're asking my honest opinion, it's risky, almost as risky as the plan that got Namira snatched up. Especially if he knows we're coming."

"And my priority will never be to kill Arhan," I said. "All I've done this past year is hurt people. Saving Namira will be my only concern if I'm going to help."

Conflict filled Efadora's gaze, and she opened her mouth as if she wanted to disagree, but said nothing. This conversation was our first real argument, I realized. The experience was strange, almost uncomfortable. If there was one thing life had beaten into me these last couple years, it was never to argue with an Adriann.

Torlo broke the silence. "If things had played out differently, we'd be wearing serf collars, loading and unloading boxes the next year over. Probably not the best idea to be throwing that gift away just to right a wrong."

He looked down, dismayed by his opposition to Efadora, and part of me wished he would look up so I could offer a nod in appreciation. He'd take both our sides if he could. "A year?" Geth asked. "Pff. Five or more, most likely. Darkwater knows their business, and they've made an art out of turning serfs into slaves."

Before reaching Xeriv, I hadn't given much thought to serfdom since I knew we'd escape it eventually, but it was impossible to put it out of my mind once I'd seen it face-to-face. On our way to the Archives, we'd caught glimpses of overseers leading strings of serfs from one side of Ravada to another. It triggered old memories of the Ebonrock, being led to one of the endless projects my home city of Som Abast had commissioned us to construct.

I knew that look of hopelessness, even from a hundred feet away. My hatred for that feeling burned white and bright. Maybe I wasn't opposed to lingering in Ravada after all.

"You have an idea," Efadora said.

I nodded. "Slavery is illegal in Mira, and Sorrelo told me on multiple occasions that the Sovereign has made it very clear to Xeriv and to other countries east of the Rift that they are never to enslave Miran citizens. It means that Xeriv has to report to the Sovereign on any serf contracts his citizens sign. The Sovereign likes to keep a close eye on those contracts so he can make sure no one is turned into a slave. And Xeriv does his bidding because they're scared of him. Since Ravada is Xeriv's capital, all the contracts would be kept here, right, Geth?"

"I wouldn't know."

"Are the serfs housed in Darkwater or in a separate building?"

"In a separate government building. Every passing's eve all serfs are shipped to whichever company they signed a contract with, then they're brought back at passing's end so they can sleep under guard by the city. But how would you know? Have you spent time in Ravada?"

"My former master worked in the Miran government," I said. "He once told me that because Miran serf contracts are so tightly regulated by Xeriv, the city does well to keep a constant check on serfs so that private companies like Darkwater aren't turning Miran serfs into slaves and getting Xeriv in trouble with the Sovereign. Xeriv is terrified of how the Sovereign might retaliate. They want to do everything they can to keep him and his primordia on the other side of the Rift." I grimaced. "The Sovereign's power is so absolute that even the threat of it from a thousand miles away can protect his citizens." My words skirted close enough to complimenting the Sovereign that they left a bad taste in my mouth.

"Wait, did you say 'former master'? Someone like you was a serf before you signed with Darkwater? Now that's interesting."

I cringed at the thought of letting slip more of my past, until I realized nothing was forcing me to keep it a secret. Just another habit hammered into existence by Sorrelo. "It's complicated," I said. What if I told these people everything?

Geth called me katsu when he saw what I could do. Maybe he knew something about the Ebonrock that could help me find them.

"Can I use one of the Archive's stores and an alchemy table?" I asked Geth.

"By all means," he said. "But only if you let me watch."

THE LONGER I thought about it, the happier I was that Efadora had convinced me to stay in Ravada. Serfdom and slavery was a blight, one that dug at me the more of it I saw. The serf barracks sat at the end of the street we stood on, operating as a prison between passings where hundreds of poor souls were forced to stay for years, and we had confirmed that it was mostly empty while the city's serfs were out and about working another passing off their contracts. If I could cure Ravada of its serf problem, at least I would have that to help me sleep at passing's end if I couldn't find the Ebonrock and save my friends.

The barracks were on the northeast side of town, in the industrial park. The air behind the building shimmered from the lava river sloughing behind it, carrying wisps of steam where condensation from the ceiling and snow flurries from the Helm of Taz'cal to the south hit the river. The street was empty, except for gaggles of cagey-looking individuals hanging around dark alleyways between buildings, watching us. None of them seemed interested in messing with our group of five. Still, it wasn't worth ignoring them. I led our group along the muddy stone sidewalk to the alley running alongside the serf barracks. A fence blocked our path two-thirds of the way back, and beyond, the ground turned ragged and uneven until it ended in a ridge where the river of lava burned and spat. I pulled a glass container tightly packed with gray powder out of my pack, along with the string that would act as a fuse. I handed both to Torlo.

"Ready?" I asked.

"Ready."

"Might take us time to set up the distraction," Geth said.

"We'll wait."

Torlo, Geth, and Shirallah left the alley and crossed the street, trying their best to act like just another pack of delinquents roaming this side of Ravada. Nervousness nipped at me—I'd told Torlo repeatedly to make sure the opening at the top of the container was big enough so that when the mixture was lit, the energy had somewhere to go. Proper energy displacement was usually the only difference between a device that caused a lot of light and noise, and a bomb.

"So," Efadora said, her voice wavering. "We haven't really talked since you woke up."

"What do you mean?"

"I mean, we've talked plenty, but mostly about this plan and avoiding Darkwater. I... never mind."

Now that I thought about it, she was right. We'd been so focused on Darkwater, I still had no idea what she'd been up to during the two weeks I was comatose. "Must have been strange while I was sick," I said. "Being stuck in a different country where you didn't speak the language."

"I spent most of my time in the Archives, actually." She smiled. "We've been trying to figure out how the Sihraan weapon you found in the ruins works. Geth can't decide if he's more interested in that, or in you."

I'd forgotten about the rail weapon. It would have been nice to have it right now. "Are you friends now?"

"Not exactly."

"I wouldn't trust him if I were you."

"I don't." She craned her neck toward the street, but the others had disappeared. "I've been reading in the Archives a lot," she said. "It's hard because most of the texts are written in other languages, but most of them are annotated in Miran. Geth says I'm picking up on languages really fast. I started reading because I wanted to try and find info on the people who kidnapped you when you were a kid."

"Did you find anything?"

"Not yet. The reading's too slow, but I want to keep at it. I think Geth would be able to help if you let him."

"It's something I was considering, actually."

"Good." She paused, struggling with what to say next. "It was… hard when you were sick."

Part of me knew that Efadora had cared about me, but hearing her say the words to confirm it left a warm, albeit nervous, feeling in the pit of my stomach. I wanted her to care, but she wasn't the first Adriann to try to convince me I mattered. "It was hard?" was all I could think to say.

She seemed equally uncomfortable. "Of course. I just…" She stopped herself as she appeared to gather her thoughts. "Sara and my father did terrible things to you, and I feel like it's my responsibility to… to atone for it, I guess? The Adrianns owe you a debt, and I'm the only one left to pay it back. So when I see you in pain, I feel like I'm responsible somehow, if that makes sense."

I swallowed hard. "Don't hold yourself accountable for what others did just because you share their blood. I'll never put that on you, and if I end up getting hurt for whatever reason, it's because I chose to." I considered her words. "I appreciate that you care about my pain, though, especially after what you told me."

"What did I tell you?"

"You told me while we were traveling out of Augustin that you don't feel anything when people get hurt. You said that you think that you're missing something, that you've never felt empathy before."

She chewed her lip in thought. "It's because of Emil, I think. He always wanted to protect you, so I do too."

I snorted at the thought of her as my bodyguard. She continued, "It really was hard with you out like that for two whole weeks. I had to figure out what I was going to do in case you didn't, you know, wake up. I had a plan."

I offered a reassuring smile. "Is there something you want to tell me?"

"I asked Geth about what I would need to do to become a cartographer."

"Oh." Efadora had left Augustin with me because she wanted to see the world—and to pay off the family debt she thought she owed me, I realized now—so I supposed it made sense she would gravitate toward cartography. "Maybe after we take down the Ebonrock, you could keep pursuing cartography, if that's what you want."

She nodded. "I think I'd be really good at it."

She opened her mouth to say more, but a sound hissed through the air. The air in the street started to glow. "Let's go," I said.

I pushed my hands into the barrack wall, and it parted with a screech. Pieces of it crumbled, sparks flying everywhere, and after several seconds I took a step back, amazed. My work should have taken minutes—for nearly as long as the flash powder was supposed to burn—but the barrier had fallen apart as easy as a sandcastle.

"In. Fast," I said. The faster work had meant much louder work, which the flash powder might not have masked. We climbed in, and I reached out and haphazardly reattached the rock. I didn't do much better than a child squishing lumps of clay together, but as long as no outside passersby looked too closely, they wouldn't think to look inside while we were still here.

"Someone's coming," Efadora whispered, and she pulled me behind a bookshelf. Rows of shelves, tables, and drawers covered the floor of the room we were in, and in the dim firelight at the other end, six guards appeared from a hallway, bounding across the floorboards toward the hole, which was now as big as a dinner plate. They stopped in front of it and spoke in their native tongue. We fell into a crouch and watched through a slit in the shelf.

All six guards headed back to the hall and disappeared. "One of them said something about going back outside, I think," Efadora whispered. "But they might come back."

"It's now or never," I said. "Let's make sure this is the right room."

I opened the nearest drawer and pulled out some papers. The documents were written in blocky Xerivian that I couldn't read. "Any idea what this says?" I asked.

"I think it has to do with properties, but I'm not sure." She pointed at a shelf three rows down. There was a sigil printed on its side, of an octopus grasping two thorny vines. "Look."

Almost half the room had shelves and cabinets with Darkwater's sigil, I realized. It didn't take long to find the serf contracts—a copy transcribed in Miran was attached to each one. I couldn't say how many were expired, but there had to be thousands of Mirans working under Darkwater's whip, not only in Ravada but throughout the rest of Xeriv. All of them Mirans who were only guilty of wanting to live outside their home country. I dug out the last two jars from my pack, these ones full of black powder. "Start spreading," I said, handing Efadora a jar. "Not too thin or the rockwood won't catch."

Efadora and I went to work, moving from shelf to shelf covering everything in powder. Firelight reflected off a glossy sheen covering every piece of furniture in the room, which I recognized as a fire-resistant resin meant to protect the papers inside. Fortunately, anything could burn if the temperature was cranked up high enough. My friends had helped me grind up batches of aluminum and ferric oxide into fine powders, which I had then mixed together to make thermite.

I discarded my empty jar at the same time Efadora finished spreading out her thermite. "Let's make ourselves scarce, yeah?" Efadora asked when I met her at the hole in the wall.

I rolled up a piece of paper and focused on the end. A flame appeared, dancing on the tip, and a tremor coursed through my body. Drawing energy from my own body to start a fire was one of the most moronic things an elemental could do, but a tiny flame didn't take much and we were short on time. I threw the paper on the closest line of thermite and wasted no time breaking through the wall once more.

We entered the alley at the same time a near-blinding light from inside cast our shadows on the opposite wall. We ran for the street but skidded to a stop when two guards rounded the corner, leading Geth, whose hands were restrained behind his back. They stopped, pointing at the light show behind us, and started shouting at us in Xerivian.

"How'd you get caught?" Efadora asked Geth, but the question went ignored. Geth had a busted lip and a black eye, and one of his captors pulled out a sword, taking to aggressively pointing it at Efadora and me in an adamant request for us to lie on the ground in surrender.

"They're telling us to listen or they'll kill Geth, I think," Efadora said.

"They want all of us alive," I said. They're bluffing."

The light brightened behind us. By now the guards wouldn't have been able to put the fire out if they wanted to, and soon it would spread to the building's other rooms. We needed to leave before whoever was inside was evacuated and joined to help these two guards.

"Could really use a hand," Geth said. He licked the corner of his mouth where a drop of blood spilled down. Despite his predicament, he wasn't scared. He looked *excited*. He met my gaze, waiting for whatever would come next. His rescue at my elemental hands, it seemed. He wanted to see my power at work.

"Do something," Efadora muttered as the guards continued shouting orders.

It was a straightforward solution to our problem—killing these guards was an easy argument to make, too, as they likely had a hand in keeping the serfs imprisoned in this building— but the thought of doing so filled me with dread. I'd killed my share of bandits on the journey out of Mira, but that had been in self-defense when I didn't have to think about what I was doing, when I only had to act. This, I couldn't do.

The two wore half helmets—how easy it would have been to crush the steel and the skulls they were meant to protect—but instead I wrenched the guard's blades away with my power, sending the steel flashing past us down the alley. I rushed the guards as they yelled in confusion, and Geth smashed one in the nose with the back of his head. He scrambled toward me desperately, and one of them grabbed him by his shirt. A blade appeared in the guard's hand, one he had yanked out of his belt, and he slashed at Geth while he held onto the shirt. Geth let out a gasp as he managed to rip himself free, and then he was stumbling into Efadora, who tried her best to stop him from falling. I ripped the second blade from the guard's grip, but this time I snatched it out of the air.

There was a long, bloody gash down the back of Geth's shirt. The wound was messy but mostly superficial. Geth clenched his teeth, and said through them, "Kill the bastards."

"Behind me," I said, and led Efadora and Geth to the street, keeping my new knife trained on the two guards. They babbled at us in Xerivian, then turned toward the growing fire when they realized they couldn't stop us. We reached the alley's mouth and ran.

Chapter 21—Efadora

WITH JAKAR AND Geth dogging my heels, the three of us caught up to Torlo and Shirallah at the rendezvous point—a little piece of Xerivian history that was an abandoned gemstone mill sitting in the glow of the northern lavafall. Gemstone mining was once Xeriv's main source of income until contact with Mira was made, then Xeriv became the gatekeepers of trade between all the eastern countries and this mysterious country west of the Rift. So began the rise of the Darkwater Trading Company.

"What happened back there?" I asked between breaths. "How'd you get caught?"

"A group of nobodies liked the pretty lights we made," Geth said. He sat on a half-ruined bench and cringed as he reached back, trying to touch his wound. "They thought we were loaded with other toys, so they tried to jump us."

"*Maj kach*," Shirallah breathed as he hurried to Geth's side and examined the man's wound. "If you'd stayed at my side, we could have run from those poor souls. But *net*, you are never listening to anyone but yourself." Shirallah turned to Jakar and me. "The gang tried to do us in with fists and violence, but the commotion caught much attention. Some of the barrack's guards who were investigating the light show got their dirty hands on Geth. Torlo and I could do naught but run."

"Is it bad?" Geth asked.

Shirallah shook his head. "It will scar, yes, yes, but it will heal." He slapped the back of Geth's head, and Geth hissed. "You must stop going off on your own. Your stubbornness has gotten the best of you once again."

Geth didn't argue, only furrowed his brows at Jakar. "You could have handled those guards a little better, don't you think?"

"You're alive," Jakar said flatly. It was almost a challenge the way he said it—to dare Geth to press the matter. For a second it seemed Geth might take the bait, but he broke Jakar's gaze and grumbled as Shirallah took a wad of cloth the man had ripped from his shirt and pressed it to Geth's wound.

What Geth didn't see was the way the light dimmed in Jakar's eyes as soon as he thought nobody was looking. Killing had become a struggle for Jakar, I knew, I just hadn't realized it had gotten this bad. What if he was forced to make a snap decision in the future between saving one of us and killing someone? Hopefully, he'd find enough grit to make the right choice.

"What happens now?" Torlo asked.

"The city doesn't have their serf contracts anymore," Jakar said. "They'll have nothing to report to Mira, so they'll be forced to release their serfs, or they'll risk angering the Sovereign." He looked to me for confirmation. This plan had been leveraged on information provided by my father—that Xeriv would never want to antagonize the Sovereign, enough for them to release their serfs if there were no contracts to show for them—and that it would throw Darkwater into chaos. I nodded. It was as good a plan as any.

"The city's going to put pressure on Darkwater to relinquish their serfs," I said. "I saw for myself how many serfs and slaves work for that company. It'll turn them into a mess if they're forced to give up most of their workforce. We'll look for our opportunity in the chaos to grab Namira."

"And then we save her and the two of you continue on your merry way?" Geth asked, his expression tight from the pain.

"Yes," Jakar said before I could open my mouth. I added, "We need to finish up our research in the Archives before we go to Som Abast, but the general idea is that we'll want to go there sooner rather than later."

"Given I'm a professional researcher, I think it's time you fill me in on what Efadora has been helping you look into, Jakar," Geth said, the pain making him sound irritable. "Efadora's been mighty stubborn about giving away any actual details about your life. She said to ask you, so this is me asking you. It's the least you can do."

The red glow from the lavafall shined through the roof's cracks, painting stripes across Jakar's face as he thought, and I tried to urge him on with my gaze. Jakar had nothing to lose, and we needed all the help we could get learning more about the Ebonrock. "Fine," he said. "I was kidnapped as a child and forced to undergo several bindings. My kidnappers forced me into hard labor so that once I was strong enough, they could send me to the Black Depths where I would dig until I died."

"Dig for what?"

"They wanted to find the Great Ones. They were fanatics about it. They use kidnapped children to help them look." He took a deep breath. "I escaped over two years ago and now I'm finding my way back so I can save my friends. I know the cultists who raised me as the Ebonrock."

Geth cocked his head. "Rha'Ghalor."

"What?"

"Eastern Cults of the Aspects, Volume Three. There's a chapter on the Rha'Ghalor, which in the Ronan tongue means Ebonrock. The Ebonrock were an organization that worshiped the flesh god Tylkoth and would kidnap children and convert them into followers, or the *tuk galang*. Tuk galang possessed great strength and elemental power, but it's said they're killed by their own power if they disobey the Rha'Ghalor in any way. Any of that sound familiar?"

Jakar nodded, his eyes intense.

"How'd you escape?" Geth asked.

"That's not something I'm comfortable sharing or something you need to know to help me."

I supposed I could blame Jakar for not wanting to talk about his flesh binding just yet. I expected Geth to argue, but it seemed he was satisfied for once in his life. I didn't expect that to last long, however.

Torlo stirred, stepping forward to kneel in front of Jakar. "Mosh zhidan teyi." It sounded Xerivian, but he pronounced the 'zh' and the 'y' too harshly.

"What?" Jakar asked.

"Hmph," Geth said. "That's—"

"Teta," I cut in. "It's what they speak in Yarokly."

Geth smiled, surprised, and warmth spread through my abdomen. It truly was a treat to have discovered talents I never knew I possessed. For years I thought being an Adriann meant ruthlessness was my de facto skill, that I needed to play to that strength if I wanted to excel in life. It turned out I was good at something else. Languages. It was hard to describe how it felt to know I could be something that had nothing to do with my family, but the feeling was good.

Torlo stood. "I was born in Byssa, but my parents were from Yarokly. The words I just spoke were the vow to a blood debt. I want to help you find the Ebonrock."

"You don't have to pledge your life to me," Jakar said, alarmed. "It's all yours."

"I can't take the words back. I wouldn't want to, anyway. I should've spoken them back in the Rift when you saved my life."

Jakar shook his head, but he couldn't summon a response. The others could pick up on his discomfort, but they didn't know why. I'm sure the last thing Jakar wanted was power over another.

"Darkwater saw you," I said to Geth. "They saw me and Jakar too. They know all three of us had something to do with the fire, and if they figure out who you are, they'll blame the Archives for the fire. Do we bother going back there?"

"Darkwater will be running around like decapitated karst chickens for now," he said. "They'll be trouble for the Archives eventually, but we mapmakers know how to make organizations like Darkwater tremble in their boots." He laughed, but I didn't understand the joke.

"Maj kach," Shirallah said. His voice was soft but deploring. "Take this seriously. Is it secure to go back?"

Geth didn't make light of the question as I expected. Shirallah was the only one in the world capable of chiding him, it seemed. "It should be," Geth said. "Maybe it would be a good idea to move now, just in case Darkwater starts putting bodies around the Archives."

"The Archives don't have guards other than the ones Ravada gives them," I said. "What's stopping Darkwater from convincing the city to let them storm the place? Seems like they've got a lot of pull around here."

Geth wiped the sweat from his forehead. He was still in pain, but he seemed to have a much better grip on it now. "Ask Xeriv what the most important institutions are in the country and they'll say the Xerivian House of Nobility, then the Dach Sepa, the House of Aspects, then the Military Academy, then the Archives, and then finally Darkwater and all the other companies that grease the country's pockets. Ask them that same question behind closed doors and they'll say the Archives, bar none. We drive the country's economy with our maps and the resources we discover. If you ever wondered why they say the pen is mightier than the sword, my colleagues and I are the reason."

As much as I liked Geth's friends, I wasn't fully convinced, but hiding in a place like the Archives when it was under surveillance was still probably safer than anywhere else in the city.

We stole several sets of clothes from a nearby cruviaq, disguised ourselves as farmers straight from the root fields in the Opal Locality, and crossed the city back to the Archives. I didn't see any Darkwater agents hiding around the fountains or under the fire-crystal streetlights along the plaza in front of the Archives, but how long would that last? The cartographers in the Archives' front room, who were bartering with representatives of some expedition, nodded to us as we moved deeper into the building. Cartographers were fierce about looking out for each other, which was one more reason I wanted to join. It was like the best parts of being in a gang, minus the backstabbing.

Geth lay on his stomach on my cot in the back room, and Shirallah found a needle and some thread to start stitching him up. Jakar dipped a rag into a water bowl in the corner, wrung it out, and draped it over his head, and that's when I noticed the exhaustion in his eyes. His sickness had turned his lithe body into something just shy of a bag of bones, though Shirallah was doing his best to make sure Jakar ate every chance he could. Breaking into the serf barracks and fleeing from the guards had been hard on him, but he didn't show it.

A little while later, after Geth was stitched up and had found a fresh shirt, someone knocked. "Geth?" a visitor asked, poking their head in. He wore a small hat, identical to the thousands of others I'd seen on the heads of the younger, poorer men of Xeriv, which had something to do with their place of worship, the Dach Sepa. "We have finished the examination of the Sihraan *ertifekt*, if you would like to discuss the findings."

"Sorry for borrowing your salvage," Geth quickly said to Jakar as he went for the door. "Efadora said it was all right."

I hadn't said it was all right, per se—Geth had strongly implied my chances of joining the Archives were slimmer if I didn't let them examine it—but I didn't correct him.

"I'd like it back," Jakar said.

"Let's go get it for you, then."

We followed Tiny Hat to the library, where the rail weapon

sat next to a pile of open books on one of the long tables meant for studying. Jakar picked it up and ran a hand along one of the two rods that made up most of the weapon. Tiny Hat asked Geth something in Xerivian while eying Jakar, and Geth answered. The man's breath caught.

"It uses the polas," Tiny Hat said. "Erm, I do not know the Miran word for it."

"Polas is…" Geth thought for a second. "It's a concept cartographers learn. It's the intermediary that lets us detect quartz."

"Intermediary, like all the rock standing between cartographers and the quartz crystals they search for?" I asked.

He shook his head. "Polas is what connects your perceptions to the crystal. It's what allows the nazil cas to track time for Ravada even though we have no sight of the moon Ulugh. It's…" He made a waving motion with both hands. "All encompassing? That's the right way to describe it."

Ulugh was what people around here called Saffar. I remembered Jakar telling me that. "Do you know what they're talking about?" I asked Jakar.

"The electromagnetic field," Jakar answered while examining the rail weapon.

"Electro… magnetic," Tiny Hat said slowly. "I have heard this word before. A proposed explanation for the lightning in the storms along Ses Pajac Voor, the Burning Mountains." A hunger appeared in his eyes, a look that reminded me of Father. This was different, I told myself. Father had wanted to control Jakar's power and the cartographers only wanted to understand it. Still, I didn't like the way those hungry eyes lingered on Jakar.

Tiny Hat continued, "We would like to study the weapon further."

Jakar offered it to me. "It's not yours to study. It's Efadora's."

"Mine? Why?" I asked.

"Because the last thing I need is a weapon, and it'll make me feel better knowing you have it."

I took it, the weight a familiar one. I'd held it at least fifty times in the last two weeks, fantasizing about pointing it at Arhan's forehead and wondering what would happen when I pulled the trigger.

"No matter," Tiny Hat said. "Geth has told me the girl expressed interest in joining the Archives as his apprentice. I will have my chance to see it again."

Jakar stiffened. "You want to apprentice under Geth?" he asked me.

Geth bristled at the way Jakar said his name, but Jakar didn't notice. I'd wanted to have this conversation privately, but so much for that. "The Archives don't accept applicants," I said. "You have to be sponsored by a cartographer to become a member. Your sponsor is the one who teaches you. But this would happen after we took care of the Ebonrock, so we can save this for another passing."

"Geth is not quite so bad," Shirallah said. He set a hand on the cartographer's shoulder. "He is quite the deal to me. He has never led me off the path when it most mattered."

Jakar wasn't listening. He'd been staring off into space, his brow wrinkled in thought, and for a moment I felt I'd done something wrong by wanting to apprentice under Geth. I understood his hesitation, even if it was wrong—Geth wasn't very good at keeping an eye on me, which I preferred, and he enjoyed getting into trouble, which I could relate to—but Geth was also my in with the Archives. Life had to move on after we took down the Ebonrock, and I'd found something I wanted to pursue, something I was good at. The wrinkle in Jakar's brow deepened, and I realized he was inspecting the pile of books on the table. His mouth parted as if he'd seen a ghost. "What is this?" he asked as he picked up a piece of paper. It was the design Geth had chalked in the Sihraan city, the one rimming the mysterious hole we'd discovered.

"That was on a sacrificial pit in the Sihraan ruins," Geth said. "You recognize it?"

Jakar swallowed. Some of the color had disappeared from

his face. "This design was carved into the base of the cage my old masters kept me in when they put me in solitary confinement. My fingers will remember those patterns for the rest of my life."

Tiny Hat asked a hurried question in Xerivian, and Geth answered. "To think I almost let you die," Geth said to Jakar. "You're just a bottomless bag of surprises, aren't you?"

"I'm glad I can satisfy your curiosity," Jakar said in a low voice.

"What are the chances that design has to do with the Unmade—what you call the Great Ones—and what are the chances the ancient Sihraans worshipped them, too?" he asked the room.

Neither Torlo, Shirallah, or Jakar wagered a guess. Disturbing as it was to think the Sihraan Empire had worshipped the Great Ones just like Ebonrock, I had to admit that the way Geth eyed the group with bright eyes, as though he could barely contain his excitement, was infectious.

A third cartographer entered the library. "*Tej rastan Darkavot.* Representatives of Darkwater Trading Company are here. They are accompanied by some of the constabulary and would like to speak with you."

All of us froze. Tiny Hat nodded and said, "I will be back shortly." He left with the other cartographer.

"Should we hide?" Torlo asked.

"If that will make you feel better," Geth said. "I'm staying here to read. There's too much I need to look into." He saw the look on my face, then added, "I'll show you some hidden passages first. We like to use them whenever we're in a pinch."

Chapter 22—Ester

ESTER CAUGHT JUDGE Abeso approaching his house on the fourth level, deep inside the Creeping Vine District where the air smelled of fresh leaves and insects chirped, triggered by the minerals that glittered in the rock above. "Pardon, Judge," she called out, leaving the maintenance alley she'd been hiding inside and hurrying to catch up.

The judge took one look at her smith's robes and paused. "Yes, Smith? How may I help you?"

"I was hoping I could ask you some questions. It shouldn't take much time."

"What about?"

"The Sovereign's visit." She'd chosen to approach Abeso because the man had acted as representative of the audencia when the Sovereign arrived in Augustin, had given the Sovereign a tour of the capital to show off the repairs that had been completed in the last several weeks. There were also whisperings that the man was not a fan of Mira's ruler. If anyone had insight on the Sovereign's visit, it was him.

He had his keys out and fiddled with them for a moment before fitting one into the lock. "Of course," he said. His politeness was cold. Colder than she'd ever felt since becoming a smith. "I'll put on some tea," he said.

Everything in Abeso's house was new, though modest compared to some of the houses belonging to the nobiletza. There was a seating area with a capybara rug and an unlit fireplace, with rich, darkly stained rockwood bookshelves lining the walls, full of heavy books. Amber quartz crystals sat on thin, five-foot-tall candelabras, filling the home with a pleasant light. The place was cozy, and Ester missed cozy. The Foundry had felt that way once. "What do you want to know about the Sovereign's visit?" the judge asked as he grabbed a kettle and brought it to the waterspout in the kitchen.

"I heard he had an emergency session with the audencia before he visited the Foundry, and I guess I was wondering what was discussed. I know it's above my station to ask, but the Foundry has been dealing with some... changes lately, and I was wondering if the Sovereign had imposed any new ordinances or laws that were equally, um, strange."

Abeso spent a minute lighting the fireplace and setting the kettle above the flames, and he said nothing the whole time. "It was an emergency session like you said, young smith," he finally said. "Of course he requested changes that would sound unorthodox to some. We have yet to announce those changes."

A silence opened up between the two as Abeso knelt in front of the fireplace and waited for the water to boil. He was clearly unwilling to talk, but Ester wasn't sure what to say to get the answers she needed. She'd spent the last few passings asking around about the Sovereign's visit, but nobody had anything useful to say beyond the fact the man and his primordia had spoken with the audencia, then spent more than a week inside the Foundry. Ester was desperate to figure out what in bowel's fire had happened while she was gone. "I know you've had a lot on your plate since the Burning," she said. "What with getting the city repaired and finding a new magnate. I know you have no good reason to help me, especially considering I broke the manservant Jakar out of his cage during his trial—"

"Wait." Abeso finally looked at her. He squinted until something clicked. "You're right. It was you. I didn't realize. Your brother helped you, if I'm not mistaken. Paid dearly for it, too."

She nodded. But of course, the judge had no idea how Damek had *really* lost his arm.

The man did something strange then. His rigidity dissolved, and the edges of his face filled with wrinkled stress. Suddenly he was on the verge of crying. He sat on the couch beside her and put his face in his hands. "I'm sorry, young smith. I didn't know who you were. I thought you were one of them."

"One of who?"

"One of the replacements."

The way he said that last sentence, full of fear and faint disgust, validated Ester's suspicions. A weight lifted off her shoulders. Maybe she was right about these smiths being flesh bound after all. "I'm not one of them," she said. "I was away from Augustin when the Sovereign visited. The Sovereign took Master Smith Mateo and the others back to Saracosta, so I'm the only one left who was part of the old cadre."

"I see," Abeso said. "I'll admit; the changes at the Foundry have been low on my list of concerns. I've received complaints from merchants and other buyers about the quality of weapons the order have been selling of late, but that encompasses as much as I've been willing to deal with regarding your brothers and sisters. There has been too much on my plate while we continue to repair the city and prepare to enact these new executive laws, so I ask your forgiveness."

It wasn't the first time she'd heard of these new smiths forging subpar weapons and tools. It was just more proof that they cared for their allegiance to the Sovereign over their sacred duties, just as flesh bound would. "Forgiveness for what?"

"For avoiding the Foundry. I've missed the last two services. I haven't been quite so motivated lately to attend."

"Of course you're forgiven. I don't mind at all. I'm sure you've had a lot to deal with." She tried to make the last statement more of a question.

He took the bait. "I shouldn't be telling you this, but we'll be announcing our new magnate tomorrow."

"It'll be someone from the audencia, or one of the nobility?"

"His name is Warren Crosby. I met him for the first time at the emergency session. The Sovereign saw fit to choose the magnate for us."

Ester couldn't help but notice that Crosby wasn't much of an Augustin name. "I can imagine that was hard on you and the others. Picking a new magnate is a big deal."

"It was more than a big deal. What the Sovereign did was unprecedented. The Adriann family ruled this territory for three hundred and twenty-seven years and it was the audencia's job to decide which family would rule for generations to come. We spent months discussing it."

If the man knew his history, he'd realize it wasn't unprecedented at all for the Sovereign to install puppets. "I can't begin to understand your pain," she said.

He shuddered, and Ester could see him opening up inch by inch. A perk of being a smith was that it brought honesty out of most people, as if the devout were above casting judgment, even though that was pretty much all someone like Ester did. It was hard not to lately, when everyone around her had frayed her to her limits. The kettle started to whine. "I'm afraid for the future," Abeso said as he moved to the fire. "I'm afraid to see what this Magnate Crosby will do to our home and how it will most benefit the Sovereign… but that's not what's making me lose sleep at passing's end."

"Are you having trouble sleeping, Judge?"

He poured steaming water into the cups on the table, and the corners of his eyes strained in thought as he sipped. "I saw something that I'm not sure I was supposed to, or perhaps the Sovereign did not care because he knew I wouldn't understand."

"Oh?"

"After I received the Sovereign and his procession at the gates, I showed the Sovereign to his villa on the second level, where he and his son Bilal were meant to stay while they were here. But there was someone there waiting for us. One of his primordia escorting a captive. Her captive seemed to be from the Barrows, by the look of his clothes. An Ash addict on his last leg, if I had to guess. This primordia must have arrived in the city before the Sovereign and hunted the man down."

Ester was too worried that anything she said would break the fragile trust sitting in the air, so she remained quiet, waiting.

"It seemed like a private thing," Abeso continued. "The Sovereign's little ten-year-old approached the Barrows man and inspected him, then turned to his father and said one word. 'Homunculus.' The Sovereign nodded, and Bilal... grabbed the man by his spine." He stared at his hand, his eyes unfocused. "It didn't make sense. The boy touched him like his hand was exploring a pile of mud. The Barrows man cried out, but one strike from the primordia shut him up, and then Bilal escorted him into the villa, followed by the Sovereign."

"Then what?"

"Then nothing. I didn't see the Sovereign again until next passing when he held his emergency session." He set his cup down and looked at it like it was the last thing he wanted now. "Bilal seems to have inherited his father's power, and I fear what that could mean. I should have said something when the Sovereign announced this stranger, Warren Crosby, as the new magnate. I should have found the courage to speak up."

"Has anyone seen the Barrows man?"

The judge shook his head. "I tasked some of the guard to look into it, but he must have traveled back to Saracosta with the Sovereign and your brothers and sisters."

None of it made sense. Bilal must have used flesh binding magic on the Barrows man, but what purpose would that have served? An Ash addict couldn't do much for the Sovereign and his son. She needed answers. There were ways she could find them, but it would mean breaking Augustin laws, and breaking Augustin laws meant betraying the throne, and by extension, the Foundry.

Laws were guidelines to what was right, not its definition. "Thank you, Judge Abeso," she said, and stood. "If I learn anything, I'll let you know."

He gave a weak nod as she left.

Chapter 23—Jakar

IT TOOK SOME manner of convincing to get Darkwater to leave the Archives—this was according to Geth, after all was quiet and Darkwater's representatives had long exited the premises—though I had little doubt they'd be back later, maybe with better proof to back their claims that a cartographer who'd been spotted with two accomplices had been responsible for the serf building burning down. Geth insisted that there was only so much Darkwater could do without hard evidence, but I was still convinced they would find some way to get their pound of flesh for what they'd lost, legally or otherwise.

Geth's associates provided us a safehouse a block away from Darkwater where we could act fast if someone spotted Namira leaving the building. At the moment we were waiting to get word from one of Geth's friends who had surrounded the trade company's perimeter that Namira was within reach. There'd been a swarm of activity surrounding the building ever since the serf barracks were burned down, but there was no sign of Namira yet.

I caught Geth in a dingy back hall with Shirallah, who was talking in a low, exasperated voice. Even while angry, Shirallah never raised his voice. Neither of them had seen me—the cartographer set a gentle hand on his companion's upper arm, then they embraced. Shirallah sniffled and wiped his nose, threw a glance over his shoulder, and our eyes met.

He left Geth's side and hurried past me, muttering, "Perac,"—an apology, I was pretty sure—before disappearing through a door. I approached the cartographer, who had been holding a stiff look of concern before he let it melt away.

"Don't mind him," Geth said. "His nerves are just fried."

"He really cares for you, doesn't he?"

"Yeah." He showed his teeth, but it wasn't enough to hide the pain. "Well, I mean, I'm not the only thing on his mind. If Darkwater finds out he was involved in the serf barracks burning down, his life in Ravada is over."

It was my fault Shirallah's house was no longer safe. There was no telling if Darkwater had figured out who'd lived there, but I could do nothing about protecting Shirallah short of tearing the trading company down to its bricks, and the last thing I needed was another reason to linger in Xeriv.

I prayed that once we had rescued Namira, it would be enough to convince Efadora to continue on to Som Abast. I needed her if I wanted to keep my elemental powers and take down the Ebonrock. I still hadn't shared with her the truth of why I needed her along, that my powers would fade if I didn't have someone I was flesh bound with in close proximity, even if the ritual with her wasn't complete. I wasn't sure when I would find the confidence to tell her, though. Her guarded way of speaking to people like Torlo and Shirallah and even Geth told me she'd been hurt by friends in the past—perhaps it had to do with that gang she'd been part of in Manasus— and that she was waiting for the other shoe to drop whenever someone was friendly with her. I didn't want her to think I was using her, even though I was. Above and below, I was a bad friend. Perhaps when the time came that we did have this conversation, she would realize I wanted her around because of how much I cared for her, too.

"You said your friends are staking out Darkwater?" I asked.

"Yes, sir."

Anxiety sat like a knot in my sternum, worsening since learning more about the Ebonrock. Before, they were an abstract threat lurking somewhere in my future, but now they felt more real, more present, which meant new levels of anxiety. It was irrational to feel this sudden sense of urgency, but still—Quin could be dying for all I knew. It was as if the chance of her death on any given passing had increased dramatically, simply because I was more confident than ever I could find her.

"I wanted to ask about the Ebonrock," I said. "They go by the Rha'Ghalor. too, right? Did you find anything else about them?"

"Maybe. Maybe not. It depends."

I straightened, acutely aware of the deviousness in his tone. "Is this the part where you blackmail me?"

He snorted. "I'm sorry?"

"You've wanted something from me ever since you figured out what I really am."

He put his hands up. "You got me. I wanted to put this off until we rescued Namira, but you're right. What I know about the Ebonrock is my leverage to get you to let me go with you to find them."

"You want to be my travel companion? That's it?"

"I'm a cartographer, Jakar. Of course that's it. Thanks to you, I now have this question burning a hole in my head. The Sihraan Empire and the cult that raised you share a connection with the Great Ones, and I have to know what it is. Did the Sihraans sacrifice their citizens to the Unmade? Imagine talking to real, breathing people who hold the answer as opposed to turning over more rocks and ruins."

I gave him a long look. "That Sihraan city is important to you. It's hard to believe you'd just abandon it."

"Yes, it's important," he nearly spat, but a heartbeat later his anger deflated. "The Archives told me that Ravada awarded the claim to the ruins to Darkwater. That cartel masquerading as a trading company is already moving in so they can get to work pillaging everything they can touch with their slimy hands. So, congratulations, you're my backup plan."

Perhaps I was acting unreasonably toward Geth. I didn't trust him enough to expect that he would always help, but he wasn't distrustful enough to betray me. There were worse things in the world than having a cartographer as a travel companion. "Tell me what else you know about the Ebonrock. Show me you're helpful and you can come with me."

He studied me, considering. "You know what? It wouldn't kill me to be on the giving end of some goodwill for once. Shores knows it would make Shirallah happy." He led me to a seating area on the second floor that had an old window overlooking a gardened plaza, and on the other side of that plaza, Darkwater. "I'll tell you that the Rha'Ghalor worship a god named Tylkoth," he said, sitting. He played with the cover of a book on the table next to him, flipping at the pages with his thumb. It was clear he was uncomfortable offering up this information—perhaps he thought if he gave up too much of his leverage, I would disappear on to Som Abast without him. "My contemporaries believe Tylkoth was the progenitor of the Great Ones, or the Unmade, or the *mora gula* if you're of Callo. Little is known of the Great Ones, which means we know next to nothing about Tylkoth. 'For the Ebonrock wax upon thee to reap the children,' as they say in Rona. 'Enslave them and drive them. Spur their flesh and roll their passions so yond might drudge and work to liberate thy doom. Tylkoth.' Tylkoth in Ronan roughly translates to 'the Great Drifter.' It's believed the Great Ones lurk within the Black Depths, so the name of their maker seems apt."

So much of what Geth said fell in line with the people I'd once known. "Do you know how to find the Ebonrock?"

"If I did, I would go looking for them myself. Maybe I'd be a member by now." He laughed.

"That's nothing to joke about."

"Who says I'm joking? I doubt they'd share their secrets

with an outsider, and it's a common strategy of the Archives anyway. We bargain with the local people and befriend them so they can teach us about the area and their culture."

"I'll be too busy killing them for you to have time to sit down with them for a chat."

He frowned. "You said you were trying to save your friends, not destroy the cult." Before I could respond, his frown disappeared and he said merrily, "But I think we can work something out before we get there."

"You sabotaged an entire caravan so you could explore some ruins," I said. "I'm not going to risk you trying something that will get me killed just so you can write a thesis on those monsters. The deal's off."

The air between us shifted. Geth thought for a moment, then asked, "Do you really want to destroy Efadora's dreams?"

I paused, trying to puzzle out what he meant. The pieces slowly fell into place. "You sponsored Efadora so you could come with me."

"Of course I did. By sponsoring her I'm agreeing to train her, and I'm not going to wait around for the weeks or months it'll take the two of you to find the Ebonrock and come back here. I'm a busy man, or I intend to be. If you don't let me tag along, Efadora's sponsorship will dry up and she'll hate you for not taking me along. You don't want that to happen, do you?"

His gaze moved to my hand—it had tightened into a fist— and his eyes flickered with fear. "You're not the only one who can blackmail," I said.

We stood there for a moment, the threat hanging between us, until he said, "And you'd be crushing Efadora's dreams along with whatever or whoever was on the wrong side of those fists." His fear fizzled away.

He knew me better than I realized. He'd called my bluff, knew that I wouldn't have it in me to hurt him simply because he was being an asshole, and he crossed his arms, waiting for my answer.

I left the room.

Efadora wasn't on the second floor, where she sometimes watched Darkwater in the unlikely chance she saw Namira leaving the building. She wasn't with Torlo either, who had refused to leave his post near the front door, waiting for an attack that everyone else was sure wouldn't come. Eventually I found her on the roof sipping on mushroom tea at a picnicking table and reading from a stack of books she'd carried with her from the Archives. Cartography had had the unintended consequence of helping her discover a deep love for reading.

"Can we talk?" I asked.

She closed the book. "Sure."

I sat across from her. I noticed the gloves she wore—they were red-brown, made from leather that looked soft, durable, and well-oiled. They didn't look cheap. "Where'd you get those?"

"Geth gave them to me. They're great for climbing and they're really comfortable. What's wrong?"

I tried to keep the discomfort off my face. "Nothing."

She pushed the book away and folded her arms, eying me, then moved her fingers around to flex the leather, almost self-consciously. "I want to talk to you, too."

"What about?"

"The cartographers kept buzzing around you like flies in the Dead Bogs, then they started bothering me when they realized you aren't a talker. Everyone wants to know about your elemental power. Why don't you explain to them how it works?"

"I told Geth about my Imbibings, and I'm sure he's told the others."

"Yes, but they don't know what elements are. They don't know that it isn't quartz they're really binding with but silicon. Why not tell them the truth?"

"What would they do with that information if I told them?"

"They'd write about it. They'd try to learn more. They're not so bad, Jakar."

"Did you know Geth only wants to train you so he can find the Ebonrock with me?"

She blinked, her brows furrowing. After a few moments, she said, "So?"

"So, he's manipulating us. He wants to learn about my old masters. They'll kill him without giving it a thought, but imagine… imagine if he learned about flesh bindings."

"Do you think Geth, or even anyone, really, is like my father? Letting people learn more about how the world works isn't always dangerous. Geth's not going to use the information to start creating flesh bindings. Besides, we don't even know if it's possible to make flesh bindings without that thing you told me about. The Child."

She still didn't know the Child's true name, Ig. "It doesn't matter. He'll bring the secrets of the flesh binding back here, then it will be a matter of time before places like Darkwater learn about it. Even if they don't have the Child, maybe they'll figure something out that will make it possible."

"You're being paranoid. But who knows, if Geth doesn't take the Ebonrock seriously enough, maybe he'll get himself killed. Problem solved."

I was used to her flippant remarks on death, but at the moment it bothered me more than usual.

"What's your problem?" she asked as she watched me wring my hands. I put them in my lap. "Something's been up ever since you woke up. I know you haven't told me you were sick because you bonded with a new element."

I went still as stone.

She continued, perhaps confusing my panic for discomfort. "I heard enough stories from Emil about the Foundry's rhidium trials to see the signs. What element did you bind with?"

"I don't know yet." Under normal circumstances I could use my Eye to puzzle out what the elemental might be, but every time I opened my Eye it nearly blinded me, it was so bright.

"It had to be my family's sword, right? The edge was made

from rhidium, and it must've bonded with something when Sara tried to execute you."

Talking to an Adriann about how much more powerful I'd become was triggering a deep-rooted instinct to shut down and shut up, but for a moment the instinct was forgotten. I hadn't considered the rhidium blade being responsible for my binding. My Imbibings with the Ebonrock had started as soon as I'd swallowed the rhidium, leaving me comatose for two passings, but this last binding had taken over two months to start and had knocked me out for two weeks. Maybe the body reacted differently to rhidium introduced to the blood instead of through ingestion.

"You don't want me to become a cartographer," she said. She was angry, but behind that anger there was pain. "Is that why you're being such an asshole?"

"It's not that. If I came off as an asshole, I'm sorry. I didn't mean to. I'm just worried."

"About what?"

"I'm worried I won't get to my friends in time and save them from the Ebonrock."

"It's been two years. Spending a few more passings saving Namira isn't going to change anything."

"I know it's unreasonable." A thought came to me, one that had been building in my mind for a while now, and I said, "That reminds me. When I see how focused you are on saving Namira, all I see is your need for revenge on Arhan. Sara was the same way. She never forgot a grudge."

Ice swept through her. "You think I'm acting like *her*?"

Her reaction caught me off guard. Her similarities to Sara were undeniable, but I hadn't realized how much she hated this fact.

Sara's betrayal had affected her in ways I hadn't known. We still hadn't talked about what had happened in Augustin and it had caused me to severely misunderstand how she was coping, I was realizing too late.

A small sound left her throat, followed by silence. She stood, moving slowly as she turned her back to me, and headed for the door. Someone blocked her path. It was one of the scouts Geth had paid to keep an eye on the Darkwater warehouse.

"Saw her. The trader woman," the man said in broken Miran. "Namira."

"Where?" I asked, staring at the back of Efadora's head as she waited in front of the scout.

"They taking her to west side. One of mine is tailing her." He frowned at Efadora and turned his attention to me instead. "He will let me know where she stops. He meet me by fishery after. We come here after that and tell you what building they take her to."

"Thank you," I said. The scout left and so did Efadora.

Why did I compare her to Sara? Only once the words had left my mouth did I realize how insensitive they sounded. My life wasn't the only one Sara had ruined.

I'd said them because deep down, I was still afraid of the Adriann name. I was afraid of the things Efadora had in common with Sara and what they could mean. Sara had broken me and I was scared of someone else doing it again.

I was still broken. This trip had only distracted me from what I'd left behind. I'd done nothing to move past what Sara and Rodi had made me do, only buried it with hard travel. Was that why I'd traveled so hard, why I never let myself rest and recover from my wounds until I fell into a coma? All I'd done since leaving Augustin was fill my head with white noise.

What if there *was* no moving past this?

I sat there, thinking of Efadora.

The tears came soon after, and they burned.

Chapter 24—Efadora

I STOMPED TOWARD Torlo, who lounged in a chair near the front room, and kicked his foot. "Up."

He leaned over to get a look at the rail weapon slung over one shoulder and my bag slung over the other. "You're packing heavy."

"Yep. C'mon."

I moved to the front door, and he asked, "Where're we going?" He pulled the pack off my shoulder and threw it over his.

"We're saving Namira."

"Breaking into Darkwater didn't work out so well the first time around. You sure that's a good idea?"

"They moved her. We just got word from one of the scouts."

"Oh." The uncertainty was clear on his face.

"You're angry," Torlo said as we stepped into the street and joined the river of foot traffic.

"That obvious, huh?"

"Is it Jakar?" He couldn't stop looking over his shoulder. "It's the only reason you wouldn't have asked for his help." When I didn't answer, he continued, "He won't be able to help if we're spotted."

"And?"

"And nothing, I guess." He continued to follow without a word. I took a moment to appreciate this, along with the fact he'd left the safehouse with almost no complaints. Even for Torlo, that was surprising. His curly hair bounced as he pushed forward beside me, and he forced a smile, one so genuine that for a moment it was like we were on any other mission. The guilt started to set in. There was no angle on his end for personal gain by helping me, or at least not one I could see. The feeling worsened, and I realized it was because I was about to put him in danger.

We crossed the city, moving along the river that ran across Ravada like a ragged scar, catching only glimpses of the water through the press of buildings. A monthly festival called Marking the Fall was about to start, which celebrated an ancient victory against Yaroklan marauders from the north, so the streets were busier than usual, full of commoners in cream-colored robes, wearing jewelry of dark blue crystal; the men wore their tiny hats while the women wore ceremonial daggers on their waists.

Turn back, idiot. You're hopeless without Jakar. Maybe I didn't know what I was doing and this would accomplish nothing, other than getting us killed. I supposed if I were competent, Namira wouldn't have Darkwater shackles around her wrists.

No. I could almost feel Jakar's accusation creeping under my skin like slime. He thought I was like Sara? I would never depend on him the way Sara had, would never force him to solve all my problems until I convinced myself to do what Sara had done to him. I was going to prove it, too.

We reached the fishery where the scout tailing Namira was supposed to rendezvous and pushed out of the crowd. The dirt lot reeked of fish, and beyond an open warehouse door, scales flashed as workers unloaded chamber cod and eel from a docked boat. The scout lurked behind a pallet of salt sacks.

"You're back already?" I asked. "You were supposed to keep watch until you were sure she wasn't moved again."

He frowned. "Ju nij rumieji."

"Oh." I thought for a moment. "Zech Namira?"

"Vichezla zo jach."

"I think he said they took Namira to the Sihraan city," I said to Torlo. "Shit." I turned back to the scout. "Why'd they take her there?"

The scout shrugged.

Fhelfire, we were barely twenty minutes into this plan and I already needed Jakar. I sat on the pallet and dug my fingers through my hair, pulling. "Shit, shit, shit."

"What's wrong?" Torlo asked.

"Hard to explain."

He grabbed one of my hands and enveloped it in his. His gaze was strained, but I realized it was empathy for the pain in mine. "Maybe think of it like this," he said. "How many people from Darkwater can be in those ruins, really? Might be hard getting in, but once we're there we'll have an entire abandoned city to hide in to find Namira."

I couldn't believe what I was hearing. Torlo was trying to convince me to do something stupid?

He kept a gentle grip on my hand, and his eyes became half-moons as he smiled, as if he were hoping he'd said the right thing. He was eager to help Jakar because of his blood vow, but he was also trying to be brave because he wanted to impress me. He liked me, and he was expecting to gain ground in our relationship by doing me favors.

So that was his angle. It reminded me of boys from my past, those who promised their friendship was unconditional until it wasn't. They had yelled at me then, angry that I couldn't give them what they wanted, having used our friendship as a guise to grow closer to me, expecting something more even though they'd insisted friendship was enough. Spurned boys were cruel. What if Torlo knew how I really felt about him? Would he become bitter, too?

"Thanks for the info," I said to the scout, and he responded with a confused look. I led Torlo off the lot to an avenue leading west, each step I took like acid. I'd take Torlo's help and deal with the aftermath later. Everything about this felt wrong, but if this was what it would take to prove to Jakar that I wasn't like Sara, then so be it.

We hiked up the hill to the west gate where twenty-foot-tall statues of King Rognach and Queen Bilfrik—Xeriv's first rulers twelve hundred years ago—were carved into the wall on either side. There wasn't much traffic around this gate—it led to a collection of root farms—so we entered the tunnel outside the city easily. The start of the path to the ruins was only a quarter mile away.

In the cavern with the side tunnel leading into the ruins, a Darkwater checkpoint sat at the bottom of the switchbacks, right where we needed to go.

I pulled Torlo behind a stalagmite next to the road. We were still a hundred feet from the checkpoint, and I was pretty sure we weren't seen. "Okay," I said. "Distraction time. Same play we did at the serf barracks." I took back the pack he'd been carrying and rummaged through it until I found the canister of flash powder. "Head to that outpost. Stay off the road and behind the stalagmites so they don't see you." I clipped off a length of fusing and stuck it through the narrow opening at the top of the jar. "That should be enough to give you a couple minutes to set it off and double back." I pointed to a grove of coral trees opposite the outpost. "Meet me there. We'll sneak through after the flash powder goes off."

He squinted at the barricades. "There are five guards. What if they don't all get distracted?"

I patted the rail weapon's strap across my chest. "That's what this is for."

He hesitated, holding the flash powder, but nodded and disappeared behind the line of stalagmites. I watched the outpost and waited until I was pretty sure they weren't looking in my direction, then bolted to the opposite embankment and jumped into the undergrowth. Tangles of orange, purple, and green lichen and moss crunched under my boots as I trudged behind more stalagmites, circled around a dark pool, and hid behind the coral tree grove. I brandished the rail weapon and aimed it at the nearest guard, who was busy balancing his sword with the tip planted in the ground while twirling the handle.

Shouts echoed from the thicket to the right of the switchbacks, and a guard climbed onto the road, pulling Torlo by the arm with his sword in the other hand. "Jach vausety stolij pisam!" *Caught myself an intruder!*

The man had caught Torlo while leaving to take a piss. *Shit.* My finger hovered over the trigger, but if I shot someone, there was no telling what would happen to Torlo. I wasn't even sure what the weapon would do. The guard dragged Torlo to the outpost, and the others gathered around him, talking too low for me to be able to piece anything together.

They jostled him around, asking questions, and when he didn't respond, they threw him to the ground. I pushed the tiny lever on the ammo pack sitting atop the weapon, and a projectile fell into place at the base of the rails. I aimed, took a deep breath, and fired.

A loud crack echoed through the cavern, and despite my terrible aim, I still managed to clip the closest guard, who fell over Torlo, the guard opposite him falling backward at the same time. The others shouted, and a heartbeat later, the thicket Torlo had been dragged out of exploded.

A concussive blast hit me like a slap to the face, the sound loud enough to needle my eardrums, and shards of stalagmites bounced off the barricade, undergrowth raining down on the outpost. All of the guards had been knocked off their feet. My ears hurt, but I was all right. I bolted across the road and found Torlo in the middle of the dazed group beneath the guard I'd shot. The dead man had a hole in his side through his leather chest guard, and the man opposite him who had fallen on his back was missing the lower right half of his jaw. The rail weapon was remarkably easy to aim—the shot went exactly where you pointed it, and the projectile was large enough to make it hard not to hit your mark. It must have gone clean through both guards.

The other three guards were coming to their senses, lifting their heads or struggling to sit up. I set the rail weapon down and cut their throats.

"Torlo," I said, shaking him. His eyes were closed and a gash on his head leaked blood. I rolled the dead man off and found Torlo drenched in blood, but none of it seemed to be his. The jar of flash powder must have exploded. I shook Torlo again and his eyes fluttered.

"My head hurts," he said softly, like a little kid, his eyes all watery.

"We need to go." I pulled him to his feet, taking care to pick up the rail weapon with my other hand without letting one of the red-hot rails touch me. Torlo staggered through the barricades as I led him up the start of the switchbacks. He stumbled but moved with frantic energy and glazed eyes, scrambling up the slope on his hands and knees whenever he lost his footing. I watched him, sick to my stomach. What in bowel's fire were we doing? We were just a couple of teenagers running headfirst into the arms of a trading company that wanted to enslave or kill us. And Torlo's head wound was clearly affecting him. He needed a doctor.

What if he died because of me?

Below, a group of people walking along the road had gathered around the outpost, some investigating the dead guards and the destroyed section of vegetation where the flash powder exploded, others watching us reach the top of the switchbacks.

"Can you keep moving?" I asked.

Torlo didn't answer, but he didn't stop. He had a look in his eyes that was both befuddled and hyper-focused on the path ahead.

The tunnels leading to the ruins had been widened with pyroglycerin and were littered with ramps and support beams for carts to fit through. Glowing amber quartz crystals hung from chains nailed to the ceiling and there were faint grooves in the rock where dozens of wheels had marked their passing. We didn't run into anyone, but the path was well-traveled. It gave me a bad feeling.

"You got that waterskin?" Torlo muttered.

I dug the skin out of my pack and handed it over. He gulped at it clumsily, lines of water piercing the sheen of blood covering the front of his body. "How are you feeling?" I asked.

"Nauseous." He handed the waterskin back. "Where's Namira?"

"In the ruins. We're going there now."

"Oh. My head hurts." He wavered, rubbing his temple and staring at one of the dangling crystals. "Can I have some water?"

That's not good.

Excited voices reached us from farther down the tunnel. "Hurry," I said, leading Torlo under the ramp behind us where we crammed ourselves into the tight space. A group of guards appeared through the slits of the ramp—they ran at us, pounding up the rockwood. Torlo wrapped his arms around me as we waited for the group to pass. He was breathing fast. "My head hurts," he whispered, scared.

We squeezed out of our hiding spot when the coast was clear. Torlo doubled over and retched water onto the rock.

"C'mon," I said, swallowing hard. The guilt almost made me vomit, too. "That had to be a whole company of guards. They'll come back this way fast once they talk to any witnesses."

He nodded. "Okay, Effie."

Magnate Bardera was the only person who called me Effie. I hated the nickname, but I didn't correct him. The gentle way he said it had a nicer ring to it. I took his hand and pulled.

No more guards stood between us and the ruins. Maybe there was hope after all. We reached the ledge overlooking the cavern and my breath caught.

Thousands worked among the white marble ruins, moving

in and out of buildings, pushing and pulling carts filled to the brim with fallen debris from the cavern's collapsed ceiling or working to repair some of the ruined structures. The city hissed and flickered with light—it seemed Darkwater had managed to repair lamps for a quarter of the city, or rather a quarter of what I could see. More ruins faded into the darkness where the floor above it hadn't collapsed. I couldn't tell how much of the steam-powered infrastructure was up and running, but it was clear Darkwater planned to get it working as soon as possible.

This was so much more than a Darkwater expedition. Half of the company's warehouse and most of their serfs and slaves in Xeriv had to be here, and for obvious reasons—the artifacts recovered here, if they were anywhere near as advanced as the rail weapon, could make them the richest company in the land. Not to mention the political implications of all these advanced weapons. Darkwater could turn themselves into a bona fide military state.

I pulled out the waterskin and poured it down Torlo's front until most of the blood was gone, then used a rag to wipe the blood from his head. At a glance, he looked like just another slave at the end of his rope. I helped him down the ramps and stairs that littered the elaborate scaffolding, and nobody paid us any heed, probably because the sheer stupidity of what we were doing protected us from suspicion. At least for now. We reached the street below and moved along the wall, down the street where there were fewer people laboring.

The flurry of activity quickly faded to nothing by the end of the second block. I turned into a half-collapsed building, and no sooner had I gotten us out of sight did Torlo stumble to his knees and dry heave some more.

I set the waterskin next to him. We were screwed. No, we were dead. Those guards would be back soon, and then the search would start. A clever person could hide in these ruins for weeks, but not this close to the entrance with a concussed companion.

Torlo lay on his back. He whispered to himself, his eyes closed. "Torlo?" I said. I nudged him, but he didn't seem to notice.

"Juromal," he said quietly. "Where's Juromal? I was wrong. Juromal."

I tried to pull him up, but he hissed through his teeth when his head bumped against the marble tile and he went limp. His eyes were closed, but still he whispered to himself. It wasn't until I saw him hurt like this did I realize how badly I didn't want him hurt at all. Fhelfire, I didn't want to care about him like this. Was it worth it to try to move him and risk being spotted, or did I need to get something of value out of this shitty plan and make sure Arhan died before we were both captured?

Torlo turned his head and dry heaved some more, and my sickness threatened to fill me up. What was wrong with me? Why would I do any of this?

Because I was a terrible person. That was why.

"I'm so sorry," I said, my voice shaking. He was too far gone to hear me.

Chapter 25—Ester

ESTER WAITED AMONG the line of smiths as everyone stood along the ridge of the trade district, looking upon the audencia as they stood on the dark rock of the chasm floor. Bursts of steam from the river punctuated the words Judge Abeso spoke, his voice struggling to carry to the thousands of Augustins rimming the chasm.

"And so I am pleased to announce the coronation of our new leader, Magnate Crosby," the judge said.

Applause erupted along the sink hole's bottom levels, and flower petals and bits of colorful moss rained down on the ceremony. When the cacophony faded, Judge Abeso continued, "May our new magnate's reign be long and peaceful. As you all know, however, the magnate's seat culminates in more than just one man or woman. It is a dynasty. And so, as our new magnate is without spouse and child, he has agreed to take the hand of an Augustin. Soon he will begin work on establishing a family that is sure to lead our great territory for generations to come."

The line of smiths watched silently, but commoners and nobility alike whispered and spoke in low voices. Ester acknowledged how smart Magnate Crosby's move was—mass distrust of electing a stranger after everything the city had undergone this past year was suddenly dampened by ten thousand fantasies of setting a family member, a friend, or oneself up with the new magnate.

Warren Crosby stepped forward and put his hands in the air to quiet the crowd. His eyes were sunken; his bangs, cut in a straight line, stuck to his forehead. Ester would've put him somewhere in his twenties, and the man had a tiny frame and frail arms. "It is a great honor to serve all of you," he said. His voice was deep and rich and accented in perfect, sterile Miran, and it carried as though it had been designed specifically for crowds. "I shall do my best to bring this city back to its former glory, to ensure every great town along the Granite Road is enriched both in what it has lost and in its safety, and to provide Radavich with the reparations they are demanding. Peace—true peace—is but a few good deeds away."

Saltier whispers made the rounds now. Tensions between Augustin and Radavich were more alive than ever—the occasional raid cracked the border hard, devastating medium-sized caravans that thought they were safe from highwaymen, and rumor had it Radavich was funding these raids. The neighboring territory refused to believe Sara Adriann had disappeared as well, insisting that Augustin was hiding her.

"Please," Magnate Crosby said. "It is necessary. Bringing peace between us and Radavich will mean easing tensions between our two territories and with Tulchi. We *must* set the example. It is the first step to ushering in another era of unity and security that will rival the decades preceding the Adrianns' fall from the throne."

Master Smith Hartlan clapped fervently, the sharp sounds echoing across the chasm. His new senior arc smiths joined in, and soon every smith was clapping and cheering. Slowly, half-heartedly, the rest of the city followed suit.

Ester's hands stayed at her sides.

She slipped away and pushed through the crowds. All eyes would be on Magnate Crosby for the next hour, which meant for the next hour Ester could be on her worst behavior.

* * *

SHE STOOD IN front of the villa the Sovereign had stayed in during his first passing in Augustin.

It was in the back of the Creeping Vine District on the second level, where the winding corridors opened into a courtyard of moss trees, fountains, and benches. There was nobody here—the eight other noble families who lived in this courtyard were at the coronation with their guards. Still, the doors to the Sovereign's villa were barred with an impressive-looking set of chains and locks. Metal rattled as Ester made easy work of it, and she pulled the chains off, letting them slide to the ground. She looked around nervously, but when nobody popped their head out of a door or around any of the corridors, she hurried inside.

Darkness filled the place almost to the brim, but in the light of the doorway she spotted a torch with stocked tinder in the holder. She struck flint to it, and her little beacon cast long shadows in the house. The Sovereign must have had all the pyremoss and glowing quartz removed. Her sandals made soft patters against the stone as she walked among ornate statues and frescoes—carved and painted eyes looked down on her from the walls and the ceiling, the air tasting cool and wet. Most of the furniture had been removed.

She came upon a circular chamber with a dais in the middle. She'd seen rooms like this in some of the fancier noble houses—the center dais often had a statue of Fheldspra, faceless and interlaced with gently glowing ruby. Five stone cubes, each with one-foot dimensions, would create a small circle around the statue, and six stone cubes, each with six-inch dimensions, would create a larger circle. The inner circle represented fire, stone, flesh, nature, and energy—the base components of the land of Ra Thuzan—and the six outer cubes represented the territories. But someone had ripped down the tapestries on the wall, removed the furniture, and pulled the cubes out of the floor, leaving the room barren. The Fheldspra statue lay on its side against the far wall, and in its place on the dais stood a large cauldron of stained glass.

Ester moved closer. Even from ten feet away she caught a coppery whiff of blood from the cauldron. It was the same smell that came off her brothers and sisters, except now it almost overwhelmed her. The cauldron looked disturbingly ritualistic, even though there was nothing interesting about it other than the smell. She peered into it, almost gagging, but it was empty.

Was a cauldron required for creating flesh bindings? If only she'd picked Jakar's brain before he left. Maybe there was another room she could check that would prove a little more revealing.

Steps echoed from the front room, and a figure entered the edge of the torchlight, the light turning his sockets into twin pools of shadow as he glowered at her. A sword hung from his grip.

"What are you doing here?" Ester asked Master Smith Hartlan. The question came out insolent, even angry.

"Your behavior these last few passings has been troubling to watch, young Jesmon. Enough to warrant keeping a close eye on you. It breaks my heart to see the disappointment you've become."

"And you would know how a smith should act?"

"Pardon me?"

Ester worried about what Hartlan might do if she reached for the sword at her hip, and at the same time, every instinct pushed against the idea of pulling her weapon against a master smith of the Foundry. "I don't think you are who you say you are," she said. "I don't think anyone in the Foundry is."

"And who are we supposed to be?" He acted genuinely puzzled, but his weight remained on his front foot, ready to pounce.

"I don't know. I've known smiths in Tulchi and Augustin, and they were different, sure, but they were the same in a lot of ways. Sometimes it feels like I'm the only smith in this city who doesn't worship the Sovereign."

"You think we worship the man?" He let out a humorless laugh. "That's a terrible thing to accuse your brothers and sisters of."

"It's so much more than that." She searched for the right words. "You all keep me at arm's length like I don't belong, or like you're in on something I don't know about. The other smiths are disconnected from everything around them. There's something missing. I want to figure out what it is."

"We're adjusting to our new lives. That is all." He stepped closer. Maybe she could draw her sword in time, but maybe not. His eyes moved from her hands to the hilt at her side to her feet, making calculations in his head.

"Where are you really from?" she asked.

"I'm sorry?"

"Tell me where you grew up. Or what made you want to serve in the Foundry. Anything from before your time as a smith."

Pain flickered across his face, the skin along his eyes and cheekbones scrunching up. "A smith's life begins anew when he joins the Foundry," he said. "Do not ask of things that are not one's business."

"Apologies. Master Smith Mateo didn't find me very agreeable, either. Did your parents worship Fheldspra and introduce you to Him, or were you raised in a secular home?"

He shuddered, his gaze falling. He was behaving like the slag-hauling smith Ester had talked to a week ago. "I... I..." he trailed off.

"Your hometown. What was it called?"

His brows furrowed. He looked determined, as though he wanted to know the answer himself. "F-Foleaf. In Saracosta. My parents..."

"Why does it hurt?"

He closed his eyes and went unnaturally still. "The Sovereign and his spawn did something to us."

"He used flesh magic on you, didn't he?"

He kept his eyes closed. "I don't know what you mean."

236

If the Sovereign had flesh bound the smiths, there was nothing that would stop him from doing the same to Mateo and the others. "The smiths who used to live here," Ester said quickly, "were they unharmed when they left Augustin? Did the Sovereign or his son enslave them the way they enslaved you?"

Hartlan finally opened his eyes. There was clarity there. "I remember now. They're dead. All of them."

"What?" Ester asked. Her voice came out small.

"Your attitude reminds me of someone I once read about," he almost whispered. The sword in his arm shifted as though he were steeling himself to strike.

Her mind reeled. All she could do was stand there, watching as he took another step closer. "Your name isn't Jesmon, is it?" he asked.

Her mind roared. Her brothers and sisters were dead. It took a moment to process his question—she thought about it, realized that admitting the truth made no difference. Nothing did anymore. "No. It's Ester."

"I figured as much. What other smith would have the gall to break into such a place? I read of you in Mateo's journal. He wrote about you extensively. He mentioned how you wanted to fight the Sovereign because you were afraid. Afraid of a great many things. Of the Sovereign in particular and what he might do."

"I guess I can die with my brothers and sisters knowing I was right. The Sovereign doesn't believe in negotiation or compromise. He doesn't respect the will of others."

"You talk of the same person who brought two hundred years of peace to Mira."

The Sovereign had brought an unprecedented era of peace to the territories, but at what cost? The Sovereign had killed everyone Ester considered family. Everyone except her real blood. And to her that was a death sentence. So long as she was alive, she would do everything in her power to carry out the sentence.

She regained her composure. She wouldn't let Mateo and the others die in vain. She would escape this nightmare and get her revenge. "Everyone commits evil at some point in their life. It's part of being human," she said. "But a leader isn't supposed to act like the rest of us. They're held to a higher standard."

When Hartlan's muscles tensed and his front foot shifted forward, she knew he was about to attack. She dove to the side and let the torch clatter to the stone, and the hilt of her sword dug painfully into her side as she rolled and sprang to her feet. She managed to pull her sword out to keep him from slicing her head in two, but the tip of his blade grazed her jaw, lining it with fire.

He sneered. She needed to interrogate him, to figure out what else he knew, to force him to reveal everything, but that sneer, that god-awful sneer, sent her moving forward before she could stop herself.

His reflexes were too quick, even for an elemental. He didn't need his metal working to help him, but Ester needed hers just to survive. He moved like a wraith in the dim light of the still-burning torch on the ground. Soon he was forcing her back, and half of Ester's concentration was set on backpedaling in a circle so he couldn't press her against a wall.

He was winning and he knew it. Ester stumbled back, and it left an opening for a killing blow, but he didn't take it.

"How long have you been working for the Sovereign?" she asked between labored breaths.

"I don't work for him," he said. "I only do what must be done to ensure peace."

"Then how long have you been *ensuring peace* as a member of the Foundry?" She needed to buy time, though she wasn't sure for what. Asking about his past seemed to work well as a distraction. "None of your Saracostan brothers and sisters could have been smiths for long. I've seen the steel you all have been making. It's as if none of you remember your apprenticeships."

"We do as well as we can while we attend to more important matters," he said, angrier than she expected, "such as calming the chaos of the masses."

"That doesn't excuse anything. The smiths are embarrassing themselves. Nobody is going to believe we're true servants of Fheldspra if we can't properly work with His fire."

"We are doing our best, despite our limitations," Hartlan said through gritted teeth.

"Limitations?"

Hartlan didn't answer, and Ester continued, speaking quickly before he could think to attack again, "There's something wrong with you. With all of you. You can't work metal. You're not elemental."

Hartlan growled like a ravine wolf, a sound so inhuman it made Ester's skin prickle. He surged forward, but not toward her—he moved for the torch that still lay on the ground, its fire almost out. She threw herself at him, knowing it could easily get her killed, but an idea had struck her in an instant and she needed to act before it was too late. She collided with Hartlan. He'd been too fixated on the torch and hadn't expected her to go on the offense, and he stumbled until he fell, tumbling into the stained-glass cauldron. Ester kicked the torch and sent it ricocheting off the wall, scattering its fuel and fire across the ground.

The light winked out, casting the two of them in blackness. Ester opened herself up to her metal working and saw with her power Hartlan's silvery blade floating before her. Hartlan's footsteps skittered across the stone, but not toward her. He was going for the front door, likely for the light where he could see her. Without any elemental power, he was as blind as anyone else here.

She followed him into the front room, tracking him through his weapon, and slashed at where she figured his body might be. He cried out and there was a meaty smack as he hit the floor. Silence followed.

Hartlan's sword came off the ground. He was still alive. There was the sound of swishing robes and sandals clacking on the floor as he brandished his blade, and he swung with vicious speed, but she was ten feet away now.

"How are you not a real smith?" she asked the darkness. She stepped closer, and his blade waved frantically, blindingly fast to a non-iron worker.

"Don't be stupid," he hissed, the words tainted with fear.

It suddenly made sense why the Foundry was forging weapons that were sub-standard—it wasn't because the smiths were shirking their sacred duties, but because Hartlan and the others weren't real iron workers. He tested the blackness with another swing, but Ester was well beyond arm's reach.

"Is the Sovereign planning to visit any of the other Foundries?" she asked.

"This isn't a conversation anymore, young smith. This is retribution for your sins. Drop your weapon."

"Answer the question and I won't kill you."

A pause. "I don't know."

"How else will he 'ensure peace'?"

"Radavich hasn't declared a new magnate." His voice quivered. "He plans to place another there, just as he did with Magnate Crosby. Beyond that, I do not know his plans."

"And our new magnate. Where did he come from?"

Silence stretched through the long seconds as the occasional drop of blood splashed against the stone, but however Ester had managed to hurt Hartlan, the wound didn't seem to bother him. More of her fear crept in. She was still terrified of the man. "Answer me," she said.

"Crosby's been here, in Augustin. Always."

"Then why hasn't anyone recognized him?"

"Because the Sovereign and his son changed him. Molded him into someone new, someone fit to represent the Sovereign."

"I don't understand."

"You would if you knew the true nature of elemental power."

Old conversations ran through Ester's head. Mateo had told her that rhidium bonded to the natural iron in the human body, and the binding allowed one to manipulate the iron around them. A smith couldn't push and pull the iron inside another person for the same reason she couldn't control a rock with trace amounts of iron in it. It needed to consist almost entirely of the element she controlled before she could affect it. Then she could bend and break it to her will.

A coldness settled in her stomach when she realized what Hartlan was implying. "People are made of elements, same as anything else. Are the Sovereign and his son bound to all the elements that make up a human body?"

"They are."

"And you're saying… they turned one person into someone else?"

"It's a messy process. Most of the meat and bone stay the same, but move the face around, change the height, and tune the thing inside your head that lets you think, and the person to come out of the process is completely new. Evolved."

Ester's chest suddenly felt too small for her heart. Her breathing rattled. Her throat felt dry, her tongue spongy. "And my old brothers and sisters? Master Smith Mateo and Senior Arc Smith Panqao? Helcia and Artur? Did they go to Saracosta with the Sovereign?"

"No."

The urge to vomit almost overwhelmed her. The only thing that stopped her was knowing Hartlan might catch her by surprise and attack her if she lost her composure. By now he would know where she was by the sound of her voice.

"Panqao," Hartlan said.

"What about him?"

"I know that name. It was mine."

There was no way the man who was once Senior Arc Smith Panqao was standing before her. Panqao was stern, bullheaded, and someone who inspired others, despite his severities. Hartlan was… much of the same. Ester choked out a sob, unable to hold it back, but Hartlan didn't advance.

"No," she choked out. "Panqao was supposed to start his pilgrimage to the Star Mines after I left Augustin."

"Spare me if I can prove it, all right?"

"All right," Ester heard herself say.

Another pause. "The Sovereign left a little more of me behind so I could keep a clear head. Mateo's journal helps as well. I read it every passing. I believe it's become an addiction at this point." A small, self-conscious laugh. "It's mostly the fear I remember. The terror that my brothers and sisters and everyone I loved would soon die, and that the erratic decisions of the young, blinded by idealism, would destroy us all."

Ester attacked in a rage, snarling as she catapulted forward. Hartlan swung fast enough to bisect her if the blow had landed, but she moved in on the back swing and felt her blade sink through flesh, all the way to the hilt. Hartlan gurgled, the wet sounds of rushing blood rising out of his throat, and then the sound of metal and flesh colliding with stone echoing through the darkness.

She waited several heartbeats, but silence enveloped her. She inched forward, almost jumping when her boot touched Hartlan's body, but the master smith didn't move. She felt for the dead torch he'd been holding and found it in a warm puddle. She brought it to the tinder box, where she stuffed more fuel into the beacon and re-lit it, and found Hartlan staring sightlessly at the frescoes on the ceiling.

The stained-glass cauldron still waited for her in the shrine room, but where it had stood innocuously before, it now exuded evil. And the scent of blood, of course. The smell of change.

She gathered her things and ran. The rational part of her knew only dark corners and stale air lurked in the villa, but a creeping sense of horror drove her out of there as quickly as possible.

Chapter 26—Jakar

THE SCOUT WHO had notified me of Darkwater moving Namira filled the doorway, his friend in tow. "We're here for our money," he said.

I'd been sitting with Shirallah on the roof of the safehouse doing my best to avoid Geth, which Shirallah had accepted without question. More than once I considered asking him what he saw in Geth, but given my history with romantic partners, I didn't have much room to judge, so I'd settled for enjoying his silent company while smoking from a pipe he'd lent me. Suyaday was my current poison—it was a calming herb endemic to Sulian Daw that I hadn't had the pleasure of experiencing in years. Letting the smoke sear my lungs while I stared at the glittering stalactites hundreds of feet above our head actually made me miss my home country.

"A little eager, are we not?" Shirallah said to the pair of scouts. "Why do you not fulfill your side of the bargain and tell us where Namira is, and then the dymium can be discussed with Geth?"

"Gorgo says he did what was asked. He met with your friend, gave her the information, so now we want what was earned."

"How is it you mean?"

The scout who had followed Namira spoke in rapid-fire Xerivian, and Shirallah moved to his feet. "Efadora and Torlo have met with Gorgo at the fishery already," he said to me.

I jumped up, my chair scraping over the tile until it tipped over. "Where did they take Namira?"

"Beyond the west gate, to the Sihraan city."

I pounded down the steps into the safehouse, leaving the scouts' protestations behind. My bags lay stuffed under my cot in our quarters, and I dug through them until I found that the compounds I'd created were missing. Shirallah watched from the doorway, and Geth appeared at his side. "Efadora and Torlo went into the ruins to find Namira," I said. "I'm going after them."

"Girl's got a backbone of diamond," Geth said, and grinned.

This was my fault. I should've known what my words would do—it took weeks after leaving Augustin before I could even say Sara's name around her. If she went for Namira right after leaving the library, that put her an hour ahead of me. I shoved my way past Geth and ran for the hidden exit.

People struggled to move out of my way as I hurried through Ravada's streets. Old Ravada was packed with people celebrating Marking the Fall. I bolted through slow crowds walking along gently sloping lawns and passed between two fortresses where the ancient battle had taken place. Hundreds of angry faces turned toward me and my disrespect. I stuck out horribly, but it couldn't be helped. A confrontation with Darkwater was inevitable anyway. I glanced back and caught a glimpse of Shirallah's head above the crowd and Geth's determined face as they tried to keep up.

The crowds in the caverns outside the western gate were thick. "Above and below," Geth said when he caught up. I stared at the wreckage at the base of the switchbacks leading to the ruins—bystanders lingered around the shattered barricades of a Darkwater checkpoint, and fractured rock and ruined vegetation lay scattered off the road where something had exploded. A regiment from the Ravada military pushed back the bystanders while others stood over a handful of bodies among the barricades. None of the bodies looked like Efadora or Torlo.

"Stay out of the way. Got it?" I said to Geth. I wasn't in the mood to deal with his dodgy remarks. He answered with a smile and stepped away, pulling Shirallah back by the hand.

I pushed my way to the front of the crowd, where soldiers waited with sharp words and sharper swords. "Where's Efadora?" I asked the closest one.

"Nast zad," he growled, pointing to the other bystanders who kept their distance.

"Where is Efadora?" I repeated, shouting this time, capturing the attention of his comrades.

The soldiers spoke amongst themselves, and I wasn't surprised when some of them tried to subtly reposition themselves around me. A darker part of me had hoped they'd recognize me. I imagined them hurting Efadora, throwing her in chains and handing her over to Darkwater, where she would be tortured for escaping the way Darkwater property never should. I pictured them killing her so they could take away her ultimate purpose. Her life and her future. A killing light burned bright inside me.

I punched the closest soldier in the throat and pulled his sword from his sheath as he collapsed in a choking heap. Fifty Darkwater guards drew their weapons, and the bystanders pushed at each other to get away, but I threw the sword as hard as I could before the regiment could react, guiding it with my power. It arced over the crowd and hit the wall next to the tunnel above the switchbacks, sinking halfway into the rock. The guards advanced, but my boots scratched against dirt as I bolted sideways. A broken stalagmite waited ahead, the top half blown off by the explosion, and I jumped, skipping off the top and catapulting myself at the wall. I crunched against lichen and bounced off the surface, sailing toward a stalactite hanging from the ceiling. I pushed off that one and landed on the top of the ridge.

A dozen soldiers huffed up the start of the switchbacks, but they paused when they saw me looking down on them. A sergeant shouted and they continued forward.

I slammed my fist on the ridge's lip and a deep crack echoed through the cavern. I jumped, sailing toward the stalactite above my head, and kicked it hard enough to cleave the rock. It sent me tumbling back to the ridge, and I hit the ground awkwardly, my head bouncing off the rock as a roar filled the air and the ground shook.

My ears rang, the sound morphing into the terrible sound of the top of the ridge and the stalactite collapsing together. The part of the ridge I'd dislodged had crumbled into dozens of pieces—a few of them were big enough to crush anyone in their path—but it was enough to destabilize the switchbacks and the path up, the debris rolling and sliding into the checkpoint. The bystanders and soldiers managed to run clear of the destruction before they could be hit by anything bigger than pebbles or the cloud of dust that spread in a wave.

Soon the cloud separated me from everyone else. It probably hadn't been wise to advertise my power like that, but it was going to be hard enough dealing with Darkwater without the enemy trying to flank me. I rubbed my head, trying to shake the ache behind my eyes, then dislodged the sword and took off down the tunnel.

Navigating the tunnels was easy—all I had to do was follow the quartz crystals hanging from chains along the carefully manicured path Darkwater had created for their carts. A breeze from the cavern up ahead hit me, and I slowed down to feel for the weapons hanging at the sides of any Darkwater security ahead.

By now I was used to the brightness of my Eye. I had the new element I was bound to to thank for the near-blinding light, though I still wasn't sure what that element could be. As I peered through the glittering spectrum, I noticed something strange.

A wall of blackness waited inside the rock ahead, like a

void lurking behind a sea of stars, and I moved closer, my lips parting in awe. The wall extended in every direction with a narrow opening where the tunnel was, but the wall revealed no hint of any elements I was bound to. It seemed impossible. Every rock contained *something* I could control, especially with my last binding. I reached the section of tunnel where the hidden wall was buried in the rock, and I dug until I found it. It was as thick as I was tall, and black. No, blacker than black, blacker than the absence of all light, and harder than diamond, though I had no way of testing it.

I closed my eyes again and noticed how the hidden wall curved ever so slightly as it extended beyond the sight of my Eye. Was it a buried dome, or maybe an orb? It couldn't be a coincidence that the one place this hidden, impenetrable wall had an opening was where the tunnel happened to be. The wall's purpose was to protect the ruins. But from what?

This was so far beyond the capabilities of a thousand primordia working together. None of them could even exert their power on this wall—it consisted of base elements I couldn't puzzle out. Whatever the answer to this question was, it would have to wait for another time.

I took off again, and another breeze hit my face, cool and wet. An opening appeared ahead, full of diffuse light, and I came to a familiar ridge overlooking a city that was far from abandoned. Everything had changed in the last month. Instead of dim light from geodes and fireflies struggling to eat at the edges of a dark, cavernous space, part of the city glowed and filled the place with ambient light. The active area of the city shrieked from ten thousand hinges in desperate need of oil, and I could see spurts of steam and shuddering copper pipes even from here. There was a distant sound of metal striking stone from what sounded like a pipe bursting. This place needed a lot of work. It would take months to repair just the technology anyone understood.

Hundreds of Darkwater employees and thousands of serfs and slaves toiled among the ruins, and worry started to set in.

Had Efadora and Torlo made it this far, or were they in one of the side tunnels? Was I too late? The scaffolding of ramps and pulleys attached to the ridge shuddered as a line of carts pulled by short-faced salamanders trudged their way up, and I took several steps back. With a running start I leapt, flying over the street until I landed on the roof of the closest building. A man popped his head out of a hole in the ceiling, then shouted something incoherent before disappearing again.

He reappeared and my heart skipped. I scrambled off the side of the building, and as I tumbled over the eaves, I heard the faint *ping* of the rail weapon in the man's hands followed by a piercing crash. I landed on the street below, and I looked up to see a cloud of dust near the cavern wall where the projectile had struck.

Of course, Darkwater found more rail weapons. How many were lying around in the ruins? Most of the city was still dormant, and who knows what secrets waited in the darkness.

The man leaned over the top of the building and aimed. I dove, and the place where I'd been standing exploded. The projectile had moved through my elemental senses, sending massive waves through the electromagnetic field, and I knew it would be far too much energy to divert if the man's aim was true.

I took off, turning a street corner before he could fire again. More Darkwater guards rushed out of a half-destroyed building, all four of them brandishing rail weapons, and they took aim as one.

I made a pushing motion, and the weapons were ripped from their hands and sailed down the white-cobbled street. One of the weapons discharged mid-air, and a projectile crashed into a pillar with a shriek as the rail weapons clattered across the rock. Shadows inside doorways and on balconies shifted and more Darkwater security appeared.

This was going to be harder than I thought.

Chapter 27—Efadora

THERE WAS DEFINITELY no shortage of goodies hiding among the ruins. I'd managed to conceal Torlo in a cubby before venturing into the darker parts of the city, only to come across weapons and armor scattered around the streets and in the buildings. The Archives had no idea what had happened to the Sihraans, and it was a question they'd been trying to answer for centuries, but my guess was that the ones here, at least, had died fighting for their lives. There were no bodies hiding in the armor or clutching the weapons, though.

I passed through marble columns and entered a building with wide steps that reminded me of the Foundry back home. The similarities in the architecture couldn't be a coincidence. Maybe there was a relationship? I smiled, wondering if real cartographers ran through the same threads of logic when they explored old ruins. A great hall waited for me beyond the main doors, with balconies along the sides and a dais at the end that sported eleven chairs. The floor seemed to have once been covered with a massive mural, but the paint had long since crumbled to colored dust. Metal rods rusted to almost nothing stuck out of the wall above the dais, and I got the impression they'd once hung flags.

This hall was for large ceremonies, and I'd seen enough chairs on raised platforms to know rulers once presided here. A lone set of armor sat in the chair to the far left, and a weapon lay discarded at the chair's foot that looked different from the one in my hand. The chamber swallowed the sound of my footsteps as I ran for the dais. The weapon had a narrow tube in lieu of two rods, and a set of coils spiraled around the tube along with a trigger on the handle like the rail weapon. I equipped my new find and aimed at a wall.

The trigger was hard to pull, and at first I thought it was broken. The longer I put pressure on the trigger, though, the louder the weapon whined. Goosebumps spread across my arms and the little hairs on them stood up. The trigger clicked, and a whip-crack sound erupted from the end.

A glowing white bolt as thin as a needle struck the wall, and the impact point turned red hot, sending bits of melted rock to the floor. "Oh, fhelfire." The weapon was warm, but not hot, and still seemed to be in the same shape—good news, considering rail weapons only had five or six good shots in them before the rods warped.

Uneasiness crept in as I thought about weapons this powerful lying around in a city whose inhabitants had disappeared without a trace. Sure, cartographers put the Sihraan's extinction event eighteen hundred or so years ago, but I eyed the yawning hall anyway. Glowing spores floated off moss that grew along the dark balconies, too faint to provide meaningful light, and I told myself that nothing more than faded decay and dust lurked inside the antechambers and hallways sprouting off the main hall. Nothing more. Right? There was no use lingering here, I told myself. This was too much dead space for my liking anyway. Too many shadows.

I hid inside doorways and behind corners as I made my way back to the lit-up portions of the city, waiting for gangs of Darkwater security to pound past. They moved fast, talking in low, panicked voices, all headed toward the ridge with the exit. Maybe it was Jakar? The possibility softened my nerves. I was such an idiot for getting mad at him, but that couldn't be helped. Whatever it was, maybe it would give me enough of a distraction to find Arhan and Namira.

Darkwater had nailed signs written in Xerivian to some of the buildings, and it was easier than I thought to guess what they meant. Karatoa, long-term storage. Karatoa, short-term storage. Yarokly, short-term storage. Byssa, late shipments. Manasus, late shipments. Was Darkwater relocating their warehouse here? It made sense, considering how much real estate it offered them, and it let them operate beyond the prying eyes of the city. In fact, they were technically in the Rift instead of Xeriv, which meant they wouldn't have to bow to any regulations. Did that mean they wouldn't have to release the serfs who were signed under the contracts we destroyed?

My lip curled. Large businesses like Darkwater would do anything to hold on to what they had.

I paused when I saw a sign labeled Nichyakoz. It literally translated to 'timing,' but Geth taught me that nichyakoz colloquially meant 'prison,' since Xeriv's nazil cas, who recorded the movements of the moon to track time, called time a prison that all countries were forced to march to. I headed inside with the coil weapon aimed at eye level, finding the place unguarded thanks in all likelihood to the commotion on the other side of the city, and found people tied to rockwood posts.

"Efadora?" Namira called out. She sat against a post next to a water bowl and a bucket for shitting, her skin spotted with bruises and her hair hanging in a ratted mess.

I hurried to her side and pulled out my knife, then cut into the rope around her wrists. "I ran into a few snags," I said as I sawed, "but better late than never."

Her laugh evolved into a mix of choking and hacking. "Are the others with you?" she asked, her voice hoarse.

"No." I helped her to her feet, and she leaned against the post. "Help," one of the other captives wheezed, and I cut the man's bonds, too. "Who are these people?" I asked as I worked my way down the line.

"Slaves and serfs who tried to escape when they moved us out of Ravada," Namira said. She grunted when she tried to walk. "Ankle's sprained, I think."

I offered her the knife when I finished, then equipped the coil weapon. "Everyone follow me," I said. Some of them didn't react, and I couldn't tell if it was because they didn't understand me or because they weren't interested in following a sixteen-year-old, but enough of them moved that the rest followed. I peeked out the front door and bolted for the other side of the street. Namira stayed close behind, but as soon as we were in the open, the others ran for the shadows in the dormant parts of the city.

"Spineless," Namira said.

"They're scared," I said. "One less problem to worry about anyway."

She eyed me, and I expected ten different colors of resentment to fill her gaze, about how I had gotten her captured and likely tortured, but her expression was unreadable. A weighty silence filled the gap between us.

The look faded. "Now we kill Captain Asshole, yes?" she asked.

For some reason, hearing the plan out loud made me uncomfortable. Killing Arhan was a deep, private thing, but when someone else said it, it gave it definition in a way that only made it sound stupid. Why go for a kill on Arhan when finding a way out or helping Torlo was the smarter choice?

But when would I find a better time? "Do you know where he's at?"

"Follow me."

We skirted the edge where darkness met the city's shuddering pipes and flickering lights, moving between carts half-filled with refuse and sleeping fountains inside barren gardens. Serfs and slaves noticed us as their overseers were distracted by the sounds of fighting and shattering rock echoed over the building tops, but they didn't point us out. I pressed a finger to my lips from the shadows, and they only offered blank and bleak looks.

It would've been so easy for them to have given us up, but they didn't. We snuck past gaggles of laborers and the occasional patrol that rushed toward the gentle boom of fighting.

"There," Namira whispered, pointing at a building against the cavern wall. "Darkwater gave Arhan his own headquarters, the prick. They think he's training some special elite regiment. He beat me in front of them for one of his lessons."

We entered the squat building, my coil weapon at the ready. We came into a square chamber, with bedrolls in one corner and a training area in the other, and Arhan was in the middle of talking to two dozen of his bootlickers. All of them turned.

"Can't hear the fighting outside?" I asked. "Or are you hoping someone else will do the dirty work for you?"

"You," Arhan said. "I should have figured. It's always you. Higher-ups thought it was the Balog Brotherhood finally making a move on this place, but they know shit-all." He wore a crisp uniform, and his auburn beard was freshly trimmed, the white streak through it as bright as the look in his eyes. He wasn't afraid. He carried a rail weapon, his underlings bearing swords, but he was smart enough to keep his weapon pointed at the floor.

"Darkwater's higher-ups are here?"

"Some of them are, and it's our duty to protect them. Best that you lay down that toy of yours and surrender before you get hurt."

That patented, smug condescension of his caused all my hatred to bubble to the surface again. "I'm going to hurt you ten different ways, and then I'm going to kill you."

"The shit you won't. Wanna know why? Because I know about the Archives training you to become one of them, and with the amount of pull I have, I've already made sure you won't get a single gig in and out of Xeriv. Everyone already knows your name and your face as Darkwater's escaped serf, and they know the kind of wrath they'll get buried under if they even sniff your direction. You'll die penniless, and you'll die as nothing. Not unless you set that weapon down and surrender.

Show me such a gesture, and I'll make sure to take you under my wing. Every guard captain needs a guide, after all. You'll have a reputation someday, even as a serf. It's not too late to start rubbing shoulders with the right people." He glanced at his subordinates as he said this last part.

The delusions of grandeur were so extreme that I wanted to vomit. I also wanted to laugh. He sounded just like Sara. She'd once tricked me into thinking money and notoriety were important, but she'd been talking to a different Efadora back then. "You have no idea why I want to be a cartographer."

"And why's that?"

His eyes flicked from me to my weapon, and even from here I could see the bead of sweat on his forehead shining in the firelight. His fear was obvious through all that bravado. I weighed my options, realized I had once again rushed into a situation I wasn't prepared for—even if I could kill Arhan, there were still all his bootlickers to contend with.

"Look at your boss," I said to them. "Look at how nervous he is."

"Fuck you," Arhan spat.

"Has he told you about me? I bet you can tell how badly I've gotten under his skin. What you don't know is that I'm only sixteen. You think you can follow someone who can't even handle a kid?"

None of them moved, but I could tell my words resonated. Arhan could, too.

"Don't listen to the bitch," he said. "She doesn't know what she's talking about."

He didn't hear the whine of the coil weapon firing up until it was too late. The white-hot beam clipped him as it sliced through the air between a pair of bootlickers, melting a hole in the back wall. Arhan's rail weapon clattered to the floor and he screamed, clenching his hand while the other guards spread out.

"Stay where you are," I yelled at everyone, using the voice I'd learned as an Augustin infanta, the one people couldn't help but listen to. They examined the coil weapon fearfully as

I continued to aim it at their captain. They could have easily rushed me, but I smirked at them despite my nervousness. "The first person to move gets a bolt through the heart," I said.

They obeyed. I was playing the hardest confidence game I'd ever been part of yet, but my time running with the gangs of Manasus had inoculated me against showing signs of weakness when my life was on the line. I could do this. I was a teenager in the middle of enemy territory standing a hair's breadth away from throwing her life away, but I could do this. Part of Arhan's rail weapon glowed from where my coil weapon had melted it, and wisps of smoke trailed off Arhan where he clutched his hand. I caught the whiff of burning meat.

"I told you I'd hurt you," I said.

"Get her," Arhan shouted, his eyes wide with pain and rage. "You're half a platoon. She'll barely get a shot or two off before you overwhelm her."

None of them moved. None of them even reached for their weapons. They were private security, where loyalty didn't work quite the same, not to mention the fear and uncertainty in their eyes, as well as a look I'd come to notice from time to time growing up. An occasional look the nobiletza had offered Father when his back was turned.

"You don't inspire them half as well as you think you do," I said. I steeled myself, pushing my nervousness even deeper as I took what would have been seen as an arrogant step forward. It got the reaction I'd hoped for—everyone took a step back. That's when I knew I had them. I had control of the room.

"On your knees," I said to Arhan, who was still on his ass clutching his hand between his thighs. "I want to look you in the eye when I kill you."

Our eyes finally met, and there was the unchecked terror I'd glimpsed once or twice since meeting him. His eyes were wet, and the tops of his cheeks puckered. "Please," he said. "I'm sorry. I got too ahead of myself. When you're on top of the hill long enough, sometimes a man forgets he can always get knocked off."

"Above and below, shut up with the metaphors and the lessons for once in your life." I looked at the others. "Do any of you really have patience for this garbage?"

Twenty sets of eyes mirrored the same discomfort. No doubt they were taught never to disparage a superior. "Just answer," I said. "He's dead anyway."

"Well…" a boy about Torlo's age, except a little shorter, said slowly. "We just let him have his fun because the job pays well and it's a good stepping stone."

"Sulf-spit," Arhan groaned.

"He is not wrong," another said tremulously, her voice thick with a harsher Yaroklan accent. "We let you say such things because it is obvious you love the sound of your voice."

And there it was. A fracturing of the delusion. Reality started to sink in, and I reveled in the way his mouth dropped and how he stared at a spot on my leg with a mixture of dumb anger and hurt. I straightened my grip on the coil weapon, and the sound brought Arhan's attention back to what was about to happen.

"Don't kill me," he said. Tears rolled down his cheeks until a rough sound caught in his throat, which he tried to swallow. "I'm not ready."

I recalled all my reasons for hurting him, savoring the moment before I pulled the trigger, and an ugly thought came to me, by itself enough to melt a hole through Arhan's face. His need to be liked reminded me of *her*, but then why did Jakar say the same thing about me? There was a flash of anger toward Jakar, but then I started to think—to truly think—about why he said it.

Trying to kill Arhan had got Namira captured. It had gotten Torlo hurt. I thought about it some more, realizing that once I'd decided Arhan needed to die, it had shaped almost every decision I'd made since. Everything except becoming a cartographer. I couldn't be moved once my mind was set on something. Just like Father. Just like Sara.

So much of Arhan reminded me of my sister—it was why I was dead set on getting my revenge on him—but all this work to get to this place, where I had my weapon trained on his forehead and all I had to do was pull the trigger, had turned me into her.

The acid in me churned. I would have loved to end this pathetic person's existence, but faults above, what would that prove? I lowered my weapon.

The captain's awkward sobs echoed through the chamber. His subordinates watched, and their fear of me transformed into embarrassment for their captain.

"Shoot him," Namira said.

I stepped away, bumping into her, but she got the hint and started backing up, letting out a grunt of frustration. The guards only watched. I was just happy others saw in Arhan what had always been clear to me.

People were supposed to feel a level of peace, or a weight lift off their shoulders upon doing right for themselves, but all I felt was a strange detachment. I'd always known there was something wrong with me—what sort of sane person feels nothing when they hurt someone, when they take a person's life?—and a thought crossed my mind, a hope that this decision would have made Emil proud. The thought finally made me feel something. It wasn't happiness, but something deeper. A contentedness? Maybe that's what doing the right thing was supposed to feel like, even if the impulsive part of my brain was warring with me to go back and burn a hole through Arhan's head.

I kept the coil weapon trained on the door as we crossed the street, but no one came out. "That was stupid," Namira said.

"Probably."

"How do we get out of here?"

The ground trembled as what sounded like half a building crashed into the ground several blocks away. "We need to get Torlo," I said. "We can't risk Darkwater finding him or him getting hurt in the fighting."

Namira protested as I ran toward the destruction, but she followed anyway.

Chapter 28—Jakar

THE PATTER OF arrows and the occasional rail-accelerated bolt dogged me through the maze of streets and buildings. I jumped and pushed off a balcony railing, pulled myself past a window and climbed the façade, shrieking projectiles blasting chunks out of the marble below. I reached the roof and sprinted for the opposite edge, then jumped to the next building. Guards shouted, trying to keep up while they gave chase on the streets below.

I landed on the parapet of a watch tower. A small force clustered along the street, all of them craning their necks in my direction, and I ducked as rock turned to dust near my face. They were getting more accurate. Those weapons would be unstoppable with enough practice. Darkwater would be unstoppable.

I descended into the watch tower, struggling to find my way through the faint glow of lightcaps, and almost tripped over one of the many suits of armor lying around the city without a body inside them. I made a cutting motion with my hand against the wall facing the street of guards, slicing into the rock as I walked the watchtower's perimeter. Stone cracked at the seam I created, then a section of the tower wall and its roof slid into the air.

City lights filled the space I was in as a twenty-foot length of marble fell to the street below. For two heartbeats all I heard was panic and the whoosh of a terrible weight, then the tower shuddered, and a great sound filled the cavern.

I climbed onto what little of the roof was left and jumped to the next building. I moved from roof to roof while dust and bits of lichen floated down from the cavern ceiling, shaken loose by the collapsing marble. Someone was shouting orders near the cavern wall, their words colored with incoherent rage, and I made my way toward them. It was time to find Efadora. The thought of killing Darkwater security had made me sick enough to my stomach that I'd held off taking any lives, but in the long run my conscience would only get me killed. I couldn't play cat-and-mouse in the ruins forever.

Two men had their backs to the cavern wall and raged at a gaggle of overseers and a few dozen Darkwater security, and I ducked when their eyes roamed the streets and the tops of the buildings. Judging by the vibrant reds and blues of their robes and the bejeweled scabbards at their waists, they were in charge of things around here. Not a rail weapon was in sight. Maybe they'd overcommitted their men to searching for me in the city.

I landed on the street next to a shivering length of pipe that whistled with steam, and the group jumped at the sound of me hitting the curb. I took a few steps toward them, trying not to startle the guards into nocking the bows at their sides. "I'm looking for someone," I said.

The men in the colorful robes spoke to each other in Xerivian before one of them said to me, "This person. How do they look?"

"A teenage girl. She's short with chopped black hair."

"Ah, yes, yes. I know of this girl you speak about. You will leave us alone if we give her to you?"

I nodded. "She's all I want."

"Yes, yes. A deal is struck. *Khasalé*. We shall fetch this girl. Wait for some moment."

The man snapped his fingers and his partner shuffled to the closest building. As we waited, I realized the silence wasn't as tense as I expected. I checked the streets and corridors for

Darkwater guards rounding the corner with weapons drawn, but all was calm in this part of the city. Colorful Robes leaned against the cavern wall with arms crossed, as if this was one of many business transactions he made each passing. Come to think of it, it was rather convenient they were holding Efadora nearby, or that the men had so easily agreed to hand her over. And why wasn't he afraid? I closed my eyes, let out a slow breath to center myself, and reached out with my Eye.

I dove to the side. There was a shriek and the sound of exploding rock, then someone was screaming. A guard's leg had been shot by one of two men half-obscured by the window behind me, hiding in shadow and the whine of steam, the rails to their weapons glowing orange in the darkness. They left their hiding spot with weapons aimed at my torso.

"You are the Iron Sorrow, are you not?" Colorful Robes asked. More screaming followed the question, the wounded guard lying in the street, his blood pouring into the crevices of the cobblestones. Concerned friends moved closer to the man, but their employer paid them no heed, pushing through the line to stare me down. "Yes, yes," Colorful Robes continued. "A Sulian man of great power books passage from Mira and signs a debt with us, only to bring trouble and despair upon Darkwater for... what? You follow an appetite you could not sate on Mira's trade roads?"

The wounded man's cries faded, and his eyes closed. I wasn't the one who hurt him, but it felt like I was, and reality came crashing down. So much pain. "I don't want to hurt anyone," I said, failing to project a confident voice. "I just want to find my sister and go."

"You have done far too much damage to simply walk away, yes, yes. There must be consequences to your actions."

Slaves and serfs alike had grouped behind carts further down the street or were hiding behind buildings, watching. They had dirty faces, ripped rags for clothing, and behind the hopelessness in their eyes, the hint of something more. My guilt faded, replaced by anger.

"You will submit yourself to sedation until we understand what it is you can do, or you will die." Colorful Robes's companion appeared with a glass vial while the two with the rail weapons continued to keep careful aim. These people had set up a trap, I realized, and I fell into it because I'd been so desperate to find Efadora and not hurt anyone else.

"No!" someone shouted. It came from one of the building's doorways, near where the men with the rail weapons stood, and a body shot out of the darkness, sprinting for the guards. It was Torlo, covered in marbled dust. Shirallah appeared a moment later, though he looked to be running after Torlo and not toward the guards. Blood coated the side of Torlo's head.

The armed men hesitated before taking their sights off me, offering Torlo enough time to close the distance. He tackled one of them and sent the man's weapon clattering to the rock, and then Shirallah was following up, reaching the second man as the guard swung his rail weapon around. Shirallah grabbed one of the glowing rails and let out a cry as he ripped the weapon away.

"Shirallah!" Geth yelled. The cartographer materialized out of the doorway and ran after Shirallah as his partner grappled with the guard. Geth was wielding a short sword, and he plunged it into the guard's stomach before the man could get the better of Shirallah. He advanced on the other one, who had left Torlo on the ground in a daze, and cut him down.

I strode toward Colorful Robes as he stumbled back and tripped over the guard with the gored leg, splashing into the pool of blood. I grabbed a handful of his robes, yanking, and ripped away a strip of cloth worth more than all the wealth I'd ever owned. I knelt next to the unconscious guard to wrap it around his thigh, above the wound. "Help him," I said to one of the others. "Also, give me that."

A guard pulled the axe hanging from his belt and handed it over with nervous fingers. I pulled my blood-slicked hands away, and he took my spot as I adjusted my grip on the axe and advanced on Colorful Robes.

The man scrambled to his feet and pushed his back to the

cavern wall. "You will not do this," he said. "I am only one of the six Darkwater *kiract*. Killing me will accomplish little."

"What is little to you is the world to someone else," I said. I'd resolved not to take a life if I could avoid it, but I had come to a realization upon looking at all the serfs and slaves surrounding us. There was irredeemable evil out there, and it needed to die, even if it killed a part of me to make it so. Sacrificing my wellbeing so that I could help the slaves and the serfs of the world was a small price to pay.

The cut was clean. The axe eased through flesh, cracked past bone, and banged into the rock behind Color Robes until it wedged itself in place. His head balanced on the axe head with a look of dumb surprise, then toppled forward. Visceral images of the Granite Road struck me, and I trembled, nearly overcome, but I managed to hold onto my composure and turn to those who'd been watching.

The slaves and serfs waiting in the wings came closer as shock, denial, and hope warred on their faces. Geth was tending to Shirallah and Torlo—Torlo looked like he'd been wounded before showing up, and sat drunkenly on the stone while Shirallah nursed his own burned hand—and Geth left their side in a rage. He grabbed the robed man holding the sedative, who struggled under Geth's grip while he dragged him to me. "Kill this walking can of garbage," he said.

I yanked the sword out of Sedative's jeweled scabbard—he was so incompetent he'd forgotten he was armed—and took Geth's place. "Not yet."

Shirallah helped Torlo to his feet and came to our side. "We must return to Ravada as soon as we are able," he said breathlessly, and offered a pained smile. "I will need to treat this burn." His palm was seared black and red, and some of the skin had been torn off. "Torlo has been concussed, too. He is unwell."

Geth moved for the building they'd emerged from, likely to grab their supplies, and said, "Run some cold water for the burn and I—"

"Wait," I said.

Geth paused. "Like the depths—"

A contingent of guards rounded a corner, huffing and running. They skidded to a stop twenty feet away and brought their rail weapons to bear. I pulled Sedative until he stood between me and them. "Tell them it's time to leave," I said.

Sedative looked from me to his guards, then to his sword in my hand, and barked something in Xerivian. The man leading the rail-armed guards asked a question, and Sedative shook his head emphatically, gesturing to the exit tunnel.

"All of you," I said to those lingering around their unconscious companion. "Collect your wounded. Find everyone else who works for Darkwater and go back to Ravada. Don't touch any of the serfs or slaves."

It was clear the death of the kiract rattled some of them enough to jump into action and obey the order. Others bristled, making their murderous looks clear, but they didn't act on it. One of the guards heaved the wounded man onto his shoulders. Those with the rail weapons still hadn't moved.

"*Isa!*" Sedative yelled at his subordinates when I tickled his back with the end of his blade. They followed the rest of the guards down the street, making their way through clusters of slaves and serfs, who backed away with heads bowed. The enslaved stood still as prey, but when the guards showed no interest in them, they watched them go, puzzled.

Geth ran for his hiding place and reappeared with a bag, pulling out a waterskin. He started pouring the water over Shirallah's burn while I brought my attention to Torlo. "Where's Efadora?" I asked.

He blinked at me and rubbed his eyes. "I don't know," he mumbled.

"We found him wandering the streets like a drunk," Shirallah said. "He will not be much use."

Geth grabbed a bandage from his pack and wrapped Shirallah's hand. The enslaved moved closer to us when it became clear safety lay in our direction, and they watched the first of the guards move up the ramps leading to the exit tunnel.

I could hardly believe it. Hundreds, even thousands of slaves and serfs were in this city, and now the fates of many were in my hands, just like in Augustin. What if my life's purpose could mean more than saving the slaves of the Ebonrock? I swallowed a growing lump in my throat, visiting a thought I'd experienced a thousand times over the years—that I would die alone with no one to care if I had ever lived at all. Perhaps it didn't have to be that way.

"You will let me go?" Sedative asked. My grip on his shirt had relaxed enough for the cloth to slip out of my blood-slicked fingers, which he'd apparently taken as a reassuring sign. I knocked him in the stomach with the sword's pommel and he collapsed in a gasping heap.

Efadora appeared at the end of a street running alongside Namira, carrying a Sihraan weapon, but it looked different from the rail weapons. "You're all right," I said when they reached us.

Efadora nodded, despite the low set of her brows. Whatever was bothering her, it seemed to fade when she brought her attention to Torlo. She set her weapon down and examined his head wound with gentle fingers. "He needs a doctor," she said. "Same with Shirallah."

"We will find one soon," Shirallah said, the words tight from his pain.

"Are you there?" Efadora asked Torlo.

He nodded slowly and smiled. She cupped his cheek with a hand and forced a smile of her own, then gave Sedative the once-over. "Where did the guards go?"

"They're gathering everyone and heading back to Ravada," I said. A steady line of guards moved up the scaffolding now, and more slaves and serfs materialized from the streets, headed our way. The headless, bloody heap of one kiract and the gasping mess of another worked like a beacon for them.

"We can't take them with us," Namira said. "Darkwater will try to take them back as soon as they step foot in the city."

Namira was in good shape, all things considered. Malnourished and bruised with bags under her eyes, but good.

Funny how she was the first domino to change so many lives. "I have an idea," I said, "but it's a big one." I turned to the enslaved, who had stopped halfway down the block, and motioned for them to come closer, but they refused. I went to them instead. "Did Darkwater stock this place with food?" I asked the crowd.

No one answered.

"Geth?" I asked. The cartographer repeated the question in Xerivian.

Still no one answered, but I could see the answer was there in several pairs of eyes. I approached the nearest slave, who took a step back, and I set a hand on his iron collar. The ring of metal clattered to the ground, his neck and shoulders underneath rubbed raw. He stuttered something in Xerivian.

"There's enough food here to feed a few thousand for several weeks," Geth said. "Darkwater was planning to relocate their company here."

"And as far as they're concerned, they're still going to," I said. "The only reason we're alive is because Darkwater employees don't want to die for their employer, but more of these—" I gestured at the kiract attempting to act invisible as he lay on the ground a short distance away—"will make their underlings regroup. They might get help from the city, too. When they hit back, they'll hit hard." I eyed the shadows in the buildings and the whining pipes. "There are probably guards and overseers still hiding in the ruins. We need to root them out. I also need to find all the serfs and slaves. It's going to take time."

"What's your plan?" Efadora asked.

She was still brooding, and I suffered the urge to forget everyone around us for a few minutes, pull her aside, and apologize for everything. "I'm going to help the serfs and slaves barricade themselves in the ruins. Then I'm going to collapse the tunnel leading here and create a new one so they can sneak in and out of the Rift."

"There's that other route," Namira said, and shot Geth an angry look. "The one Geth ignored when he was escorting the caravan. It'll give Darkwater a path here."

"I'll take care of that tunnel too."

"Darkwater will know where to blast, and there's the rub," Geth said. "They can afford however much pyroglycerin they'll need to reopen the tunnels."

"Please," a woman said, stepping forward. "This plan of yours is a good one. You set us free, and you give us the Sihraan weapons. Some of us will gladly kill any who seek to take away what it is you are offering. This is *khasalé*."

She offered her neck to me, and I set a hand on her collar until metal clicked. "That settles it," I said. "Geth, Namira, Efadora, can you find the slaves and bring them here? I'll remove their collars if you can't find keys. I'm going to hunt down any Darkwater stragglers in the meantime and kick them out."

Some of the slaves frowned, but my mind was set. I wasn't about to let anyone with a Darkwater patch die because they'd picked the wrong company to work for. Some of them undoubtedly deserved it, but separating the thugs from those looking for a paycheck would be impossible. Meting out more death wasn't something I was capable of at the moment, besides. Already I could feel the killing of the kiract eating away at the base of my chest, pushing flashes of unwanted memories from the Granite Road onto me, memories of blood and death.

Sedative threw his hands in front of him when I approached, babbling in Xerivian. I dragged him to his feet, led him to the crowd, and threw him toward the woman I'd freed and those standing beside her. He stumbled into them, but they caught him with rough hands. "You should collect as many weapons as you can and prepare for your stay in the city," I said. Geth repeated the words in Xerivian. "And put him to work if you'd like. It's time he earned some callouses."

"That is unwise," Sedative said. "A deal can always be made, Iron Sorrow."

He continued speaking, but his words were stifled by the enslaved pulling him deeper into the crowd. He cried out, the sound swallowed up by the commotion. "Arhan's a few blocks that way," Efadora said, pointing while she continued to brood.

"He might have some friends with him, but I don't think they'll fight back."

I realized that might have been what was bothering her. He must have escaped her again and she was itching for a chance to kill him once and for all. If she couldn't find the chance, I would do it for her. It would destroy me to do so, but I would do it if she asked, and I would never let her know how it affected me. It was the least I could do. "What do you want me to do with him?"

She shrugged, but I could tell there was a lot going on under such a simple gesture, and the conflicted look in her eyes deepened. "Nothing, I guess."

"Nothing?"

"Let him live his miserable little life. I'm over what he did."

She was annoyed with herself, I realized. I had no idea what would compel Efadora to spare Arhan, but whatever the reason, I would try to talk to her about it. By this time next passing, I hoped for us to be on the road to Som Abast once again, which meant there was time for me to make myself available to her. There was so much to talk about. She deserved my trust and she deserved to be listened to, and I'd spent far too long not giving her enough of either.

I stepped closer. "I'm sorry."

Her expression cracked. For a second it seemed she was going to cry, but she reined herself in. "Don't be sorry. You were right."

If she meant I was right about comparing her to Sara, I didn't know what to say in response. It had been a mistake ever saying those words. She was so much more than her sister, so much more than the Adriann name, and part of me had been too scared to see that. I almost wimped out at the last moment out of fear she might recoil, but I closed the rest of the distance between us and pulled her into a hug. "I'm sorry," I repeated. "You deserve better."

"No, I don't," she said, her voice muffled. She hugged me back.

Chapter 29—Ester

ESTER CLUTCHED AT her coat, trying to shake off the chill that wouldn't stop dogging her as she hid behind the ghost mushrooms in the sixth level gardens. After a few passings of muscle-cramping and snot-running cold, she was willing to sleep inside a forge at this point. Judge Abeso entered the gardens, and once Ester made sure an armed escort wasn't following on his heels, she left her hiding spot.

Judge Abeso flinched for the weapon on his belt but paused when their gazes met. "Apprentice Ester?" he asked, looking her up and down. Her dirty and bedraggled form was humiliating, but it did offer anonymity.

"Are any of the sixth-level guards nearby?"

"No. Did you follow me?"

"I swiped your itinerary from your assistant's home. Saw you liked to come here the same time every week, so I figured I'd wait it out."

"You're wanted for murder, young Ester."

"Are you saying that because you're going to turn me in?"

He studied her. "Did you do it? Did you kill Master Smith Hartlan?"

Despite everything she knew—despite the truth about what

Hartlan really was—the man had been appointed leader of Augustin's Foundry, and she had killed him. Stupid, irrational guilt kept her from holding back the truth. She nodded.

Abeso checked over his shoulder. "No, I won't turn you in, but I'm likely the only one in the city who wouldn't. One half of Augustin wants justice for Master Smith Hartlan and the other half would no doubt cash in on that chasm-sized bounty on your head. You're lucky Princepa Sara destroyed the Fiador Fianza, otherwise you'd be dead or captured by now."

"I know all of that. It's why you found me playing Mushroom Man here instead of waiting outside your house."

He stepped back and gave her another once-over, cringing, then pulled a piece of wadded-up cloth out of his jacket pocket. "I always bring a snack with me on my walks. Are you hungry?"

Ester unfolded the cloth and scooped at the hummus inside, desperate. She didn't slow down until it was gone and there was nothing left to do except lick the cloth. To Abeso's credit, he didn't show his disgust as he watched her. "You look like death," he said. "What happened?"

She ran her tongue around the inside of her mouth, searching for the last bits of hummus, and used the time to think about what to say. "I broke into the villa the Sovereign stayed at on his first passing here. The master smith followed me. He told me things before I killed him, about my old brothers and sisters, and the new magnate."

She'd prepared for two passings to have this conversation, diving into the story before she could second-guess herself. If there was anyone in Augustin she could trust it was him, though that wasn't saying much. By the time she finished, Abeso was sitting on the cap of one of the bigger mushrooms. "*Imposile*," he said. "You're saying the Sovereign turned this beggar he found… into the new magnate? A more reasonable explanation is that you've gone crazy, young Ester. Have you considered that?"

"If you knew how elemental power worked, you'd realize

it's limitless. I barely understand it myself. Besides, look at what you witnessed during the Sovereign's visit. It adds up."

Abeso wrapped his coat tighter and hugged himself, staring into the mid-distance. "So, if Magnate Crosby is what you say he is—a homunculus?—and so are Augustin's smiths, what do we do?"

"I was hoping you'd tell me." She double checked the garden's entrance, but still saw no unwanted visitors. The courtyard they were in opened directly onto the ridge, but the foliage that made up the front wall was thick enough that someone had to be looking hard to get a good look at her.

"I wouldn't even know where to begin," Abeso said. "I could tell the audencia that Magnate Crosby and the smiths are imposters, but they would only laugh me out of the chambers. I would ruin my reputation and likely put myself in mortal danger, and for what? Saior Crosby will still be magnate. Those monsters will still control Augustin's Foundry."

Her face started to burn. "So then we let these things control the magnate's seat and the Foundry and we pretend everything is fine? The magnate ushers in an era of peace while the smiths enforce it, then we live happily ever after? People need to know what the real cost of this peace was."

Judge Abeso scoffed, but before he could retort, Ester leaned over, letting out a ragged sob. That tightness inside her that had been mounting since returning to Augustin had finally squeezed her until she couldn't take it, and now tears poured from her, dripping onto the mosaics of the garden's walkways. Her brothers and sisters were dead. No, it was worse than that. Every time she thought of Master Smith Mateo, or the senior arc smiths, or Smiths Reeda and Daltano, all she could picture was the Sovereign twisting and shaping their meat and bones until they were unrecognizable.

Abeso watched uncomfortably, but Ester didn't hold it against him. Smiths only lost their composure during their rhidium trials. They were always the comforters, never the comforted. "The Sovereign will have to do much more than install puppets in the magnate's seat and Augustin's Foundry to ensure peace," he said. "Augustin is only one of six territories he has to contend with. Radavich is having problems of its own, and Tulchi and Manasus are looking to take advantage. War may yet come to Mira."

Ester took several shaky breaths and wiped her nose. "Hartlan said the Sovereign is going to place a magnate in Radavich, too."

Footsteps echoed off rock—four people entered the gardens, and they paused at the sight of Abeso and Ester. Ester's hand went to her hidden blade, but Abeso grabbed her wrist. With another look, she realized the newcomers were teenagers, and one of them carried a bottle of root wine. Abeso wrapped an arm around her shoulder and turned their backs to the group, leading her deeper into the gardens. It put them in a corner, but Ester didn't fight.

"Fi cosa," he cursed lightly. "Pray that none of them recognized me. It'd hardly do me any favors if the public or my wife got word I was rendezvousing with a strange woman in one of the upper gardens."

"I'll stick to praying they didn't recognize *me*."

"I wouldn't worry about that. You can spot a smith a mile off by the way they stand, and you've done a good job of moving just about as opposite as one can."

She hadn't realized that smiths carried themselves a particular way, and she was too tired to figure out why that subtle technique was now lost to her. "Listen," Abeso continued. "The Sovereign is far from finished with exerting his influence on the territories. If he's placing another magnate in Radavich, he might extend that solution to Tulchi, too. Tulchi took control of Radavich's western border after Jakar killed Radavich's magnate and Sara Adriann razed the Granite Road. If Radavich's future puppet is anything like Magnate Crosby, they'll bend over backwards to make Tulchi happy. That could be enough, but it might not. The territories are at a tipping point. There's word too of Magnate Bardera of Manasus trying to seize control of the eastern trade routes to put an end to the outrageous tariffs Radavich placed on her territory. All this disarray among the territories has made the Sovereign furious at his primordia. Apparently, they have not been taking their responsibilities as enforcers seriously."

"Tulchi took control of Radavich's western border? Do you know if Tulchi took control of Radavich's gas veins there?"

"I don't know. I'm sorry."

Ester's family lived within a passing's walk from the border where Radavich's largest gas vein resided. Tulchi purchased gas from Radavich that they used to boil seawater from the Sea of Daggers, so it would make sense for them to take control of the veins. And living that close to such a contentious area put her family in danger. Or perhaps she was just being paranoid. The last thing her parents, and especially Damek, wanted was to get involved in political conflicts. They would find a way to stay out of it.

"Then there are the ruin folk to consider," Abeso said.

"What do you mean?"

"Ruin folk have been raiding towns in south Manasus and Byssa, and the Sovereign intends to 'deal with them' after his trip to Radavich's capital."

"They're raiding towns to stockpile weapons because they want to mobilize against the Sovereign."

"You're sure?"

"Yes. I wasn't here when the Sovereign visited Augustin because I was hunting something the ruin folk stole from the Foundry." Ester's frown wasn't quite so intense this time around while thinking of Breach and his friends. Hopefully, they would be on the move once the Sovereign put his energy into hunting them down. She wasn't sure when her anger with Breach had faded. Probably around the time the Sovereign killed all her brothers and sisters.

"Can you sneak me out of the capital?" she asked. "I have a plan."

"Does it involve high treason?"

She opened her mouth, but Abeso put up a hand. "That was rhetorical. Getting you out of the capital would already be enough of a betrayal to the audencia. Plausible deniability might save my life someday."

He was actually going to sneak her out? She almost couldn't believe it. It was a shot to the moon, but maybe it wasn't too late to help Breach turn his friends into iron workers. It was her only shot to make the Sovereign hurt the way that he had hurt her.

Chapter 30—Efadora

THE TWELVE BELLS of the House of Nobility tolled throughout Ravada, signaling mid-passing and for all Xerivians to face the House grounds and give thanks for fifteen minutes. It was our cue to move our asses.

Jakar and Torlo piled the last of our supplies into the cart while I prodded the Dead Bog buffalo to get moving. It lumbered toward the road leading out of Ravada, taking its sweet time, and I poked it in the rump again with the wooden rod until it picked up the pace. The people in this part of the city hardly noticed us as they gave their silence while facing the center of town, a few of them stepping out of the way.

"Mind taking the reins?" I asked Geth, who sat next to me. "I'm a little small to be leading an eight-hundred-pound buffalo up this hill."

Geth took the reins and brought his attention to the road that would take us up Ravada's southeastern slopes, beside the Helm of Taz'cal, and out of the city. He'd been skulking nonstop since Shirallah had ended their relationship.

"Want to talk about it?" I asked.

"I'm sure a girl your age has felt this way many times and knows exactly what I am going through," he said.

274

"Fine. You're right. I've never had my heart broken, but that just means now's your chance to explain the problem with boys and why I shouldn't touch them with a ten-foot pole, right? You'd be saving me trouble."

"Life is pointless without love," he said angrily.

"Yeah, you're really selling that idea."

By showing his face to Darkwater, Shirallah had ruined any chance for a safe life in Ravada, but he hadn't wanted to come with us to Sulian Daw, either. Instead, he had stayed in the ruins with the freed serfs and slaves to help them establish a community and oversee their defenses. Jakar had fortified the ruins with natural barriers, but we all knew it wouldn't last. I still didn't understand why the two had broken up, but before doing so, Shirallah had forced Geth to promise one thing—to help Jakar save his friends from the Ebonrock.

"Let's stick to a business relationship only, then," I said. "You're still going to teach me how to become a cartographer, right?"

"At least until Jakar gets what he needs, then I'm coming back here and you'll never see me again."

Geth was a manipulator and a schemer, but I could tell Shirallah was the most important thing in his life. There was nothing I could do or say to convince him to finish my training after the Ebonrock were taken care of when it meant he could return to Shirallah, so I would take what I could get. "Fair enough. I'm excited, either way."

"Me too," he grumbled.

This close to the Helm of Taz'cal, I could see the hole to the surface that fed the mountain of snow, letting me catch a glimpse of the stars. Wind whipped up flurries of snow that rained down on our cart, and I could see patches of ice here and there on the road ahead, but Geth did a good job avoiding them. Jakar sat on the back of the cart beside Torlo, studying the city as we slowly rose above it. A look of relief spread across his face. We'd stayed in Ravada for way too long, thanks to my stupid vendetta, but at least we'd passed through the other side relatively unscathed. Torlo was feeling like his old self, minus the tenderness of the stitches on the side of his head.

I turned in my seat and pulled out a book from the cart. "Hey," I said to Jakar. "I never told you about what I found on the Ebonrock."

He crawled to the front of the cart and wedged himself between two bags. "What?"

"A while back you told me about that creature in Sulian Daw's lake that created your flesh binding. I think it lives inside the lake because it feeds on the algae in there."

His cheek twitched upon me mentioning the creature he called the Child. It was the one thing that seemed to bother him as much as the Granite Road. "I don't know how that helps us, but thank you."

"This book says that the tuk gulang helped their true masters find food. Maybe once you save your friends, those things will starve to death."

"The Ebonrock would wait decades before coming back to Sulian Daw to kidnap the next generation of elementals. The Child was living at the bottom of Obsidian Lake all that time without any help, so as far as I know, that won't work."

"Is the next step in your plan to find the Child?" Geth asked, a degree of his misery forgotten.

"Only if that book can't tell us where the Ebonrock is."

"Stop!" someone yelled from down the hill. Jakar whipped around, but it was only Namira running to catch up. Geth pulled on the reins and the buffalo snorted before coming to a stop. Namira stopped and struggled to catch her breath, then threw the bag that had been hanging over her shoulder into the cart. "Looks like there's just enough room on there for me," she said.

"I thought you were suing Darkwater," Jakar said. "You said you were going to get rich off what they did to you."

"I was, until Darkwater told Ravada I was a known associate of the Fist of Kaedis."

The Fist of Kaedis was what they were calling Jakar now. Kaedis was the Aspect of water who in the Xerivian religion made all of Ra Thuzan's tunnels—her statues lined the streets of the Tanzanite District, a woman with a porcelain mask and a sword of ice who often took the form of a salamander. She was also the spectre of death. Jakar didn't seem bothered by the nickname, but of course it was miles better than the Stalker of Cragreach or even the Iron Sorrow.

"Darkwater dug my grave, but all of you handed them the shovel," Namira said, climbing into the cart. "So instead of Darkwater paying me back, all of you are going to. I'll be taking this cart as payment for Geth causing this whole mess in the first place, I'm taking that buffalo as payment for Efadora getting me captured, and three grams of dymium or its equivalent for helping keep Torlo alive in the Rift."

Torlo said, "Fair enough," at the same time Geth said, "Eat batshit."

"Don't worry," she continued, "I won't be collecting until after you're done helping Jakar. But I promise I'll be taking it."

"Works for me," I said. "We won't be back to Ravada for months, though. That a problem?"

"Course," she said. "I travel for a living, remember?"

"You were born in Sulian Daw but didn't you say you grew up in Ravada? What about your family?"

Her mouth hovered open as though she wanted to respond but wasn't sure how. "I have a son but he does his own thing these days, so I do mine."

We'd been slumming it together in the city for two weeks before Darkwater captured her, and not once had she mentioned her son. I'm sure there was a reason. I was well versed in the art of dropping the subject when it came to problematic family members, so I didn't push it. Her bedraggled hair had been washed out, she wore a fresh change of clothes and her eyes were bright, and her bruises weren't quite so ugly as before. It was good to see her on the up and up. I was happy to have her with us, too, and as a professional traveler, she probably had some insight on the journey ahead. "Two weeks and we'll be in Sulian Daw. Should we expect trouble on the way?"

"I've never traveled a road that was completely safe," she said, "but the one to Sulian Daw isn't so bad, as far as bandits are concerned. The wildlife can get aggressive, so bandits aren't keen to camp off the beaten path. We keep a smart head and we'll be fine."

As we traveled the tunnels east of Ravada, we came across our fair share of travelers we paid close attention to, but according to Geth, Darkwater was still so focused on the ruins that they'd never send agents out of the city's east entrance.

"Someone might be following us," Jakar said.

"Where?" I asked, scanning the white-glowing vegetation and the shimmering heat of a magma vein behind us.

"I don't know," he said. "Just a feeling."

"Sounds like paranoia," Geth said.

"Can't blame him," Namira added.

The tunnels were wide and made avoiding people easy—if there was someone really following us, we'd have plenty of warning if they decided to do more than watch. In Mira, traveling alternated between sprawling caverns and twisting tunnels, but here most tunnels were cavernous, and the caverns themselves could be big as sinkholes. One such space was a canyon entirely exposed to the surface with a dense forest, its vegetation climbing almost all the way up its thousand-foot walls, with water cascading from a pitch-dark sky. Geth called it the Twilight Canyons and said it extended over a dozen miles.

"Rain," Jakar said as we attached poles and a tarp above the cart beneath the protection of the tunnel's edge.

"That's where lightning comes from, right?" I asked.

He nodded. "And your coil weapon."

According to him, the coil weapon shot a projectile super-heated by electricity. The perfect weapon against the kadiphs.

I knew he could take on anyone at this point with his new bound element, but there was a warmth to knowing he considered me his ace in the hole, just in case.

"Did you figure out what element you bonded with?" I asked as the buffalo pulled us along the single wide road stretching from one end of the chasm to the other. I had to raise my voice over the sound of the rain hitting the tarp.

"I can't use my Eye to figure it out because everything's so bright," he said, "but I have my suspicions. If Sara stabbing me started the binding, it makes sense that the element came from steel." He spent a moment thinking. "I think it was carbon, but that should be impossible. The more abundant an element is inside someone the more likely they'll die binding to it, and carbon is one of the most common elements in the human body. It should've killed me a hundred times over. Carbon's the only answer that makes sense, though."

"Isn't all this 'element' talk still hearsay?" Geth asked. He was acting more like his old self these last few passings. "These are theories that one group of scholars in Rona came up with, and even they said it's impossible to prove most of what they postulate."

"There are many things in the world that can't be proven. The best you can do is come up with a hypothesis that makes correct predictions, and the Element Hypothesis has done a damned good job with that so far."

Geth dug through his pocket and pulled out a vial of liquid that glowed a faint blue. "So, when one of us cartographers undergoes their Delineation, what element's responsible for that?"

"Silicon," Jakar said. "Where'd you get that?"

"The Archives. Where else? It's for Efadora."

So Geth wanted to keep his word after all. I imagined what it would be like drinking rhidium and how painful it would be, but if Jakar could do it, so could I.

"The Archive's binding ritual is called the Delineation?" Namira asked.

"That's the modern name. The old tongue name is 'Colche Ditrac', which means 'They Who Seek to Transcend.' Not a fan of that name, though."

"Pretty strange name. Sounds awfully spiritual for a group of secularists."

Geth returned the rhidium to his pocket. "The Archives aren't officially non-religious, but yes, I agree. The Archives' start goes back to before the end of the Sihraan Empire. Early cartographers followed this dogmatic idea that we needed to find and repopulate the abandoned empire."

"Seems weird that the oldest organization in existence, which specializes in gathering knowledge, wouldn't know what happened to the Sihraans."

"On any other passing that would sound like criticism, but moods aren't meant to be soured in places as beautiful as this." He took a deep breath of the wet vegetation. "You're right. It is strange. That's why cartographers like myself love studying the Sihraans so much. My ancient predecessors searched for ruins because it was their spiritual obsession, while I'm doing it because they did such a shitty job at it."

The first passing's eve we camped halfway through the Twilight Canyons, on a rise overlooking a plain of bioluminescent mushrooms as big as houses, next to a ruby vein in the wall that kept the area well lit. I sat on my bedroll, watching Torlo unroll his. His movements were awkward, and he winced from bending over. I couldn't stop staring at the bandage wrapped around his head.

"I never said sorry for dragging you into the ruins," I said to him. A bag of jerky was in my hand, and I offered it to him.

He sat on his bedroll and took the bag. "Why apologize? I made my decisions. The doctor said I'd be fine, besides."

I didn't deserve to be let off the hook, and his grace made me think of the realization I'd had, that he had a thing for me. It had bothered me at first—what if Torlo wasn't nearly so kind as he made himself out to be, and would change like the other boys did when I spurned them?—but then I realized how foolish the thought was. Torlo was kind through and through, whether he was talking to me or Jakar or any of the others.

He ripped at the jerky with his teeth, and I watched him chew. He had a strong jaw, and I found myself studying its definition, along with his narrow nose and high cheekbones. He met my eyes and smiled, and I realized what I'd been doing.

"Can I at least make it up to you?" I asked. "Let me take your guard shifts."

"All right. Sure. Thank you, Effie."

I headed back to my bedroll, lying on my side so I could watch Torlo stare at the sky, watching the rain fall. Even though it had happened almost a month ago, I started feeling guilty for the way I'd treated him when we first met. He had clearly moved past it, but still I found it eating at me, suffering the urge to apologize to him. There was so much I wanted to say sorry to him for.

Oh fhelfire, I liked Torlo.

I spent a good while watching him watch the rain, enjoying how he marveled in the simple pleasures of the world around us—simple pleasures that had drawn me toward becoming a cartographer—studying his lashes whenever he blinked, tracing the line of his profile as he stared up, his hands cupped behind his head.

Eventually I lay on my back, wishing this passing would last forever. I looked from Jakar, who cupped water out of a pond to wash his scarred and battered torso, to Geth and Namira, who argued over the best way to season ridge-venison as they bent over a fire, then at Torlo once again, a warmth stirring my gut. I'd always known there was something missing in me; it was why killing never fazed me, how I could still fantasize about killing Arhan, or why I could manipulate my way through the Augustin nobility and the gangs of Manasus. So how had I managed to surround myself with these kinds of people?

I didn't deserve them.

Chapter 31—Jakar

SULIAN GUARDS, MOUNTED atop Spiral Horned Yaks—animals bred to be as deadly as the cruel-looking spears the guards held—siphoned us and everyone else along the narrowing road as we rounded the bend into Som Abast. I glanced at the road behind us, trying to catch a glimpse of the person I was worried might be tailing our cart, but as usual I saw nothing. It had been based on a feeling and nothing more, I had to admit, but those feelings were what made me such an effective killer for Sorrelo Adriann. Maybe Geth was right and I was just being paranoid.

Fiery light appeared ahead, and I caught a glimpse of Saristra's Tear hanging from the city's massive ceiling, its shadow touching the back wall of a vast cavern. I could taste the cold, wet Sulian wind, its smell fresher than any air in Mira, and on it rode the sounds of the city, rising above the ambient noise of the travelers around us. All of my senses were assaulted with familiar sensations, and it filled me with dread.

For a decade, the Ebonrock had instilled in me an intense fear of leaving this city. That fear returned, a knee-jerk reaction, and it left me shaking as our cart rolled along the gentle slope that would bring us into the Bejiya Bel, the trade district. What if the Ebonrock was still waiting for me after all this time? What if my punishment for two years of freedom would be worse than anything I could possibly imagine?

Geth watched me, puzzled, but I shook my head so he wouldn't ask. Our cart descended the forty-foot-wide road along the city's northern wall, but even all this space could barely accommodate all the travelers. The city was a common pit stop for western travelers from Xeriv, Karatoa, and Yarokly on their way to Rona to the south. Efadora's attention was sharp as she watched for any hands that tried to dip into our uncovered cart, though I wasn't too concerned. Sulians rarely stole—to steal meant giving up a piece of one's nam'asa, which was like a combination of honor and a person's soul. Incidentally, this belief created a great excuse to look down on the city's sabadra, or their poorest. My parents were sabadra. We stole to survive, and as a result we could never build up reputation enough to get jobs. Even if we had never been caught stealing, it was assumed at some point or another that we had.

My home country hated sabadra. It was why they sold a handful of them to the Ebonrock.

"I've never seen so many people in my life," Torlo said. "They're like ants swarming an ant hill. How could you stand living here?"

"Be careful," I said. "Sulians are very proud of their city. An insult that would get you a sneer in Mira will get you a length of steel to the gut here."

"Is that why people back home think Sulians are savages?" Efadora asked. She didn't sound judgmental—she carried that relentless curiosity she'd been displaying more and more alongside her studies with Geth—but I cringed anyway, checking for eavesdroppers. Nobody around us looked Sulian, though, or seemed to speak Miran.

"That's a part of it," I said. "Nam'asa is like spiritual currency, and offending someone is like stealing some of what a Sulian needs to ascend to one of the better tiers of the afterlife.

So Sulians might get violent at times. They're afraid of what will happen to them in the afterlife if they let certain offenses slide. Respect goes a long way around here."

The city didn't look much different from how I remembered it. The Raval District was bigger, now almost reaching the wall that I'd helped build with my old friends by the cave's mouth. I tried to find the Ebonrock compound on the shores of Obsidian Lake, but the manufacturing district blocked it from view.

My dread worsened when we entered the streets and a chaotic bag of old memories hit me left and right. The ginger smell of turmeric. The teal and crimson quilts being sold that were covered in curving, flourishing designs meant to signify the foundation of the world that the Makers built. The piercing stares of the vendors—in Sulian Daw, it was considered rude to glance away from someone whose gaze you caught, so vendors took full advantage of this.

Already an angry woman had approached the back of the cart where Torlo sat, carrying a quilt and trying to harass him into buying it. "It's rude not to hold eye contact," I said to him. "Tell her 'Anas,' a few times. It means something along the lines of 'I'm really, really, really sorry.' And be emphatic when you say it."

"Is she going to stab me if I say it wrong?" he tried to ask over her spitting words.

"I'm ninety percent sure she won't."

Torlo found plenty of motivation to sell his words. She scoffed and stalked off, and Torlo was smart enough to keep his eyes glued to the ground.

"I thought those intense looks you give were because you were always mad," Efadora said to me.

Before I could answer, Geth said, "That's an important lesson to remember, Efadora. People often like to ascribe other cultures as being inherently happy, or submissive, or angry, but really, it's due to the tics of their cultural norms. We all hurt and fear and rage and celebrate. People are all the same, really. At least where it matters."

Efadora gave a thoughtful nod. "Where to?" Namira asked.

"Head west toward the back of the cave, where the lake is," I said.

Namira gave the buffalo a command and patted it on the rump. She'd already taught it her own special commands and refused to tell us what they meant in preparation of staking her claim on this cart, though it wasn't too hard to figure the commands out. "Could be for the best we rest up and recharge," Geth said. "You know, before we potentially run into a group of elementals each as powerful as yourself and led by a group of sociopaths with bodies that are literally as hard as rock. Would hate to do that on an empty stomach."

"All of you can stay behind," I said. "I can't wait any longer. I have to see this."

"You aren't leaving us on the sidelines," Efadora said.

After a few blocks, my shaking had gotten so bad that I finally said, "Let's stop for a minute."

Namira brought the cart to a halt in front of one of the hundreds of coffee cabanas that littered the city. I ordered the group drinks, and it wasn't until then did I realize how rusty my Sulian was. The proprietor made a fuss about us trying to use Xerivian currency, but he relented. We drank at a table in front of the cabana, and I was grateful for the caffeine and the wind that I could use to blame for my trembling if need be.

"This tastes like shit," Namira said.

"Never had Som Abast coffee before?" Geth asked. "It's one of Sulian Daw's main exports. A drink for only the richest nobility in Mira, and here we are drinking it for next to nothing."

"Well, all coffee tastes like shit."

"It's perfect," Efadora said. "It's hot enough that I can almost forget all this wind whipping me around. Is it always this cold?"

"Only near the walls and the back of the cavern," I said. "In the center of the city where the buildings are packed close together, you barely notice it."

A silence followed, and all of them watched me while I sipped on my steaming cup.

"Are you sure you want to do this?" Namira asked. "We can always wait until next passing."

"Of course I want to do this. It's why I'm here. Why wouldn't I?"

Another silence, this one awkward. "You look terrified, my friend," Torlo said.

I couldn't help but glance over my shoulder. I'd been doing that a lot since entering the city.

Everyone offered me looks of varying sympathy, except for Efadora, who seemed to struggle with guilt. She knew my history with her father and sister, and while 'awful' couldn't come close to describing what they'd done, their abuse was nothing compared to what awaited me if I'd never escaped the Ebonrock. I'd done a good job forgetting this fact up until now. What if the fellowship recaptured me and the kadiphs found a way to rebind me? It was all I could think about. Strange how easy I could compartmentalize my abuse by staying far, far away from the people who caused it, but how the triggers of returning to Som Abast had caused all those walls to crumble.

I focused on memories of old punishments, dwelling on them until phantom pain crept up the base of my skull and squeezed. Knowing Quin and the others would have to endure that pain again and again before I found them was enough for me to down the rest of the coffee. There was no logical reason to feel so strongly that they were still alive and waiting to be rescued, but I felt it anyway. It had infected me right down to my bones. They needed my help. "Let's go."

We parked the cart in a lot to an abandoned leather working shop a quarter mile from the Ebonrock compound, and Namira stayed behind to watch the cart while Efadora, Geth, and Torlo insisted on coming. We followed the road running along Obsidian Lake, moving around warehouse workers towing loads of building material, and I stared at the black waters. Was Ig lurking down there? I still hadn't told Efadora and the others its real name. I couldn't tell if it was the coffee, but I was becoming hyper-aware of everyone around us, checking

286

for anyone who gave us more than a glance. My anxiety made it hard to walk in a straight line. I couldn't stop fidgeting.

The outer perimeter of the Ebonrock compound was marked by a wall torn down to the first row of bricks, and a plain of dirt, emberbrushes, and bad memories waited for us on the other side.

"By the look in your eye, I'm guessing this is it," Geth said.

I flipped a piece of brick over with my boot. Hundreds of miles traveled and several near-death experiences to reach this moment, and all that I'd found was dust. I'd tried to steel myself for this possibility—a lot could happen in two years and I'd always known the Ebonrock traveled from city to city to recruit elementals—but still I felt the despair creep in.

"I bet the city cleared the compound out so they could sell the property," Efadora said. "Unless Sulian culture doesn't value making money."

The area I was once obsessed with escaping hardly looked bigger than one of the nicer villas in Augustin. Funny how such an unassuming place had birthed some of the most powerful elementals in the world. "What now?" Torlo asked.

I reined myself in. I was sure that the Ebonrock was still here, even if their school wasn't. "I think Efadora's right. The property likely went back to the government. The Ebonrock was working with them when they kidnapped me and the others as children, so *someone* working for the city must know something. We'll start by finding whoever manages this property." I grimaced. "The Ebonrock stole over a hundred Sulian children. Four out of every five of those kids died. You can't get away with something that awful without leaving a trail."

"That many kids died during the Imbibings?" Efadora asked. "You never told me that."

"You sound concerned," Geth said. "Are you second-guessing your decision to become a cartographer?"

Efadora chewed on the inside of her lip—a nervous tic of hers—until the lines in her face settled. "Not a chance."

"Good." Geth pulled the vial of rhidium out, and he flipped it in the air, unconcerned with it slipping and breaking. "It takes a special kind of dysfunction to survive a dance with rhidium. Just look at the smiths, or my colleagues, or Jakar." He held the vial up, letting the red light of the Burning Mountains turn the blue vial purple. "You're not normal enough to let a funny little thing like this kill you, are you?"

"I'm not sure why, but you just made me feel better."

"So, are you ready?"

"For what? The rhidium?"

He nodded.

"This isn't the time or the place," I said. "In fact, this is probably the worst time and place to be making Efadora comatose for two to three passings."

"I'd say it's the best time. Doing it on the road would've been stupid, and you need a bit of time to find the Ebonrock, yeah? Best do the Delineation while Jakar hunts and we're bunkered down. We won't be finding out where your old friends are in one passing."

"Isn't it too early?" Efadora asked. "I've only been studying for a month."

He snorted. "The Archives aren't the Foundry. You're not expected to memorize the Sky Scrolls dozens of times or prove to an arc smith you've got the zen of a juiced-out gypsum addict. Cartographers learn as they go." He handed her the vial. "Besides, even if it was early, who's going to stop us?"

There was a longing in Efadora's eyes, and my first reaction was to answer with an emphatic *no* and throw Geth in the lake for good measure. The thought of the rhidium killing her made me sick. Instead, I spent a few moments in silence separating myself from my history with the Adrianns, and forced myself to acknowledge that this was Efadora's choice, not mine. She needed to know I trusted her, and that meant trusting her decisions.

"Let's get this over with, then," she said with a shaky breath.

Chapter 32—Efadora

JAKAR LED US to the center of the city where stern-faced people packed the streets, who moved with the kinds of strides that dared someone to get in their way. It seemed like Sulians were very deliberate in everything they did—I'd read that from mid-passing to passing's eve they worked harder than pack animals, then took full advantage of their leisure time. Things were starting to wind down in this part of town as the passing came to a close. Here the buildings were taller and blocked light from the Burning Mountains, and in the shadows, streetlamps dotted the curbs, similar to the gas lamps in Manasus and Radavich. These lamps had glass that spiraled down the length of the poles and were full of fireflies that glowed white instead of red. Namira parked the cart in one of the tight alleyways, and I draped a blanket over my coil weapon while we lugged our stuff inside.

Jakar got us a room at one of the inns. Our room was filled with red-stained wood and reeked of crisp persimmon, and the glass window, which faced the Burning Mountains, was stained so it filtered in a brighter shade of light. Now I understood why Som Abast translated to "Bloodreach." It was like a stain wherever the light touched. "You had enough to pay for three passings?" Torlo asked.

"No, but we'll figure something out as we go," Jakar said.

"Maybe you'll save yourself some money if the binding ritual kills me," I said, and jumped on one of the beds. Now that I was in the room where I would Delineate, my nerves started to set in. "So, what first?"

Geth smoothed out a blanket under the window and knelt in front of it, bowing his head and whispering quickly as he moved an index finger along its edges. "What are you doing?" I asked, but he didn't answer.

"To think all this time he tried to convince us he wasn't religious," Namira said.

"I'm not," Geth said. He stood, and the easy attitude with the calculating eyes he always sported had died, replaced by total seriousness. "I'm respecting tradition, is all. It doesn't matter if I'm atheist or not. Everything in my life comes secondary to the Archives." He motioned me over. "Lie down."

"Already?" I asked. I lay on the blanket and found it the perfect length. Fractals were woven into the fabric, and at first I thought they were meant to be quartz crystals, but the longer I looked at them the less sure I became.

"Nava Yasi Ma," Geth said. "Say it."

"Nava Yasi Ma."

"Slower. Draw out those syllables. You'll repeat it one thousand, four hundred and eight times, once for each rumored town and city destroyed by Ra'Thuzan through upheaval, time, memory, or otherwise, claimed by the days when the maps of the world were full. Ruins we vow to seek and knowledge we vow to reclaim."

"Fifteen hundred times? What if I lose count?"

"That's all right. Just keep it up as long as you can. You'll know when you're finished."

I almost laughed, but something in Geth's eyes told me that was the last thing I wanted to do, so I closed my eyes. "Nava Yasi Ma," I breathed. "Nava Yasi Ma…"

A little while later, somewhere between six and seven hundred, I heard the swish of cloth over metal. "This really is something," Geth said. "Any clue how it works?"

"What was that word you used in Ravada?" Jakar asked. "*Polas*. This weapon wreaks havoc on that field. Enough to disrupt an elemental and their power, I'm thinking."

More swishing of cloth on metal. I opened an eye and saw Geth polishing the coil weapon. "Interesting," he said. "Yaroklan texts say that deep within Ra'Thuzan, the forces that be are so strong that some elements transcend the three states of gas, liquid, and solid to become a fourth. Just takes enough heat or a strong enough *polas*. Really fucks with you, though, if you do manage to create it. But that's all hearsay, since no one knows how. Say, you wouldn't—"

"No," Jakar said. "Channeling heat like that would kill me. Even if I tried, I wouldn't be able to do it alone."

"Unfortunate." Geth turned the coil weapon over. I'd seen fathers look at their newborns the same way.

"Makes you wonder what killed the Sihraans," Namira said. "If anyone was equipped to deal with existential threats, you'd think it'd be them."

"You can't shoot at a disease if that's—"

"Shit," I whispered.

Torlo sat up. "What?"

"Nothing," I said, closing my eyes and going back to chanting. I'd lost count. Again.

An hour later, I moved onto my elbows. "All right, I'm done."

"That was quick," Geth said.

"I'm a fast talker. Learned from my family." In truth, I'd given up after losing count for the eighth time.

"How do you feel?"

"Good." Regardless of how dumb and pointless rituals seemed, I couldn't remember the last time I'd felt this calm. I'd spent the last several minutes listening to the slowed beat of my heart and chanting in rhythm with it, and somehow, I felt more grounded. Centered. Maybe I'd try the mantra again if I ever needed to relax.

"Lie back down," Geth said. He flattened the edges of the blanket, knelt over me, and started whispering to himself, too low for me to hear. His index finger traced my body, moving counter-clockwise, and I picked out a word here and there, but it didn't sound like any language I'd heard before. Jakar watched with a frown. If *he* was puzzled, then maybe this ritual was stranger than I thought.

"I'm good at treating bindings," Jakar said, as if sensing my unease. "I'll be close."

Geth's voice rose until he started singing from his throat, low and guttural. He slowly moved a hand into the inside of his jacket, and I heard the sound of metal sliding against leather. A knife appeared.

Jakar stepped forward. "Stop."

Geth had been staring at my stomach while chanting and singing, and his eyes didn't move from that spot when he replied, "I stop and this won't happen for Efadora. This is how it goes."

"You're going to hurt her?"

"Of course I'm going to hurt her. Ever tasted rhidium before?"

Jakar stood halfway between us and the bed, ready to take another step forward. "It's all right," I said. "Just humor him."

Geth's throat singing started up again, and he touched the tip of the knife against my forehead, holding it there until it burned and I felt warm blood drip down the side of my head. The hilt of the blade was carved from bone and looked like the head of an animal I didn't recognize.

Jakar fidgeted, conflict warring on his face. "Really, it's all right," I said.

"Carving into the flesh is supposed to open a pathway to allow the polas to enter your body," Geth said without looking up. "It allows you to forge a connection with it."

"That makes no sense," Jakar said. "None of this was part of my Imbibings."

"Do you know what doesn't make sense? That you can exert a force on steel or quartz or whatever else you're bound to and it doesn't push back. Ever hear of the law of motion?"

Jakar didn't answer. None of what he said made much sense to me, but I was too focused on the knife to comment.

"All actions create equal and opposite reactions," Geth said. "That's physics. Whenever Efadora pushes against quartz, this sacrifice of the flesh will let her disperse the reaction into the polas around her instead of it pushing into her. You do the same thing, even if it's not a conscious choice. It's why you can push a boulder ten times your size without getting flung backward to kingdom come."

"You're sure that's how it works? The Ebonrock didn't tell me any of this."

"Yes. The Archives don't know everything, but they're trying their damndest to fill in the gaps." This time, Geth spoke with a little less patience. "Respect the process. I'm almost done, anyway." He finally looked away from my stomach and met my eyes. "Repeat after me, yes?"

I nodded.

He said a string of words and waited, the knife poised over my stomach.

"I don't understand," I said.

"Just try your best."

He said it again, and I repeated it slowly, fumbling my way through the alien language. As soon as I finished, his knife made seven superficial cuts—six slices around a middle point, like a star. I only caught a glimpse of the shape before blood welled out and covered it.

"Take out the rhidium," he said.

I pulled it out of my pocket, the movement making my stomach sting. My forehead still felt wet and warm. Geth took the vial and pulled out a quartz pebble. "You can't hesitate, all right?" he said. "The rhidium is going to try to react with the air as soon as I unstop the vial, so I'm going to drop the quartz in and you have to drink it right away. Too slow and it's going to kill you. Got it?"

"Of course," I said, failing to mask how close I was to calling it quits.

The cork popped, and in one fluid movement the pebble splashed into the vial as he was bringing it to my mouth. The rhidium tasted cold and greasy, and my instinct was to spit out the rock, but I forced it down and laid my head back.

My stomach hurt, but I was pretty sure that was from the nerves. "When does it start?"

"Give it a few minutes."

Geth wiped the blade on his pant leg and sheathed it, then left my side. Jakar grabbed a bowl of water and rag and took the cartographer's place. He touched a finger to the water, and after a few moments dipped the rag in the bowl before dabbing it onto my forehead. It was ice cold.

"There's going to be a chemical reaction first," Jakar whispered. "The rhidium is mixing with your stomach acid, making it more acidic until it starts burning holes through your stomach lining. It's going to hurt, but it's also going to heal. The rhidium is going to spread through your body, looking for the part of you that's the same as the part of quartz it bound with. Once the binding starts, your body is going to turn on itself and try to kill an illness it thinks it has. All we have to do is manage the symptoms."

"Why are you telling me this?"

"Because willpower is important. It's what's most important now and I'm not sure why. If you know what's going to happen, then that means you can quantify it and it becomes less scary. That's always been my secret to beating these things. Knowledge is power, or something like that."

I nodded. His brows furrowed, an intense concern in his eyes, and for a moment I wasn't quite so scared of what was coming. "I haven't been fair to you," he said.

"About what?"

"Everything. Ever since we left Augustin. I kept thinking you'd turn out like your sister, that I couldn't trust you."

I barked out a laugh. Once upon a time I might've been upset talking about Sara, but I realized that tender spot had healed. "I don't blame you. I was stupid for reacting how I did when you compared me to her back in Ravada."

"You're not her, you know."

I wanted to force out a laugh—to show him how ridiculous the idea was—but the sound caught in my throat. I knew I wasn't her, so why did hearing him say that hit so hard?

"Why did you let me come with you to Sulian Daw?" I asked. "You could've said no, and I would've gone to Manasus with Meike and Carina. You could've ditched the last Adriann and washed your hands of my family once and for all."

His eyes lost focus, and for a second I thought he'd forgotten the question. "It's complicated," he said.

"Doesn't seem like it would be."

Guilt flashed across his eyes, but no, that couldn't be right. "You don't let tragedy bother you," he said. "I want to learn how to make death stop bothering me."

He still had nightmares, so I couldn't say I was surprised. "Not being bothered by death isn't a strength. It makes me want to do bad things sometimes. I'm not a good person."

Of all the reactions I'd expected from him, smiling wasn't one of them.

"What?" I asked.

"You're just like your brother." He ran the cold rag past my ear and along my jaw. "People who are naturally good won't change the world, because there will always be bad people to take advantage of them. But those who turn away from their bad impulses to do the right thing? They're the ones who make a difference. And they have the stomach to do what's necessary to the bad people when it's required."

It was a nice thought, but it was hard to believe the world needed someone like me. Hearing Jakar say that I would make a difference in the world filled me with warmth, though.

"There's another reason I brought you along," he continued. "I like being around you. You're fun. I never got much of that in Augustin."

His words cut me in a way that was new and strange. Not only did he think I was strong, but he actually enjoyed my company? That's what friends were supposed to say, but I'd spent so long hanging around people like the Titanite gang and my sister that I'd forgotten that fact. The only other person who'd ever said they liked my company had been Emil.

He frowned. "Is it the pain?"

I wiped the tears out of my eyes. "No."

Pain cracked the inside of my abdomen like a whip, and I clutched my stomach until my knees were pressed to my chest. My vision went fuzzy and the inside of my temples pounded, and when I could see again, my teeth were covered with the slime of vomit. "It's starting," I croaked.

"It started twenty minutes ago," Jakar whispered. His voice was far away, as though it were at the end of a tunnel. He still kneeled over me, holding a rag now thoroughly stained red. Most of the water was gone from the bowl. "Remember," he said quickly. "I'm right here. You're going to be all right. I'm here for you."

What felt like a coil weapon discharging in my abdomen struck again, making me scream.

Chapter 33—Jakar

"SLEEP DEPRIVATION IS gonna kill you," Torlo said.

Efadora's seizures had stopped hours ago. Nevertheless, I hadn't moved from my spot, to the point it felt as though a stake was being driven through my lower back, but I still couldn't bring myself to leave her side. "I need to keep her head cool or her brain will cook itself," I said. "She can't lie on her back, either, or she might choke on her vomit."

"Both easy things to manage," Namira said. She sat on the side of the bed she'd slept in and yawned. "The question is if you trust someone to look after her for you. Aren't you supposed to be chasing down the Ebonrock?"

I offered a hand to Torlo and he helped me to my feet. I almost stumbled but caught myself and stretched. "Yeah... you're right. Can you watch her, Torlo? Her water needs to be changed every hour. It helps if you talk to her on occasion."

"Shouldn't you rest?"

"Not in the mood, so I might as well be productive."

"You shouldn't go into the city by yourself."

"I grew up here. And I can defend myself, if that's what you're worried about."

"You get all sorts of attention if you use your power, though.

Could be smart to have someone watching your back so you can keep a low profile."

I would've preferred having Geth along—he knew Sulian culture and could speak the language—but he had left a couple hours earlier to investigate the city. Namira sighed. "Just go with him, Torlo. I owe Efadora for saving me from Darkwater."

"I thought that's what the cart was for," I said.

"Well, I've always been bad at math." She moved to Efadora's side and swept a sweaty bang out of the girl's face. "I have plenty of practice at caring for a child. This won't be an issue."

Namira had mentioned she had a son, and Efadora suspected they'd had a falling out. I nodded. "We won't be long."

"Get me a fresh change of water before you leave."

We stopped at one of the coffee cabanas, then walked several blocks to Som Abast's downtown area where the country's seat of power operated. "Why is this rockwood so soft?" Torlo asked, feeling the side of one of the buildings, which had been painted white with red trim.

"It grows above the ground, near the Burning Mountains. People cut it down and bring it here."

"Wood growing above the ground? Really? You're not pulling my chain?"

"The surface isn't so dangerous near the mountain range, from what I hear."

"Are the Burning Mountains really burning? Is that why it's warm enough to go outside?"

"No one knows. I used to hear rumors about people crossing to the other side, but you know how some people are. They'll say anything for fame. Most say there isn't a way through."

"Not unless you were an elemental who could make a path for yourself."

I pressed a hand against the side of the building, wondering if my theory about binding to carbon was right. My hand sank into the wood as easily as breaking the surface of a pond,

298

and I pulled back immediately, leaving a shallow imprint. Fortunately, nobody noticed except for Torlo. It seemed there was no denying it at this point. I had bonded to carbon.

"Jakar?" he asked. "If Efadora's Delineation ever started to turn bad, there'd be signs, right?

I tried not to let Torlo's anxiety feed into my own. I took a step back and tried to look at it as if Efadora was just another child I'd grown up beside in the slave school. "Her odds are good," I said. "Never a hundred percent, but a high pain tolerance usually tells you someone is going to make it through. And Efadora's suffered a lot of pain."

"What happened to you two? Before we met, I mean."

"Her family hurt the both of us. Then we left."

"You'll make sure she doesn't get hurt like that anymore, yeah? Aside from that rhidium business, obviously. I can tell she really struggles sometimes."

I nodded. He wore his infatuation with Efadora on his sleeve, and while I once would've discouraged it given the circumstances of how I'd come to know him, I'd warmed up to the idea. He cared for people without abandon. This world didn't allow people like him to exist, yet here he was.

We found the Office of Buildings and Codes and entered the properties department, where the lobby smelled of incense and had plush seating with exotic plants lining the walls. "I'm interested in buying a property next to Obsidian Lake," I told the man at the desk, speaking slowly as I tried to remember my Sulian. "The city owns it, currently."

"Which one would that be?"

"I don't have the address. I'm sorry. All I know is that it's on the south edge of the manufacturing district."

"A commercial property? Undersecretary Rhulkaur is who you'll want to talk to. I'll see if he's available to meet with you."

The assistant disappeared. "I know that name," I whispered to Torlo.

"Lucky us."

"He met with the fellowship of masters sometimes."

The prospect of finally meeting someone associated with the Ebonrock wiped the eager look off his face.

The assistant returned a few minutes later. "Follow me."

Undersecretary Rhulkaur had lost weight since I last saw him almost four years ago—loose skin hung off his face where fat had once been, making him look old and worn down as he worked at his desk. He still wore his cape of white grotto-wolf fur over fine silk shirts, but the fabric was frayed and old. The rug in his office was so soft I thought I might sink through it, and glass cabinets with old Sulian wood carvings stood against the walls. I shook the man's hand, and Torlo and I took a seat opposite him in front of his desk. "Ah, *modah*, how may I help?" he asked.

He didn't recognize me. "There's a property I'm doing some research on," I said. "I'm thinking of buying it. I don't have the address, but it's on Obsidian Lake, just south of the lumber mill. Last I remember, there were three buildings and a wall there, but it looks like pretty much everything was torn down. Do you know where I'm talking about?"

He frowned. "What about it? You said you're looking to purchase it? It's not for sale."

"Then I'd like some information on the last owners who occupied the property."

"Why?"

"I need to find them."

"They are not ones to be found easily, nor would they be keen on visitors."

"Maybe, maybe not. I'd like to join their organization, if possible."

The man stared at me for several moments, tapping his pen against the table. "I'm not sure what you're trying to say, but once again, that property isn't for sale. There's no other way for me to help you, sadly."

I tried a different tactic. A more direct one. "We met once."

"Oh? I work for the city. I meet many people."

"We didn't meet exactly, but you met my masters. It was several years ago, back when you were hiring them to have their slave children build for the city. I was one of those kids."

Rhulkaur froze, then tried and failed several times to come up with a response, his mouth opening and closing.

"You know about the Ebonrock," I said. "The Rha'Ghalor. Tell me where they are."

Again, he didn't respond, and with each second he grew more uncomfortable. His arm shifted subtly, and I could tell he was feeling for something under his desk. Torlo straightened ever so slightly—he couldn't understand what we were saying, but he'd noticed the rising temperature in the room.

"Leave now," Rhulkaur said. "I cannot help you, and I do not know what you're talking about."

I left my chair, dragged it to the door, and wedged it under the handle. He watched in disbelief, the fear on his face intensifying. "Guards!" he screamed.

I grabbed the edge of his desk and heaved. It fell toward him and nearly pinned him to the wall, but he slipped to the side, wedging himself in the corner where Torlo and I could keep him. A sword was in his hand—he must've been holding it while behind his desk—but despite the fact Torlo and I hadn't brought weapons in with us, he was still terrified.

"Last chance," I said. "I need to find them. They took my friends."

"I misheard you just now," he said. It sounded as if he was talking to himself more than to me, and his voice wavered from the words, beads of sweat trickling down his forehead.

I glanced at Torlo. He seemed as confused by Rhulkaur as I was. Either Rhulkaur truly was a coward or he could sense that I didn't want to kill him.

"I'm sorry," he cried out as he jumped at me. "Don't hurt me!"

He attacked, his movements desperate and his eyes pleading. I leaned backward, feeling the blade slice through the air in front of me, and I punched the man in his throat on the back swing. He choked and tumbled to the floor.

While Rhulkaur lay there gasping, someone knocked on the door, yelling, "Is everything all right, undersecretary?"

Rhulkaur wheezed in response.

There was more pounding on the door followed by demands to open up. Rhulkaur struggled to his feet, clenching the sword in one hand and holding his throat with the other, and stumbled at me again. His eyes were wild, but whatever desire he had for mercy wasn't enough to stop him. The blade sliced downward, and I palmed it to the side, this time punching him in his wrist. He took a few drunken steps backward and sniveled, tears in his eyes, but he picked the blade up with his other hand. "I don't want to die," he cried. Someone on the other side of the door must've heard, because they were throwing themselves against the barrier now.

Something wasn't right. Rhulkaur's words didn't match his actions. Nobody that scared and inept at fighting would come at me so recklessly unless they were more terrified of something else.

"Tell me about the Ebonrock," I said.

The question injected him with a new wave of energy and terror, and he swung awkwardly. I didn't even need to use my elemental power to block it. I grabbed his wrist, twisted it until he dropped the blade, and caught it before it fell to the ground. He stepped away and I waited. Then he did exactly what I was afraid he would do. He, an unarmed, injured man, came at me again, his fear peaking.

I knocked him on his stomach and put a foot on the small of his back, then knelt down and grabbed his shirt collar. The tip of the short sword sliced through the fabric, revealing flesh riddled with pale scarring, like lightning spreading from the base of his neck.

"You misunderstood me," I said. "I was asking about the Ebon Raiders."

"What?" he said.

I rolled him on his back. "The Ebon Raiders. Ebon. Raiders. That's who I was asking about. They're a group of bandits near the Sapphire Hollow, out by the border. I was not asking about whatever it was you think I was asking about."

The man shuddered, but his body relaxed. I backed away, and he slowly climbed to his feet. "Thank you," he said, tears falling down his face as he nursed his broken wrist. "You knew?"

"Better than anyone." I thought bitterly about how effective their Word was at forcing Rhulkaur to keep the Ebonrock a secret—he could either manage to kill whoever was asking after the cult, or he would get himself killed. "Again, I don't know what you're talking about," I said, hoping it would help him relax. "Do you think you can convince the guards this was just a misunderstanding?"

He jumped a little when the door shuddered, but nodded. I handed him the short sword.

"What's happening?" Torlo asked.

"We'll talk about it later," I answered in Miran. "He's going to open the door now and convince the guards to let us go."

"We can trust him?"

"Never, but what choice do we have?"

"Fight our way out. You're good at that sort of thing."

"No," I said.

Torlo and I moved to the corner of the room, and Rhulkaur rested the sword against the wall beside the door so he could use his good hand. Two guards rushed in, almost sending him on his butt, but he raised his hand and said, "Stand down. Everything is all right."

"What happened?" one of them asked. He looked from Rhulkaur's torn shirt to the wrist he was nursing, then to us. I folded my hands in front of me, trying to come off as non-threatening as possible.

"They're brothers of an ex-partner," Rhulkaur said. "They were just upset about me ending it, and rightly so. We sorted it out."

The guard noticed the sword leaning against the wall. "Did you?"

"It was a heated argument. Nothing more. Let them leave the premises. They won't be coming back."

I motioned Torlo toward the door. He didn't budge at first, but he eventually got moving. Rhulkaur gave me a mixed look of thanks and confusion as we walked past.

"I can't tell if that went well or not," Torlo said when we were on the streets outside.

"It did us more good than bad. That man was flesh bound. Words fade over time, so either someone from the Ebonrock is renewing his Words or there's something about flesh magic I don't know."

"What does that mean?"

"I'm not sure. There might be lives at stake here other than my friends', though." How many people walked the streets of Sulian Daw, bound to serve the Ebonrock under penalty of death? What about in other countries the Ebonrock had visited, like Rona, Karatoa, and Callo? And those were just the places I knew about. This was now much bigger than freeing some elementals.

"Strange, isn't it?" Torlo asked. "To leave this network of flesh bound behind when the Ebonrock won't come back here for years and years." He spoke with his gaze on the ground, trying as usual to avoid eye contact with feisty vendors.

"They did it because the flesh bound are doing something for the Ebonrock," I said. I couldn't help but look west, toward Obsidian Lake.

Chapter 34—Efadora

I woke to the sight of blood.

No, it was just the light of the Burning Mountains and the stain of the wooden ceiling above me. I definitely woke up to the taste of blood, however. And vomit.

"Ow," I tried to say, but it came out as a moan. Torlo was dozing against the wall and Geth sat against the side of a bed, reading one of the books I'd brought with me from the Archives. He caught my eye. "Sleep well?"

I tried to say, "You know it," but the words I forced out of my mouth sounded more like, "Lfhflg."

Torlo woke with a start. "Efadora," he said, rushing to my side. "How're you feeling?"

"Alive," I managed.

Both of them helped me over the next ten minutes, Torlo massaging the cramps out of my legs while Geth spoon-fed me some sort of spiced mush. "Where's Jakar and Namira?" I asked, once I was sure I could fully form sentences.

"There're some people in the city flesh bound to the Ebonrock," Geth said. "Jakar and Namira are tailing one of them, trying to figure out what they're up to. We should be doing the same thing, but we were waiting for you to wake up."

My new elemental sense was there, like a muscle that had suddenly popped into existence, but one I still wasn't sure how to use. I focused, trying to engage it by closing my eyes, and for a second, I thought I caught a glimpse of something glittery.

"You won't feel much," Geth said. He must've figured out what I was trying to do. "There isn't quartz around here for you to see. Wait until we're on the ground level, closer to the rock."

I tried to stand but failed. "I don't know if that's a good idea," Torlo said. "You're pretty beat up."

"Yeah, I'm pretty beat up after lying here for, what, two or three passings?"

"Just under two."

I tried again, and this time I was able to get to my feet and rest against the window frame. "I need to help Jakar. Did you say there are flesh bound people walking around Sulian Daw working for the Ebonrock?"

"We've spotted about a dozen so far. We don't know what they're supposed to be doing, but we haven't spotted any cultists in the city yet. Jakar and Namira are following a woman who works for the city's utilities, and there's a street sweeper Jakar asked us to check out."

"It only takes one person to tail someone. Why are both of you here?"

"Torlo doesn't know the city, and there was a misunderstanding the last time I went out alone," Geth said. "Jakar kindly requested that we go in groups now."

Torlo rolled his eyes. "Jakar figured out that if you mention the Ebonrock to someone who's flesh bound, they'll attack you on sight. Geth thought it a good idea to start running through the city shouting the name. The upside is that he managed to find two before they almost killed him."

"I thought we were trying to keep a low profile," I said. Standing soon became too much, so I moved to the bed and sat on it in a fit of coughing. There was no way members of the Ebonrock didn't know we were here by now—they had to be in the city if they had flesh bound servants walking around, since Words faded, given enough time.

"They should've been back by now," Torlo said after an hour. "Should one of us look for them?"

"Didn't you mention a street sweeper?" I asked. "Let's find them. We'll leave a note. I'm sure Jakar and Namira are fine."

Geth didn't hesitate to grab ink and paper from the desk in the corner. "All of us?" Torlo asked.

"I just need a bite and one of those coffee drinks and I'll be back to normal in an hour, tops," I lied. My whole body felt like one giant bruise, but I was eager to test out my new elemental sense and I never did well cooped up inside for too long.

We tracked down the street sweeper, whose name was Bhata, while she worked her shift cleaning trash and patches of moss off the curbs near Sulian Daw's manufacturing district. She looked too normal to be a slave bound by flesh magic to a secret cult society, but once upon a time I thought Jakar was just a quiet, boring servant Father had picked up to make his court more exotic. The first two hours of surveillance were boring, but it gave me a chance to recover some of my strength. By the time Bhata finished her shift, I barely had to hold onto Torlo's arm for support whenever I got dizzy.

The three of us tailed her from half a block away as she headed toward Obsidian Lake. "Still think she has no idea we're following her?" Torlo asked.

"She's walking like a drunk," I said. "Did anyone see her drinking?" Minutes after leaving her job, she had started to waver as she moved, as though she was sick or under the influence. She turned off the road and onto a footpath that ran along the back of a tanning shop, toward the lake's edge, and we hid behind the building and watched her descend the small hill to the rocks along the shore. She sat on a rock and stuck her feet in the water.

"Looks like she's just enjoying her time off," Geth said.

"Notice how bad the wind is?" I asked. "She's only wearing a shift. She has to be freezing."

The woman sat for ten minutes before climbing off the rocky shore and continuing along its edge. A hundred feet before she reached the property edge to the old Ebonrock compound, she stopped and bent over. That's when I noticed a wooden rectangle on the ground that was almost invisible from the road because of the sloping shore. Up swung a metal door she'd grabbed onto, and she climbed into the hole.

"Jakar didn't think to check the shore?" Geth asked.

"That door isn't even on the property," I said. Geth left our hiding spot, headed for the trapdoor, but I grabbed the scruff of his shirt. "What are you doing?" I asked.

"I'm a cartographer. What do you think?"

"We shouldn't go in without Jakar. I don't even have my coil weapon."

He shrugged my hand off. "Cartographers don't depend on others to do their jobs for them. If they did, we'd be dust and a memory. Can you take care of yourself or not?"

"Of course I can."

"Good answer."

Geth's habit of working alone didn't mean he was stupid enough to walk into a situation like this blind without more help. It didn't make sense. "Why are you really doing this?"

"Because it might be my only chance. I've been waiting weeks for a chance to learn more about the Ebonrock, but Jakar made it clear he'd rather destroy them than learn from them. The Ebonrock worship the Great Ones, and so did the Sihraan Empire! What if they know what happened to the Sihraans?"

Geth had grown more animated as he was speaking—the words sounded suspiciously rehearsed, too, as if he'd been waiting for this moment. So this was the Geth Jakar had tried to warn me about in Ravada. Depths below, I should've known these were Geth's true colors after that shit he pulled in the Rift.

"I know how to work my way around a bit of danger," Geth continued. "Assuming there is anything to worry about. The Ebonrock have been gone for months. I'm just going to poke my head around a bit while we wait for Jakar to show up, all right? You're welcome to join me."

I turned to Torlo. "Go get Jakar and Namira. Wait for them at the room if you have to. Can you find your way back?"

Torlo grabbed my hand, gently but firmly, as if afraid I was a bunny about to bolt at any moment. "Come with me."

"It only takes one to play messenger." I didn't want to tell him the truth—that I was afraid of what Geth might find down there and that I didn't want to see him hurt. A voice in the back of my head, the one that sounded far too much like Sara, told me that caring for Geth was only me being weak, me being someone who hadn't grown up and learned the hard truths of the world, but still I couldn't stand to watch Geth go. He was almost at the trapdoor now. Fhelfire, what had happened to me? If this was back in Mira, I would have waved Geth goodbye and laughed at his stupidity.

"I don't want to leave you," Torlo said.

"It won't be for long. I believe in you."

His hands, which had always been so soft, felt rough as they held mine. This trip had hardened him. Even though things were moving much too quickly, this moment slowed as I looked into his eyes, wishing we'd had more time together, just me and him. My heart quickened, and I felt it rise in my throat before I swallowed it back down.

"It's not like the Ebonrock have been hiding down there this whole time," I said. "They left Sulian Daw. Now go get Jakar." I pulled away, hurrying after Geth as he disappeared into the hole.

Chapter 35—Jakar

"WHO ARE THEY?" Namira asked after a few minutes of us watching the couple working the fruit stand in Tradevein Plaza.

"My parents."

"Oh. They look... normal, considering."

We continued to watch. Following the utilities worker had been a bust—the man had finished his shift and gone home, where it looked like he'd remain for the rest of passing's end—and Namira and I had talked about heading back to the inn before I'd realized we were near Tradevein Plaza. The place my parents frequently lurked, and the place I'd been begging at when the Ebonrock threw a bag over my head and knocked me unconscious with meaty fists.

My parents worked feverishly bagging up and bartering with the customers around their booth. This passing was a popular time to buy fruit, apparently. "I don't remember my parents ever owning a business," I said. They'd always spent their off time complaining about the lack of work, and it wasn't until I was older that I wondered how much time they'd spent looking. What really surprised me was the fact they were sabadra—scum of the land in the eyes of Sulian

Daw—and now they were operating a business in one of the well-to-do areas of the city.

"When was the last time you saw them?" Namira asked.

"When I was eleven. So, fourteen years ago."

"Go talk to them. They probably miss you."

"They sold me to the city for drug money, and that's how I became part of the Ebonrock."

A long silence followed. It was the first time I had ever said those words out loud, and it brought back corrosive memories. I'd been angry at the Ebonrock for torturing me, but what they'd done was in their nature. The hurt my parents inflicted had gone far deeper—it was hard to put into words how it felt to have the two most important people in my life betray me the way they had.

"They're doing well," I said.

"Is that a good or a bad thing?"

"I don't know."

"They can be totally different people compared to who they were when they raised you. Maybe they regret things."

"Maybe."

"I can talk to them. I'm a mother, so I know how important you standing here could be to them. You know... if they've changed."

"How's your Sulian?" I asked.

"I haven't lived here since I was a kid, but it's passable."

She left my side before I could stop her, but I was too afraid to attract my parents' attention if I went after her. So I hid. A fountain carved in the shape of Fedsprig—Sulian Daw's version of Fheldspra—sat in the plaza's center, and I put it between me and the fruit stand. The god was carved to look like a vaguely shaped bipedal creature made of magma, with water flowing out of its palm that had glowing bits of red moss. Fedsprig was a monstrosity, likened to a form that could truly take on the Great Ones, and He provided plenty of coverage to hide from my parents.

Namira reached the front of the line and struck up a

conversation with my parents, but I was too far away to hear anything. Every time she gestured in a way that made me think she was pointing in my direction, I ducked. Was she talking about me? She stayed for a few minutes, then headed off with a bag of fruit in hand. It took her a moment to spot me behind the fountain.

"What did you guys talk about?" I asked quickly.

"I just asked them about the business. How they got started and whatnot. Told them I transported goods like theirs and that I was thinking of setting up shop in Sulian Daw, if they were interested in expanding their reach."

"You… networked?"

"Of course. It would be weird if a complete stranger was asking about their personal lives without good reason. They started up their fruit stand business about ten years ago. They've been having trouble staying open because old debts are eating into their profits. No, I didn't mention you, but you might want to know what they named their little fruit stand."

"What?"

"Jakar's Juices."

I sat on the edge of the fountain, trying to sort out what that meant and what it meant to me. Did they regret selling me off? It was the only explanation. Did it change anything?

"Old debts?" I asked, taking my face out of my hands.

"I didn't ask. It would have been strange to pry. Given what you told me about them, I'd guess they got in deep a long time ago when they were feeding their bad habits."

"Do they look like they still use?"

"Hard to say. I'm sorry."

I crossed the plaza, angling my body away from my parents until I reached the northern steps and headed for the hilly part of Sulian Daw near the cavern's north wall. "Where are we going?" Namira asked.

"My old home. I need to see if they're still using."

Walking around Obsidian Lake gave me the jitters, but traveling through this part of Sulian Daw felt strangely nostalgic. Nostalgic was too strong a word, perhaps. The tiled streets changed to dirt, colored with bands of red light and shadow, and buildings rose and dipped with the land. We came to a depression where several fifty-foot-tall mounds waited, covered in hundreds of holes like Swiss cheese. Paths spiraled to the top of the mounds, and people covered them like ants. This was the Nochi district. Home of the sabadra. It was one of the districts closest to the Outside, and biting wind whipped at us in staccato gusts. Most of the people around here wore little more than rags, but they didn't seem to mind the wind. I followed a path up one of the mounds, squeezing past people moving the other way, until I came to a hole I could pick out of my dreams. I ducked inside and Namira followed.

The place was much smaller than I remembered—just a simple living space carved from clay. The bed took up almost a quarter of the home, and there were a few wooden dishes in the corner and a water bucket. Stacks of papers were under the bed, which seemed to be for the fruit stand business. Other than some knick knacks, the place was empty.

"They're clean now," I said. "I remember this place being full of trash and clutter. The walls also had this acidic smell to them that came from the pipes they smoked. The smell's gone."

"A lot can happen in fourteen years."

I sat on the bed, trying to think, trying to puzzle out how I felt, but my thoughts bounced back and forth, from miserable memories living in a house of drug addicts to the torture of the slave school, back and forth, from the life that was stolen from me to the knowledge I would have grown up to be a futureless sabadra anyway, back and forth, from the surprise of this sudden confrontation with my past to knowing deep down that I'd been drawn to my parents all this time. It wasn't fair. My freedom to choose had been stripped clean with my flesh binding, but my choices had been taken away long before then. I'd never had a say in the person I was to become, whether that was sabadra or… whatever I was now.

But would I change the past? I tried to imagine who I might be if my parents had never sold me, and that's when I found my answer. Whoever that man might have been, it wasn't me. It was a stranger I would never recognize. Not only that, but in a life where everything had been taken away from me, the one thing that had become my unassailable possession had been my identity. No one, not even me, could take that away.

The sound of steps and the rustle of fabric entered the house, and a figure crowded into the doorway. The sullen-looking man froze. "Who are you?" he asked.

"Who are you?" I countered.

His hand went inside his coat pocket, and I could feel the steel hiding there. "Are you here to collect on Yega and Jedke?" he asked.

"Yes," I said, thinking quickly. I rose from the bed, trying to stand menacingly. "Maybe I'll take some of what they owe from you. Who are you?"

He raised his hands in a calming gesture. "Relax, please. I work for the city. It is not in your best interests to threaten me."

"Why are you here?"

His smile was brittle. "It really is none of your business."

"My... Yega and Jedke work a fruit stand in Tradevein Plaza. Tell me why that is, given they're sabadra."

"They performed a great service for the city many years ago. The city awarded them a business license as part of the agreement."

A great service many years ago. "What did they do?"

"Again, that is none of your business."

"Was it when they sold their son to the city?"

The way he stiffened was all the answer I needed. "Are you really here to collect?" he asked.

"No."

Steel flashed in his hand, and I pushed Namira behind me. She fell on the bed as I grabbed the man's knife hand and twisted until the weapon fell to the floor and he cried out in pain. I grabbed him by the front of his coat and slammed him against the wall. "Why are you here?" I asked.

His eyes watered from the back of his head hitting the wall. "I'm… here to deliver subsidies."

I dug through his pockets until I pulled out a coin purse, and I turned it over until a dozen vials slipped through the drawstring and clattered to the ground, all of them cracking and oozing clear, viscous fluid on the ground. "Above and below," Namira said. "That's Elyan Ice."

"What?"

"It's called the Drug of the Free Market. Leaders of Darkwater and other big businesses use it. Hyper-productivity and euphoria in one, from what I hear. In Sulian Daw they call it Lightning in a Bottle. People would kill for those vials, Jakar. It's the most expensive drug on the market."

It took a moment to compare her words with what this man had said. I slammed the city worker against the wall again. "You called them subsidies," I said. "Was that another part of that great service my parents did fourteen years ago? They get set up with a little business in a nice part of town and free drugs to boot?"

His eyes widened. "You."

"Me?"

"How'd you escape the Ebonrock?"

I grabbed the knife off the ground and jammed it into his abdomen before I had time to think. He gasped, and I pulled the knife out and stabbed again. And again. And again. Blood covered my hand, then my arm, then it was in my eyes and I had to wipe it away before I stabbed again. It wasn't until Namira was screaming did I realize I'd been screaming myself.

I stepped back and the man crumpled to the ground, his chest a ruin. The vials were submerged in blood. Namira watched me in horror, flicks of blood staining her shirt and hair, and I dropped the knife, stumbling back, almost slipping.

"We need to leave," a voice said. It was mine.

I took her hand, and she let me, but I wasn't sure if it was because she trusted me or because she was too terrified to resist. I led her out of the hole and found people outside their hovels watching us. Some gasped and others ran. We stood halfway up the mound, the ground thirty feet below us, and I picked Namira up and jumped. She screamed again, but my power let us touch the ground smoothly. I took off running with her in my arms.

It was impossible not to draw attention to ourselves as I took us along the outskirts of the Bejiya Bel near the exit out of the city. A deep-set canal cut against the cavern wall, and I jumped down and moved along its precarious banks, the ground level of the trade district a dozen feet above our heads. Eventually I found a spot with an alcove. I set Namira at the water's edge and backed away.

Blood was smeared along the back and the side of her shirt, and I took in my gore-slicked body. I studied myself, watching the tears splotch onto my forearms, leaving little windows of pain. A whine left my throat as I tried to say something, to let her know she didn't need to be afraid, and I finally managed to croak out two words. "I'm sorry."

She didn't answer, just looked at me with a range of emotions. I was too ashamed to hold her gaze, so I stepped into the water and started working to clean off the blood.

"I've never seen you that angry before," she said.

I tried to come up with a response but resorted to scrubbing my shirt instead.

"Are you all right?"

My voice was quiet. "No."

She joined me, slipping her own shirt off. In her undershirt, she grabbed a rock and went to work beside me. The shock of what had happened wore off, and I scrubbed miserably, thinking of how after all the time I'd spent telling myself I wouldn't kill unless necessary, I had brutally murdered someone in a simple fit of rage. And it had been far from necessary.

"I've seen many things in my long years," Namira said.

"You caught me by surprise, so I apologize for my reaction, but I promise I've seen worse. You can talk to me if you'd like. No judgment."

The prospect of talking about this didn't sound as overwhelming as it used to. "I felt fine until we got here. Well... fine for me."

"You never processed it."

"What my parents did? I did process it. I've known for years what they did."

"Knowledge only gets you halfway. Acceptance is something else entirely. All you did was dig a very deep hole so you could put it all somewhere quiet."

It was strange hearing someone else puzzle out the motivations behind my behavior, and it made me realize how little reflecting I'd done lately. These past few months had been strangely freeing, despite the hardships, allowing me to live from passing to passing without thinking about the Granite Road or the Adrianns. However, it left me unprepared to confront what waited for me here.

We scrubbed at our clothes for half a minute. "My son died," she said.

I stopped. I waited patiently for her to continue, her expression starting to scrunch up as she recalled a memory, until her face relaxed as if she had regained something she had almost lost control of.

"It'll be six years next First Northern Sway," she said. "He got sick. I never found out of what, only that it took eighty-four passings after that first terrible cough before I lost him. And I was with him for almost every hour of those eighty-four passings, feeding him once he couldn't feed himself and cleaning up after him when he was too weak to go outside." She wrung out her shirt. "I got into the transportation business because I found I felt all right whenever I would leave the country, but every time I came back to our little place in the Tanzanite District, I would fall apart. I could barely hold myself together. I realized that walking away from a problem can trick you into thinking you've worked through it, when in reality all you've done is walk away from its triggers."

I turned, causing her to flinch. She offered a look of apology while I tried to keep the guilt from eating me alive, and I asked, "What do I do? What did you do?"

"There's no easy answer to make you feel all right with what happened. You just have to accept what is. In your case, I suppose you'll have to accept that we're all flawed, your parents especially."

"Should my parents be punished?"

She grimaced. "Enough talk about what the people who did the hurting deserve. This should be about what the victim deserves, and I suspect far too few people have given that enough thought when it comes to you. You deserve what your parents couldn't give you. Flesh and blood aren't a prerequisite for love, you know."

The knot in my throat grew. I knew she was right, of course—I'd found love and kinship among the kids I'd grown up with in the Ebonrock, but I'd thought I could never experience that again once they were taken from me. Maybe that's why I had fallen so hard for Sara. After years of loneliness I'd been desperate to connect to someone. Emil was the only person I'd truly loved, but I realized perhaps that was no longer the case.

I loved Efadora. I loved her just as much as Emil. It didn't matter if we didn't share blood, she was my family, and I would do anything for her. I couldn't deny my growing fondness for Torlo, either. I didn't know Namira very well, but I found myself hoping I could change that, too.

"Thank you," I said. I couldn't look her in the eye.

She set a hand on my shoulder while I hunched in the water cleaning a pant leg, the gesture slapping against my wet shirt. "You'll be okay. Maybe not soon, but eventually. Surrounding yourself with good people is the best medicine for such wounds."

We spent the rest of our time in the canal in silence. My shirt and boots were a lost cause, so I threw them in the river.

I picked up Namira, offered her a warning, and she sucked in a breath as I leaped out of the canal and landed on the streets of the trade district. The blood on my soaked pants had turned into faded stains, but without my shirt and with Namira dripping beside me, we looked more like a freak show than a couple wanted for murder. It was another mile back to the inn, and people stared at us the entire way, making no effort to hide their disgust. We looked like sabadra, so no one was afraid of offending us. More than once we had to dodge into an alley or double back to avoid patrols. We slowed down a block away from the inn.

"Isn't that Torlo?" Namira asked.

Torlo, who had been hanging around the entrance to the inn with a panicked look on his face, spotted us and broke into a sprint. He ran into several people on the way through, and they spat curse words in his wake, but he ignored them. When he reached us, he said through ragged breaths, "I just came from the lake."

"The lake?" I asked.

"We found a hidden entrance going under the compound and Geth decided to go in. Efadora followed."

Ice filled my stomach, and then I was running. My flesh binding was created under the Ebonrock compound, and if the kadiphs and the fellowship didn't collapse those tunnels when they demolished the buildings, it meant the tunnels still had a purpose. And its purpose was evil.

Chapter 36—Ester

NOBODY ATTEMPTED TO kill or even stop Ester as she came onto the ridge overlooking the ruins of Mulec'Yrathrik. People didn't scurry about the ruins this passing—in fact, she couldn't spot anyone among the worn-down towers or the ancient rubble stained green and brown. For a moment, she wondered if the Sovereign had put his Ruin Folk Extermination plan at the top of the list and already passed through here, but then a woman down the hill exited the gutted innards of an outpost and grabbed for a spear leaning against the wall, yelling something in the old tongue.

"I'm here in peace," Ester called out. The woman stopped several feet away, not attacking but not lowering her spear. "Why here?" the woman demanded.

Ester slid a hand into one of her saddlebags and pulled out a vial of glowing rhidium. "I'm looking for Breach. Is he still here?"

More ruin folk appeared, wearing bits of armor that were so horribly made, it almost hurt Ester to look at them. They forced her off her mount, and it took effort not to resist them as they led her fox and the rhidium away and escorted her down the hill. They entered a building without a ceiling, its rubble cleared out, where Breach stood at a table covered in a giant map. Several ruin folk were with him, wearing more poorly smithed gear. Breach's mouth fell open when they locked eyes. "You're here," he said.

"Yep. I'm here. I changed my mind. If you need the rhidium, you can have it."

"What's wrong?"

She barely heard the murmurings of the ruin folk as they spoke to each other in their native tongue—she only had eyes for Breach, who stared at her with nothing but worry in his eyes. She'd missed him dearly, despite not trusting him, knowing that if he ever betrayed her again he would at least try to protect her as he did it. It was a screwed up way of looking at things, but her mind had been all sorts of broken lately. The way he was looking at her only solidified the relief she felt upon seeing him again.

"She bring Anjia's Tears?" one of his companions asked. He was a tall, lanky man with a bushy beard and surprisingly high-quality leathers. "We leave immediately. Can catch up others."

Breach strode toward her, dismissing the words of his companion with a hand. He stopped a stride away and examined her more closely, as if checking to see if she was hurt. "Ester, tell me what's wrong. Did something happen in Augustin?"

The concern in his voice seemed to pique the interest of his friends, enough to wait for an answer, and before Ester knew it, the words were tumbling out. As she spoke, not hesitating to include every little detail between the moment she returned to Augustin and the moment she left, she found that she craved the way the horror grew on their faces, how it was no longer her and Judge Abeso bottling up the truth, the pressure mounting until she wanted to burst into tears for the tenth time. Before the loss of her brothers and sisters she had cried only once in five years, and that was when Damek had almost died, but lately it seemed like it was all she could manage.

But it didn't have to be this way anymore. Judging by the look on everyone's faces, they believed every word, and it dulled the despair that had shadowed her for weeks.

"Vampire," a squat man with a puckered scar on his cheek said. "What did Sovereign's child call beggar man?"

"'Homunculus.' Bilal said 'homunculus' before they kidnapped and changed the beggar into the new magnate."

The man rattled off some words in the old tongue and Breach translated. "That's a loaded word around these parts. It's an old one. Older than the Sihraans. It comes from legends about soulless and malformed creatures created by demigods, pulled from the rock and the water around us. About as ancient and evil as it gets." Breach stepped closer, enough for it to almost feel intimate, and he asked in a low voice, "Are you ready to discuss this? If you need rest, let me know."

As much as she appreciated his concern, making sense of all this was the only thing she cared about. She gave a small nod in thanks. "I thought there was nothing older than the Sihraans this side of the Rift," she said to the others.

The tall, bushy-bearded man laughed. "Humans six times older than Sihraans, at least."

She wondered about the reasoning behind his math, but found she was pretty tired of dark and evil things at the moment. "Did you ever use the rhidium you stole from me?" she asked, peeking at the map on the table. It was of Mira, with pins indicating landmarks, most of which were concentrated in and around Saracosta.

The lines in Breach's face darkened from some memory. "We used what we knew about the Foundry's Trials and a few volunteers tested it. It didn't work."

You mean people died. "Figures. How did you go about it?"

Breach explained, and Ester was shaking her head by the time he finished. "Dying is always a risk with rhidium, but that probability skyrockets if it accidentally binds with something else inside whatever material you used," she said. "Judging by the shit-forged steel I've seen, their deaths were guaranteed."

Breach nodded in deference, despite the jab, and Ester regretted her rude tone. She couldn't remember the last time she wasn't in a bad mood. "If you could show us the right way, we'd appreciate it," he said.

"No time," the companion said. "We ride. Catch up to the others. Drink Anjia's Tears there. Show them how, too."

Ester gave Breach a questioning look, and he said, "All the battle-ready ruin folk left here a week ago. They're headed for Saracosta. They're going to start a guerrilla war by attacking resource nodes to crash Mira's economy."

"Crashing the economy will hurt a lot of people indirectly."

"We can't brute force the Sovereign and his primordia out of power, so our plan is to undermine his ability to run the country. Sow discord until his citizens go to him for help, and when he can't, things will eventually sour." He gave a brittle smile. "It turns out when the people demand reform, it can create powerful change. Just look at the fall of Sorrelo Adriann." He turned to one of his associates. "Our people will have splintered in a dozen different directions by the time we catch up, so riding after them won't work. We need to do the trials here."

Ester found the tiny, unmarked area on the map in southern Tulchi she'd been looking for. "I call the shots if you want my help, and I say we're doing the trials in these ruins. It's best for those undergoing it to be somewhere familiar. After that, we ride—" She planted a finger on the spot she'd been eying— "here."

"Why?" Puckered Scar asked.

"Mira's treasury is there. You want to crash the economy? Go where they make the currency."

Breach and the ruin folk shared a look. "Know this place, how?" one of them asked.

"My brother Myrilan is an assistant treasurer. I'm not supposed to know about the treasury's location, but the last time I saw Myrilan, we got in a bad fight and I may have memorized the directions he was given to get there."

"Seems strange you'd do that," Breach said. "What was the point?"

The question reminded Ester of the kind of person she'd been before committing herself to the Foundry—the kind who'd been jealous of Myrilan for landing such an important and lucrative job, and for playing with the idea of showing up to the secret treasury unannounced, hoping her initiative might garner interest. She'd realized back then it would've only gotten Myrilan fired, but she knew enough now to wonder if it would've gotten them both killed, too.

Nobody outside her family knew she'd been a loyalist before discovering the Sky Scrolls and joining the Foundry—back when her need to belong to a group had almost led her down a terrible path, until the smiths taught her how evil the Sovereign really was. A disgusting secret she would take to the grave. "I knew it was important information at the time, so I figured it'd be worth remembering."

The ruin folk didn't question that she had a brother working for the Sovereign. Even they assumed her smith-like hatred for the Sovereign superseded her relationship with Myrilan.

Breach spoke in the old tongue in a tone that suggested he was making requests, and one by one, his companions left. "They're going to gather up everyone I want to turn into metal workers. While they do that—"

"Don't call them metal workers," Ester said. "Please."

He nodded, and his hand twitched toward her, almost as if he was going to grab her hand, but he caught himself. "I know how big a deal this is, so thank you. It means the world to me."

A silence passed between them, and Ester found herself a little moved by how he considered every word she spoke. He'd always acted like that, but she hadn't appreciated it until now. "Did you finish that weapon you were working on in the Tear?" she asked.

"You remember that?"

"Of course. I could tell it was important to you."

"I'll show you, but promise you'll keep it a secret. I'd rather word not get out, even among my friends. Those leading the ruin folk have a frequent habit of acquisitioning anything that might help the cause, and my project has grown quite dangerous. I'd hate to see them take it before it's properly tested, and hurt themselves."

He led her to an antechamber, which was full of bits of metal, tools, glass, and a cot with blankets thrown haphazardly on top. The weapon lay on a table beside the cot, and he picked it up. "I still need the right power source, then I'll calibrate the weapon so it properly channels the energy."

"Why is it so hard to find a power source?" she asked.

"I've found it already, actually. I've even experimented with it. It's rhidium." He tossed the weapon on the bed and threw the blankets over it, as if embarrassed. "Why do you think rhidium glows? Light is energy, if you remember that first conversation we had at the Guild. Rhidium's energy is exceptionally powerful, and you don't have to eat it to take advantage. Unfortunately, I ran out of rhidium before I could perfect the thing."

"I guess it's a good thing I brought more."

He shrugged. "I have something else I want to show you that you'll find more impressive. This you should also keep a secret."

"You really don't trust your friends."

"It's not like that. They just like to make fun of anything they don't find useful, and I don't want to hear it from them."

They headed into the ruins, beyond the perimeter where the overgrowth had been cut back and maintained, to where moss, vines, and plants with flowering bulbs of light ran rampant and grew in tangles that grabbed at their feet. They reached a stone ring lined with torches, and Breach approached a strange contraption waiting in the center. "One of your Guild experiments?" Ester asked.

"Not in the slightest." He bent over and gave it a pat. It was a dome that came up to his knees and was made of rusted copper, but not nearly rusted enough given its probable age. "This place used to be infested with fire beetles and a pretty nasty trapdoor spider, but I cleared them out and found this amazing bit of technology. Watch." He pushed a hidden switch and it started to hum.

"What does it do?" she asked.

"Just wait."

The dome opened, revealing a complex system of gears, cogs, and dozens of tiny lenses that gleamed in the torchlight, brand new, which was probably Breach's doing. Then beams of light shot out of the contraption, focused through the glass.

The contraption surrounded them in a dome of light that ended at the ring's edge, filled with hundreds of sparkling pinpoints. "It looks like the sky," Ester said, exploring the dome. The inside was mostly empty space, the projected light concentrated at the edge. The faux stars disappeared whenever she stood between them and the contraption.

"It *is* the sky," Breach said. "A projection of it. All the constellations and nebulae are accurate. What I don't get is how this device refracts light. But the most fascinating part is this." He gestured to the dome's center, above the contraption, where several balls of light were rotating.

"What is that?"

He pointed at the smallest ball of light, which was red, as it rotated around the second smallest ball, which was half blue and half red. "I think the red ball is Saffar," he said. "And the thing it's circling is Ra'Thuzan."

"Ra'Thuzan? As in…" Ester motioned to the ground around them.

He nodded.

The second smallest ball—Ra'Thuzan, apparently—rotated around the largest and brightest ball in the light show, which was as big as Ester's fist. "So what's that?"

"I don't know. Something like that would fill up our entire sky, but look at this." He pointed at the second largest point of light, which was white and almost three feet away from the other balls. "That's Ceti. I would bet my Guild membership on it. In fact, I'm sure about all of this, that we're looking at Saffar rotating around Ra'Thuzan, and Ra'Thuzan rotating around… whatever that is, and that giant ball of light and Ceti are circling each other, like a never-ending dance."

Ester eyed Ra'Thuzan, and noticed it was half blue, half red. "The blue side is always facing away from the giant ball," she said.

Breach looked closer. "You're right."

She set her hands on her hips and gave the spectacle another once-over before saying, "It's pretty. Why are you showing it to me?"

"Because you and I find many of the same things interesting."

He was right, as usual. Her inquisitive mind was often drawn to the things he was working on, to the concepts he loved explaining.

"But that's not the real reason I brought you here," he said, picking up a metal rod lying on the ground. "This is what I wanted to show you." He tossed the rod at the contraption and a spark crackled through the air, accompanied by a flash of light, and the contraption darkened. "It builds up quite a charge when you turn it on. Lost all the feeling in my arm the first time I tried to turn it off."

Electricity. "Can you move it?" she asked.

"Not this one, but there were a handful of other working devices we found around the city that could build up a nasty little spark. Obviously, they're not intended as weapons, but beggars can't be choosers."

She remembered the way Nektarios's body had flexed, his eyeballs nearly popping out of his head after Jakar had shocked him and proceeded to cave his skull in.

"I'm happy with the discovery, too," Breach said. "We wouldn't have put the effort into finding this stuff without your heads-up. Together, you and I can turn the tide against the primordia."

She smiled. Happy wasn't the right word to describe how she was feeling; more relieved. Hopeful, too, that they had a real shot at hurting more primordia, and warm with the thought she was in the presence of someone who wanted the same things she did.

She crossed the distance between them and hugged him.

"Thank you," she said when she pulled away.

"I—" He opened his mouth and shut it again. "I figured you were just here for revenge. That you'd be furious with me because of what I did." Even after all these weeks, guilt made it hard for him to look her in the eye.

"It's all right," she said. While she had forgiven him, she had to admit that weeks spent being strung along while chasing the rhidium, being lied to every step of the way still smarted a little, but she had tried her best to understand where he was coming from. She tried not to think about how if she'd been in the capital when the Sovereign showed up, Mateo and the others' fates might have turned out differently.

No, she was being naïve. All that would have changed is she would be a homunculus with the rest of them.

"It doesn't feel all right," he said.

She couldn't help but think about how it was just the two of them, alone. She didn't know how the ruin folk would react to her romancing one of their own, but it's not as if they would know if she chose to act on her feelings. She eyed his lips, studied the wrinkles around his eyes. No one so young should have had such wrinkles. It meant he spent a lot of his time worrying, trying to take care of the ruin folk he wanted to protect.

"I told myself I'd make it up to you if I ever saw you again," he said. "And now that we're together again, you're already promising to help with the rhidium trials. I'm in an endless debt, it seems." He didn't seem bothered by the idea—in fact, there was a hint of amusement in his tone. Was he flirting? Breach was a man so focused on complex ideas and big pictures, Ester wasn't sure if he'd spend his time on something so inane as flirting.

Whatever the case, now wasn't the time for her to figure it out. There was work to be done. "Start by promising me you'll never lie to me again."

"I promise, Ester."

His eyes glimmered, and Ester turned to head back before she thought too hard on what that look meant. *One step at a time.*

Chapter 37—Jakar

BLACKNESS GAPED AT me as I stood at the top of the steps leading into the underground compound. All darkness was the same, technically, but there was also a flavor to this darkness I know I wasn't imagining. Motes of dust floated in the red light, falling into the inky hole that swallowed them. It took effort not to turn and walk away.

I folded my hand into the other to stop it from shaking. "Grab some emberbrush," I said. Torlo ran off, and I forced myself down the first few steps. "Efadora?" I called out in a hoarse whisper. "Geth?" I didn't want to alert anyone who might be a threat, but I was also unsure how to go about finding Efadora or Geth. Only my echo answered my call.

Torlo returned with three branches, their wood dancing with light like smoldering embers. The glow wasn't bright enough to see more than a few feet in front of us as we reached the dungeon's floor, but it'd have to do. The place smelled wet, rocky, and long abandoned, and once again the memories came, ones that made my heart sit at the bottom of my stomach. This place had broken me. I had dissolved here, down into a thousand pieces, and left to wallow in something resembling a mind. Was I really any different now? How could a couple years make a difference when I'd spent a decade training to become the person Ig had turned me into?

What if I was too broken to do this?

Dead torches hung in sconces that lined long, winding corridors, and minerals embedded in the walls glittered from the light of our branches. "Efadora?" I called again, this time quieter. We reached another set of stairs, our boots slapping the stone as we descended them, twice as loud in the silence. I paused. I asked Torlo and Namira a question with my eyes—whether they'd heard the faint scraping coming from a hallway to our right—and they nodded. I moved down the hall before I could second-guess myself, and turned into the closest chamber.

Two people stood in front of a row of cages, one of whom was working at a cage's latch, and they turned. One of them was the flesh bound Namira and I had tailed last passing. The woman's face scrunched up with fear. "Please," she said. "Leave. Leave now." The other one tensed, less afraid, his weight onto his front feet.

"We can't," I said.

"Please," she repeated. "They'll make me hurt you."

This was Undersecretary Rhulkaur all over again. Their flesh bindings would compel them to protect this place, but this time around there was nothing I could do to stop what would come to pass—I had to keep looking, I had to find Efadora.

"I'm sorry," I said.

They attacked.

Daggers flashed in their hands, and Torlo and Namira scrambled back. I palmed the first dagger to the side and knocked the man out with a clean hit under the chin, feeling the woman's dagger slide along the fabric of my shirt below my arm, close enough for the rough edge to leave a stinging line on my skin. I twisted, ripping the blade out of her hand, and clocked her in the temple with the dagger's butt. Both lay on the ground, unmoving.

"Open one of the empty cages," I said. "They won't be out for long." There were five cages against the back wall, three of which were occupied, and the bedraggled, sullen prisoners watched us as I dragged the first of the flesh bound into the cage Namira opened.

"Help," one of the prisoners whispered in Sulian. He and the other two shielded their eyes from the emberbrush light.

"How long have you been down here?" I asked, grunting as I set the second flesh bound next to his friend.

"A long time," he said. His face was gaunt but not emaciated, his knees knobby, and his hands desperately shaking the bars. "Help. They're going to kill us."

I locked the cage I put the flesh bound in and released the three prisoners. Torlo and Namira helped them out—there were three men, all of them naked, with bruising on their legs and sores on their skin. "What were they going to do with you?" I asked.

"We don't know."

"I was here before these two," one of the others said. "There were a couple before me, got led off several passings apart. Don't know what happened to them."

I led the group into the hall, the flesh bound stirring as we left, and we reached the stairs in the main hallway. "Help them outside," I said to Torlo and Namira. "I'll keep looking for the others."

Deeper into the compound I went, poking my head through rotted doorframes with my emberbrush and moving up and down the tangle of hallways, but I found no sign of Efadora. I descended another set of stairs and reached a fork I'd seen time and again in my dreams. I went left and found the entryway at the end of the hall. The one from my nightmares.

The door was open. "Efadora," I said. She and Geth were at the table of metal boxes along the left wall, and they turned. Relief flooded Efadora's face. "Thank Fheldspra," she said.

"You should have waited for me."

Guilt flashed across Efadora's face. "I'm sorry."

Geth gestured at the boxes. "Do you know what these are?"

I crossed my arms, trying to decide how angry I was. Excluding the three flesh bound, all was quiet down here. There was still the mystery of what they had planned for the people in those cages, but for now it seemed Efadora was safe. "You earn my help when we work as a team."

"I'm a cartographer," Geth said flatly. "If I want to put my life on the line for what I do, I'm going to do it. And Efadora *chose* to follow me. Now are you going to answer my question or not?"

My attention moved to the glassy, still pool behind them, and the ball that was forming in my chest doubled in size. My anger fizzled, overshadowed by the fear looming over me, over this room. I didn't want to be here anymore, but I was struggling to articulate it. Namira's words came to me, and I realized it was old trauma rearing its head, refusing to let me speak.

Geth took my silence as stubbornness. "It's fine. I'll figure it out myself," he said. He bent over the boxes, the metal in surprisingly good shape, and followed the tangle of wires that led to the pool of water against the back wall and to a chair covered in stains the color of rust.

"It's not safe here," I finally managed to say as I stared at the chair. "Ig lives here."

"What?" Efadora asked.

"The Child."

She eyed the pool of water, her brows furrowing. "Maybe we should go, Geth."

"We just got here. There's still so much for me to do. For *us* to do. Now's your chance to prove your salt as a bonafide cartographer.

"We can at least find the others. Jakar's right. We should stay as a group."

"What do we need them for?" Geth kept his eyes on the boxes, running a hand along their backs. "The danger won't change. Keep that in mind if you want to be a cartographer.

When you're in the unknown, hesitating is what gets you killed. You gotta be in and out as quick as possible."

I tucked my hands under my armpits to still their trembling. Despite my fear, Geth was right. This was why we were here, to learn more about the Ebonrock and to find a way to track them down.

I started scouring the chamber, looking for documents or for a way to turn on the boxes. The last time I was here, people had been working at them, pushing buttons that were built into the table's surface, inputting information, though how it worked was lost to me. Colors and writing had covered the glass on the boxes' fronts when they were working, so maybe they could tell us what we needed to know, if we could somehow turn them on.

Geth grabbed a miniature lever protruding from the rock next to the desk and pulled. I jumped at the sharp crack that echoed through the chamber and at the spark that flashed on the water's surface. "What was that?" Efadora asked.

The water rippled.

"Back," I said. Geth obeyed, responding to something in the tone of my voice, and he and Efadora came to the door to stand beside me.

"Should we go?" Efadora whispered.

She shifted uncomfortably when I didn't answer for several seconds, but then I managed to give a weak shake of my head. My terror wanted to send me scurrying in the opposite direction, but I had to remind myself that I was strong, that I could do this. We were here for a reason. To stop the Ebonrock. That included what was hiding inside Obsidian Lake.

"You should leave," I said to her.

"Not without you."

"Shit," Geth whispered as a pale bulb of flesh broke the water's surface. Higher and higher it rose, thicker than a man, now thicker than four men, until it nearly touched the ceiling. It glistened, bulbous and ghostly, and a chill ran down my neck. More points broke along the water, and tentacles slithered out, hovering in the air. They swung lazily back and forth, moving toward us as if searching.

"Into the hallway," I said.

They moved without question, and I reached toward the ceiling. The ground began to shake, the air roared, and rock crumbled as dust blew past us. I backed up to dodge the rubble filling the room as it sent shards of rock flying into the hallway. I gritted my teeth, concentrating. Collapsing the ceiling had weakened the rock between us and the city above, and if I wasn't careful, I'd start a chain reaction that would kill us all.

I joined the other two at the bottom of the stone steps. "Did you kill it?" Efadora asked.

No other elemental could have survived a cave-in like that, excluding perhaps the primordia. I concentrated, and found to my horror that the tumor in my Eye was now moving through the debris, barely hindered. A fleshy appendage began to grow out of the wall of rubble.

"That's a no," Geth said.

Ig pushed into the hallway without trouble, leaving in its wake a cacophony of grinding rock and the cracking of compression fractures. It was no longer a lengthened bulb—it moved like a snake out of the rubble and into a pile on the ground, then stretched, touching the walls. It filled half the corridor, a six-foot-tall block of flesh coming for us, moving at a toddler's pace.

Efadora pushed Geth up the first step. "*Now* we need to go."

We hurried up the steps and almost ran into Torlo and Namira. "The prisoners are out," Torlo said. He glanced down the steps. "Is something down there?"

"Yep," Efadora said. "Get moving."

The five of us jogged through the snarl of hallways, Torlo in the lead. He stopped and bent over, searching the floor. "I put down some pebbles to mark the way back," he said. "They're gone."

Two flesh bound materialized from the darkness, masks of pain on their faces, one of them holding a short sword. They charged. The woman, who was unarmed, tackled Torlo, lifting him off the ground and barreling into the rest of us, and I pushed at the steel in the other's hand, sending the sword flying. Efadora used her knife to send the man crumpling to the ground in gasps of agony.

"Oh, Fhelfire," Torlo said. Ig entered the edge of the brush light, the wall of flesh slithering toward us. The woman who had tackled Torlo was closest to it, but she didn't move. Only watched the Child calmly. The one Efadora had stabbed stopped moaning from his wound, moving into a sitting position to wait.

"C'mon," I shouted at the woman. I knew she didn't want to be here, was only fighting us because she was afraid of the flesh binding's punishment, but she didn't appear afraid of the Child, only continued to sit there like an obedient servant. That's when I saw that one of the Child's appendages had gotten hold of her foot.

She met my eyes, her expression dumb. I couldn't even imagine what Ig was doing to her mind in that moment. Skin fused as Ig overtook her, and it lifted her off the ground as the woman's legs, then her waist, then her arm melded into it. The flesh bound opened her eyes when half her torso had been absorbed, and she thrashed her remaining arm, her eyelids fluttering. She was going into convulsions. Her face flattened, stretched as her head was absorbed until her eyes, nose, and mouth floated on the wall. Then she was gone.

"Evil," Namira choked out. We backed away and watched as the Child reentered the edge of the emberbrush light and reached the second flesh bound. The man sat in a pool of his blood, staring in awe, then the fusing began again.

Efadora grabbed the short sword off the ground and we broke into a run. "I'll make an exit if I have to," I said. It would be risky—a cave-in might kill some of us, and there was a chance we'd be coming up under a building which could collapse. But it was better odds against Ig.

Geth was running in front, and he stopped abruptly. The hallway ended at another, built perpendicular, and a wall of flesh was moving through it from left to right. The wall stopped. A lump formed on the surface, transforming into an appendage that pushed toward us, searching.

We headed back the way we had come. Efadora held my hand, and when I noticed her palm slick with sweat, I knew in my soul that whatever happened here, I would get her out. The emberbrush's glow and the featureless hallways and the speed of our running switched on one of my deep-rooted instincts—that animalistic need to survive—until it pushed out almost every other thought and all I could hear was our ragged breathing and the scraping of our shoes.

Torlo rounded the corner and cried out as he collided with the Child. He tried to pull away the hand he'd used to stop himself, but it wouldn't budge.

"Makeitstopmakeitstopmakeitstopmakeitstop," he screamed. It swallowed his hand to the wrist. His eyes rolled into the back of his head, and his knees gave out, but I caught him. "Efadora!" I yelled.

Efadora didn't hesitate. She brought the short sword up and swung down on Torlo's forearm. Hot blood splashed across my face, and she swung again, sending me on my back and Torlo on top. Namira and Geth scrambled to help us up before Ig could reach us. Torlo's eyes were closed, his body limp, and I grunted, throwing him over my shoulders. As I ran, the front of my pants became wet as Torlo leaked blood all over me.

"Fuck," Geth said when we ran into what had to be the tenth room in a row. This one had a cage in it, identical to the one I'd spent weeks in after my flesh binding, with whorls and patterns etched into the plateau of rock it sat on, and the bars. "Fuck, fuck, fuck," the cartographer said, pacing back and forth.

I set Torlo against a wall to give my burning legs a break, then started fashioning a tourniquet with a strip of cloth. Torlo's eyes were half closed, and he didn't respond when I tried talking to him, though he appeared to be conscious. It could have been shock, or it could have been from Ig touching his mind. I prayed that the Child hadn't done anything permanent.

"Can you make an exit?" Namira asked.

"Maybe," I said, "but then what?"

"We survive," Geth said. "What else?"

"Yes, we survive, but then it follows us into the city." That electric shock had woken Ig up from its slumber inside Obsidian Lake, and whatever the Ebonrock had done to put it back to sleep after it served their needs, that knowledge was lost to us. "It didn't stop when it absorbed those flesh bound, so maybe it won't stop when it leaves the compound."

"So you're saying you won't get us out of here?"

My gaze settled on the cage in the back of the room. Its bars went from floor to ceiling, with a raised platform made of a gnarled, ancient material I couldn't puzzle out. I gripped the bars and pulled with all my elemental might. It moved, but barely—it was made to keep people like me in, but people like me weren't usually bound to a seventh element.

"What are you doing?" Efadora asked after a few minutes, her voice steeped in panic.

A length of material snapped away, and I rolled my shoulder, trying to soothe the pain. "Making a weapon," I said, then rushed past them, into the hallway.

Only two turns brought me to the fleshy, blocky mass slithering its way in search of the group, two foot-long tentacles sweeping the ground before it. I dodged between the writhing masses and stabbed the Child before dancing away.

The weapon resisted as I pulled it out, but it ripped away instead of staying attached, just as I'd hoped. Ig spurted humanlike blood onto the floor and my shoes, and I stabbed it again and again, the tentacles writhing and curling in on themselves. For a second, it seemed to recede. The Child struggled to absorb the weapon the same way I had struggled to break it off the cage—it was bound to the carbon in the material, just as I was—but it couldn't exert control over the other elements in the weapon, and so couldn't stop it as I plunged it in and out of its body. Alien blood soaked into my clothes, my face, my hair, but I blocked out the sensation, tearing into flesh.

The ground rumbled and rock screeched. I leapt away as the ceiling came crashing down, and I rolled across the floor, rubble bouncing off my body. I recovered, coming face-to-face with a wall of pristinely smooth limestone instead of one of rippling, gory flesh. The ringing in my ears faded and I caught the sound of flesh sliding against the opposite side of the limestone.

The group was waiting for me when I returned. "Is any of that yours?" Namira asked, her mouth hanging open.

I wiped a hand along my neck and flung away the blood. "No. I think I slowed it down, though."

There was a shuddering in the air that sent the hairs on my arms—the hairs not matted with blood—standing on end. Everyone looked to the door.

"The Ebonrock could talk to it, yeah?" Geth asked. "So maybe we can, too?"

"Why would we want to?" Namira asked, shooting him a look as though he was an idiot.

"When you can't fight them, join them," he said, then quickly added, "I don't mean literally join them. Just see if we can do a bit of negotiating."

Even under the looming hand of death, Geth still wanted to learn from the Ebonrock. He didn't have the faintest clue what he was dealing with. "It can't be reasoned with or bargained with," I said. "Its mind comes from a place we will never understand, and if we try to, it'll only break us. The last time it spoke to me, my mind was lost for months." I glanced at Torlo.

"But have we tried? Seems we're short on options here."

"You're welcome to go shake its hand if you want," Namira said, doing a poor job of hiding her disgust. She turned to me. "I have faith that you'll get us out of this, my friend."

Despite the panic that was starting to set in among the group, Namira seemed to truly believe I could do this, even if I didn't. "I wounded it pretty badly," I said. "It could be dying, for all we know."

"It's not dying," a weak voice said. Torlo was awake, his back pressed against the wall, one of his eyes stained red and random muscles in his body twitching. Efadora rushed to his side. "Are you all right?" she asked.

"It's absorbing—elements from the rock," he said, his words stilted. "Healing itself. It—needs more than what's around it—though. It needs us to be whole again."

"How do you know?"

His eyes rolled around in their sockets. For a second I thought he might seize, but his gaze found Efadora again. "It joined with me. I—learned much from it. It's coming. Jakar's—right. It won't stop with us."

My plan had failed. Black winds. My instinct to dig us out of here warred with the stronger instinct to keep Ig trapped here, away from Sulian Daw, but would it find its way to the city eventually? How could I kill it? It was bound to almost all the same elements I was.

But the seven elements weren't the only weapons at my disposal.

"I know what to do," I said. "Stay here."

"What's your plan?" Efadora asked. I must have been doing a poor job at masking my feelings, as she grabbed my wrist in distress, to stop me doing whatever it was she thought I was going to do.

"Just trust me," I said, trying to sound as confident as possible. I handed her my makeshift spear.

She looked ready to argue, but I took off before I could give her a chance to protest, as leaving her behind was already hard enough. I was worried I might actually listen if she told me to stay behind. The voice in the back of my head screamed not to leave them alone in this maze of a tomb. I plunged into the hallway again, and four turns later the Child appeared at the edge of the emberbrush's glow, the light reflecting off the sheen of blood and dirt covering its body. Several appendages segmented like spiders' legs dragged it forward, and it moved almost as fast as a walk now. It rippled, as though sensing me.

I threw a rock at it and fled, glancing over my shoulder to make sure it was following me, seeing its legs striving in my direction like fingers on a hand. I widened the distance then crashed into the wall, the rock crumbling with an ear-piercing shriek. I started digging.

The tunnel turned into an oven, its surface a faint red as I dug as fast as I could, the path I made awkward and uneven. A dark mass filled the entrance to the hole ten meters behind me, lit by the tunnel's dull glow. I dug harder. It was moving faster than I was. Sweat drenched my hair and my temples pulsed with pain.

I reached the loose rubble filling the flesh binding chamber, bursting out of the hill to find myself standing at the edge of the summoning pool. I took a few long, even breaths, then dove in. The water was like ice, easing the stinging from the scrapes littering my body, numbing my extremities as I swam through the black cavity. My Eye helped guide me through the blackness. When I was surrounded by nothing but sparkling elements churning and flowing around me, I knew I'd reached open water. I opened my eyes to find bioluminescence covering the lake floor, creating shadows of fish and other wildlife that called this place home, and a clump of glowing blue fungus rimming the mouth of the underwater cave I'd exited.

My lungs strained as I waited. Ig appeared, moving toward me, its spidery legs replaced by two fins that flapped lazily, propelling itself toward me. The water around me was cold—unbearably so—which meant I couldn't increase the intensity of my power by much. But I didn't need to. I reached out a hand.

Ice started to crystallize around the Child as I funneled the energy out of the water around it, diverting it toward the surface, turning the water above me into a column of bubbles.

The crystals around the Child expanded, interlocking into a layer that crusted the Child's flesh, thickening with each second. The added weight pulled the Child down, and two more appendages sprouted from the mass and started flapping along to keep it from sinking.

The growing ice clung to the first two fins until they were immobilized, and Ig sank, bouncing off the lake floor, the twenty-foot-long monster already half covered in a growing sheet. My lungs screamed, but I kept drawing heat from the water, now redirecting it into a depression I was creating at the bottom of the lake. The boulder of half flesh, half ice rolled to the bottom of the depression, and a dozen more appendages sprouted from the back half of the Child, some with two, three, four joints, lengthening until they were needle-thin, waving as they tried to reach me, but I floated just outside of reach.

The ice entombed the Child and stuck to the lake's floor and continued to spread like a fungus. Spots appeared in my vision, and I came to a sobering realization. I was too good at ignoring my pain. I would pass out long before I reached the surface.

A monstrous shock wave shot through the water, vibrating my body and sending me careening through churning bubbles, then everything went black.

Chapter 38—Efadora

"IT'S—FOLLOWING HIM to the lake," Torlo said.

I'd been squatting beside him, checking the wound on his arm to make sure he wouldn't bleed out, wondering if we were all about to be lunch. "How do you know?" I asked.

"He'll drown," he said. He twitched every time he opened his mouth, his eyes rolling little in his head.

"I can almost see him, right on the edge," Geth said. He stood against the back wall, a hand on the rock and his head tilted slightly. "The Child's swimming after him."

I joined Geth, struggling to reach out with my new senses. After a few moments, the darkness behind my closed eyes gave way to light—twinkling stars that smeared the insides of the wall. Concentrating more, I noticed polygonal ridges along the smears. Quartz deposits in the rock. I extended my senses beyond that, finding more twinkling lights floating and moving like they were being pushed by the wind. It was Obsidian Lake, I realized, and the element I was bound to filled the water almost to the brim.

"It's the algae," Geth answered. "It's why the water's so black. If you look, you can see Jakar and the Child swimming through it."

I tried to ignore the way Geth sounded more fascinated than anything else. The swishing, twinkling lights moved erratically around two voids—one vaguely human-sized, and one a lot bigger. What was Jakar trying to do? He'd led the monster away from us, but it wasn't going to stop until either it or all of us were dead.

"Why do you think he'll drown?" I asked Torlo with a strained voice. "We don't know what his plan is."

"The black waters have taken—many people over the centuries. It's the cold and the—darkness. Ig told me."

"How much did Ig tell you?" Namira asked.

"In a moment, it—learned all that I am or ever was. The connection worked both ways."

I had to trust that Jakar knew what he was doing, but the certainty in Torlo's voice ate me through. What if Jakar had bitten off more than he could chew, and all I did while he was dying was sit here and do nothing?

"Help Torlo out of here," I said, then left them, carrying my emberbrush and moving in the general direction of the exit.

I used my senses to guide me—without the Child chasing us, I could move methodically, taking time to memorize the invisible brush strokes of quartz inside the walls and remembering the patterns if I accidentally double-backed. After a few frustrating, hair-pulling minutes, I found the first staircase leading to the top level, then climbed out of the trapdoor onto the shore of the lake.

I picked my way along the rocks at the water's edge and tried to extend my senses out again, but they couldn't reach wherever Jakar and the Child were. I steeled myself and jumped. The water slapped me like Kaedis' icy hand, but I gritted my teeth and swam. The temperature was doing its best to lock up my muscles, and I distracted myself by searching the algae blooms. *There.* A human-shaped void was sluggishly treading water below me. It had to be Jakar. He'd been underwater for more than a few minutes, long enough for a normal person to risk losing consciousness, and he was still a good thirty feet under. I took a deep breath and dived. Twenty feet down and the bioluminescent light at the bottom of the lake started guiding my way. I swam furiously at Jakar's fuzzy shape, hoping he'd turn around and see me, but by the way he was moving, it looked like he was about to run out of breath.

A boom shivered the water, slamming into my body and leaving me disoriented. The water turned into a pandemonium of bubbles, and I almost lost sight of Jakar through the chaos. He'd stopped moving. I reached him, my hands almost numb as I struggled to grasp the back of his shirt, but I pulled and kept swimming.

Fhelfire, I wasn't strong enough to get him to the surface. Panic seized me. I grabbed his face and shook it, but his eyes wouldn't open.

The water cleared enough for me to see the bottom again. Fire ripped through part of the rock, a glowing magma flow sending black plumes billowing to the surface. Nearby, a hill of ice grew out of the ground.

Adrenaline injected me with a new burst of energy. I pulled Jakar toward the nearest plume, and the water quickly changed from unbearably cold to uncomfortably hot. My heart lurched with joy when I realized the current of warm water was pushing us to the surface. Daggers stabbed at my eardrums, but the pain was quickly forgotten as we floated up, up, up, the water clearing, my face breaking the surface, my abdomen almost seizing as I took a ragged breath of delicious air. The relief was short-lived. It took all my energy to keep Jakar's purpling face above water, and the shore was still too far away.

A slab of glassy ice bobbed onto the surface in front of us. I desperately swam to it, then managed to unsheathe the dagger from my belt and stab it into the ice. It was a precarious thing trying to cling to the ice while holding onto Jakar, and treading water was still exhausting, but it was manageable. I kicked us toward shore, trying to ignore the fuzzies at the edge of my vision.

Vague shapes climbed out of the hole on shore, and a distant thought acknowledged one of their outlines jumping in the water. A voice said something a moment later, and I realized the shape had swum out to us. I tried to respond, but my mouth wasn't working. I tried to focus on the person, but I couldn't figure out who it was. They spoke again, grabbing onto Jakar, and I was able to puzzle out that it was a woman's voice. Namira, then. How nice of her, I thought.

"Almost there," she cried out. I tried to kick harder, then realized I'd stopped moving a while ago. My legs weren't working.

I WOKE UP in a cocoon of warmth and my body aching.

People surrounded me. I was propped against the back of a building by the lake's edge, a fire roaring a few feet away and my body tightly wrapped in a blanket. Someone had taken off my clothes. I didn't mind, though, considering how the dry warmth of the blanket was pure bliss. Jakar lay next to me wrapped up in the same fashion, his face no longer purple.

Torlo was propped against the wall beside me, cradling his now wrapped wound and staring at the ground, whispering to himself. Geth and Namira worked the fire and spoke with a pair of strangers accompanying them. The Sulians rummaged through their bags, and they pulled out poultices and medicines and offered them to Geth, who dropped a handful of coins in each of their hands.

"How's that head?" Geth asked when he glanced over at me.

I blinked hard, trying to bring my vision back into focus. "I feel drunk."

"You're still thawing out. You'll feel better soon."

My vision returned enough to see the frothing water on Obsidian Lake. A mound of ghostly flesh crusted with ice floated several dozen feet offshore, and I almost jumped out of my blankets. "The Child," I croaked.

"It hasn't moved since it came up," Namira said.

"Dead?" I asked. I couldn't help but look at Torlo.

His cheek twitched. "Jakar trapped it. It got—desperate, killed itself by accident. Pulled energy from its own body to—break the ice."

"Cratered half the lake, too," Geth said.

That's when I noticed the crowds of people clustering along the circumference of the lake, pointing. We were half-hidden by the shadow of the building we camped against, and the spectators didn't notice us, or didn't make the connection between the dead Child and our group. It was hard to tell if the Sulians bartering with Geth suspected anything. They left me and Jakar changes of clothes and left. Namira stirred the fire and Torlo continued to whisper to himself, rocking back and forth. My stomach sank.

"You're going to be all right," I told him.

"No, I'm not," he whispered.

After several minutes, I started to feel like a normal human again. Jakar shifted, waking with a start, and his eyes moved wildly before settling on the dead Child. He studied it for a long moment.

"I'm alive," he said, but I couldn't tell if he was talking to us or to himself.

"You can thank Efadora for that," Geth said.

Jakar scowled at him and said nothing.

More time passed until I had the energy to stand and limp behind a stack of old crates with my change of clothes. Jakar did the same after I finished, moving like an old man, and we could hear him groaning from behind the crates.

That could've gone better," he grumbled when he joined me beside the fire.

"Had some trouble dressing yourself?" Geth asked, grinning.

"I was talking about that." Jakar pointed at the Child.

"Ah. Well, you can say that again, then."

Jakar was now glaring at the cartographer. "No more jokes. We went into the Ebonrock compound without a plan or Efadora's coil weapon because of you."

"*I* went in knowing what I was doing. *You* went in without a plan or the coil weapon. Don't hold me responsible for your actions."

I cut in. "You've been acting like a dick lately, Geth."

"I'm a cartographer, in case you didn't notice, which means the Archives are my priority, bar none. Jakar would fuck with my chances to study the Ebonrock if I let him, so pardon me for taking a bit of initiative."

"You almost got us killed," Jakar said.

"And yet here we are."

Jakar moved to his feet, his joints cracking, and advanced on Geth. The cartographer stiffened where he sat, but didn't move, calling Jakar's bluff. Jakar lashed out with his foot and hit him in the chest, sending him on his back. "No more," Jakar said. "I can't trust you to look out for anyone other than yourself. You're staying away from us."

Geth moved to his elbows. "I think you're overreacting."

"You're going to collect your belongings and walk away. As soon as I lose sight of you, you make sure that we never meet eyes again."

Geth's usual airy confrontation dissipated when he seemed to realize that Jakar was serious. He frowned. "I made a promise to Shirallah to help you, and I'm not planning to let him down."

"You already proved that learning about the Ebonrock is more important than your promise."

"You're acting the fool. You need me. Efadora needs me."

I chewed on my bottom lip. Did I need him, though? Part of me liked him, but I couldn't deny that he'd pulled an asshole move. He couldn't play nice with the idea that Jakar wanted to destroy the Ebonrock before learning more about them, and it had forced everyone to rush into the fight with the Child. And I'd gotten the most important piece of what I'd needed from him. My Delineation was done. True, I couldn't join Xeriv's Archives as an official member if we left Geth behind, but he'd already admitted how decentralized the Archives were.

I could always show up at a different one, make up a story about how my mentor was killed, and ask for a new one. It was manipulative, but at the moment I didn't mind being that type of person. "Shitty behavior begets shitty consequences," I said.

"Are you going to send Torlo away, too?" Geth asked, his cheeks red. "Look at him. It's obvious the Child fucked with his head. Probably turned him into one of those slaves that tried to kill us. He's more of a danger than I am."

Torlo didn't speak up to deny the accusation. Only stared at the ground and whispered to himself.

"He's not the only one in this group who's touched the Child," Jakar said, leaning over. "He's strong. Now, get anywhere near us again and I'll burn you." His breath smoked between them, his gaze sharper than glass.

The reality of the situation seemed to finally sink in, and the cartographer's face fell. "Fine."

Jakar sat next to me while Geth picked himself up, brushed the dusty footprint off his shirt, and said, "I need to grab my stuff from the inn, but I'll be gone before you get back."

"Take the coil weapon and I'll find you."

"Sure, sure."

I expected Geth to get angry, or maybe show a bit of fear, but he only frowned to himself, a range of emotions warring on his face. He left the fire and disappeared behind the corner of the building. "Good riddance," Namira said.

We sat around the fire in silence, everyone stewing in their own thoughts. I couldn't stop thinking about Torlo. I refused to believe what the Child had done to him was permanent, and my stomach lurched if I spent too much time thinking about it. I moved next to him. "I'm here if you need me," I whispered.

He didn't answer, but after a few moments, he rested his head on my shoulder. I wanted to do more—to talk to him until I knew without a doubt that he would be all right, to hug him and never let go until he knew without a doubt that he would get better—but sitting next to him would have to do.

I laced my fingers through his and squeezed, and he squeezed back.

"What now?" I asked.

"Jakar's wanted for murder," Namira said. "He can't stick around here."

I gave Jakar a questioning look.

Jakar gave a summary of what happened in the Nochi slums, and it quickly became clear there was a lot to unpack behind what had happened and how he felt about it. He showed no interest in diving into it, though. "Wouldn't be too hard to convince the guard you kidnapped me," Namira said. "I did do a lot of screaming. Maybe I can stay here without getting hassled by the guards—if they find me."

"What's that supposed to mean?" I asked.

"It means this is where my adventure ends." She tried to make the statement casual, but the regret was there, her words warbling. "I grew up in Kenah, a small city not far from here. I have family there I can track down. They can help me get my business back on its feet."

"You have family nearby? When's the last time you saw them?"

"Before I moved to Ravada, when I was a girl. Traveling with all of you made me realize how much I miss them. In a good way," she added quickly.

She struggled to meet my eyes, which was funny because of how much she'd helped us, so there was no reason to feel guilty, *especially* considering all the horrible things we'd put her through. What I'd put her through. "Thank you," I said. "I'm sorry again about Darkwater. I'm going to miss you."

She smiled. "What happened in Ravada had to happen, I think. It got me out of there for good. So don't feel bad."

We spent the next several minutes watching the city guard launch boats onto Obsidian Lake and paddle toward the Child.

"We're lost again," Jakar said. "We don't have a lead on the Ebonrock anymore."

349

"Maybe the flesh bound are free now with the Child dead," I said. "Maybe they know where the Ebonrock are."

"I can—find them," Torlo said. "The Rha'Ghalor."

We all looked at him.

"Father," he said, staring at the dirt. "I can feel Him. He's far, but I think. I think I know—where to go. He has your friends, Jakar. All of them."

I wasn't too thrilled to meet 'the Father,' whoever or whatever that was, but I did my best to keep the nerves plaguing me off my face. Geth had been a wild card, but he was capable, and finding our way felt like a crap shoot without him. There was something wrong with Torlo, too, so it was hard to say how much we could count on him the next time danger came knocking. Then there was Jakar. He almost died defeating the Child, and supposedly the Child was just a spawn of the Great Ones. He'd also have to protect us from the flesh bound elementals he grew up with, all of whom were as powerful as he was, while also dealing with the kadiphs.

The more I thought about the plan, the more doomed it felt.

"Better get going sooner rather than later," I said in as chipper a voice as I could manage. A bit of optimism might go a long way when spirits were this low, even if dread sucked at me as I said the words. Jakar gave a tired smile, nodding, and pulled himself up.

Part 3

Chapter 39—Ester

THE ENTRANCE TO Mira's Treasury of Springs waited at the other end of the cavern—a massive facade almost fifty feet high and a hundred feet wide, all for an entrance a fraction of its size. It was how Ester knew the place was Sovereign-made. Whenever the country's ruler exerted his will on the land, he had this innate need to create great works of architecture, even in hidden places where few could appreciate the labor. It had added to his allure once upon a time, but now Ester saw only self-indulgence.

Breach coughed into his palm. "You see anyone manning the battlements?" he asked while our group hid behind a lichen-encrusted boulder off the side of the road.

"Nen," Miyaz said. "Who to guard secret against?"

He had a point. People had to know about the Treasury of Springs in order to attack it. The place was a secret, and for good reason—all of Mira's coins were minted here, and by attacking it, it would throw the country's economy into flux while securing funds for the ruin folks' rebellion for years to come. It was the first and most important step in destabilizing the Sovereign's rule.

She waved for the group to follow, leading them single file

along the edge of the cavern through the mossy undergrowth where insects swarmed them. It took all her willpower not to swat and make a ruckus while the others barely seemed to notice the pests. They reached the start of the cut stone—a towering buttress that would've taken dozens of man hours to shape, but which couldn't have taken the Sovereign and his sycophants more than a few minutes. Ester heaved herself onto the foundation and climbed the start of the curving arch leading up the facade.

The group scooted along the one-foot lip as it arched over the treasury's main gate and the balconies above it. Wood smoke along with the sounds of voices and soft shoes scuffling against stone reached Ester as the group took its place over the first balcony.

She gave the signal and dropped. Fourteen pairs of leather boots slapped against the floor a heartbeat after hers, and for a moment the group faced a cluster of administrators lounging on chairs and sofas, who were half-dressed and smoking pipes, neither group speaking. Ester swallowed, her adrenaline pumping as she scanned the room for Myrilan, but he wasn't there. Then came the eruption of shouting and scrambling. She rushed inside as the first of the administrators screamed for help, and she grabbed him by the scruff of his professionally tailored shirt, then threw him at the ground hard enough to rip the fabric near in half and make his face hit the floor with a meaty smack. "Don't," she said, and slid out her sword, pointing it at another man crawling for the door.

She secured the room with help from her friends. Miyaz stood over their captives, most of whom whimpered on the floor misted with nervous sweat. "How many guard?" he asked.

"There're a couple hundred on staff, last I checked," one of the more confident-looking ones said. "They'll scrape Therm like you off our boots soon enough."

The tip of Miyaz's boot smashed into the administrator's cheek, sending him reeling. Ruin folk didn't take kindly to the insult—it compared them to the rotten-smelling hydrothermal vents that occasionally sprouted up from beneath Mira. "For now, you Therm on mine," Miyaz said, and scratched at the puckered scar on his cheek. He turned to Breach. "Dupelo e'multima."

"The man's lying," Ester said. "There aren't two hundred."

"What makes you say that?" Breach asked.

"People lie to smiths all the time because they hate disappointing them. Serve in the Foundry long enough and you develop an ear for exaggeration. Besides, you really think they'd garrison two hundred soldiers for a place no one knows about?"

Miyaz pushed the administrator on his back and set a boot on the side of his face, slowly putting weight on it. "How many?"

"Shifshy."

"Sca?"

"No more than fifty," one of the other captives said. "Why are you doing this?"

"That's none of your concern," Breach said. "Just go with it."

"Is it a Foundry uprising?"

"No," Ester said quickly. "This has nothing to do with the Foundry." She touched her blade to his neck. "I'm not associated with them anymore. Call me a rogue smith if you want. All right?"

The man nodded. Ester's heart was pounding, but she did her best not to show it. The last thing she wanted was to put more of her brothers and sisters in danger. If there were fifty men garrisoned here, that could pose a problem for her oredancers—her name for her new friends who'd undergone the binding ritual, taken from the extinct cult that introduced the Foundry to the rhidium trials over a thousand years ago. "Where are the assistant treasurers' offices?"

A small sound escaped his throat as her blade tickled his clavicle. "Er, assistants don't have their own office, but they work in the Office of Canopies helping the directors of finance."

She heaved him up. "You're taking us there."

Their group split up into three groups of five—Ester's group entered the halls first, with Miyaz planning to follow a couple minutes later while Breach's group stayed behind to watch the captives and squeeze them for more information. Ester navigated the halls with the administrator's help, passing elaborate fountains, glowing quartzite on pedestals sculpted into perfect spheres, and furs and paintings that covered the occasional wall from floor to ceiling. Every new hallway brought about a moment of panic as Ester half expected to run into her baby brother. She still had no idea what she would say or do to him, but figured she could wing it.

They came to a wider hallway with a set of double doors and words carved in the rock over them that said 'Office of Canopies.' A squad of guards lounged against the walls, conversing and looking half bored, and they turned at the arrival of Ester and her group. Two of the men wore black fighting leathers—a strange getup for guard duty. Their faces and hands—the only skin not covered by clothing—were even stranger. Every square inch was covered in scar tissue, so bad that their bald heads didn't seem capable of growing hair. At first Ester thought they'd been horribly burned, until she saw the lines in the chaos of scars. It was as if they'd been cut thousands of times.

"Who are you?" one of them croaked.

Ester threw her escort to the side and pulled out her blade.

The contingent of guards—there were six of them accompanying the two scarred men—pulled out their weapons, too. The normal soldiers carried short swords or grabbed spears that had been leaning against the wall, but the scarred men pulled out sabers hanging from their backs. Ester advanced, two of her oredancers flanking her, and she prepared for the swipe of a saber as one of the scarred men charged her.

She dodged his blade by a hair's breadth, and on his backswing she sent the tip of her sword stabbing at his gut. She felt the tug of an invisible force push at her weapon, and her attack moved awkwardly along his side. Her oredancers traded blows with the other guards while she and her attacker took a step back and reassessed each other. He was probably as surprised as she was. The man was bound to iron.

The other scarred man decapitated one of her oredancers. Dhulf had been the oredancer's name, and he'd been a man Ester had spent the last two weeks riding beside and trading jokes with. Now beads of his hot blood were splashing against the side of her face, and rage moved in to replace her shock. She jumped forward, knocking aside a spearhead aimed for her chest and slashing at the first scarred man before he could settle into a proper fighting stance.

A scarred man hacked off Whetson's arm while a guard stabbed him in the kidney with a spear, and Kelkir snaked his way past the spear tips and gutted two spear holders, sending mailed bodies and spear hafts clattering to the floor. A scarred man whipped around and slashed Kelkir across the back. Ester stabbed at the scarred man's thigh, feeling the push of his power, but she turned the blade so it bit deep into his leg as it passed. It left her open for the second scarred man, but Rorgrand was suddenly there to block the vicious hack. Before he could back off, though, the scarred man got in close and buried his saber in Rorgrand to the hilt. Icy fear needled its way down Ester's spine when she realized how outmatched they were. Her oredancers were still getting used to fighting with their power, and these scarred men moved like they'd been born with it.

Kirlen, her last oredancer, dispatched the final non-elemental guards. The scarred man with the wounded leg tried to swing at her, but he slipped in the blood now coating the ground and hissed in pain when his knee cracked against the rock. Ester managed to hack at his side, and he screamed, his damaged vocal cords making him sound more like a cat. He crumpled to the ground. Ester quickly repositioned herself so that she stood at Kirlen's side, facing the last surviving soldier. The second scarred man.

"My subordinate is finding help as we speak," he croaked. "Surrender or I'll kill you both."

The administrator she'd taken hostage was probably sprinting for the nearest set of reinforcements. She leapt at the man, Kirlen following. He dodged their attacks like water, splashing through the blood as he backpedaled, but Ester pressed hard. His power wouldn't do him much good if they backed him into a corner.

He pulled something off his belt and flung it. Ester barely had time to notice a disturbance in the elemental field before light and sound enveloped her, heat searing her face as a concussive force flung her back. She slid until she crashed into a body, then scrambled to her feet, panicking while she waited for her vision to return and her dizziness to fade.

She regained her bearings to the sound of Kirlen screaming in anger, despite the blossoming wound on her face, and slashing at the scarred man who had taken a hit from the explosion too. She struck him down with a meaty hack.

Ester limped to her companion. Kirlen's neck and the side of her face were red and blistery, but she barely seemed to notice. "Are you okay?" Ester asked.

She nodded. "Never better. Kill ugliest man alive."

What the scarred man had done didn't make sense—he'd thrown some sort of handheld bomb and used his elemental power to trigger it, but Ester had felt no presence of iron inside the bomb before it had gone off. Had he been bound to more than one element? "That's going to hurt like fhelfire later," she said to Kirlan, cringing at the woman's burn. "Let's move."

They entered the Treasury of Canopies and closed the door behind them, sliding one of the broken spears through the handles. The air was warm and wet, the ceiling covered in vegetation and moss, with running water that ran through miniature canals along the floor. One corner of the room had a garden with shin-high mushrooms and bushes. Another corner had three rows of desks, along with whom Ester assumed to be the senior financiers and their assistants, who were currently pointing swords at them.

"You know who was outside guarding the door, right?" Ester asked.

Some of them nodded.

"They're all dead," she continued. "You really think what you're doing is a good idea?"

Their swords clattered to the floor.

"I'm looking for Myrilan. Myrilan Selenitea."

They shared a look, but none of them answered.

"Doesn't ring a bell, eh?" she said. "What about Myrilan Watertracer? I know he works here, or that he did at some point. If you lie, I'll know."

"Myrilan is gone," one of them said. "He left about a week ago. Went home."

"Why?"

"It was privileged information."

She rushed for the group and grabbed a discarded sword before driving it into the desk one of the financiers had been leaning against, pinning the man's shirt to the wood. She had her own sword under his chin before he could try to rip his shirt away. Her heart raced. "Deciding to withhold information wasn't your best line of thinking."

"Please, miss," he cried out. "I meant it was too privileged for us to know. Myrilan was forced to go under orders of the Imbued."

"The Imbued? What are those?"

"Th-the men you just told us you killed."

The scarred men. The financier whimpered as blood from beneath his chin rolled down her blade, and Ester stepped away. "Keep this room secure," she told Kirlan. "I'm going to find the others and help them."

Her mind raced as she searched for her friends. Why would Myrilan be forced to go home now, after years of being away, while being accompanied by the Imbued? Either the Imbued had heard about her murdering Master Smith Hartlan, or above and below, they found out she and Damek were involved in Nektarios's disappearance. Maybe Mateo had told them after he was turned into a homunculus? Those were the only two explanations.

More disgust filled her with every step. These past couple months had changed her—turned her into someone who had put her need for revenge above everything else. She had been so focused on shedding blood for every one of her lost brothers and sisters that she'd barely given her real family a second thought. Now they were in danger.

She followed a trail of bodies until turning a corner and coming to an antechamber with a half-open vault filled with iron bars. "Breach," she almost shouted, running to the group of bloodied oredancers in front of the vault. They stood over several dead guards, one of whom was a scarred man, and Breach applied pressure to a deep gash in his arm.

"Can't say I'm surprised to see one of those around here," Breach said, nodding at the scarred man.

"You knew about them?"

He frowned. "Did you run into others?"

Ester gave him a rundown of her confrontation and of the captives Kirlan was overseeing. "We should return to Miyaz," Breach said. He coughed hard into his hands and wiped away the spit from his mouth. "We'll need more oredancers if we're going to secure the rest of the place, and in case we run into any more of these." He nudged the scarred man's boot. "Our contacts in Saracosta told us the Sovereign has been conducting experiments on soldiers to make them stronger. Looks like it worked."

Two of Breach's group of five had been killed, and Breach left one behind to guard the vaults. Ester led him and Dreamer, Breach's last remaining oredancer, back to the lounge area.

"Where others?" Miyaz asked, pursing his lips at all the blood.

"One is guarding some captives in the Treasury of Canopies, and one is guarding the vaults," Ester said. "Everyone else is dead."

"We killed about half the garrison so far, if we weren't lied to about the numbers," Breach added. "We'll need your help, though, if we want to take the rest of the compound. There's been a development."

Breach relayed his and Ester's run-ins with the scarred men, and by the time he finished, Miyaz was furious. "Why not warn us?" he asked the administrator who had provided the information. He didn't give the man a chance to answer, though. He stabbed him in the gut as he tried to squirm away, and the man howled and clutched at his stomach.

"You," Miyaz said, pointing his blade at another administrator, his weapon streaming blood onto the tile. "Tell us other special guard locations or you die."

"They're in the furnace minting standards," the man said in a tight voice. "There are three left. I can't say how many normal guards there are."

"Any other surprises, I come back here and kill all," Miyaz said, addressing all the hostages. "Got it?"

A dozen voices started speaking at once, spilling everything they knew, but the information wasn't helpful or new.

Breach stayed behind with one other to guard the hostages and to stitch himself up, and Ester followed Miyaz and the others to the furnace. Miyaz poked at the administrator who guided them, eliciting the occasional hiss. It was hard for Ester to focus on the task at hand—every minute spent here meant another minute her family was in danger. All she wanted to do was flee this place and ride hard for home. It couldn't be more than three passings away.

A wall of heat hit them when they entered a vast chamber with a line of furnaces in the back, where almost two dozen men and women worked on smelting metal into coins and stamping them with the Miran standard's design. Three of them worked without their shirts on, covered in scars and their backs glistening with sweat. Nobody had noticed the group enter. Miyaz pulled the administrator's head back by the hair and slit his throat, then let him tumble to the floor.

Ester hated this. There was nothing satisfying about it anymore; it suddenly seemed brutal and sickening. Miyaz gave them a signal, and the group crept toward the workers. Halfway there, someone noticed them and shouted, but their voice was muffled by the roar of the furnaces. Ester launched herself forward, running for the nearest Imbued, who was in the middle of drawing molten metal out of a vat. As he was turning toward the commotion, she collided with him and sent him falling into the liquid metal.

The second Imbued took a sword through the back, and the third managed to dodge swings from two oredancers before one blade took off his arm and another cut one of his legs out from under him. The other workers scrambled to grab tools to defend themselves, but they weren't fighters. They quickly surrendered.

"He's still alive," Dreamer said, and pointed at the dismembered scarred man. Miyaz had Ester and one other drag their enemy away from the noise of the furnaces to the opposite end of the chamber.

"What is nature?" Miyaz asked the man.

The Imbued looked from Miyaz to Ester and the others in silent confusion, and Miyaz let out an exasperated sound. "You ask," he told Ester.

"He wants to know where you came from," Ester said. "Did the Sovereign make you?"

The man shook his head. "Bilal."

"The Sovereign's son?"

He nodded.

"He's just a child. You're saying a child did this to you?" she motioned at his torso. Blood pooled from the stumps of the man's arm and leg, and Miyaz instructed Dreamer to make two tourniquets.

"Bilal is not a child," the Imbued said, his voice weak and strained.

Dreamer started to tie the first strip of cloth above the man's stump of an arm, but the Imbued's eyes rolled into the back of his head and he went limp.

"Ester, take three. Find last guards," Miyaz said.

Ester did as she was told and rooted through the rest of the compound, hoping both to find and to avoid any other scarred men. There were none left. They tied up the guards who surrendered and dispatched the ones who refused to drop their weapons, then gathered all their captives in one spot.

"I need to leave," Ester said to Breach and Miyaz. Breach had managed a haphazard stitching for his wound, which Ester found impressive considering he had to do it himself. "My brother's traveling to my hometown under orders of those Imbued," she continued. "It might have to do with the primordia I killed."

Miyaz made a motion with his hands. "This too important."

Ester opened her mouth, more than ready to argue the point, but Breach said, "She's given you plenty. She told us how to find this place. She showed us how to perform the rhidium trials, for Brexa's sake."

Miyaz pursed his lips. "Spread thin. Cannot hold place if she leaves."

"Then destroy it now," Ester said.

The leader's face hardened. The plan was to pillage as many resources as possible to help fund the ruin folk's future operations, then leave the place in ruins. "No."

"Attacking this place was never part of the original plan," Breach said. "We'll make do. Ester's family is in danger. Are the territories' families not the people we're trying to protect?"

Ester resisted the urge to walk away, cursing Miyaz to the depths while he deliberated. "See in your eyes you go regardless of what say," he said. "Fine."

Breach nodded in thanks. "Let's go," he said to Ester.

"You want to go?" she asked.

"You've made a world of difference to this cause. Enough that I could spend years paying it back and still come up short. I'd like to start working on that debt now."

Miyaz shook his head in disbelief. "Leave and you reveal true priorities."

"You'll be angry at me for a while, Miyaz, but I'll bear it." He patted Miyaz on the shoulder, who stiffened at the gesture. "Unconventional paths are my bread and butter, remember? It's how we got Ester and the rhidium in the first place." He turned to Ester. "Wherever you go, I'll follow. To the bowels of Ra'Thuzan and back, if it comes to it."

Her despair lessened in that moment, and she pulled him toward the exit. He gladly followed. It was time to focus less on the cause and to prioritize the people that the cause was meant to help. People she had spent far too long neglecting.

Chapter 40—Jakar

A HAND SHOOK me awake, sending me bolt upright, and I pulled my fist back without thinking. It was Efadora, backing away as she eyed my hand.

"Sorry," I said.

"There's something wrong with Torlo."

Torlo had been sleeping several feet away, near the cliff's edge we'd camped beside in preparation for our several-hours-long descent. He was muttering to himself and twisting on his bedroll until his blanket wrapped like a snake around his body and neck.

"He's still asleep," she said as we stood over him. "I gave him a few small kicks and it didn't do crap."

I knelt next to him and listened. He was speaking words I didn't understand, but it didn't sound like his native language, Teta. I climbed on top of him, held his head still, and slapped him.

His eyes fluttered open, and he sneered at me, reeking of hatred. Then he blinked hard. "Ow. What are you—doing?" he asked as he rubbed his cheek.

I helped him up and brushed the dust off his shoulders. "You were scaring us. Bad dream?"

"I don't—dream anymore."

He packed up his belongings silently, and Efadora and I watched him, eventually following suit. After what little we had was packed in our bags in preparation for the descent, Efadora followed me to a spring at the other end of the cavern to fill our waterskins while Torlo chewed on mole-rat jerky.

"He's getting worse," I said.

She stared at her reflection as her waterskin gurgled under the pond's surface. "Yeah."

"The Child might've infected him."

She didn't argue. She couldn't. Ig had obviously affected Torlo in some irreversible way—now the boy spoke in stilted sentences, walked with a limp that came and went even though there was nothing wrong with his legs, and his eyes always swept the ground in front of us while we walked. Efadora still struggled with the change, even though she would never admit it—she almost never left his side and would keep a close eye on him whenever he walked more than a dozen feet away from us. Was it a stretch that the Child had imprinted some of itself onto him? It had once rewired my brain, so maybe it had rewired his, too.

"He's just struggling," she said.

"Is your head or your heart saying that?"

She capped the waterskin a little too hard, splashing water onto the ground. "Head."

We returned to camp. We'd traveled light since leaving Sulian Daw, since Namira kept the cart and the buffalo, and I was starting to worry about food. We were deep in uncharted territory, somewhere north of Sulian Daw and east of Yarokly, where the plants and animals looked unrecognizable at best and deadly at worst—the animals had strange patterns on their scales and were brightly colored, which usually meant they were poisonous—so I wasn't interested in giving them a taste. Torlo insisted we were close, though. The Father was near, and with Him, the rest of the Ebonrock and the elementals they'd enslaved.

Beyond the cliff's edge was a circular hole and no sign of a bottom. We smeared bioluminescent paste onto the seams of our leathers until our clothes emitted a teal glow that kept the darkness at bay. Torlo tried to help Efadora nail the anchor into the cliff's edge, but his hands were too shaky. "Is that safe?" I asked. I had deferred to Efadora's expertise since I didn't know the first thing about climbing, but the knot she'd tied didn't inspire confidence. She had fed the rope through the anchor and fastened it on the other side with just a stick. It wasn't even tightly wrapped around the stick.

Efadora yanked at the rope and the stick was pulled perpendicular against the anchor. "It's called a fiddlesticks and it's how we'll get our rope back if we want enough of it to get to the bottom. We'll be fine as long as there's weight on the line." She patted at the dust on her legs and arms, glanced at Torlo as he stood there trembling, and swallowed. "Alright, so I've got the most experience, so that means I'm in charge. First things first—impatience is what'll kill us over anything else, got it?"

Torlo and I nodded.

She ran us through how to use the equipment, which took me ten minutes or so to memorize. Mostly. At least I'd be able to make my own handholds in the rock if things got too risky. "What's this called?" Efadora asked Torlo, holding up what I was pretty sure was the quickdraw.

"The runner," Torlo said.

"Good." She eyed us, then sighed. "I guess there's nowhere else to go but forward. Or down."

She fastened herself to the line and leaned off the edge until she was almost horizontal, then pushed off, disappearing below the lip. Torlo hooked himself up next and followed on shaky feet. I tailed the group, almost slipping as I leaned back. Efadora was already near the end of the rope at the edge of the darkness. Torlo was only fifteen feet below me, but it looked more like fifty from this angle. The height started to make my head spin. I closed my eyes and focused on pushing off, then realized I needed my eyes open to see where I'd touch rock again. Butterflies filled my stomach as I rappelled several feet.

Efadora pulled a stick out of the collection she'd stuffed into her pack, then finished securing the next anchor and transitioned to the next rope. She waited for Torlo to reach her, keeping him close as usual. I transitioned last, then Efadora called out from thirty feet below: "Okay, give the first rope a jiggle and the stick should fall out."

The stick did fall out and the rope smacked me in the shoulder as it dropped, but I managed to keep a hold on it. We slowly and awkwardly transferred the rope to Efadora so she could fasten it to the next anchor.

The descent was slow and exhausting. After what felt like hours, we had managed to make it only two hundred feet or so. Sweat mixed with the bioluminescent paste and made it run, dimming the light, and there was still no sign of the bottom.

Efadora once again transitioned to the next rope and anchor, waiting as Torlo rappelled to the bottom and reached her, then the boy paused, his legs trembling. He said something, but I couldn't hear him.

"What'd he say?" I called out to Efadora.

Efadora squinted at him as if she was trying to parse out his words, and he continued talking, the words coming out faster and faster, until I realized he was speaking in that strange language again. Then he dropped like a stone. He collided with Efadora, sending her off the rope shrieking, and they disappeared into the darkness below.

I jumped.

Cold air blasted me as I fell into blackness. I cut through the air, and a faint glow appeared in the pitch dark, which grew into two terrified people struggling to cling onto each other. I grabbed for Torlo, hooking my hand onto his shirt before I could lose him in the darkness, and I pulled him and Efadora close. He tried to speak, but the gale stole his words. The walls became a glittering blur in my Eye, but the void below extended into eternity.

Darkness gave way to rampant growth—fireflies that glowed white instead of red swirled around moss, and fronds slapped at us as we sailed past. The plant life illuminated a sheet of glass below that rose up fast. I pointed my feet downward and the other two did the same.

Pain knifed my body as I cut through the water. For a few seconds I floated there, coping with the stinging sensation wrapped around my body, then something else crashed into the water. Our packs. Efadora and Torlo swam inside crystal clear water illuminated by rotten logs that glowed green and blue at the bottom.

I swam for the shoreline and pulled myself onto the rocks, helping the other two as they struggled onshore. Efadora lugged out her sopping wet pack, and I dived in to grab Torlo's. Soon we were dripping on the rocks while I stoked a fire to help dry us off. At least we weren't cold—an ambient warmth filled the cavern, a helpful sign that we were deep inside Ra'Thuzan.

"What was that?" I asked Torlo.

"My hands don't work—that well," Torlo said, refusing to meet my eye. "I slipped. I'm sorry."

"You were talking to yourself before you fell. What were you saying?"

"I wasn't talking."

Efadora caught my gaze, hers full of fury. I was being aggressive with the kid, but I wasn't sorry. I knew what it was like to have someone else's will wiggle its way into my own, knotting up my desires, and I needed to know Torlo wouldn't put us in danger when we were this close to the Ebonrock. What if he had let go on purpose to try to hurt Efadora?

No, I was being foolish. Right?

"Where to?" Efadora asked Torlo. The boy picked himself up and took an awkward step forward. "Not far," he said.

"Please tell me there's a way to help him," Efadora whispered as we walked a short distance behind Torlo.

"You'd need another spawn of the Great Ones to untangle whatever they scrambled inside of him," I said.

A small whine left her throat, and she watched Torlo take a lurching step over a rock. "It's like he's been replaced."

Replaced. I tried to keep my face level. What defined a person, anyway? Change enough in their brain and they become someone else entirely. It made me wonder what kind of person I had been before my flesh binding, and if the Child had scrambled my wires without my realizing. I had to consciously choose to obey or disobey a Word, but as I thought about Torlo insisting he didn't talk to himself, it made me wonder if I'd ever done something and been unaware of it.

Being forced to do something you didn't want to do could be traumatic, and the brain did funny things to protect itself.

"People deal with trauma in lots of different ways," I said. "Just act normal. It'll help him remember who he is and what he likes about us. Don't let him forget we're here for him for the long haul."

"All right. Yeah. That's a good idea." She frowned and focused on walking.

"We're close," Torlo said over his shoulder. The first signs of human influence appeared—the tunnels turned into smooth angles and sharp edges, and the ceiling was made of rippling, pale blue rock, and was bright enough to give the place an ambient glow. It was limestone, but no limestone I'd seen before. Unkempt vines grew along the ceiling, drooping down to brush against our shoulders and ears, but the roots had been carefully planted into waves and whorls. The place was all corners and corridors, with ceilings barely a foot above my head and rooms that could've been supply chambers, or bedrooms, or prison cells. Whatever this place was used for, it hadn't been occupied for centuries. Dripping water and the occasional fluttering of wings kept us company, and I focused hard on picking out any unfamiliar sounds until all I could focus on was the sound of my heartbeat.

My guard slipped the longer we walked. After an hour, I started to wonder if we'd find anyone at all.

"This place goes on for miles," Efadora said.

"You still know where we're going?" I asked Torlo.

He had been whispering to himself with his arms wrapped around his body. "This is—where the Ebonrock lived—a long time ago. They move a lot. We'll catch—up soon."

What would compel a group of people to dedicate generations toward finding lost gods? Fanatics were more determined than the average person, I supposed, but convictions couldn't last forever. What were they hoping would happen when they found the Great Ones?

A vibration made the ground tremble, so faint I was the only one who noticed. A hundred feet further and the vibration happened again, enough for Efadora to perk up. "Was that a quake?" she asked.

Pebbles and dust fell from the ceiling, and Efadora brushed dirt out of her hair. The ground shook again. And again. "Not natural," I said.

Torlo kept whispering to himself, getting a little louder as we reached the source. The tunnel widened and turned into a series of stone steps with veins of amber crystal growing along the walls, and crooked lines were etched into the stone, zigzagging and breaking up the contours of the tunnel, disorienting me enough I almost slipped. It was as if the whole place had been designed to play tricks on my eyes. The stairs slithered down until the ground leveled out and brought us onto a ridge overlooking a cavern twenty feet below. The place brimmed with human activity. I ducked behind a line of old crates and the others followed suit.

A lavafall on the cavern's left side, along with torch stands scattered across the ground, set the cavern ablaze with light. To our right, elementals molded and blasted away at the wall, the rock showering them with sparks and spouting wisps of flame. They wore little more than rags, and sweat glistened on their grimy, scarred skin. Several people in leather armor waited behind them, either keeping a steady supply of waterskins moving toward the elementals or carrying boulders to piles waiting on the sidelines. The kadiphs. At the far end of the cavern, a pool of water ran the length of the opposite wall, where half-spherical structures made of metal, like domes on stilts with wheels, lined the pool's edge.

Rocks filled the pit of my stomach. This was it. I counted over a dozen elementals and seven kadiphs, but that must have made up only a fraction of the Ebonrock. I spotted a hall entrance next to the lavafall, which had to lead to the lived-in parts of the compound.

"Stay here," I said.

"You're not going down there, right?" Efadora asked. "We just got here."

"There's only seven of them. I can take care of them before the others show up, then we can run back into the abandoned parts. Dismantling the Ebonrock piece by piece is the best way to do this."

She set a hand on my shoulder, but there was tension there. "No offense, but you're an idiot. Just start by taking a breath, then we'll make a better plan. That's what you're always telling me to do, right?"

My heel tapped against the rock. For all I knew, the elementals down there would be able to make a run for it if I killed the kadiphs fast enough. "I can do something to help, finally. I can help *right now*."

"You don't know that. If you go down there without talking this through with me first, you'll be a giant hypocrite. Also, I'll shoot you."

Her hand rested on the butt of the coil weapon. I didn't think she'd shoot me, but that didn't exclude the possibility of her whacking me in the head with it. Maybe I was being impulsive. Jumping without looking seemed the only way I'd find enough courage to face the Ebonrock, though. Even now, I was worried I'd start trembling too much to stay loose for a fight, and the acidic taste of vomit sat on the back of my tongue.

"Fine," I said. I took a deep breath, which helped, but not much.

Torlo was whispering again. "Not so loud…" I said, turning around, but I trailed off when I saw his mouth wasn't moving.

The whispers grew louder. They spoke in a language of syllables that ran together like a pile of worms, too fast and fluid to be human. Something caressed the back of my head, like a breeze or an insect, and I slapped at it, whipping around. There was nothing there. The sensation intensified until it felt like fingers pushing at the base of my skull. Applying pressure.

"Oh no no no no no," I said, scrambling for the exit.

The voice shouted, loud enough to make the world tremble and my legs to turn to jelly. No, I'd imagined the ground shaking. I didn't understand the words, but I felt their intent in my marrow. I wasn't allowed to flee.

I didn't want to flee.

Why would I? This was where I needed to be. This was where I belonged.

Efadora watched, horrified, as I left our hiding spot. She grabbed for my pant leg, but I ripped myself away and headed for the stairs and catwalks leading below. For a second her horror infected me, but it was fleeting. I was home. Whispers spoke in a continuous stream on the edges of my mind as I descended the wooden steps. Efadora called after me, restrained, and then the sound of her and Torlo's boots scraped against the rock and faded into the exit. I reached the bottom of the stairs and strode toward the center of the cavern. The kadiphs and elementals stopped what they were doing to watch. The thing that compelled me—the owner of the whispers crawling inside me—exited the hall beside the lavafall, entering the cavern's light. The only thing I wanted in the world was to approach it, but I couldn't help but acknowledge the smallest voice in the back of my mind that screamed at the sight of the thing before me—telling me to race after Efadora and Torlo and to hide. To cower in the darkest corners and pray I would never have to see this creature again.

It was bipedal and towering, its mass distributed in a way that made it look like a humanoid trying to walk on its hands.

Teeth ran along jagged crevasses that littered its flesh, and in those crevasses' shadows I saw eyes. Hundreds of them.

The slaves watched, the hope and surprise that had first crossed their faces gone, all of them compelled to witness, in the same way I was compelled to come closer. Needed to come closer. The creature resonated power in a way the Child didn't. This had to be the Father. I stopped several feet away, and now with my task completed, a sudden terror overcame me. Why had I wanted to come near it? I turned away to run as fast as I could, but its whispers rose to a firm, guttural command. The need to stand where I was became overpowering. It felt good, to the point I laughed with giddiness, the high-pitched noise ringing through the cavern, joining the gurgling of the lavafall.

"I recognize him," a voice said. It took a second to realize the voice wasn't inside my head. Someone had been walking beside the creature and I hadn't noticed. When we locked eyes, my mind went blank.

"You," I said. It was her. Strands of gray ran through frizzy brown hair pulled into a ponytail, and deep grooves of wrinkles and scars slashed across and around her face. Whorls and alien patterns were etched into her leathers, barely visible in the black material. It was the same design from the Sihraan city, one I'd been seeing more and more since the start of this journey. I should've taken it as a warning. Her expression was full of glee.

"This is the last place I thought I'd see you," said the kadiph who had stopped my escape attempt from the Ebonrock years ago, who had forced the flesh binding on me, who had been one of the orchestrators behind everything wrong with my life. "Mira must have been quite the shit hole if you crawled back to us."

The need to kill overwhelmed my desire to stand still. The ground trembled with my power, and I launched forward, striking at her as the ground swallowed her feet, rooting her in place. My knuckles made contact with her neck, but it was like punching glass that wouldn't give. She twisted her body and grabbed hold of me, her feet breaking through the rock. Alien words squirmed inside my head, and even though the sounds made some small part of me want to vomit, the sudden need to stop struggling was so strong, I shuddered from the pleasure of going still.

"It's better than sex, isn't it?" the woman whispered in my ear while she had her arms wrapped around me, pinning my hands to the front of my body, her grip stronger than stone. "That's what the slaves tell me, at least." She let go, and I stepped away, the lingering buzz of pleasure fading. With my task fulfilled, all I wanted was to sprint for the stairs again, but was that because I wanted to leave, or because it would force the Father to give me another command to stay?

"Why are you here?" she asked.

Whispers rode on the tail of her question, and I almost moaned in relief at the opportunity. "To save my friends," I said.

The woman barked out a laugh. "Oh, dear. That might be the most pathetic thing I've ever heard." She turned to the Father. "Let me talk to him. I'd love to get to know him better. Learn where he's been."

Spiders skittered over my brain, sending chills up my spine, and I almost jumped with excitement to go with the kadiph. I had to stop myself from telling her everything on the spot, since talking here wasn't the command. She led me to the hallway, and I had to resist the urge to tell her to hurry up.

Chapter 41—Ester

ESTER'S HOMETOWN OF Stonegate was built against a steeply sloped wall. Dozens of buildings were carved into the rock with ramps and stone steps linking them, as well as pulleys to move cargo and people up and down the town. Halfway up, there was a path leading under a naturally formed archway and out of sight to the right, where a small Foundry would be waiting with its sole smith and a handful of volunteers. Ester's parents' home was to the left on the opposite end of town, near a waterfall that sprayed mist onto the buildings. Ester was torn between where to head to first. Help from another smith wouldn't hurt, but the idea of roping in someone new from the Foundry who could get caught in the Sovereign's crossfire made her sick.

Townspeople watched the two of them as they trotted into town on their foxes and up a series of zigzagging stone steps, but Ester wasn't certain they recognized her under her hood. "You're sure you can't get that rhidium weapon working?" she asked.

Breach shook his head, his hand on the lumpy satchel hanging from the fox's side where the weapon lay. "No can do. I need time we don't have."

He'd fiddled with the weapon almost nonstop between the ruins and the Treasury of Springs, even claiming to have made a breakthrough right before they attacked the treasury, but everything had happened so quickly since then, along with Miyaz confiscating the rest of the rhidium so Breach couldn't work on it on the way here. Breach had been willing to delay his potentially groundbreaking discovery, but now Ester wondered if it would've been worth waiting a bit longer so he could get the weapon working first.

She recognized several faces the closer they came to her childhood home, which was strangely reassuring. Maybe nothing bad had happened yet. Her old house was four levels up, almost underneath the waterfall, with vines growing in the crevasses of the brick facade and an overhang to protect the inside of the home from mist. The front doors were thrown open, but Ester's parents had always liked it that way, open to anyone who wanted to poke their head inside to say hi.

Someone left the shadows within, and Ester's mother came out to greet them. She looked the same as always, with deep wrinkles in her face and gray-threaded auburn hair pulled into a severe bun, and she wore her favorite set of robes with beetle carapace sewn into each shoulder. "Ester?" she said, stunned.

Ester pulled her hood down. "Hi, Mom."

"Damek returning was hardly a surprise, but to see Myrilan and then you, all within a week? It's a reunion."

"Where's Myrilan? Did he come alone?"

"Why wouldn't he have? He's on vacation." She grabbed the reins of their foxes and led them into the cobbled alley next to the house with a hitching post at the end. "Who's your companion?" she asked as they dismounted.

"Xander," Breach said. "Member of Augustin's Guild of the Glass. Your daughter has been humoring me as a travel companion."

"Oh?" She looked him up and down, and Ester caught a glimpse of disbelief in her gaze, which the woman quickly masked. "You'll have to tell us all about how my daughter's been humoring you while you're here."

Ester hurried inside. A rug covered the stone floor, woven with an illustration of a creature that was part pigmy bear, mole-sheep, silt-cat, bat, with the head of a human to finish it all off. Some people might've found the sphinx eccentric if they could even figure out what the complicated mess of body parts was, but Ester knew it to be the god her parents worshipped, Terias. Knowing Myrilan and his cronies were here, these advertisements suddenly seemed like a very bad idea. The Sovereign's loyalists were known for their casual cruelty toward anyone who was different. "Where's Damek and Myrilan? Is everyone safe?"

"Ester?" a voice called out. Her father walked into the front room, wearing an apron stained with black blood and holding a shard of exoskeleton. He looked as if he'd been in the middle of scooping meat out of some sort of giant bug. Ester suppressed the urge to gag—her parents had progressed to eating the things they worshipped now. They'd gotten worse in their children's absence.

"I'm looking for Damek and Myrilan," she said. "It's important."

"We haven't seen you in two years and that's the first thing you say when you get back?" her mother said as she entered the house, Breach in tow. "Why don't you sit down so we can catch up? Damek and Myrilan should be back in a couple of hours."

"Tell me where they are. I need to talk to them."

Her father set the chitin down and pulled off his apron, wiping the blood off his hands. "Tell us what's wrong."

Ester gave them a paraphrased version of events—she still couldn't admit her hand in the primordia's death, only saying that she was in trouble with the Miran government and they had killed her brothers and sisters back home. "The smith here might be in danger, too," she said. "Every Foundry in the territories could be in danger."

"Ah," her father said, the skin around his eyes tightening.

"They can't really be in danger, right? The government's never raised a hand against the Foundry. They're the only religion he openly tolerates."

He was hiding something. For a moment Ester wondered if her parents were helping Myrilan, but the idea sounded ridiculous. They were as wary of the Sovereign as she was angry. "Just tell me where Myrilan is. Damek might be in danger."

"Why would they peg Damek as a threat?" her mother said. "They'll take one look at his disability and realize how ridiculous the whole notion is."

"Don't talk about Damek like that."

Her mom continued talking as though she hadn't heard. "And you think Myrilan would betray you two? Don't be so paranoid."

Frustration bubbled up, threatening to make Ester explode. Five minutes back and she already remembered half the reasons she'd left. They never knew how to listen. In their eyes, their extra years of wisdom superseded every opinion their children had, no exception. Not to mention how they treated Damek. Myrilan and Damek had always been timid growing up, but since Damek was older, they'd learned to focus their attention on him. And he'd been right about everything back in Augustin—his injury had only made it worse. "Tell me. Where. They are," she repeated.

Her mother paused, reacting to something in Ester's voice. "We don't know," she said. "They've been disappearing every passing since Myrilan got here. They go who knows where. We're just happy they're finally bonding, considering the three of you had such a hard time getting along before you moved out."

"I'm going to look for them. Promise me you'll keep an eye out for anyone who doesn't look like they're from around here. Myrilan didn't come here alone."

She marched out of the house before they could respond, across the cobbled road until she stood at the parapet overlooking the cavern. Patches of forest and giant mushrooms littered the ground far below, with a river and several tunnels leading out of the cavern, along with two lichen farms by the river's edge. Handfuls of townspeople traversed the space but none of them resembled her brothers or Miran soldiers. If Myrilan was interrogating Damek, where would he take him? Somewhere quiet, probably, away from prying eyes.

But her parents had said they were returning after each passing. Damek would've fled the first chance he got if he was in danger, or at the least, he would've given their parents the impression something was wrong. Whatever Myrilan was doing to their brother, it was subtle.

"Any clue where they would've gone?" Breach asked as he came up beside her.

"There were some spots the three of us liked to go when we were kids," she said. "I think I'll check there."

She turned down an alley halfway across town and reached a set of stairs leading up to a small ridge near the ceiling. It took her and Breach to a path leading into a maze of tunnels where the people of Stonegate grew dates and maize in tiny, enclosed grottos. Some side tunnels provided access to the river that fed into Stonegate's waterfall, and Ester turned down one of these, retracing steps from ten-year-old memories. She and her two brothers had been close a long time ago, but then she and Myrilan had become fascinated with the primordia and the Sovereign, dreaming of becoming powerful enough to move mountains. Damek had pulled away from them, and that's when the fighting had started. Then Myrilan, the golden child, the youngest and smartest of them all, had landed a job with the Miran government, and Ester grew bitter feelings toward him. In her despair, she found the Sky Scrolls and its passages on how circumstance was irrelevant to a good, fulfilling life, that hard work within the Foundry could create a calling for anyone—a message she desperately needed during that time of disillusionment. In the weeks leading up to Myrilan's departure for the treasury, when Ester became more devout toward the Sky Scrolls and was first taught to be wary and even afraid of the Sovereign, things had gotten vicious between them.

Ester heard a pair of echoing voices and her heart leapt into her throat. She stopped at the tunnel's end and peeked into the cavern beyond. Damek and Myrilan sat on two boulders by the water, Myrilan speaking in a low voice, the echoing and the rush of water making it impossible to hear. Damek appeared troubled, but he wasn't in danger. He wore a leather cap over his stump, held in place by a strap that crossed diagonally to his other shoulder. Myrilan was in the middle of explaining something to him, leaning forward and moving his hands around to emphasize his points. Myrilan's face, or at least the side Ester could see, looked the same as always, powdered up and covered with enough makeup to make his skin look flawless and porcelain smooth. That was the style among the Saracostan aristocracy and those loyal to Mira, and was a style Myrilan had been particularly drawn to. He'd been bullied incessantly as a kid—Ester and Damek had done what they could to fend the bullies off, but they could only do so much, and Ester suspected Myrilan had developed an obsession for his self-image after years of being torn down, brick by brick, by his peers. He looked good; the style fit him well.

Myrilan turned to look behind him, and Ester caught a glimpse of the scar running down the side of his face, a scar no amount of makeup could cover. The scar she had given him the last time they'd seen each other. She followed his gaze to the back wall, where more tunnels led upriver, and found a man and woman dressed in all black leathers with faces full of their own scars, approaching her brothers.

Ester left her hiding place without thinking. The Imbued noticed her first, stopping and moving one foot behind the other, trained to make themselves smaller targets. Myrilan and Damek jumped to their feet. "You're here," Myrilan said.

"What are you doing to Damek?" I asked.

"Talking," he said, the look in his eyes hardening.

"And what are they doing here?" I asked, motioning toward the Imbued.

"They're my guests."

"That is your sister?" the female Imbued croaked. She and her companion's hands flexed, ready to pull the sabers off their backs.

"Well, ah—" Myrilan said, trailing off. His gaze shot from me to the Imbued, and he looked like a firefly caught in the glow of magma. Why was he so nervous? Why not just tell them she was his sister? "She... is," he finally said.

The Imbued pulled out their sabers and Ester drew her sword. Behind her, steel slid against leather and Breach moved to stand next to her. Myrilan rushed forward and put himself between the groups. "Wait, wait, wait," he said. "We don't know if she had anything to do with the primordia's disappearance. Let's not get ahead of ourselves."

"You told us you believed she might," the female Imbued said. "That is why we're here."

"And I've been talking to my brother these last few passings trying to make sense of things. I've appreciated your patience, but you knew coming here that there'd be a chance I was wrong."

"You gave us the impression that chance was very small." She spat at the ground. "You said you could sweet-talk the information out of your sibling, but it seems he sweet-talked you instead. You are incompetent. Disgusting."

Anger flashed across Myrilan's face until he looked away, cheeks flushed. Old habits made Ester step forward, and she imagined the feel of cutting the tongue out of the woman's mouth. Both Imbued brandished their weapons. If they made one move to hurt her brothers, she would kill them both.

"You had your chance to do things your way," the male Imbued said. "Now that the smith is here, we will take over."

Damek grabbed Myrilan and pulled him out of the way as the Imbued ran forward. Myrilan let out a desperate yell to get everyone to stop, to just wait a second and talk, but Ester and Breach were already meeting the Imbueds' blades. The Imbued struck more carefully than they had at the treasury—they knew Ester was an iron worker, and apparently, they thought she was responsible for Nektarios disappearing. What they didn't anticipate was Breach blocking a side swipe and riposting with almost blinding speed—a move Ester had been teaching him. His edge bit through the man's vambrace and into the meat of his forearm.

The woman knocked Ester's blade to the side and Ester repositioned to protect herself from the woman's sword arm. Instead, the Imbued struck with her offhand. Ester felt a disturbance in the electromagnetic field a split second before the woman's fist connected with her chest, causing Ester's world to explode.

The concussive blast knocked Ester off her feet. She rolled back, and when she came to a stop, her chest heaved as she tried and failed to inhale. Fire filled the lower right side of her torso too. Her rib must've cracked. A pair of hands pulled her up while she was still struggling to breathe, and the Imbued punched her, filling her vision with white.

Ester regained enough of her bearings to see the ruined knuckles on the Imbued's gloves, the flesh torn and bloody. The woman must've stuffed whatever explosive element she was bound to into her gloves. The woman punched her again, but Ester's lungs were still seizing too much for her to do anything about it.

"You will tell us what happened," the woman croaked.

She let Ester go, crying in pain as she grabbed at the knife Damek had buried in her shoulder. She swung her sword wildly as she did so, but Damek danced away. Myrilan still stood off to the side, frozen and watching with wide eyes, and the male Imbued pressed his attack on Breach, who had put his back to the river. Half of Breach's neck was slick with blood.

Damek saw Breach struggling. He turned from the woman as she kept trying to reach for the knife and bolted for the male Imbued. He tackled the man from behind and they both crashed into the water as Breach stumbled out of the way. The two men quickly disappeared under the fast-moving current.

"No!" Ester gasped, clambering toward the river. She dived into the icy waters and quickly lost herself to the chaos.

The walls, floor, and ceiling of the underground river punished her, pounding at her legs, side, and arms. The noise was deafening, the water pitch black. She hit another rock, spinning, and her stomach lurched with the sensation of free falling.

She hit the pool of water one terrifying heartbeat later. In the back of her mind she knew she was in Stonegate's cavern now, and she flailed for anything that remotely resembled a shore. The Imbued's hand gripped her and pulled with enough strength to drag her onto the rock. She lay there in a daze, her head pounding as she slowly centered herself, but found Damek kneeling over her instead of the Imbued. He watched the waterfall's base with narrowed eyes, waiting for another Imbued to come riding down after them.

"Where?" was the only word Ester managed to say, but her question was answered when she saw the male Imbued lying halfway out of the water several feet away, a knife protruding from his neck. The weapon was made from rockwood.

Damek wiped his drenched locks out of his face. "We need to move. That woman's probably going to take the long way around. You need a new weapon." He helped her up, and she gasped from the stabbing pain in her ribs. He retrieved his rockwood knife, cleaning the blade and returning it to the sheath hidden under his shirt. He'd been practicing during their months apart.

They struggled up the levels of Stonegate, the residents watching, alarmed, as they passed. Some tried to ask what was happening, others called out her and Damek's names, but Ester ignored them all. When they reached the fourth level, Ester turned right while Damek tried to go left.

"Where are you going?" Damek asked. "Mom and Dad have

weapons in their shed."

"I want Foundry steel," Ester said, and hobbled under the archway of rock, along the path toward the little chapel at the end of Stonegate.

"You won't find Foundry weapons there," Damek said when he caught up. Ester was about to ask what he meant, but the words died in her throat when she took in the sight of the chapel.

Its red-and yellow-stained glass windows had been shattered, and vines with colorful flowers grew out of the jagged holes. A miniature forest of mushrooms and bushes that buzzed with insects covered the plateau next to the building, and past the chapel, rampant overgrowth had taken over the tiny pool that had once been full of lava. Mist and moss dictated much of Stonegate's aesthetic, but here, plant growth had grown wild and unchecked—a breeding ground for all sorts of dangerous flora and fauna.

Ester pushed through the front doors. She had expected the place to be abandoned, but found several men and women in dark blue robes, tending to vertical gardens covering the walls. Busts of grotesque creatures on pedestals littered the floor, and where there had once been a statue of Fheldspra sitting on the dais at the other end—the Foundry's crowning landmark in Stonegate—there was a new statue, half-completed, of an abomination. Of Terias.

"What... is this?" she asked.

"It was Mom and Dad," Damek said.

"Ester!" a voice called outside the Foundry. It was Breach, and he was running toward them, a palm pressed to the wound on his neck.

"Are you all right?" Ester asked. "Where's the woman?"

"She's following." He bent over, chest seizing in wracking coughs, and when he recovered, continued, "She has two more Imbued with her."

Chapter 42—Ester

A GROUP IN all black appeared at the end of the street, and Ester pulled Damek and Breach into the building, the motion sending a dagger of pain digging into the right side of her chest. Breach closed the doors behind them and looked around for something to stick through the handles, but there was nothing.

"I can't fight that well," Ester said. "I think my rib's broken."

"Can any of you fight?" Breach asked the cultists.

They shook their heads, some of them angling themselves behind busts or self-consciously making their bodies smaller. "Simple followers of the Burrowing Sphinx," one of them said in a heavy accent. "Pacifists."

"Pacifists?" Ester asked. "Did any of you touch the weapon stores in the back when you moved in?"

Again, they shook their heads.

Ester rushed to the back, trying to ignore the horrible ache in her torso. In a low room beyond the main audience chamber awaited a stone-cold hearth with bellows and an anvil covered in moss. Beside the cobwebbed tool stand was a door, and Ester touched her hand to where the internal lock would be until she heard a click. The door creaked open to reveal an untouched array of weapons on the other side. Damek moved for the dirk while Breach traded his old, chipped side sword for one that gleamed brand new in the mushroom light. Ester grabbed a bow, tried to draw the string, and when that made her side catch on fire, she went for the crossbow instead. "Help me load this," she said to Breach.

They entered the audience chamber, and Ester rested the crossbow on the lectern, aiming it at the door. The cultists kept to the shadows, clearly understanding that it likely wasn't for the best that they flee out of the very spot Ester had her weapon trained. "I shouldn't have abandoned you," she said to Damek. "I'm so sorry. All of this is happening because of me."

"Don't be sorry," he said. "I made it hard on you back in Augustin for no reason. I pushed you away." He snorted, keeping his eyes on the door. "I was so miserable that first passing we parted ways. I didn't realize until you were gone how horribly I'd been acting toward you. Making you take care of me, always sulking."

"Anyone in your position would have felt that way."

"But the point is to move past it eventually. I used to feel you were so disappointed in me."

Ester started to argue, but he put a hand up. "I know you weren't, but thinking it pulled me out of my rut. I swore to myself I wouldn't rely on you like that ever again. I've been feeling pretty good about myself lately." He showed his teeth.

His optimism was exactly what Ester needed to hear, she realized. They would fight their way out of this, one way or another.

The front doors swung open as the Imbued entered. They lined up on the landing—one of them was the woman who had managed to get the knife out of her back, who carried the wound quite well—and each had a saber in their hand. Myrilan pushed past them.

"Please, for the love of Mira, stand down," he said. Ester couldn't tell if he was talking to them or his companions. "You got lucky, but it's not going to happen twice. These soldiers listen to my commands, but they won't hesitate to attack if they think it's in the best interest of the Sovereign."

"It certainly would be," the female Imbued said, voice trembling with anger, but she didn't attack. Even after that sad display of fighting Ester had exhibited earlier, they were still wary of her. To them, she was the person who had disappeared a primordia.

"Damek," Myrilan said. "Remember my offer. I can make you whole again, but you have to put your weapon down."

Damek's brows furrowed. He responded to the words with longing in his eyes, whatever they meant, but he didn't move.

"Myrilan didn't see what just happened," Ester said to Damek. "You saved my life from one elemental and killed another. Myrilan and Mom and Dad are all full of shit. None of them actually bother to open their eyes and really look at you past your injury. You're the same person you've always been. Fearless. Don't listen to Myrilan."

She couldn't tell if her words had meant anything—he blinked hard and frowned to himself, but he didn't move.

"Don't do this, Ester," Myrilan said, his voice cracking. "I was stupid and said the wrong thing to my superiors that resulted in all of this." He gestured at the air around them. "I'll pay for it, but just set your weapon down so you can tell them this was just one big misunderstanding."

"And what did you tell your superiors?"

"That you fit the description of someone who was spotted with Nektarios the last time he was seen in public, during the Burning of Augustin. My soldiers are mad, but they attacked you first and you defended yourself. If you navigate this situation the right way, we can all walk away without any fighting."

Dear Myrilan and his hatred for fighting. As a kid, he would freeze whenever the other kids started pummeling him, and it didn't matter if Ester told him that it only made matters worse. Even now, he didn't recognize the hate in his soldiers' eyes that would soon override whatever command he gave them.

"I'll tell them I lied," Myrilan stuttered. "That I was only looking for clout. My coworkers at the treasury never take me seriously, just because I'm not from Saracosta, so I saw this as a chance to contribute to the primordia's search. It was impulsive. I didn't even think of the ramifications before the words were out of my mouth."

The stances of the Imbued changed subtly as the two men and the woman glanced at their superior, disgust in their eyes. It was clear they didn't believe him—and Ester didn't, either, knowing he was desperately trying to deescalate—but the weakness they sensed in him was eroding the last of their will to obey his orders. And if he kept talking, it would probably get him killed.

She needed to shut him up, to keep the Imbueds' attention on her. "I killed the primordia Nektarios, representative of the Sovereign," she said loudly, her words filling the chapel. "The Iron Sorrow helped me, and we dumped Nektarios's body in the capital's river after we were done."

Myrilan's lips parted in surprise, and he kept silent for once as emotions cycled across the Imbueds' faces. Shock, fear, anger, and finally determination. Myrilan looked ready to be sick. Well, she certainly had their attention now. Ester aimed the crossbow at the man on the far left and pulled the trigger.

The man was fast, and he was bound to iron, but few iron workers could fully divert crossbow bolts. He grunted, but the bolt only managed to graze him before pinning his shoulder guard to the wall. Myrilan ran out of the way and the other two Imbued catapulted forward. Breach threw himself at the man and woman, despite knowing he could barely take on one, despite knowing it was suicide, and the sight sent Ester into a frenzy. She barely felt the pain in her chest as she pulled back the string of the crossbow, loaded another bolt, and lifted it up. Breach managed to survive in the handful of seconds that passed, parrying a blow from one and dodging a swipe from the woman. The Imbued moved slower from the wound in her back, but not by much. Damek covered Breach's left side, and the Imbued Ester had pinned to the wall undid his shoulder strap and moved to join his companions.

"Stop it!" Myrilan screamed.

The two already attacking were smart enough to ignore Myrilan, but the one heading into the fight paused for a second. Ester took full advantage. The bolt *woosh*ed between Breach and Myrilan and tore into the Imbued's abdomen. The scream that came from his lacerated vocal cords was nightmarish.

The bust Breach had been using to cover his right side shattered to dust and sprayed pebbles across the floor from the sword of the last male Imbued. Damek managed a parry, but his blade was knocked out of his hand by a vicious two-handed swing from the woman. He backed up, leaving Breach exposed on the left side, and in Ester's mind's eye she saw how easy the woman could step to Breach's left and skewer him while he tried to fend off the other Imbued. And there was nothing she could do.

The male Imbued grunted as a rock hit the side of his head, and Breach stepped back to focus on protecting himself from the woman. One of the cultists had picked up a piece of debris and thrown it, a wild look in his eyes. "Do not desecrate this place," he yelled.

The male Imbued marched toward the cultist. With an upward swing he sent blood splashing up the wall and ceiling, and the cultist hit the floor. Four nearby cultists screamed, and the Imbued set himself on them next.

The female Imbued pressed the attack on Breach, and the wound on her back seemed to be the only reason Breach was still alive. Damek ran for his dirk on the floor and Ester tried to pull the crossbow's drawstring back, but the motion amplified her pain tenfold. She had made the crack in her rib much worse, she realized.

"Help us, please," she said to the handful of surviving cultists.

"We're only followers," one of them said as he held himself. His attention went to the entrance, hope flickering there, and Ester followed his gaze.

Her parents stood on the landing. They watched the male Imbued wipe off his sword, standing over the dead cultists before moving to help his companion, and rage filled their eyes. They spoke, but it was in no language Ester understood, and their hands and fingers made complex motions while pointed at the ceiling, as though they were controlling marionettes.

Something moved among the shadows on the ceiling, between branches and leaves. Quartz light gleamed off black carapace, and then the creature struck.

It was faster than any piece of steel in the hands of an iron worker. Extending from ceiling to floor, it grabbed the female Imbued between its pincers, who screamed until the sound rose to a pitch Ester couldn't hear. The creature squeezed, and the top half of the woman's body snapped from the bottom, leaving legs and part of an abdomen to spill onto the dusty Foundry rugs. Breach cried out as he jumped away, but the creature had already returned to the ceiling's shadows with the top half of the Imbued between its jaws. Two heartbeats later and it was gone. Ester recognized it as a sand striker— they lived in the deeper parts of Mira and were to be avoided at all costs. And her parents' cult had brought one here to live in the ceiling.

Despite the remaining Imbued standing there alive and well, who had frozen at the explosive violence, Ester's parents brought their attention to Myrilan, who hid behind the door next to them. "You let them kill them?" their mother asked, on the verge of tears. "Our friends?"

The Imbued jumped into action. He ran at Ester's parents, and time seemed to slow down as Ester could do nothing but watch. First the man's bright, steel sword plunged into her mother's chest, right where her heart was. Then the blade was out and cleaving her father's head from his shoulders. Blood spattered Myrilan's face as he watched with wide eyes.

The Imbued glanced back at Ester as she ran at him, and he pulled a familiar object out of his jacket and tossed it. For a third time Ester was hit by heat and a concussive blast, but this time she was ready, and she tried to brace herself as she was thrown back. Fire bloomed on a dozen points on her arms and face. She lay on her back for a few moments, then forced herself up and assessed the blackened spots on her arms. This bomb had contained shrapnel, and the bits of iron had singed her, but hadn't penetrated her skin.

Damek had been smart enough to hide behind a pillar, Breach behind a bust. Breach helped Ester to her feet while Damek approached their parents and shuddered until he broke down into a heap of sobs.

A distant part of Ester—the part of her that was pulling away from this moment with each passing second until she was like the sand striker watching from above—knew that the image of her father's head on the ground next to his body, and the look of agony in her mother's dead eyes, would stay with her for the rest of her life. She would see this image in her dreams and when she was awake. Every time she would try to summon a happy memory of them, this was what she would see.

And it was Myrilan's fault.

Her brother was gone. She wasn't sure if he'd fled on his own or if the Imbued had forced him along, but she took mechanical steps around the blood pooling under her parents and exited the Foundry, checking the streets. The Imbued and her brother had disappeared. The cold and logical part of Ester heard townsfolk shouting—the rest of her was still inside the Foundry—and she moved for the parapet. She caught glimpses of a stone fox running down Stonegate's level before shooting out of the main gate, carrying two people.

Damek's sobs grew louder. The cultists were leading him and Breach outside the building. "You shouldn't have to see this," one of them said when Ester rejoined them. The man put a hand on her shoulder and frowned, and she realized she had been staring at him. He waited for her to speak, and when she didn't, only watching him calmly, he continued, "We can deal with this. They were our leaders. They'll receive the best death rites we can offer."

Ester almost shoved the man away. Why were they even discussing this? Her parents' bodies were still warm. Their blood hadn't even finished draining onto the stone. Again, she imagined their ruined bodies, butchered like mole-rats, and nausea made her lightheaded. And who was this man to decide that Ester and Damek's parents deserved the rites of a *cult*?

A thought stole her mounting anger and heat flooded her cheeks. It wasn't her religion, but it had been her parents'.

"Take them away from here, please," the cultist said to Breach. "We'll come find you when we're done cleaning up."

Breach guided Damek by the shoulder, and he grabbed Ester's hand, pulling. Ester looked at him stupidly—there was so much to do, and they were just walking?—but she followed.

"I FOUND SOMETHING important," Breach said as he entered the home.

Ester had been sitting on her parents' couch, knees pulled to her chest as she stared at a wicker basket on the other side of the room that she had woven for her parents when she was eight. She had been staring at it for hours. Breach's words stirred her out of her trance, and she realized she couldn't hear Damek crying in the back room anymore. He must've fallen asleep. She stared at Breach instead of the wicker basket, and his brows scrunched up as he met her eyes before joining her on the couch. He was holding a satchel.

"The Imbued left some supplies behind. I found some correspondence from the Sovereign's son, Bilal. I don't think Myrilan knew that the Imbued had orders to find and capture you. They were supposed to take you somewhere after they captured you. If it's any consolation, I don't think anyone knows that Damek helped you kill Nektarios."

Ester had already lost interest in the conversation. The home was filled with trinkets and paraphernalia from her parents' cult—it reminded her of how open they'd been about their beliefs, and how gross the concept of a sphinx was to her, simply because she didn't understand. She'd spent years trying to understand, then had given up when she'd become a member of the Foundry, when she could've spent all that time accepting her parents for who they were and enjoying her time with them. So many wasted years. She thought of when she first told them she planned to join the Foundry.

They'd been happy that she had found something she loved and wanted to pursue.

She would live the rest of her life in regret, but she would never forget that her chance to mend her relationship with them was gone forever because of Myrilan. He had killed them.

"Ester," Breach said. He set a hand on top of hers, which had been resting on her knee. "They were going to take you to the Star Mines."

It took time to process his words. The Star Mines? But the Sovereign didn't know where the Star Mines were. *She* didn't even know. Only the Foundry's pilgrims, the senior arc smiths, and the master smith were privy to that.

Then she remembered her Augustin brothers and sisters and what had happened to them.

Breach held up the parchment scrawled with writing. "It's strange. Bilal is, what, eight years old? And he's already experimenting on people, creating Imbued, and coming up with these schemes. He doesn't write like a child."

The writing was cursive and elegant. It reminded Ester of some of the executive orders written in the Sovereign's own hand. On the reverse of the parchment was a detailed map with instructions to get to the Star Mines.

"Why?" Ester asked. It was the first time she had spoken since leaving the Foundry chapel.

"Why... did they want to take you to the Star Mines? What

do they even want with the place? The letter doesn't say. But we could find out." He made a hacking sound into his palm, violent enough that his hand started to tremble, but he wiped his palm on his pant leg and pretended it hadn't happened. The man was coming down with something, and had been carrying it since before they'd reached the treasury.

She nodded. Of course she wanted to know what Bilal wanted with the Star Mines. If it gave her the opportunity to kill the Imbued who had killed her parents, or to make Myrilan hurt for what he'd allowed to happen, she would gladly take it.

Chapter 43—Efadora

WE WAITED INSIDE a tunnel alcove, listening to the footsteps of the kadiphs approaching. The skin of my knuckles stretched painfully from squeezing the handle of the coil weapon, the oiled leather soaked with my sweat. If it came to it, I'd jump out and attack without hesitation. Torlo waited silently, shaking, ready to do the same. I could paralyze one of the kadiphs, but several deadly seconds would keep me from taking a second shot. What else could we do, though?

The kadiphs spoke a few sentences in their own language. The words were wispy, interspersed with hums that reminded me of the thrumming melodies that were popular with the older crowds in Byssa. The language was beautiful, melodic, and even a bit delicate. Almost singsong. I knew the Archives would find that bit of information fascinating, and I did my best to commit the sounds to memory, parroting their conversation by mouthing it to myself. It helped reduce my anxiety over my possible death in the next minute.

The kadiphs continued onward. After a few minutes of silence, I exhaled hard, the sound whistling through my teeth. "I wonder how long until they just say 'Screw it' and start collapsing tunnels."

"This place is—too precious to them. Even the abandoned parts."

We turned down a corridor leading away from the kadiphs, and after about a mile inside this endless maze, we reached a room with a massive tablet in the center, the top of it etched with what looked like a map, three- to four-inch hills and valleys carved into it. "Why did Jakar go with them like that?" I asked.

"Because he wanted—to," Torlo said, his eye twitching. "When I'm close, I can overhear the Father give commands. They're not—like normal Words. It changes Jakar's will until—the task is done. It's why those kadiphs came after us so fast. He told—them about us as soon—as the Father asked."

"Well, then we're fucked. Deeply, horribly fucked. You're saying Jakar *wants* to help the Ebonrock now?"

"He wants to complete whatever—task the Father gives him, but he's probably pretty miserable—outside of that."

"You don't have to call that thing Father, you know. It sounds creepy."

"That's—what he is. He birthed all the—Children the Ebonrock use to create flesh bindings around—the world."

"Is he one of the Great Ones?"

"No, just a spawn." He started breathing hard, as though it'd taken a lot of energy to say so many words, and I helped him sit against the table map.

"Do you need anything?" I asked. "Are you going to be okay to run if the kadiphs get on our tail again?"

"I don't know," he said.

A traitorous thought crossed my mind then. What if he wanted to be found?

Shut up, you idiot. Torlo started whispering to himself again, and something lurched in my stomach. I would've done anything to see the old Torlo again. I hated the Child for what it had done to him. The Ebonrock had stolen any chance for him to live a normal life—for him to run again, or to stop twitching, or to use both his hands, or to smile. I just wanted to see him smile.

"The Child told me many secrets, even if—it didn't realize it was," he said.

"What are you saying?"

"That there's—a way to stop Father."

"How?"

"His will can be changed. I—can change it." He was breathing harder now. "It requires a ritual. The right words to be spoken. Words are powerful here. I just need to get close enough to the Father before the—Ebonrock kill me."

"Good luck with that."

"There's always a kadiph with Him. And Father can call out to the elementals for aid too, and—they'll be there in less than a—minute. *You* could disable Jakar, though."

"I could?" I asked, even though I knew the answer. An answer that made me a little sick.

"Complete the binding ritual between you and him. Give him a conflicting command—and he'll be punished."

The thought made me uncomfortable, but what else could we do? The idea of Jakar killing us without hesitation was a hard idea to swallow, and we needed a way to protect ourselves against him. I didn't see any other choice. "That doesn't solve the problem of everyone else."

"It doesn't."

The tapping of faint footsteps reached us from one of the halls. The steps weren't heavy like the kadiphs', which explained why we hadn't heard them until the person was almost on us. We tiptoed for one of the side rooms and managed to hide only a few seconds before the person reached the room. Boots scuffed stone as they circled the room, then they stopped.

"I guess I'll announce my presence so I don't scare Efadora into accidentally killing me," the voice said.

I hurried into the room. "Geth?"

The cartographer looked the same as the last time we'd seen

each other, with a pack strapped to his back and a bandana tied around his forehead to keep the sweat out of his eyes. He grinned. "I'm glad I found you. Judging by all the commotion in the tunnels, you two are pretty popular."

Torlo limped out of the side room. "Did you follow us here?" I asked.

"Had to keep my distance otherwise Jakar would've turned me to paste, but I knew you guys would need help, even if Jakar didn't want to admit it."

"But how'd you find us *here*?" I asked. "We're surrounded by miles of tunnels."

"I've been nearby." He pointed at my gloves. "It helps that your gloves are laced with quartzite dust."

I moved my fingers, flexing the material. Of course the gift wasn't just a gift. Geth didn't make nice gestures. He'd been afraid we would ditch him back in Xeriv. "Thanks for coming then, I guess. But I call bullshit on you wanting to help out of the kindness of your heart. You didn't want to pass on an opportunity to study the Ebonrock."

His grin leveled out. "It wasn't just for that, thank you very much," he said. "I told you I'd made a promise to Shirallah. I'd sooner die than go back on my word to him."

I supposed Jakar would understand why Geth was part of the group again, assuming we snapped him out of his little trance. I explained to Geth what had happened to Jakar and just how hopeless things were looking at the moment, and he barely reacted to the idea of Jakar being captured—by the time I'd finished, he'd already switched his attention to the table in the center of the room. "This looks like a map of the Black Depths," he said. "Most of it's unplotted, but I recognize part of the outline. Looks like the Ebonrock are having a hard time getting very far into open waters."

"I hope you know you're not helping your case at all. Let's focus on helping Jakar, all right?"

It seemed to take Geth effort to wrest himself from whatever train of thought he'd had. "Sorry. You guys are trying to figure out a good time to attack, right? Jakar's bound to an extra element, which makes him more powerful than all the elementals here, and you know he'll spill the beans as soon as that Father thing decides to ask. It'd make sense that the Ebonrock would want the rest of their elementals to have the same edge Jakar does."

When Sara had stabbed Jakar back in Augustin, she had unwittingly discovered the safest way to bind to the elements—by injecting the rhidium into the bloodstream instead of ingesting it. Jakar knew this now, which meant that the Ebonrock might know as well.

Geth grew more excited. "If the Ebonrock start binding their slaves to carbon, it'll mean we'll have a whole bag of elementals comatose from an Imbibing in the near future, right?"

"That's assuming they know to ask Jakar," I said. "And I doubt they'll have everyone undergo the binding at the same time." The plan was terrible, if I was being honest with myself, but it was better than nothing. Facing some of the elementals instead of all of them was still suicidal, but not as suicidal as our plans before Geth showed up. "Do you think shooting the Father with this will hurt it?" I waved the coil weapon at Torlo. He half-twitched, half-shrugged.

"I've been thinking a lot about that," Geth said. "The Sihraans obviously knew who the Great Ones were, enough to incorporate them in their culture. What if the Great Ones had something to do with the civilization's disappearance? What if the Sihraans were using what you're holding to defend themselves? Big threats need big weapons to deal with them."

"That theory isn't based on any direct evidence," I said. "It's also dumb."

He smirked. "The first part of what you just said is what I would expect a real cartographer to say."

"What—" I started, but faltered when a distant shriek echoed through the halls, followed by the ground trembling.

"That sounded uncomfortably close," Geth said.

The shriek started again. It was the sound of rock grinding violently against rock. It wasn't the regular rhythm of elemental digging, either—there was a cadence to it, and it was a cadence I'd grown familiar with in my travels with Jakar.

I stepped toward the entryway. "Where are you going?" Geth asked.

"Someone's fighting, and they're elemental. What if Jakar and his friends got free?"

I hurried into the hall, not bothering to see if the others followed.

Chapter 44—Jakar

THE KADIPH LED me toward the line of diving bells that sat at the water's edge in the cavern. Other elementals trudged out of the tunnels, forming into packs of three in front of the bells, some watching me with hateful or resentful looks. They were probably trying to understand why a person would be stupid enough to come here and throw away their freedom. Through my excitement to reach the diving bell and fulfill Father's request, despair plagued the edges of my mind. I'd told them about Efadora and Torlo, and I'd told them gladly. The kadiphs could enter the cavern with my friends' bodies slung over their shoulders any minute now, and it'd be my fault.

"Would you believe me if I told you I feel bad?" Krisenth asked. "Belief and conviction are delicious motivations, and I know that's why you're here. I respect that. I can sympathize with having your beliefs crushed to powder. It can't be a good feeling."

I said nothing. We reached our diving bell—an open-bottomed dome that we would climb inside from underneath, which sat on four poles with hardwood wheels—and I had to resist the urge to wade into the water and climb inside, as Father wished, after Krisenth signaled me to wait. "What I'm trying to say is I wanted to provide a gesture. An olive branch, if you will. The sooner you accept the reality of the situation, the easier it'll be, and hopefully this will help alleviate some of that hopelessness."

A kadiph appeared, towing a figure with hands bound by rope. My stomach dropped. The two reached us, but Quin kept her eyes on her feet, scowling.

"Quin was next up for the rhak'dar, but I asked to have her switched," Krisenth said. "You can thank me later."

Quin finally noticed me, and her mouth fell open. Her brown eyes were as bright as I remembered, the whites intense against her grimy face. Scrapes covered her arms, her muscles toned from years of laboring for the fellowship of masters and the kadiphs.

Krisenth motioned to the bell. "Ig, into the diving bell. In you go, too, Jakar."

It was a strange thing to hear my old command word, but of course it would be used to control the elementals raised in Som Abast. I spotted Krisenth's flesh sacrifice—it had been carved into the back of her left calf muscle, the name of Som Abast's Child in the center, surrounded by whorls that matched the design on mine and Quin's backs. Every kadiph's flesh sacrifice matched the scars of the elementals they controlled, with two elementals assigned to one kadiph, but Krisenth's flesh sacrifice didn't affect me, as Sorrelo Adriann had stolen her spot as my master two years ago. Knowing she could never give me a Word was a small pleasure.

Quin was untied, and she approached the shore and stepped into the water, the other kadiphs and elementals doing the same. I followed. Inside the diving bell, a chunk of glowing white rock hung from a rope, and the seating that ringed the inside of the bell was long enough to fit four people. I sat opposite Quin. Krisenth climbed inside to sit next to us, then let out a satisfied sigh. "You'll learn to enjoy these trips in the bell," Krisenth said. "It's very calm, unless you're the type who can't handle the sound of their own thoughts. That tends to become a problem with some of the elementals. What you'll be doing is pushing this bell with Quin's help. You'll obey my instructions on where to go and what to do. Sounds simple enough, right?"

I said nothing. All I could think about was the person sitting opposite me, the woman I'd traveled all this way to find. I'd finally found her.

"Take us out," Krisenth said.

Quin's power nudged the diving bell forward, followed by the muted squeaking of wheels inside the water. The water rose until the pocket of air inside the bell stopped it from rising any higher, plunging our legs into the ice-cold bath up to the tops of our shins, and I could sense the diving bell moving toward an underwater gate. The other capsules did the same, quickly moving ahead of us. A sudden eagerness overcame me, and I added my power to Quin's—Father had instructed I help push the bell and to listen to any direction provided by Krisenth—and the bell lurched, tilting until it threatened to tip over. Quin gasped, gripping onto a handle and trying to correct the mistake, but the bell was too heavy for her to do it alone. The diving bell quickly righted itself with my help.

"It's awkward work at first, but you'll get used to it," Krisenth said.

Quin caught my eye, and there was a question there. Had she felt how strong I really was?

We reached the first fifty-foot-long iron gate, which slid to the side with the combined willpower of the elementals in the other diving bells. We rolled into the pressure chamber beyond, then closed the first gate before opening the second. I could sense open water waiting for us on the other side. The second gate opened and our bell creaked from the water pressure magnifying a thousand times over. The glowing rock reflected off the water's black sheen as we rolled along the bottom of the Black Depths. I couldn't sense anything around us except for trace elements floating in the ocean and clumps of glowing silicon that must've been algae. Did something ancient and massive lurk out there, waiting for us to find it?

"You're fast," Krisenth said.

I almost panicked upon realizing I'd been pushing the diving bell far faster than the others, and Quin said, "He hasn't been worked like a pack animal for years like the rest of us have. His mind is fresh."

"A fresh mind couldn't move like this," Krisenth said. After a few tense moments, she let out a *hmph*. "I always knew you were special, Jakar. Keep up the pace. At this rate we'll outpace our record by at least a couple miles. Father will be very pleased."

Krisenth brought her attention back to the oily dark water and I tried to force myself to breathe evenly. Not once had the subject of my abilities been brought up during my interrogation—as far as they were concerned, any Ebonrock elemental who underwent the trauma of another binding ritual would surely die—which meant the Ebonrock had no idea I was bound to another element. Again, Quin gave me a strange look. I tried to think of something to say to fill the void, but all I managed was to leave my mouth hanging slightly open. Sometimes there was just too much you wanted to say, and you had to surrender yourself to the feelings that washed over you. With each moment I held Quin's gaze, though, more of my desire to help Father was washed away. The feeling never lasted. The need to follow Father's Word always came riding back.

I was surrounded by people who perfectly understood the pain I'd gone through, people who could sympathize when I told them about the terrible things I'd been forced to do back in Augustin. It was a soothing thought, in a way. Maybe getting captured wasn't the worst thing to have happened.

I sighed and rubbed my eyes. *Of course* being captured was the worst thing to happen. My mind was starting to play tricks on me. I needed to focus on Efadora and Torlo—if they weren't captured yet then they would be soon, and I couldn't let that happen.

"Where were you?" Quin asked.

"He was flesh bound to some nobleman halfway across

the world, running errands and slitting throats," Krisenth answered for me. "Empty chores, all of it. Country politics are so… hollow, don't you think?"

Quin and I only looked at each other. I was coming to realize that perhaps Krisenth loved hearing the sound of her own voice. She continued, "I can't imagine living a life with so little meaning, with no aspirations to uncover the gears that turn the world."

"You were flesh bound to someone that wasn't a kadiph, or Father?" Quin asked me.

"Clever, what he did," Krisenth said. "He should have been mine after the Child changed him, but he finished the flesh binding ritual with whatever smith-loving Miran rescued him from his hole. Fortunately, we always have Father as a redundancy."

"I'm talking to Jakar," Quin said. "Isn't that why you put us in here together? So we could catch up?"

Krisenth shrugged but stayed silent. Quin brought her attention back to me. "I can't believe you came back."

"I wanted to save you and the others," I said. "It's the only thing I've wanted since I freed myself from my last master."

"I don't want to be saved."

I didn't know how to respond. She must've noticed my shock, for she said, "Not until I kill her," and nodded toward Krisenth.

The kadiph took a break from picking her nail and gave Quin a mild look. "I should have Father order you to like me. That way I wouldn't have to deal with your constant, irritating threats. You won your second chance to avoid the rhak'dar experiments, so don't waste it."

"What are those?" I asked.

"Do you remember when we first met?" Krisenth asked. "Remember anything strange about my appearance?"

"Your hands were made of rock."

She nodded. "Father likes to experiment on the kadiphs, to see if he can gift his most faithful with bodies that are immune to the frailties of flesh."

"But he's lost faith in his faithful," Quin said.

Krisenth bristled. "No, he is branching out with his experimentation. That is all." She held her hand up, the one that had once been made of molten rock, a look of longing in her eyes. "The experiments have failed for the kadiph. My body rejected the gift."

"Maybe you're just unworthy," Quin said.

"Ig, quiet while I finish speaking with Jakar."

Quin sat there with her mouth shut, and Krisenth continued, "Father believes an elemental might be able to withstand the change. Three elementals have sadly passed, but he remains optimistic. Quin was supposed to be next but I pulled her out of the queue so you two could be reunited. I told you I'm not without mercy."

"What's the point of it all?" I asked.

"An indestructible body is our potential solution to dealing with the Ebonrock's greatest enemies."

"I'm willing to bet your enemies could be my friends," I said. "Who are they?"

"I've heard a thousand versions of your snide comment already," she answered, dodging the question. "Your contempt is going to pass eventually. Unless you're Quin, of course. But that just means the rhak'dar will be in your future, and who knows, maybe we'll actually find success with you as a subject."

Silence settled between us again. I thought about pressing the issue to figure out who the Ebonrock's enemies were, or to learn more about the rhak'dar, but disgust with myself slowly replaced my lingering curiosity. I hated the itch of excitement I felt pushing the bell as fast as it would go— anything that would fulfill Father's needs. Was this what Ash addicts, or even my parents, felt when they used? An intense, compartmentalized compulsion surrounded by self-loathing?

The ground started to slope upward and Krisenth straightened. "We're already at the Fingers? Amazing. We covered the distance in less than a third of the time."

I could sense a vague outline of the Fingers—twisting columns of rock that grew out of the ocean floor, shepherding us to the northeast. We kept going, navigating the terrain as it became more treacherous and threatened to tip us over. I was able to keep us stable and progress at a steady pace, though. Krisenth was alert the entire time, demanding updates on our outside surroundings while tapping her fingers excitedly against the bench.

"Stop," she said. The bell came to a rest, and she slid the goggles she'd brought with her over her eyes. "We're at the Crescent Pyres. A series of volcanoes we've only been able to survey from a distance. I'll be back." She sank into the water.

Once her head disappeared, I didn't waste time. "Is there anything we can do to escape?"

To her credit, Quin didn't act awkward now that it was our first moment alone, just gave me a long look. "What do you think, Jakar?"

I stared at the water, clenching my jaw as I thought, my disappointment seeping in. It was a stupid question, but it had to be asked. I was stuck here.

"As soon as we're within reach of Father, we surrender ourselves completely to whatever he wants," she said, her voice kinder now. "There's no fighting it."

"It doesn't matter that I'm not bound to a kadiph? What about the fact I'm bound to another element? I could bring the caverns down by myself if I had the chance."

She took a moment to answer. "So that's what's going on with you. Father doesn't know?"

I shook my head and proceeded to explain to her how Sorrelo completed the binding ritual in Krisenth's stead and bound me to his family, how my binding passed on to his children once he died, and how Sara had inadvertently bound me to carbon.

"Carbon should've killed you ten times over," she said when I finished. "And your old master—Sara, was it?—trying to kill you is what broke your flesh binding with her?"

"I don't suppose you can bait Krisenth into trying to kill you."

She blinked hard at the churning waters, thinking. "Don't tell anyone what you just told me. The kadiphs can't know that they can bind their elementals to a seventh element."

"I won't," I said, but the last part of that sentence hung unspoken between us. *Unless Father asks.*

"Who are the Ebonrock's enemies?" I asked. "Maybe they can help us."

"They're the Mazesh, or that's what they're called around here. They're worshipped as gods in most places, I believe. Fedsprig is one of them. I think He's called Fheldspra in that country you've been living in."

Krisenth broke the surface and climbed onto the bench. "We're surrounded by lava chutes, and I can say for certain they aren't natural."

"Someone built them?" I asked.

She shrugged, but her body quivered with excitement. "This is the closest we've gotten to the Pyres, and it's the first time I've noticed how uniform it all is. I couldn't find a single place to get past those ash clouds. Almost like they're a barrier." She pulled the goggles off her face. "To think I'm the one who found this. With your help, of course, Jakar."

The darkening, disconcerted look on Quin's face contrasted with the twinkle in Krisenth's eye. The twinkle disappeared when she studied the two of us. "I'll never understood your lack of interest in finding the Great Ones. That's the real enigma."

"I think the whole 'enslavement until death' thing is souring everyone's curiosity," I said.

"Finding them means answers to fundamental questions. What if I told you the existence of humankind is thanks to these gods?"

"Are we heading back, or no?"

Krisenth shook her head in disappointment, but to her credit, she didn't speak for the rest of our trip back to the enclave. We reached the double doors and emerged into the cavern, which felt strange and empty. We were the first ones back. Father's voice invaded my mind, licking its corners with His tongue. *We found something*, I said, and when He asked what, my heart sped up with a hunger to answer. Quin's eyes fluttered as Father infected her, too. I tried to ask about Efadora and the others, but there was only coldness between us. I could feel His presence, but it was purely alien—trying to initiate communication with him was like trying to break through a massive wall extending into eternity.

"You'll work on excavations while I speak with Father about my discovery," Krisenth said. "I'll be back soon with a plan in mind."

Quin and I worked side-by-side at the end of the cavern, forming the start of a new tunnel that would be the next section of the enclave. Neither of us talked. Something had changed in Quin since we'd discovered the lava chutes—she was more somber, stuck in her own head, and barely looked at me. The Ebonrock was finally making progress, and that fact made her despondent.

I wished I could take it all back, to see that last bit of fire Quin clung to that had irritated Krisenth so much. Seeing her gutsiness was what helped me cling onto hope. Just like old times back in the Ebonrock.

I broke and bent the rock, sparks showering over me and pricking my scalp and forearms, and I wondered if finding the Great Ones could be worthwhile. I wasn't hurting anyone, after all. To stay here was to live a life without killing.

No, no, no. I was only thinking that because Father's will was snaking its way into my brain again. He didn't have control over all of me—only when he gave me a Word. The rest of the time I was my own, and I needed to use that time to plot our escape.

Over time, though, the thoughts came creeping back, insidious. The mindless digging was therapeutic, in a way. I didn't have to think about my problems. I didn't have to think about anything at all.

* * *

HOURS LATER, THE kadiphs led the elementals into the living area of the enclave. We passed through a room that stuck out like a sore thumb compared to the rest of the manmade compound—it was a small, naturally formed cavern with stalagmites and stalactites littering the floor and ceiling, with a pool in the corner. Father was in the pool, limbs writhing in pleasure. The water was saturated with green vegetation, and I realized He was eating.

"He eats constantly," Quin said. "We harvest the algae for Him when we're not digging."

So Father didn't consume people after all. The thought made Him slightly less horrifying.

I shook my head. I was humanizing Him, continuing to slip. I couldn't let myself do that.

We washed ourselves in a bathhouse, ate nutrient-rich mush that the kadiphs made us, and then we were brought to our bunks. Within minutes of lying down, the sound of feet padded in my direction, then a figure in the darkness pulled at the sheet covering my body and slipped in front of me. Quin. My heart thumped in my chest—I was naked and so was she, but she had no problem pressing her back against me, the skin on her shoulder cool against my mouth.

"I missed this," she said quietly.

We'd held each other like this all the time back in the Ebonrock, albeit clothed. It was commonplace in Sulian Daw, and it was one of the few ways I could ground myself when times were chaotic or violent. I realized that living in Mira had acclimated me to the way they expressed affection, though, because all I could think about was what it would be like to kiss her.

Was my Miran relationship with physical touch tricking me into thinking I was attracted to Quin, or had I felt this way all along?

I wrapped my arm around her and hugged her closer. "I still can't believe I found you."

"You shouldn't have." Her anger at my arrival wasn't there, as it had been earlier.

"I'm sorry for coming."

She squeezed my fingers. "Don't listen to me. I'm being unfair."

"These last couple years have been... hard. I hurt a lot of people. I came here because it was a chance to help the people who need it the most."

"Tell me about the people you served," she said. "Tell me about Mira and what it was like living free from the Ebonrock."

I told her what I could, whispering so I wouldn't wake the others. I wouldn't have been surprised, though, if those closest were listening—some of them looked at me with more curiosity than resentment now. Whenever I reached parts of the story I struggled with, Quin would give my hand a reassuring squeeze.

"That woman loved you," she said.

I bit back a muted laugh. "Sara did awful things to me."

"Yeah... she did. She had no right to fall in love, what with the power she held over you. That in itself is abuse."

A painful sucking sensation appeared in the back of my sternum, and I tried to swallow it down. I was lying on my back now, with Quin's head resting on my chest, and she caressed my stomach with a finger. "Serving the Adrianns wasn't good," I said.

"That boy Emil didn't sound so bad." She placed a firm hand down, as if trying to say, *I'm sorry you had to lose him.* After a moment, she asked, "What about that other Adriann girl? Efadora?"

I couldn't help but smile. I continued my story, talking about how I'd fled Augustin with Efadora, our adventures through the Rift, Namira's rescue in Ravada, and our time in Som Abast. Some of the bunks around us creaked when I described the fight with the Child.

"She sounds like a special girl," Quin said. "And she's stranded somewhere in the enclave?"

My anxiety over Efadora's fate returned in full force. "I don't know how to help her. If she was wise then she would have left."

"And if *you* were wise, you never would've come. I'm suspecting she might follow your example and try to help you out of a hopeless situation."

Quin was right, and it made my anxiety worse.

"You shouldn't have come," she said again. "You're going to die here, just like me. Just like everyone else."

The side of her face rubbed against my skin as she shifted for more comfort, and I noticed the warm wetness on my chest. She was crying. I squeezed her tighter and pressed my cheek against the top of her head. My feelings for her deepened with each passing moment, but I reminded myself again that moments like this had been normal when I'd lived with her in the slave school. We used to hold each other all the time to cope with our misery.

"We can escape this," I whispered.

She sniffled. "Do you know something I don't?"

"Just that things move from order to chaos all the time. Believe me, I saw it firsthand. Whether it's Augustin or Mira, or how energy itself works, or even the fact Fedsprig is the deity of chaos and He's all people want to worship these days. It's just the way of things. Eventually the Ebonrock will slip and we'll find our chance."

She snorted. "By your logic, your plan when you came here was supposed to fall apart. We're right on track."

I touched my lips to her temple tenderly, the gesture so automatic from being overcome with the need to kiss her. She didn't pull back, and it was too difficult to see her expression from this angle. "And now I'm here," I said, breaking the silence, "which means we're back together and you can help me figure this out. Maybe you were the piece that was missing all along."

She answered by nestling into me.

Boots on stone entered the room, and an outline of a kadiph

filled the doorway. "Up," Krisenth said. None of the other elementals moved—she was Quin's master and my unbound master, therefore the command was for us alone. We climbed off the mattress and slid our pants and tunics on, then I followed her from the room. She led us through the maze, walking smartly.

"You're upset," I said.

"We just found the four kadiphs we sent after your friends. They're dead. How dangerous are your companions, really?"

On the wake of her question rode Father's voice. It roared to the point I couldn't hear the sound of my own thoughts, and I faltered, falling to one knee and rubbing at my ears. "They can't fight the Ebonrock," I said. A pleasurable chill ran down my spine from answering, and I hoped Father would ask something else. Anything. I just wanted to help Him.

"So they had a Sihraan plasma cutter and nothing else they might've scavenged from the ruins? It's just the girl and the boy?"

"Yes," I said. "Didn't you say kadiphs were vulnerable to plasma cutters?"

"Don't be stupid," she said, standing over me. "Your friends would've had time for one shot, and even then, it would not have killed. It doesn't explain the dismemberment or the crushed skull, either."

There was fire in Quin's eyes, and it stirred something in me, momentarily pushing away the need to serve Father. Killing four kadiphs didn't mean much when a small army of elementals and Father were around, but killing four kadiphs shouldn't have been possible, either. Something out there was happening that I didn't understand, and it signaled hope.

"None of that is our concern at the moment," Krisenth said. "Father is excited. He has a job for us. We'll be going to the Crescent Pyres in short order, but before we do that, Jakar will be undergoing a rhak'dar procedure."

Chapter 45—Efadora

THE TUNNEL SHIVERED and the rock shrieked so powerfully it hurt my ears. I slowed down until I was walking carefully, wondering if getting tangled in whatever I was hearing would be the worst idea I'd had yet. Even though we had to be miles from the rest of the Ebonrock, it wasn't impossible that they'd heard and were already running in this direction. I turned a corner to a chamber almost as big as a cavern, where lines of pillars rose from floor to ceiling like a grid. Twenty-foot-tall sculptures filled up the center of the chamber, the sculptures nauseating masses of limbs and eyes, with vines and moss slowly overtaking their discolored surfaces.

A body collided with one of the sculptures, cleaving off a shard of rock as it bounced off.

The body crashed to the ground and picked itself up, shaking the dust out of its hair. It was one of the two kadiphs who had been hunting us, with a crooked nose and cropped black hair. Near him, a disemboweled body lay in pieces in a pool of black blood—even from here I could pick up the aroma of chemical burns. Through the grid of pillars to my right, someone screamed. It was a woman, the other kadiph who had been hunting us, and she was in the middle of trying to pry a glowing blue sword from the hands of a barrel-chested man almost seven-feet-tall. The barrel-chested man hissed through clenched teeth, his white hair plastered to his face, as he slowly overpowered her and drove the sword deep into her side. A third kadiph with balding gray hair punched at the barrel-chested man's side, but he wasn't strong enough to stop the giant from skewering the woman.

"Ah, fuck," I whispered, my heart in my throat, staring at the Sovereign's primordia as the woman ripped the rhidium blade from his grasp—the fact it protruded from her side seemed to give her extra leverage—and she stumbled away. Aronidus let her go and turned his attention on the balding man, punching down on his leg hard enough to turn a normal person's flesh and bone into ground meat. It only made Balding Kadiph let go with the sound of pained frustration. A blur rocketed across the room and Crooked Nose crashed into Aronidus, picking him up by the legs and carrying him off.

What should I do? What *could* I do? Crooked Nose carried Aronidus into the marble wall hard enough to make dirt rain down from the ceiling and causing the stone to spider web. Aronidus faltered, and Balding Kadiph jumped on him from behind and wrapped an arm around his neck. Crooked Nose swept the primordia's legs and knocked him off his feet, and Aronidus fell to the ground, thrashing to get out of Balding Kadiph's chokehold, but the kadiph's grip had to be stronger than iron. Aronidus's face purpled.

I aimed the coil weapon, swallowed my fear to take a level breath, and squeezed the trigger. The weapon whined, then the air popped as lightning arced across the chamber and struck Balding Kadiph in the side. He let go of Aronidus and clawed at his wound, his skin charred black, and seized into convulsions. Crooked Nose catapulted himself my way.

Time seemed to slow as the kadiph rushed me. I aimed between his eyes, but the bluff didn't scare him off. The coil weapon wouldn't charge in time. Something crashed into him from behind and sent him skidding across the floor until he hit the wall several feet to my right. Aronidus had thrown Balding Kadiph, who was still paralyzed, at Crooked Nose.

Aronidus was on us a heartbeat later. He picked Crooked Nose up and threw him down, then stomped on the man's face, cratering the stone beneath the man's head. A second stomp turned his face into a bloody ruin, then Aronidus straddled him and wrapped his massive hands around the kadiph's head. Aronidus roared and bone collapsed, sending blood and viscera into his face.

He didn't waste time. He picked Balding Kadiph off the floor, the kadiph's limbs bent at unnatural angles from his convulsions, and squeezed his neck. The chamber became oddly quiet as I stood there, too scared to run, too scared to speak, as Aronidus watched the life leave the kadiph's eyes. He let go, and the man's body was like a boulder hitting the ground.

A cry of pain echoed through the cavern. The woman kadiph was at the other end near the mouth of a tunnel, lying in a pool of her own blood as another woman stood over her, holding the Adriann family's meteor blade.

Sara.

Sara aimed the meteor blade at the kadiph as the woman put her arms under her and tried to push up, but collapsed. The kadiph didn't try a second time.

It wasn't until the woman stilled did I realize I was halfway across the cavern to Sara, out of breath and my heart pounding. Sara noticed me and the air changed, thickening until it was like butter. "Reunited at last," Aronidus said in his boyish voice, now standing several feet behind me. His footsteps had been dead silent.

"You weren't doing me any favors," I said.

"I was not talking to you." He studied the sculptures around us, which towered twenty feet in the air and created two concentric rings, the outer one with six sculptures and the inner with five. The sculpture in the center of the room, the tallest and thickest of them all, almost reached the massive troop of lightcaps growing on the ceiling that illuminated the cavern. The center sculpture was vaguely humanoid, but it wasn't Fheldspra or any other deity I recognized. Some of the others were easier to pin down. The outer ring had to be the Great Ones, considering how awful the statues looked and there were supposedly six of the monstrosities lurking in the Black Depths. The inner ring was simply deposits of different minerals cut into columns.

"Do not run," Aronidus said. "Come, or I kill you."

Again, he wasn't talking to me. Geth and Torlo appeared around the corner of the tunnel I'd come out of, taking careful steps toward us. Geth had his dirk in front of him, but held it about as confidently as a toothpick. Torlo was weaponless, and watched the ground with his arms wrapped around himself as he shuffled forward.

They joined us, and Aronidus said to me, "I have been looking for this place for a long time. Thank you."

"For what?"

"For leading me here."

It all fell into place—the comments Jakar had made during our ride to Som Abast, when he thought someone was following us. It had been Aronidus and Sara all along. Aronidus let out a sharp whistle, and Sara came to join us, leaving behind a trail of sizzling blood that dripped from the rhidium blade.

Somehow, Sara looked exactly like the person I remembered and almost like a stranger. It was the first time I'd seen her hair matted and disheveled—it was usually so smooth that it could probably undo its own knots. Dirt streaked her cheeks and there were bags under her eyes. She'd always had the curves in the family, but she'd lost so much weight that it had changed the shape of her face. The biggest difference was in her eyes. She could usually have a staring contest with a statue and win. It wasn't that her gaze was intense—it was always cool instead of hot, and she never seemed uncomfortable letting someone have all her attention. Now she gave me only furtive glances, and she stood like she was embarrassed to be here. Or guilty that she'd fucked up my one request to never see her again. She handed Aronidus the meteor blade.

"When did you start following us?" I asked, my voice weak.

"Since the Xeriv capital, after that spectacle Jakar put on in Ravada with his power. I would like to thank Sara for convincing me to go to Ravada in the first place—she was certain it would be the best place to pick up your trail, and she was right. You Adrianns are a clever bunch."

I wondered why he had brought Sara along instead of killing her, but I suddenly lost interest in talking about anything involving Sara. The conversation fizzled. Aronidus didn't talk—it was almost as if he was giving me and Sara space for our reunion, though the idea of a primordia being that courteous was laughable. Torlo stepped in. "The—kadiphs might know there was a fight here. We should move."

Aronidus moved past us, heading the way we'd come, not bothering to check if we were following. Geth gave the sculptures a longing look and went after the primordia. The rest of us were a lot less ambitious to follow, until Torlo limped after and we got moving. Sara's footsteps echoed behind me.

Aronidus brought us to a room made from naturally formed rock, with glass figurines half shattered and left discarded across the floor. Someone had carved whorls and mesmerizing patterns on the ground, which made me dizzy if I focused too hard on them, and the air smelled faintly of fish, the back corner of the room stained green and brown. It seemed someone had stockpiled vegetation here, long ago, now so old that it turned to dust under my boots.

"When Sara first told me the manservant would come here, I believed it was to remove his flesh bindings once and for all," Aronidus said to me. "I've since concluded this could not be the case, as bringing an Adriann along would only bear the additional risk of being enslaved again."

His expectant gaze made it clear he was asking a question. "He came here to save his friends," I said. "He kept me around because he knew I wouldn't complete the binding between us."

He snorted. It was an ugly sound, so ugly it was almost funny. "That is not the only reason."

"What makes you say that?"

"The tuk galang lose their power if they are separated from their masters. And so it is with you and the manservant, even if you cannot give him a Word. Your sister has confirmed this."

"What?"

"Jakar would lose his powers if he was separated from you for more than three passings."

I glanced at Sara, and she nodded.

I tried to take even breaths but realized it was harder than it sounded. It wasn't the usual sinking feeling that accompanied the realization that someone wasn't who I thought they were. This time it was a gaping hole in my chest. All this time Jakar had let me believe he'd kept me around because he enjoyed my company, but it was because he needed me so he could fight the Ebonrock.

There was always an angle.

"This is interesting," Aronidus said. "You are not the manservant's master yet?"

"No," I said quietly.

He showed his teeth, amused, but the expression was wooden. "What's so funny?" I asked.

"I have spent these last months in my travels deciding whether to kill your sister. My decision was to allow her the chance to make peace with you and the manservant as payment for pointing me in the manservant's direction, then I would kill you both."

I stiffened, the skin on my spine prickling. The coil weapon was ready to fire, but Aronidus was so close I'd barely have time to think about raising the weapon before he wiped me from existence. "*Planned*? As in past tense?"

"You have earned your life."

The relief was short-lived. "What about Sara?"

"She has been given her chance to speak with you. Where is the manservant?"

"Gone." I explained the situation with Jakar working for the Ebonrock now, trying to wrestle with his refusal to tell me how his powers worked, feeling for one traitorous moment that his kidnapping might have been a bit of karma rearing its head. Did that make me an asshole? It seemed like a lot of that was going around.

"This is an unfortunate development," Aronidus said when I finished.

"Right," I said. "What are you going to do with Sara, since she can't 'make her peace' with Jakar?"

"A good question. What do you think I should do?"

Some distant, rational part of my mind recognized that Sara deserved to die. Not even for what she had done to Jakar, but because of what her army had done to the Granite Road and Augustin. But part of me couldn't stop my pulse from quickening and my breath from going shallow. I pictured him ending her life in the same brutal fashion he had ended the kadiphs'.

"Let her live," I said.

"And who are you to deny her a fate she has earned?"

"You wouldn't feel a little bad about killing her? She's been your traveling companion for months now."

"She is dirt to me, as are all masters. I could crush her and feel nothing, as I've felt with every man and woman I have squashed. If you have nothing else to say in defense of her life, then I see no reason to keep her alive."

"Please don't," Sara croaked.

Aronidus backhanded her. The movement was lazy, almost as if he was raising his arm to brush the hair out of his eyes, but there was enough force behind it to send Sara off her feet and crashing to the ground.

"My command stands, even now at the end," Aronidus said as Sara picked herself up. "All words are poison in the mouths of the masters, and so you have lost the right to yours."

Blood covered Sara's mouth, and she sucked at it. The muscles in her forearms clenched like she was ready to fight for her life, but the look on her face made it clear she knew how hopeless that would be.

"Wait," I said. "You need her."

Aronidus crossed his arms. "Explain."

"She's elemental, right? That means she can be useful against the Ebonrock, especially since you can't use your own elemental power."

Aronidus's eyes narrowed. "Interesting words that you choose," he said. "Explain."

The cartographer part of me—the part that loved solving puzzles—was eager to share my theories, even though revealing one of the primordia's closely guarded secrets could be hazardous to my health. "You and the other primordia are flesh bound to the Sovereign. I saw Otalia's scars when we met in Lo Toddul. I'm guessing that probably means you also lost your elemental powers when you abandoned the Sovereign and came here. Were you trying to find the Ebonrock because you want to break your bindings to him?"

Aronidus's expression tightened. Over the span of a few moments, he went from standing solid as a boulder to hunching in anguish. "You… you know." He paced to the other side of the room and kept his back to us. Sara was looking back and forth between Aronidus and me, mulling over the revelation. A small sound left her mouth as if she wanted to interject, but she knew better this time around.

"I cannot discuss this topic in plain words," the primordia said without turning around.

Because of a Word. "There are other ways your power is being restricted, aren't there?" I asked. "The Sovereign's been using a Word to stop you from using your power outside of the territory you govern. You governed Manasus, which would've made you powerless as soon as you stepped outside that territory. It's why you couldn't find my family in Augustin and instead put a bounty on our heads. Why?"

He turned around. In the ruddy glow of the lightcaps, I could've sworn the skin around his eyes was red. "Man is not made to live so long." He spoke slowly, navigating some hidden minefield. "Our bodies are built to last, but eternal health in the muscles and organs is a simple matter compared to health of the mind. Many of us have... degraded. You have met elders who have succumbed to invisible illnesses, yes? We are in a far worse state, thanks to the centuries. We would kill each other if we could." He seemed to physically chew on his next thought, and when he was satisfied, spoke again, this time even more slowly. "We each have our domains. The territories. To stray into another's would be suicide. Nektarios would have destroyed me if he knew I was walking his roads. The Sovereign gets what he desires by setting it up this way—the primordia ensure peace in Mira while leaving one another to his or her machinations."

"Seems like your boss left a glaring hole in his strategy, considering you were able to walk off whenever you wanted."

"You speak of that which you do not know. Become master of another for a thousand years and you'll realize that if you keep the leash too short for too long, your subject will become useless. The most effective leash is the one that's comfortable. The Sovereign made concessions." He rubbed his jaw, almost self-consciously. I knew the man was human, but he still seemed above such gestures. "But yes, he has been unusually lenient as of late," he said. "You may thank his growing focus on his son, Bilal."

"Wait," I said. "I thought the Sovereign was only two hundred years old."

"Once again, you speak of that which you do not know."

The Sovereign had created Mira two hundred years ago, but I supposed that wasn't any real indication of his age. "Well," I said. "No need to worry about Nektarios killing you on his home turf anymore."

"And how do you mean?"

"Jakar killed him."

His expression darkened, his gaze flitting to the coil weapon in my hands. "I see."

The tension in the room tightened like a wire. I thought the death of a rival would've relieved Aronidus, but it quickly became apparent I'd been way off the mark. "Er, question,"

Geth said. "Back in that other room, you said 'reunited at last' like you were talking about this whole place." He waved at their surroundings. "Were you one of the Rha'Ghalor?"

Aronidus didn't take his attention off me for a few more seconds. My stomach dropped when he finally did. "I cannot discuss this topic in plain words," he repeated.

"I hear you loud and clear. Let's say, hypothetically, that you are Rha'Ghalor. Then getting anywhere near them probably isn't the best idea, unless you're trying to turn out like Jakar."

"This descendant holds no sway over me."

It took a moment to understand. The Father was a "descendant" of the Great Ones, if I'd interpreted his words correctly, whatever that meant. I knelt in front of the rotted vegetation and picked up a piece, examining it while I tried to think of a plan. It glittered in my Silicon Eye, like the algae in Obsidian Lake. "Geth thinks the Ebonrock are going to perform more binding rituals once they find out that Jakar's bound to another element, so we should wait until they're incapacitated to attack the Father."

"Such an action will take weeks to take place," Aronidus said. "The Rha'Ghalor do not store their rhidium caches here. The caches travel with them as they move from city to city collecting children to convert."

"Okay, then that plan is out the window," I said. "These tunnels are going to be swarming with kadiphs as soon as the Ebonrock find those people you killed." I eyed Sara, who wore the same hollowed-out look I used to see on Jakar all the time before I moved to Manasus. I needed her to act like her old self again, that way I'd feel better about hating her. Not this beaten down shadow.

"What does Sara think we should do?" I asked Aronidus.

Sara perked up as the primordia eyed her. The man nodded.

"I've got something," she said in a scratchy voice. "It's not much, but it's a starting point."

* * *

TORLO PRESSED THE tip of the blade against my skin. "Are you— ready?"

"I said don't give me time to think about it, remember?"

The knife went to carving, moving slowly over my shoulder blade. Two fiery slashes followed. I grunted and almost yelled out, but bit down on the strap of leather Geth had been nice enough to offer me. Torlo started on the letter G next. Then came the whorls and the lines, identical to the scar on Sara's forearm. He drew the blade away and pressed a rag to my wound. "Done."

"That's it?"

"That's it. You willingly—sacrificed a part of yourself. To break it, you'll have to do the—opposite, and sacrifice him."

He meant try to take Jakar's life. I couldn't help but check on Sara, who sat in the wings sharpening everyone's blades with a rock, but she was pretending like she wasn't listening. I pushed myself off my stomach and sat up, reaching up to take the rag and push it against the *Ig* carved into my flesh. Torlo was trembling so hard he could barely keep the rag on straight. "I don't feel any different," I said.

"An elemental of soul, not of matter," Aronidus whispered. He stood in the shadows, firelight glinting off the whites of his eyes. "What you control is precious. Misuse will earn you horror and death."

I couldn't tell if he was threatening or warning me, but I hoped it was the latter, since the whole point of binding with Jakar was to misuse it. "I bet you know all sorts of interesting tidbits," Geth said to the primordia. "Would you ever be willing to do a one-on-one with me? After we deal with this business with the Ebonrock, obviously."

Geth shrank under Aronidus's gaze. "If we succeed," Aronidus said softly, "my business will be with the descendant alone. Then I am gone." He turned to Torlo. "You guarantee the descendant will be of sound mind and body after you perform your ritual and break its hold over its servant? I will speak to it when Jakar and the others are unleashed and its worshippers dead."

Torlo nodded. "The ritual won't kill it, but it'll destroy—the flesh bindings."

It was hard to piece together Aronidus's relationship with the Ebonrock, but the man had offered hints here and there when the mood struck him. All of the Children spread throughout the world to create flesh bindings for the Rha'Ghalor were splinters of the Father, which explained Jakar's connection to the monstrosity. Aronidus's bindings had been created by the Father's predecessor, another descendent, though, and that descendent was dead. I'd asked if the Sovereign had had something to do with it, but Aronidus hadn't been able to confirm or deny it. I wasn't even sure if he wanted to answer.

With the original creator of his flesh binding dead, Aronidus couldn't go to that descendant to sever his tie to the Sovereign, but he hoped the Father might know something about flesh bindings that could help him. He reeked of the need to interrogate the thing—fidgeting whenever he talked about the descendants, flaring his nostrils when the topic of going back to Mira came up—and I couldn't help but feel a little sad watching Aronidus barely contain his desperation. A stupid thought, but I couldn't forget how he'd stopped Otalia from killing us in Lo Toddul.

We gathered our things and headed out. Aronidus guided us—there was a pattern to the compound only he saw, and he led us through tangles of hallways and corridors, stopping at random when he sensed something none of us could hear.

"Do you get the feeling Torlo isn't telling us everything?" Geth asked quietly as we walked.

"No," I said, sharper than I planned. "Quit projecting."

"I'm not projecting."

"Yes, you are."

After a second, he said, "Maybe you're right. I'm trying to be better, you know. I do feel bad about Som Abast."

"Don't be. It happened and it worked out. Not much else to say there."

"And that's how I know you'll be a good cartographer," he

whispered. "The best of us aren't the best because we know how to pick our way through some old caverns. It's about our constitution. Cartographers are put in a lot of hairy positions, so it pays to have feathers that are unrufflable."

"I thought ditching you meant I couldn't be a cartographer anymore."

He slapped me on the shoulder. "I'm all bite and no bark, Efadora. I say a lot of things I don't mean. You'll just have to promise to ditch Jakar afterward if you do want to stay under my wing."

I would've given a snarky reply to the suggestion if it had been any other passing, but I found myself attracted to the idea. I'd do what I could to save Jakar, but I was still bothered that he'd kept me close so he could remain elemental. I wouldn't forget that.

I made the mistake of slowing down enough to give the impression I was walking alone, which a certain someone tried to take advantage of by speeding up to walk beside me. I gave her a look that made it clear what I thought of the idea, then sped up myself to walk beside Torlo, who limped several strides behind Aronidus. "You doing all right?" I asked.

"Always," he said, squeezing his fist over and over as he kept bringing his arm to his chest and letting it fall to his side.

Before I could think about it, I found myself blurting, "I miss you."

A few awkward moments followed. "Please—don't do that," he said.

"Do what?"

"I'm the same—person. Geth thinks I'm strange because I got hurt and act different. I've been sad. Really—sad. But only because I wish what happened never did. I'm getting—over that, though. Nothing on the inside's changed, so please don't act—like it has. It only makes things harder for me."

I walked in silence, the heat of shame creeping up my neck. I hadn't considered that maybe Torlo hadn't changed just because the Child had scrambled him up, but because he was depressed. And who wouldn't be? It was a hard thing to lose what he'd lost, and we were just making it worse by acting as though he was surrounded by eggshells.

My hand slipped into his, my heart thumping. At first he had trouble holding on, but then the trembling in his arm calmed. For a second, it was as if his affliction was gone. Everything inside me wanted to try to catch a glimpse of his eyes to see what he might be thinking, but I was terrified to look over. A year ago, someone as kind and as giving as Torlo would've been a match made in fhelfire for me, but now he was all I could think about. Did that mean something in me had changed?

"Geth thinks there's something you're not telling us," I whispered.

"They're right."

I pulled away. He offered a half grin—the first time I'd seen him try to smile since Sulian Daw—and continued, "Aronidus won't be able to talk to Father. It can't—be communicated with, not unless they're flesh—bound together."

I checked to see if Aronidus had heard, but he was too busy checking the corridors up ahead for any lurking kadiphs. I swallowed the knot in my throat. "Can't imagine he'll be happy about that when he finds out."

"No. Not—at all. But all of this is pointless without his help anyway, so we'll cross—that bridge when we get there."

Chapter 46—Ester

RIVULETS OF SWEAT slid down Ester's neck and back, the heat evoking pleasant memories hammering steel alongside Artur in the Foundry. Damek wedged a waterskin between his thighs while he rode, and uncapped it to pour water into his mouth and over his sweat-soaked hair. He'd long ditched his shirt, the leather of his arm cap stained dark. Breach stopped the three of them at the ridge just beyond the tunnel's mouth. "Careful," he yelled over the roar of the cavern. "It's a long drop."

Ester nudged her stone fox to the rocky ledge and leaned in her saddle to peer over the side, her ribs aching. With places like the Tear or the pits of Byssa, the windy black void at least tricked her enough for her to pretend she wasn't walking next to a very, very long drop. Here, however, the magma did an unfortunate job of illuminating every nook and cranny of the cavern. The distance from one side to the other had to be more than fifty Augustins wide, and the depth perhaps another twenty. The ground shivered from the largest lavafall Ester had ever seen, which gushed from a river of fire that poured out of the ceiling at the opposite end, dropping past the plateau below and into the lake at the bottom. The sweltering heat swirled to the top of the cavern, stirring up enough wind to whip around dust and ash that disappeared into hidden cavities above. Ester slid off her fox and studied the plateau that waited halfway down. To its left, the cavern wall was honeycombed with red glass and volcanic rock, hosting a series of tunnels of billowing smoke—water vapor, meant to keep the rhidium inside from oxidizing before it was mined.

Ester dropped to her knees and pressed her forehead to the rock. This was a sacred place not meant for her eyes. All her growing doubts about the Foundry, about Fheldspra and the world, disappeared upon witnessing Fheldspra's terrible power. Here was just a glimpse of a domain that trembled with enough energy to consume the world over if He were so inclined. Spending too much time away from the Foundry had pulled her away from Him. She'd been due for a little humbling.

"For some reason, this seems like a worse idea than attacking sociopathic primordia," Damek said.

Ester stood and wiped the dust from her forehead. "It's a much worse idea."

Breach pulled out his refractor—a long tube filled with glass—and aimed it at the plateau, squinting into it. "I'd say about a thousand in the Sovereign's colors are down there."

Ester offered her hand and Breach handed the refractor over, and she wiped ash from the lens with her sleeve before peering through it. The plateau spanned only a quarter of the cavern, but that still made it several times larger than the floor of Augustin. People crawled from building to building like fire ants, too small to make out, but even at a glance the Sovereign's men had to outnumber the Foundry's pilgrims ten times over. She couldn't say for certain how many smiths were here, but put their numbers at less than a hundred—a handful of them milled around the largest building, which looked like some sort of meeting hall, with the rest hidden somewhere in the settlement.

"I wouldn't call it cowardice if we turned back now," Breach said. He leaned on his knees and let loose a few wracking coughs, then wiped at the ash sticking to his face, which left black streaks. He pounded his chest and cleared his throat. "This is a few orders of magnitude above what you signed up for."

Ester snapped the refractor shut and handed it back. "We're here for Myrilan. That crowd down there is a gift, actually. Should make sneaking in and out easier."

Both her companions nodded without complaint. A plan like theirs was long odds, but she and Damek had nothing left to lose, and not even an army could stand against Breach's optimism. Ester failed to suppress a glance toward Breach, who swigged from his waterskin and washed ash from his beard. She had so much to say to him, but it had been weeks since there'd been a good time to say it. Reuniting with Damek had reminded her of something important, a point driven deep into her heart after the death of their parents—to keep close the people you cared for the most. Breach just didn't know he was now one of those people.

They backtracked a quarter mile, where the heat was more bearable and where water trickled from cracks in the walls of an alcove. Ester touched a finger to the water and tasted it to make sure it didn't taste like sulfur or any other harmful sediments, then they tied up their stone foxes next to the spring and donned the Imbueds' garments they'd pillaged at Stonegate. She pulled out a vial of dirty green liquid—distilled benthic willow—and downed it. The ache in her ribs faded within minutes. Breach had his pack slung over his shoulder, the sharp angles of his experimental weapon pushing against the fabric. "You sure that's worth bringing along?" Ester asked.

"About as worth it as that little trinket of yours."

Ester readjusted the strap to her pack, the tiny contraption of metal and wire jumbling around inside. It was an artifact from Mulec'Yrathrik, with a switch that let it build up a nasty shock once it was turned on. Breach was of a mind that it used to be the base of a lamp that didn't need fire or bioluminescence to glow. More junk than a weapon, but she'd brought it along anyway just in case any primordia were lurking. "Good point."

"To answer your question, the worth of it depends on if I can get into the mines. Rhidium is the secret ingredient to get this thing working, but I suspect it's the unrefined stuff I need to get it firing."

They picked their way along the path that spiraled down the great cavern. The trail weaved in and out of the wall, offering places to hide and a chance to reassess the threat below. "I see a few dozen Imbued scattered around the army," Damek said as they lay on their stomachs on the path's edge. "Do you think one of them's the one who rode off with Myrilan?"

"Maybe. I don't know," Ester said. All the Imbued looked the same to her. "I don't think it matters. The Imbued probably brought Myrilan to Bilal to report on what happened at Stonegate. The child prince seems like the best place to start."

"Perfect," Damek said with an edge of bitterness. "Maybe we should just kill ourselves now and get it over with."

Black winds, please be with Bilal. A black rage had been building inside Ester since leaving Stonegate, and she would jump at the opportunity to take it out on the child prince if she had the chance. She'd kill him—hold white-bright steel to his mouth to make him suffer before she did so, his age be damned. He was responsible for the deaths of her brethren and her parents. Myrilan had had a hand in the latter, and for that she would ruin his life, too. Tear it down stone by stone, starting with the deaths of everyone he answered to.

Breach let out a *hmph* as he stared into the refractor, frowning.

"What?" Ester asked.

"You saw those smiths hanging around the meeting hall, right? They keep disappearing inside, one by one. I haven't seen any come out yet."

"Interrogations?" Damek asked.

"Maybe," Breach said with careful mildness. "Unless Bilal's in there."

Nausea crept inside Ester. If Bilal was making more homunculi, that would explain the aimlessness of the army while they waited for him to conduct his work. "We do this now," she said, and pulled herself to her feet.

Near the bottom, the trail came to a series of ledges with steps to traverse them, Foundry runes carved into the ledge faces. Squadrons of soldiers guarded the ledges. "Your business here?" the sergeant asked, his words watery as he eyed Ester's disguise.

Ester had moved the black cloth over her mouth, and hoped her gaze was adequately piercing. "With the prince," she said in as scratchy a voice as she could muster. A tickle in her throat almost made her cough.

"Ah, right. Of course." He shuffled to the side so he wasn't blocking the top of the steps. "I have to ask these questions, you know. I hope you understand."

None of the soldiers commented on the lack of facial scars, or on Damek's wound, but the questions were in their eyes. Ester tried to ignore them. Rocky outcroppings littered the start of the plateau, and among them a hundred stone foxes chirped, barked, and growled at each other, standing side-by-side in neat rows where soldiers tended to them, giving them food and water.

"Any chance the Sovereign is here?" Breach whispered, even though the roar of the cavern made it impossible for anyone more than twenty feet away to hear them.

"Bilal likes going his own way, I think," she said. She'd read the dead Imbueds' correspondence a hundred times already—the Sovereign had traveled to Radavich to appoint a new magnate, but Bilal had splintered off to head to Manasus to deal with the ruin folk. And now he was here. She still couldn't imagine him as an eight-year-old child. She wondered if they knew the ruin folk were in Saracosta desecrating farms, poisoning the capital's underground springs, and burning the natural gas veins the territory used for lighting. Saracosta would have no idea the ruin folk were behind it, either—as far as they knew, the land was simply going bad. And soon they would go to the Sovereign to fix their unfixable problems.

The deeper into the plateau they got, the less interested the soldiers became. The army was preoccupied with busy work, carrying pails of water from a nearby tunnel or running training drills. Every soldier was covered in sweat and misery. Refuse from rations littered the ground, and gardens lay trampled where fireweed, grapes, and silversword flowers had been flattened under a thousand pairs of boots. Oddly enough, the Star Mines looked untouched, a solitary footbridge separating the misty tunnels from the rest of the settlement.

"Look," Damek said, nudging Ester. An Imbued had exited a domed hut made of mole-rat hide, a leathery old man in white pilgrim's robes following him. "Why don't they fight back?" he asked.

"Your twilight years as a smith involves the mines, kinship, and prayer," she said. "Nothing else matters, not even our feelings toward the Sovereign."

"And if they find out what he did in Augustin?"

"…that could change things."

This was no longer a simple matter of revenge. If Bilal really was playing god with Ester's brothers and sisters, she needed to save them first, kill the boy second. Or maybe she could take care of both at the same time. "Here's what we do," she said. "The smiths are probably being held prisoner in these huts. We'll convince them to fight, then we coordinate an attack as one. Try to focus on the meeting hall before we're overwhelmed."

"Sounds like a shitty plan," Damek said. "Significantly less shitty than trying to assassinate Bilal on our own, though."

"Wait," Breach said. The domed hut sat next to a carved path that led to the footbridge and into the rhidium mines. "I'm going that way."

Some nearby soldiers watched them, but Ester couldn't tell if it was out of curiosity or suspicion. "It's already three of us against several hundred. You want to make the odds worse?"

"You trust me, don't you?"

She almost laughed at the question. "You're funny, *Xander*."

"Well, do you?"

She gnawed on the inside of her cheek. "Take Damek with you."

They crossed the footbridge while Ester shouldered her way through the furs draped over the entrance of the hut, resting her hand on the hilt of her blade. There were no guards inside. Just a handful of smiths, sitting on the ground with their backs against the walls, wrapped in blankets and coughing to themselves. It was surprisingly cool inside—a jagged lump of ice sat in a hole in the center, wisps of steam curling in the air, the ground it sat on somehow dry.

"Are you okay?" Ester asked the group.

An old woman with wiry white hair, skin that hung from arms corded with muscle, and rosy cheeks was rubbing at her lower back, and she grimaced at Ester. "You shouldn't be here. It's not safe for our kind."

Ester's disguise wasn't the best, but it wasn't *that* bad. How had the woman sniffed her out? "Did they do something to you?" she asked. She noticed none of them were restrained, and all of them either wore pained expressions or struggled to clear the phlegm from their throats. "Are you sick?"

The woman wiped dribble from her mouth. "It's a cost you would never know until you made your pilgrimage, young smith. The cost of doing what we love. A privilege to spend our final years perfecting our craft and loving our brothers and sisters, to be as close to Fheldspra as one can. A price happily paid."

"You're saying that the Star Mines are killing you?"

She coughed, nodding. "Rhidium kills all us smiths in the end, one way or another."

A shiver ran down Ester's spine. "I have friends in the Star Mines."

"A single exposure will do little. You have to work around rhidium for months before the sickness comes. Do not worry."

None of the smiths in Augustin had ever gotten sick, but the Foundry had kept their rhidium stores behind locked doors, far away from everyone. She thought about all that time she'd carried those vials in her pack, though she felt fine. For now. Then she thought of how much time Breach had spent tinkering with the element, trying to make it work with his new weapon, and remembered the cough he'd developed after.

"You need to leave," the woman said.

Ester peeked through the curtain, but there were no Imbued coming their way. "I'm rescuing you."

"Rescue us from our home?" asked a decrepit smith with limp white hair. "You know better than to ask us to abandon this place, young smith. We will dispel the Sovereign's ilk, one way or another. It's just a matter of finding the right words."

"The Sovereign's son isn't bringing you before him to negotiate. Has anyone who's shared an audience with him returned yet?"

They shook their heads.

With a trembling voice, Ester recounted the events at Augustin's Foundry, sticking with the annotated version while checking outside the hut every several seconds for any approaching Imbued. The pilgrims' reactions were a mixture of denial, shock, and horror. "So I'm pretty sure Bilal isn't here to talk," Ester said when she finished. "He might not even want the rhidium. We're all just his playthings."

The woman—the senior of the group, it seemed—struggled to her feet. "I have no intention of surrendering my body to that monster," she said, her body quivering from anger or her failing health; Ester couldn't tell which. "He won't cheat me from a worthy death."

The others stood. Relief flooded through Ester, but the feeling was short-lived. She was in Augustin again, the deaths of her brothers and sisters staring her in the face, and she experienced a sudden, intense aversion to losing more of them.

"I have to get you out of here," she said, even though she knew it was a losing battle.

"You know that won't happen, young smith," the woman said, smiling sadly.

Finding Myrilan had become an afterthought once she realized the smiths were in danger, but convincing them to escape was a lost cause, she realized. A fight was imminent.

And a fight was necessary, even if it felt awful. War was just hurt people hurting more people, the pain extending into infinity, but sometimes the alternative was worse. She would just have to atone for her sins when she reached the next life and destroy Bilal in the meantime.

"He's coming," one of the men said. The door flapped to the side and an Imbued appeared, pausing mid-stride.

Ester's rockwood knife was in her hand and plunging into the meat beneath the Imbued's jaw in one fluid motion. The man struggled, his eyes rolling into the back of his head, and she pulled him inside as he clawed at her arms. Blood bubbled over the front of his black fighting leathers, and she tossed him toward the center of the hut. He bounced off the block of ice and landed on his back, the knife still stuck in his head.

"These are more of Bilal's experiments," she said, pressing two fingers to her cracked rib. It didn't hurt, but it had started to click if she turned too far to the left or right. "They're bound to steel and like to use explosives. I don't know why their skin is cut up."

The lead smith rattled the sword away from the Imbued's belt while another smith pillaged the dagger strapped to its ankle. Ester retrieved her rockwood knife and wiped it clean. "I'm going to rally the other smiths," she said. "The plan is to attack the meeting hall. That's where Bilal is. We'll have to move fast before his army can react. I'll try to find you some weapons in the meantime."

"They'll come looking for him eventually," the woman said, nudging the Imbued's boot. "You need to go now."

Was there a faster way to convince the other smiths to fight? She set a hand on the furs, about to pull them aside, when a voice called out, "You'll come out of that hut slowly with your arms raised."

She shared a panicked look with the others. She gave the

furs a light brush until she caught a glimpse of the other side—a dozen soldiers waited outside with their lieutenant at the front, who was flanked by two Imbued. Those in the army closest to the squad watched on with interest but seemed otherwise unconcerned. They must've assumed some of the smiths would put up a fight eventually, maybe even expected it, but didn't take the threat seriously. But how did they know something had happened?

"You'll leave your weapons behind," the lieutenant continued, his voice almost inaudible over the lavafall, hair whipped about by the wind. "The punishment for murder is a like fate, but we will show mercy to those uninvolved. Those who stay inside willingly implicate themselves."

"They must have used the Great Ones' magic to know of this demon's death," a smith said, then bent over, hacking.

The old Ester would've agreed, but she'd learned a lot about the nature of magic in recent months. The Imbued had to be connected to each other somehow. Maybe through the carvings in their flesh? According to Jakar, that's how the connection was made between him and Sara and Sorrelo Adriann.

"It's going—" she started, but her words faded when an ache appeared in the space between her eyes. She rubbed at her temples and the smiths shuffled in discomfort, groaning. "Black magic," a smith grunted.

A low whine left the hairs on Ester's neck standing, and it grew higher in pitch until the sound disappeared. The soldiers outside started shouting. Boots on stone charged past the hut, and she realized they were running toward the Star Mines.

She made a blood-smeared cut with her rockwood knife into the hide of the wall facing the mines. On the other side of the footbridge that connected the plateau to the Star Mines, Damek and Breach were hunkered down at the mouth of the Star Mines' entrance, half-hidden by mist. Breach was aiming his weapon at the soldiers advancing on him and Damek, the glass chamber on the weapon's stock glowing a ghostly blue, and the weapon discharged, blue smoke shooting out its sides as it rattled in Breach's hands. Ester's headache faded. A platoon of soldiers and Imbued had been making their wary way over the footbridge, double-file through the chokepoint, and they flinched when Breach took the shot. When nothing happened, they continued advancing.

Breach's weapon hadn't worked. "We need to help my friends," Ester said. Some of the soldiers were passing near their tent as they prepared to cross the footbridge, but none of them noticed Ester. She started widening the hole. "We'll hit them from the side."

"What's that?" the lead smith asked at the same time Ester heard the distinct sounds of retching.

Half of the advancing line of soldiers doubled over, vomiting their rations onto the path or crumpling into a heap, holding their stomachs. Some stumbled out of line, walking like drunks until they collapsed.

Breach was shouting something at Damek, smiling, and the two of them disappeared into the smoke. Beyond Ester's field of view, the rest of the army could be heard yelling and scrambling into formation. The advancing line—those who hadn't been hit by whatever invisible projectile Breach had shot, at least—struggled to recover, but they didn't look too thrilled to step onto the footbridge, despite Breach and Damek having disappeared. Even the Imbued hesitated. "My friends have a minute, max, before they're overrun," Ester said. Breach had somehow managed to take out dozens of soldiers with a single shot, but that was peanuts compared to the rest of the army.

"Warn the others," the lead smith said, testing the sword she'd pillaged from the Imbued by swinging it, the metal moving in a blur. "We'll help your friends."

Breach reappeared, the back of his weapon glowing blue once again. The line of soldiers stopped to brace themselves this time, and the smiths jumped on the chance, charging through the hole and over the garden of coffee beans behind the hut. The smiths were old, they were slow, but as soon as they were running past the soldiers, they moved like water around the glinting metal that tried to poke and bite at them. One even managed to disarm a soldier and steal his weapon. One of the Imbued jumped at the group and tackled a frail man to the ground, and then his dagger was pinning the smith in the dirt through his back. The others broke free of the front of the line and raced across the footbridge. The lead smith, who now took up the rear, spun with a flash of her blade, and Ester barely caught sight of the arrows as they bounced off the bridge's handrails and tumbled into the abyss, cleaved in two.

A headache sprouted behind her temples and a faint whine rose out of the roar of the cavern once again. Soldiers let out panicked shouts, raising their shields even more, and then blue smoke was shooting out of Breach's weapon, the metal shaking. Several seconds of fear and confusion followed as soldiers tried to figure out if they'd been struck by another of Breach's invisible projectiles, then they were dropping or crying out in drunken pain.

She moved the black cloth over her mouth again, tightened the strap to her satchel while taking a deep breath, and pushed through the furs. The squad and the Imbued that had been standing in front of the hut had disappeared. Archers scrambled to form a line, but they were focused on the mines, not her. Soldiers deep in the army had collapsed with bloody vomit staining the fronts of their leathers, and Ester realized that whatever Breach was shooting, no amount of flesh or shield managed to slow it down. The occupants in the meeting hall at the other end of the settlement still hadn't emerged.

Battles like this were about momentum. They were desperately outnumbered, but if they were relentless, they'd make the other side suffer before they were overrun. Hopefully, the smiths who had joined Breach and Damek could hold the footbridge long enough for her to rally the others. She broke into a sprint toward the nearest hut.

Inside, an Imbued was in the middle of tying rope around the wrists of the pilgrims, the smiths voicing their outrage. The woman jumped to her feet as Ester launched herself forward. Ester was ready this time—she wasn't much good at hand-to-hand combat, and she was wounded, but she'd been training for this moment. She tracked the Imbued's gloved hand as it cocked back and flew toward her center of mass. Her left hand caught the woman's wrist while her right chopped at the crook of the woman's elbow. The Imbued caught her own hand under her chin at the same time the powder inside her glove exploded.

Ester had turned her head away, but heat and sound still smashed into the side of her face as she tumbled back. She fell halfway out the front door, and rushed to her feet, warm liquid running down the side of her face. Her ear rang and her fingers came back red when she touched them to her head. The Imbued lay on her back, her head blown apart, white bone stark against charred and bloody flesh.

The elderly smiths struggled out of their bonds. "What have you done?" an old man asked, incensed, but despite his anger he moved to Ester's side to keep her steady. "You're responsible for the fighting outside, yes? Now we have no hope of dispelling these people."

Ester rubbed at her side—she'd fallen sideways on her satchel and landed on the metal inside. She had no doubt she'd be in a lot of pain if she survived this. "They were going to kill you anyway," she grunted.

"You can't be serious," one of the others said. "The Sovereign's let us be for two hundred years. They wouldn't dare touch us with ill intent."

She examined the dead Imbued, the smell from the woman's charred flesh acrid enough to burn her nostrils. Breach suspected the powder they were bound to was magnesium. "Bilal is not like his father."

Something screamed outside. No, a dozen voices screeched in unison, the chorus bone-chilling and inhuman. Ester opened the curtain, and her stomach dropped.

The Great Ones' evil did exist after all.

At the end of the line of huts, where the meeting hall sat near the edge of the plateau, the ground had been cleared of soldiers, save for those who had exited the hall. The hall doors had been thrown open, and in front of the building stood a monster, propped up by a dozen sets of limbs. Human arms and legs. Its body was long as a scorpion's, its skin wrinkled and hanging off the bone. Its tail glistened with red muscle and bone, and at the end hung a lumpy orb. Heads, Ester realized. All fused together, facing outward, with their mouths hanging open in a perpetual state of surprise. The eyes were clouded over, sightless.

"Dear father of the core," one of the pilgrims whispered. They'd filed out of the hut behind Ester. They whispered prayers to themselves, passages from the Sky Scrolls meant to ward off the Great Ones' evil.

Bilal stood behind the monster, hands politely folded against the small of his back. He wore a hooded cloak embroidered with runes and patterns, and under the hood he watched with a lazy, slack-faced smile, as though he were high on Ash. A lithe woman in climbing leathers stood next to him, watching with barely suppressed disgust. She had a full head of hair, but it was gray and wiry like the pilgrims', despite the flawlessness of her face. Her feet were set like she was ready to spring into action, even though she carried no weapons. Her body reeked of potential energy, filled with promises of explosive violence. Ester had only seen one other person carry themselves with the same power and confidence. She was primordia.

"*That's* what you'll become if you don't fight," Ester said, pointing at the monster. She swallowed down the bile that had risen in her throat.

"The boy will pay for this," one of the smiths said. They all joined Ester, ready to fight. Ready to die.

Chapter 47—Ester

ESTER THOUGHT SHE had come to terms with what the Sovereign and his son had done to the smiths in Augustin. She'd spent weeks meditating on it, praying to Fheldspra, accepting over time the fact that she would never see her brethren again. Loss was a part of life, and she'd been unfortunate enough to experience it a little earlier than some.

It turned out she was dead wrong about her feelings. The monster's muscles rippled and flexed as it seemed to eye the nearby army, humanoid in shape and anathema in attitude, and all Ester could see in that wrecking ball of faces was Mateo and the others, screaming and roaring in anguish and horror as Bilal and the Sovereign bent and broke them, molding them the way a potter worked a molding wheel of clay. The images surrounded her, threatening to hamstring her and flatten her to the ground.

Then the feelings faded, filed away in dark places. They'd come for her again, she knew, once things went quiet.

She put all her focus on Bilal. By stopping him, she'd inflict a blow on the Sovereign that would hurt him and his cause more than anything the ruin folk could come up with.

The monster screamed again. A dozen voices sang as one, and for a moment the army forgot about the mines. Soldiers shouted and shied away from the meeting hall, their lines thrown into chaos, and Imbued punched and kicked to move everyone back in line. Bilal clapped, his smile stretching from ear to ear.

A hand gripped Ester's arm, belonging to a wispy-bearded pilgrim with watery eyes. "We have to destroy it," he begged. "Whatever happens, we can't let them go on like that."

Them. The ball of faces twitched as though they were in agony. Did some vestige of her brothers and sisters still exist in there?

"We'll end their suffering," she said.

The monster crawled forward, the palms and soles of its hands and feet slapping against rock. In lieu of pincers it had elongated, broken femurs, the jagged tips moist with marrow. It turned its body and swung its tail. The ball of faces reached out at the line of soldiers and struck the head of one man and the chest of another, spraying blood onto the others and sending the dead flying.

Bilal laughed. "It works," he shouted in his small, treble voice. "It listens." The ball connected with another soldier and those nearest him tried to flee, pushing past each other. This time the Imbued didn't stop them. Lengthened pincer-bone gutted one soldier and gouged the shoulder of another.

"Why?" Ester asked. It was all she could think about. "What's the point?"

"Some men would do anything to discover the limits of their potential," one of the smiths said. "It's in their nature."

"He's just a child, though," said another.

Bilal turned his gaze on Ester and the smiths, his eyes lidded like he was drunk or stupid, and he shouted something at his monster. It paid him no heed, barreling toward the army, and he shouted again. The primordia stepped up as though she wanted to help, but Bilal spat words at her and she froze. Bilal hadn't flesh bound his creation, Ester realized.

Two more groups of smiths materialized from the nearby huts. "Group with them," she said. "Find weapons. Hurry!"

"Iron is what will save us, not steel," an old man said, and the others nodded.

She didn't understand, but when the group joined the others and hurried behind the huts, trampling over the manicured soil, she followed anyway. The flesh monster skittered across the rock and crashed into the press of soldiers, and the army was torn between advancing on the mines and dealing with the horror at its flank. An Imbued managed to lumber past the fallen bodies collecting at the chokepoint of the footbridge, and the smiths protecting Breach and Damek rushed to meet him before he could finish crossing.

The smiths led Ester along the edge of the plateau, where the rock rose and fell sharply enough that she was climbing as much as running, and they reached the back of the meeting hall. She caught a glimpse of the Red Forge on the other side of the hall—a monster of a hearth over ten feet high sitting at the plateau's edge—with several anvils in front of it, surrounded by two rings of cubed stone.

Three Imbued rounded the corner of the hall, cutting them off.

"Careful!" Ester shouted as one of the Imbued stuck his hand in a pouch on his belt and pulled out a ball of iron. The ball went flying, but Ester had warned her brothers and sisters of the trick beforehand. They all stuck their hands out, pushing, and the ball careened off the ridge, exploding in a flash of light and almost blinding them.

The Imbued pulled out their blades and advanced. "Surrender," one of them croaked.

Breach had said something in Stonegate about the Imbued who had taken a tumble with Damek over the waterfall— something about how lucky Damek had been that the man hadn't been carrying any magnesium powder. Ester spotted a line of pails next to the hut closest to the meeting hall, where soldiers had been stocking up from the settlement's well. "Distract them," she said, and ran. One of the Imbued launched after her, but the smiths moved themselves between the woman and Ester.

When Ester picked up the pail, the Imbued were busy tossing

around the smiths, who cried in pain as frail arms and legs hit the black rock. One smith struggled to his hands and knees, and an Imbued kicked him in the face, sending him rolling and beads of blood and spittle flying.

"Piece of shit," Ester muttered, and moved into an awkward run with the pail hanging at her side. The Imbued didn't notice her until she was flinging water at the closest two, who stood over the prone smiths, blades prodding at the elders' backs. The men froze, letting out panicked gasps and trying to rip off their belts and gloves. Two heartbeats later, they exploded.

The blast sent one broken body tumbling over the plateau's edge. The other flew several feet in the air, tumbling like a ragdoll, and bounced off the meeting hall's back wall. The smiths grumbled and moaned from disorientation, but looked largely all right, thanks to having been forced to lie on the rock. The third Imbued—the one who'd avoided the water—had been quick enough to dive away from his friends. He picked himself up, blade in hand.

A body collided with Ester from behind, smashing her to the ground. She caught herself with her hands, but her skull still bounced off the rock and her arms scraped across the ground until she came to a rest. Hands pulled her up, and in her daze, she realized that a company of soldiers had arrived. Someone wrenched her arms behind her, then the man was shouting in panic.

The company of soldiers had gained control of the situation for all of fifteen seconds before everything was thrown into chaos. Dozens of men and women in white robes swarmed the soldiers, carrying blades and smith's hammers. The rest of the pilgrims. Ester scrambled through the violence until she reached the meeting hall's wall, then leaned against the material as she limped along the edge of the building. She drifted away from the fight and tried to catch her breath, her scrapes awash with pain dulled by the benthic willow. The smiths seemed to be holding their own, but these were normal soldiers they were fighting, not Imbued, and the bulk of the army still waited in the middle of the plateau. She wasn't even sure if Bilal's monster was still distracting the soldiers.

She got her answer when she heard the sound of naked hands and feet hitting the rock quickly enough to make one continuous sound.

Bony, bloodied spears rounded the corner of the hall, followed by the fleshy amalgamation they were attached to. The monster blocked the Red Forge, filling her view, but before the ball of faces could appear and see her, she slashed at the hide next to her and jumped through the gap.

The body moved in front of the slit of light, but didn't come ripping through. Ester sat in the low light of the meeting hall for several seconds, trying to put a cap on her rising panic, then moved to her feet.

The place reeked of blood, dust motes dancing in the light. Someone had shut the doors, and the roar of the cavern was so loud, it was almost as if there wasn't a battle raging outside. Then Ester saw the pile. It lay in the corner in a perfectly circular depression in the ground, blood pooling at the bottom. Arms, legs, torsos, and strips of meat. She couldn't see any heads.

She vomited on the rune-patterned rugs. She wiped her mouth and checked the hall again—the building was circular, with tables, chairs, four support beams, and braziers that hung from chains with smoking blocks of ice. Myrilan wasn't here. Not whole, at least.

The entrance cracked open, and a figure slipped inside. They stared at each other until the silence was broken by a dozen screams outside.

"I know you," the primordia said.

Ester backed up until she was touching the ripped edges of the wall. "I doubt that."

"You have his freckles. The treasurer. He was supposed to bring you here. Curious, that."

Ester slipped a hand into her satchel. If she wanted a real shot at killing Bilal, she'd have to take care of the primordia first. "Is Myrilan here?" she asked.

"No. He never showed, yet here you are."

Ester thought the news would frustrate or upset her, but all she felt was relief. She wasn't supposed to feel this happy that Myrilan was safe from this horror. "Your master is doing some terrible things."

"I thought that once, you know, but I've grown numb to it over the years. I have to, being in my position."

"That boy… he's evil."

"A chip off the old block, as they say."

"Is he, though? He's not just a child, is he? The Sovereign did something to him."

The primordia studied her, but Ester couldn't tell if the woman noticed her gripping the metal in the pack. "Bilal is the result of the Sovereign trying to play god. To create something out of nothing."

"He's not just a homunculus, is he?"

She shook her head. "Something made from scratch. An impossibility, given the complexities of the human mind and body. But the Sovereign is very old. He's had a long time to perfect his craft."

"And Bilal is supposed to be perfect?"

"No." There was a hint of sadness in her voice. Did she disapprove of what Bilal had done? "Bilal's penchant for human experimentation is an incredible irony," the primordia said. She turned her head toward the pile of flesh. "His current fascination is with the crust's unnatural fauna. He thinks to add to it. To become a creator much like his father, much like others in the ancient past."

"What do you mean unnatural fauna?"

"The world of Ra'Thuzan has been changed and broken and remade by man many times over the eons. This land has been irreversibly scarred by the ability to bind with the elements, and its animals are one such byproduct. A necessity for us to survive in a world that is underground. Bilal thinks to come up with a few species of his own."

Ester's best bet was the element of surprise—for the

primordia to attack so she could pull out her weapon as the woman met her. She clicked on the switch on the bottom of the metal plate, taking care not to touch the wires poking out the center. "Thanks for the information," Ester said. "You're very giving."

"I doubt what I tell you will matter for very long."

The plate thrummed quietly, and Ester tried to catch a hint of whether the primordia had noticed. "Kill me, then. I can't live in a world where Bilal can be allowed to turn my brothers and sisters into his playthings."

"The Sovereign *has* tried to stop him, but children are willful. He is doing what he can to fix Bilal's temperament, but I'm of a mind that he's only making it worse." She strode toward Ester, but her hands were folded behind her. "Bilal hasn't told me to kill you yet, so I don't feel terribly compelled to at the moment. Once his fun with his homunculus is over, he'll kill you all without my help."

"Help me kill him first, then."

Her laugh was sharp. In the middle of that sound, Ester could've sworn she heard a choked sob. "You know nothing."

"I know plenty, actually. It sounds like your leash is loose, at least for now. There has to be enough wiggle room in your Words to nudge the odds in our favor."

The woman's mouth parted in surprise, but she shut it when the homunculus let out another chilling screech. "He can't be killed, even if I could help. Even if all of my brethren could help."

"There has to be something."

She shuddered, and her eyes rolled into the back of her head. She wavered. "The only gift I can give is your life for just a little longer. Now leave."

Ester pulled her hand from the satchel. She saw in the primordia the same expression she'd seen on Jakar the first time she'd met him, when she saved him from the river. The anguish of being forced to live in a world that was nothing but cruel to them. It was a terribly stupid association for her to be making at the moment, yet there it was. It was enough to steal her confidence. She slipped out of the tear in the wall and entered the heat outside.

The homunculus crashed through one of the huts, sending beams and cloth flying. Its flesh had purpled, riddled with bruises, but it continued to stab and flail at smiths and soldiers alike. Somehow the smiths had managed to put the monster between them and the rest of the army. White-robed bodies littered the ground, and out of the dozens of smiths who had come to fight, nine were left standing. Through the chaos wrought by the homunculus and the soldiers scrambling to get out of the way, an army several hundred strong still gathered on the plateau. Ester couldn't see if Damek, Breach, and the others were still alive.

Their momentum had finally slowed.

One of the smiths, his face twisted in pain as he clutched an arm, caught sight of Ester and yelled at the others, motioning in Ester's direction. The survivors rushed to meet her. "Young smith," he said. "We need your strength. Follow us."

They passed behind the meeting hall and into the open, but the army's attention was still on the homunculus, which tore through the line of huts. The smiths reached the Red Forge, and one of them pointed at one of the cubes comprising the two rings. "Throw that in."

Ester grasped the cube and pulled it out of the rock, straining—it was pure iron, the surface pockmarked and its edges biting into her hands. She lugged it to the forge and dumped it inside. The smiths took their places around the hearth. "Protect us," a smith said.

Ester checked the soldiers—they had already noticed them, grabbing the attention of their sergeants and pointing toward the forge. "I'll try." She took one of the smith's swords and held her rockwood knife in the other hand.

Fires sprouted among the coals, and Ester realized the smiths were reaching toward the lavafall with their metal working, drawing heat from the iron mixed within. They were using one of the basic tools of their trade, channeling heat into the metal, which allowed smiths to create perfectly tempered steel. Ester couldn't begin to guess what they were up to. The cube, already red, brightened to orange, the air around it shimmering.

Bilal passed through the line of soldiers and pointed at Ester, laughing. He spoke, and five Imbued appeared, separating themselves from the army. A company of soldiers moved to follow them. The soldiers took their time approaching the Red Forge, walking almost leisurely, some of them chatting with each other. One of them let out what looked like a nervous laugh. Some studied the homunculus, then smiled. That monster was pure horror, yet the men seemed to be adjusting to it. Such was the nature of war, Ester noticed. The horror either numbed you or came for you in the quiet further down the road, a fact she knew too well.

A figure hit the ground nearby, cracking rock, and the primordia eyed her through the strands of hair that had fallen over her face. "Fight her off!" one of the smiths yelled, his voice cracking.

Ester grabbed for her satchel lying on the ground, but like before, the primordia didn't move.

"Smart, what they're doing," the woman said. "The company I keep lets me forget what people are capable of."

"You mean metal working?"

"I mean self-sacrifice. Pointless at times, but it lets you do the impossible. On occasion."

A smith crumpled to the ground, shuddering in convulsions. Ester pulled the plate out of her satchel, ready to smash it into the primordia, but the woman continued to study the ring of smiths. Had she attacked the smith without moving? It took a moment to realize that the smith was dying from heat death, the act of funneling too much energy from one source of iron to another. It was a danger elementals were told to be wary of; one of the arc smiths had warned Ester about it when she'd first become a metal worker, but this was the first time she'd witnessed it.

The primordia frowned at the pathetic piece of rusted metal in Ester's hands, then her attention moved to the forge. The iron glowed white now, hot enough for Ester to feel the heat from twenty feet away. A strange look crossed the primordia's face. Hope.

The Imbued reached them, the company coming to a stop several strides behind. The primordia faced her underlings. "We kill or save for the prince?" one of the Imbued croaked. Despite the heat, their faces were free of sweat, whereas the soldiers wiped damp locks from their foreheads. The smiths were drenched, their robes clinging to their frail bodies, but they continued like nobody was watching.

Metal flaked under Ester's fingers and floated to the ground. The fight was lost.

"A good question," the primordia said. She'd been thinking. "Neither, I'd say. They seem to be doing an adequate job killing themselves for us." As if on cue, another smith dropped.

"I do not understand. The prince asked us to deal with them." The Imbued frowned with his eyes. "So we deal with them. We cannot leave them be."

"Sure we can. It's easy. I'll show you." Her sword flashed in her hand and it cleaved through the man's neck, spraying blood over the black leathers of the Imbued next to him. The primordia struck her victim's neighbor with enough force to bisect him, sending both gored halves hitting the floor. The other three scattered.

The woman set herself on the company of soldiers, who were slower to react. Ester watched on, almost forgetting to breathe, seeing the terror in the men and women's eyes before the primordia's blade took the life from them. She carved a path through the company until the crowd parted and the rest of the army came into view. Bilal included.

The boy screamed and the primordia collapsed. The soldiers continued to flee, but the ground trembled and dark cracks formed along the ground as waves of rock rose on both sides of the company, cutting off their escape. Ester watched with a mix of awe and horror as Bilal waved his hands like a conductor in a concert hall, the rock rising and falling in tune with his movements. What Jakar had done in Augustin didn't hold a candle to this boy's power. Bilal continued to yell, red-faced, and the company halfheartedly moved to reorganize as the rock corralled them.

Ester turned to face the brightness behind her. The molten iron floated out of the forge, a ball of liquid like a miniature Ceti, guided by the seven surviving smiths. They continued to pour heat into it, and the iron swirled, convulsing into a chaotic mass. Shrinking. It was starting to evaporate. To make iron hot enough to turn it into gas… Ester didn't realize that was possible.

But they didn't stop. Still they gave it more heat. One of the smiths let out a gurgled gasp, falling on her face, dead. Her body seemed to pass through some invisible bubble surrounding the floating star of iron, and her hair caught fire and the skin on her head bubbled and melted. The ball of light floated toward Ester.

"What is this?" Ester shouted over the ball's humming. The smiths had carefully condensed until they stood in a circle just beyond arm's reach around the iron, containing the unimaginable heat inside the orb.

"Concentrate," the old man yelled back. "Creating this has weakened all of us. You're the only one strong enough for this next part."

Through the intense brightness, Ester could see the iron glowing with all the colors of the spectrum, almost putting her in a trance. The sound of another smith hitting the ground snapped her out of it. With her Eye, she watched as the iron in this new state of being, iron that had passed from a solid to a liquid to a gas to something new, wreaked havoc on the field around it, threatening to tear through the smiths' control at any second.

"Hurry," the old smith struggled to say, trembling. "Take it. He's coming."

Bilal strode across the rock, the ground rippling away from his feet like water in a shallow pond. His primordia lay comatose at his feet, and what was left of the company moved in formation behind the boy. Past the rest of the army, Ester caught a flash of a moving hill of flesh—the homunculus attacking Breach, Damek, and the other smiths at the Star Mines.

The iron came to rest above her palms. The iron was just a fraction of what they'd started with, yet what was left seemed to contain more power than the lavafall roaring past the plateau. The smiths cried out, two more of them crumpling to the ground, and Ester panicked, throwing the iron with all her might.

It sailed through the air like a shooting star. Rock and fire swirled around Bilal, and the boy threw out a hand like he wanted to catch the iron, but the element moved beyond the pilgrims' influence, exploding. A shock wave blasted the cavern, shaking Ester to her bones, and as she flew back, she caught a glimpse in her mind's eye of the iron in this fourth state ripping through the electromagnetic field, immune to Bilal's attempt to stop it.

She collided with a wall of stone. She was an expert at being flung through the air by explosions at this point, managing to protect her head. She had smashed into the Red Forge. When she recovered, she rose to find half the army on fire. So much screaming and so much pain. The ground continued to tremble, turning her legs to water. The circle of smiths had disappeared—the explosion must have thrown them clear of the plateau.

The rock jumped down, almost knocking Ester off her feet, and the sound of crumbling rock pierced the roar of the lavafall. The plateau was breaking apart.

The middle of the plateau was the first to go. A section as large as a city block dropped and a hundred soldiers went with it. Ester ran for the path leading off the plateau, where foxes that had managed to rip themselves from their restraints bolted up the trail. Damek and Breach ran along the opposite ridge, having ditched the weapon and the rest of their gear, and behind them, the last of the smiths fought the homunculus, trying to protect the nearest soldiers who were running for the trail, even as the ground threatened to fall away.

Ester reached Damek and Breach. Whether it was because of their disguises or because people had stopped caring, footmen raced past them, huffing it up the trail and almost knocking their group to the ground. The noise of the collapsing plateau intensified, almost loud enough to shatter Ester's eardrums. She grabbed Damek and Breach's hands and pulled them up the path.

A piece of rock as big as Augustin's capital splash into the magma, sending dark red globules up the sides of the cavern. The heat worsened until Ester felt her ankles, wrists, and the side of her face blister, and the soldiers around them screamed, their gear offering them little protection. She continued to scramble up the trail with those few who managed to bear the pain.

Three-quarters of the way up, Ester's vision started to swim and she had to stop. Most of the settlement had disappeared into the lake, and bodies lay scattered among the remnants of the rock far below, having succumbed to the heat. "There," Breach said, pointing.

Several figures stood on the opposite side of the cavern, on a ridge that should've been impossible to climb in such a short amount of time. They were too small to make out, but Ester could just about see that one of them was substantially shorter than the rest. On a different ridge, the homunculus was pushing itself into a crevice until it disappeared.

"We should leave before he comes for us," Ester said.

As soon as she had said the words, a dark hole appeared in front of the distant group. Bilal had burrowed into the rock, moving it as easily as sand.

Chapter 48—Jakar

"You won't kill him, right?" Quin asked Krisenth.

"That's for Father to decide," she said as she led us through the low tunnels, moving almost too fast for us to follow without jogging.

The tunnels opened to a room with high ceilings shrouded in darkness and pillars carved from volcanic rock, embedded with epithets in an alien language and shiny from obsidian. A place built for ceremony, it seemed. "Why would He want to kill me?" I asked.

"Simply a hazard of the rhak'dar experiments. They are usually performed on kadiphs, who have bodies that are better built for such trauma. Who knows, though. Perhaps you'll survive. If not, Father can always recycle you."

My gut stirred at her words. I was used to my mind being invaded, but my body was a different story. The last time that happened, the Child had created the flesh binding and the experience had nearly broken me.

A guttural voice rose from the depths of my consciousness. It licked the folds of my brain, bathed in the warmth of my spinal fluid. I wanted this. To take on a new form and use it to serve the Great Ones in whatever task they had in store for me.

I put on a burst of speed, almost overtaking Krisenth in my eagerness to reach the nursery, where all rhak'dar experiments were performed.

Gemstone veins ran through volcanic pillars, glowing from the reflection of lit crystals that covered the ceiling, carved into starbursts. The room we entered was almost featureless, save for the opposite wall, where a layer of flesh covered the rock. It didn't seem to grow from the wall. It was the wall.

"Come now," Krisenth said, sensing my hesitation. "It won't bite you. Quin, you stay back. It *will* bite you. Very, very hard."

I was meant for this. Father said so. I slid my shirt over my head and then my pants dropped to the floor. I took two steps forward and the wall rippled in several places, as though shuddering in anticipation. I stopped.

"Nerves getting to you?" Krisenth asked. "I can give you a little kick if you'd like."

"No," I said. I wasn't entirely sure why I'd stopped. That voice in the back of my head—the part of me that was desperate to escape this place—was now screaming at me, loud enough to break through my need to serve Father. I was here to save Quin and the others, to get them out of this dark hell. I needed to save Efadora and Torlo. *Efadora*, I thought. I needed to fight Father so I could find her.

Past Krisenth's shoulder, Quin stared at the ground, white-knuckled and trembling while she glowered. She was fighting her own demons, too. The voice in my head willed for her to jump in—to help me rip Krisenth apart before I touched the nursery wall—but Quin didn't even look up.

"Quin?" I asked.

She met my eyes. Her eyes were glassy, and she looked as though she wanted to hold me. "Yes?" she asked.

The way she said the word—carefully, her voice shaking—was enough for the last of my courage to disappear. Father's will was too strong. "Nothing," I said. The voice in my head was gone, and happiness rushed in to take its place as

I approached the wall. The surface stretched toward me in several places, as if metal rods were pushing into it from the other side. Protrusions elongated into tentacles, and they swung back and forth, searching. I stepped closer and opened my arms to let them take me. They wrapped around me in a loving embrace.

Where they made contact was like spikes burrowing into my skin. A needle for every pore. I opened my mouth to scream, but my lungs weren't working. The sensation spread like a wave of fire, as though someone were pressing a red-hot poker against each nerve in my arms, the back of my skull, the back of my body. The edges of my vision darkened, then flashed white, then darkened again, and I looked down to see a tentacle gripped around my arm, fusing with the skin.

Another managed to push through the back of my head, and then I was gone.

Pain.

Ecstasy.

It was pulling. Pulling my skin. Spreading it. Constricting. Tearing me apart. Gone gone gone gone gone

Tightening. Tightening. Tightening

Under me. Under me. Under my muscles. Under me. Inside my organs under me. Coating my bones under me

Bones. Recycle. Precious precious precious precious to eat use give us what Elvar would not offer we are worthy we are worthy Father bellowing

Noooooooooooooooooooooooooooooooooooooooooo

Give it back Give it back

Stretching and compressing more and more and more and more and more and more and

My eyes are open. Krisenth. Quin. Standing and watching. Quin and her hatred. So hate so hate so hate so I reach out. To comfort. Recoils. My arm. My arm? It protrudes. Grasps for Quin. I am the waaallll

"Nursery works quick," Krisenth says to Quin. "He's already halfway done."

Two more kadiphs fade into the light. Ra'Thuzan's blood sits in a wheelbarrow, bright and flaring with the breeze. They set the wheelbarrow a foot from me. The wall. Me the wall me the wall. Father speaks. I reach out to claim Ra'Thuzan's blood. Flesh meets molten rock and the wall shudders. Agony and pleasure. I'm stepping away, a million million million connections break one at a time. The last one snaps. The wall wants to reclaim me, and I want it to. The loss, bottomless. Infinite. Take me back, please.

I am a man standing in a room. I am Jakar.

"And there we have it," Krisenth said. The words were mild, but there was an uneasiness masked behind them.

My arms were still in the wheelbarrow. I pulled away from the magma, but it kept sticking to my skin. My skin wasn't skin anymore—it was dark rock, craggy with molten fire, and it reached halfway up my bicep where it turned to flawless gray skin. The blemishes on my shoulders were gone. I turned my body every which way, trying to find a hint of imperfection, but every scar had been scrubbed clean. Even the scars from my flesh binding were gone.

Quin's eyes roamed my body, but they were more inquisitive than anything else. "Did it... hurt?" she asked.

I nodded.

"Pain of the most exquisite kind," Krisenth said. "The elementals who failed the rhak'dar couldn't handle so much pleasure and agony, but of course Jakar was the one to make it through. His true talent isn't his elemental power, I reckon. He's a master of his pain."

The masters at the slave school had said as much. It was the reason why I was always the first child to wake after the Imbibings. It had never felt like much of a strength, until now. The gift of the rhak'dar was unlike anything I could have imagined.

"Do you feel it?" Krisenth asked, a hunger in her voice.

"The reservoirs?"

I opened my Eye, but the sky of white fire surrounding us glowed just as bright as before, which I supposed made sense. My elemental power hadn't changed, but now I possessed two wells of energy to pour into my power. Father's voice squirmed in my head, and it prompted me to draw energy from my new gift. Wisps of fire flared from the crags of my arms as I pulled in the magma's heat. Panic seized me as I was torn between obeying Father and wondering how long it would take for the energy to rip me apart.

Deeper I drank in the heat, yet nothing happened. My body could store more of it, I realized. Much, *much* more.

It suddenly made sense why the Sovereign's primordia were so powerful. Their bodies were made of flesh and bone, yes, but it was denser than steel. More mass meant more room to store energy. And now I had the body of a kadiph. Of primordia.

"Why did They give me this?" I asked, glancing at the wall.

"Father has always wished for his servants to break free from their prisons of flesh," Krisenth said. "It'll let them better fight the enemies of the Ebonrock. However, it's risky to have a slave wield the powers of an elemental as well as the body of a kadiph."

Her eyes shone with jealousy. Not only did my body seem to accept my new molten limbs, but I was now both kadiph and elemental. And it was risky for me to hold so much power, she'd said. But why? All I wanted, all I could ever dream of wanting, was to help Father.

Fight now, a voice in one of my mind's dark corners whispered.

Father's voice cocooned me, whispering to me what needed to be done. I marched for the exit, and Krisenth made a point to move to the front, like she was showing me who the leader was, but it was all the same to me. My eyes fluttered from the pleasure of making my way toward the capsules.

THE WATER AROUND our legs churned, oily black, as our diving bell raced across the ocean floor, the metal creaking, the glowing white rock swinging from its rope, my power magnified by Ra'Thuzan's blood. I started to glimpse a limit to my wells of energy when we were halfway there. We slowed down so I could pace myself, and I noticed the fire in my arms darken a degree. The waters calmed and Quin pushed her wet bangs out of her face.

"What are you thinking about?" I asked her. I didn't care that Krisenth was here. I needed to know and Quin had been too quiet.

"Order to chaos," she said.

She had been wracked with concern throughout my transformation and since, but apparently she'd held onto her determination, too, looking for an angle. And there was one. Four kadiphs were dead, after all.

"It's the eve of a new era," Krisenth said.

"Is it?" I asked.

"If this proves successful, we may truly find what we've been looking for after all this time. You're the first iteration of a new tool, my friend, assuming you survive your new affliction or if Father doesn't decide to recycle you."

I examined my arms again. The rock was black, wisps of steam curling from the surface. "Why would this kill me?"

"Your arms are made of fucking lava, Jakar," she said. "One wouldn't consider that conducive to human health. The minerals will bleed into you and poison you. The one elemental to make it through the rhak'dar barely lasted a passing before Father had to recycle him. I kept my hand for almost a year, so you can hold onto some hope, considering your new body."

"You sound upset," I said.

"The Ebonrock was betrayed the last time elementals were given the kadiphs' gift, so of course I'm upset."

"I didn't think it was possible for one of your flesh bound to betray you."

"It was centuries ago. Another time, when the rules were lax.

Six elementals were given bodies of the kadiph, and an outsider came in and stole them away. Destroyed Father's predecessor. That outsider became ruler of Mira, if I'm not mistaken."

The Sovereign fought the Ebonrock? And had stolen six elementals, too? Those had to be his primordia—Nektarios and the others. Shock at the revelation was overshadowed by the disgust I felt toward someone betraying Father's kin. *There's a way to break free*, that voice in my mind's dark corner whispered.

"And you're the first elemental in history to suffer Ra'Thuzan's blood," Krisenth continued, worked up in her annoyance. "You don't believe in the Ebonrock, yet you've become the strongest of us. But it is Father's will. He believes you can reach the Ebonrock's enemies, those who have moved beyond our grasp."

The Mazesh, she was referring to. Gods like Fheldspra and the others worshipped throughout Ra'Thuzan. For the first time in my life, as I studied my arms of molten rock, I believed that Fheldspra might exist. The potential of elemental power truly was infinite, along with the type of life it could give you. What if Fheldspra had once been a man?

"If Father wants me to destroy his enemies, I will," I said, the words placating. Father hadn't commanded me to fight his enemies yet, and so the notion still disgusted me.

She leaned back. "Your lack of conviction bleeds out of you like an open wound. To think that you won't respect this gift the way I would have. When the Great Ones send you after the Mazesh, they will eat you alive."

The first of the Crescent Pyres appeared on the horizon of my Eye. With Quin's help, I navigated the slopes leading to the first of the pyres until Krisenth signaled us to stop. The water swirled around our legs, bubbly and smelling of sulfur. Krisenth slid her goggles over her face and handed me a pair. "Stay close. You'll be disoriented at first, and this isn't the type of place to be taking a wrong step. Got it?"

I nodded.

She dove into the water and I grabbed my goggles, the metal becoming hot under my fingers as I slid them on. "Jakar," Quin said, touching my shoulder. "They won't keep you alive if this works. Father will recycle you. He would sooner turn his kadiphs into elementals before letting you keep your new form. He knows it's too dangerous to give someone like you so much power. If there was ever a time for chaos, it's now."

Every second Quin's hand was on my shoulder was one second I couldn't fulfill Father's wishes. "Let go," I said.

She pulled away. A tiny voice in my head raged through the giddiness at obeying Father's Words, but I couldn't summon the willpower to apologize. My hunger to obey sent me plunging into the black depths.

Pain lanced through my eardrums and a sudden pressure pushed my goggles against the skin around my eyes. Near-darkness swirled around me, and as soon as I lost contact with the diving bell, I was lost in the froth. I tried to feel for the familiar metal, but it was gone. Panic set in. I flailed, my boot colliding with something hard and causing it to shatter. A hand grabbed the back of my neck, squeezing, and I resisted the urge to lash out.

An amber glow appeared in the murk. It was Krisenth offering glowing quartz. I took it and tried to focus. Through my panic, I hadn't realized I could've used my elemental power to find the diving bell. Krisenth let go and motioned for me to follow.

I couldn't see more than a foot beyond the crystal's glow, but I could see an outline of the landscape with my Eye. We approached a rise, and beyond, vast plumes of energy rose through the depths. Godly amounts of energy. Just a fraction of what Ra'Thuzan was expelling every second would have been more than enough to rip me apart if I drew from it before my transformation. Krisenth grabbed my shoulder, pointing, and I knew what I had to do. I jumped off the ridge, plummeting toward the sea floor a hundred feet below, sinking like a boulder. I hit the ground hard enough for the sediment to swallow me up to my stomach. I tried to struggle free and another wave of panic set in.

The chutes were close enough now for me to feel their warmth. The fingers of my power reached out, and I felt an ocean of energy waiting. My arms flared, bright enough to make the water around me glow, and suddenly I could do anything.

I kicked out of the sediment, flying toward the chutes. More appeared in my senses, arcing away like a crescent. They were evenly spaced—too even to be natural. Together, they created a uniform wall of billowing black smoke, like the edge of an ocean-sized cage. I collided with the base of one and braced myself, drinking in more heat.

My arms were like veins of fresh lava bleeding out of a ruptured chamber. Energy filled my muscles until my bones shivered and heat warmed my throat. I was pure, elemental fury. Fury wielded by Father and offered to the Great Ones. To think there was a time when I thought I was meant for anything else. Had I even existed before the Ebonrock?

The question provoked a slew of faces to appear in my mind's eye. Efadora's, set with grim determination. Emil's kind smile. Torlo's gritted teeth, gladly suffering the pain he could save from his friends. The corners of Namira's crinkled eyes as she offered a hand and kind words, despite what it cost her. Quin and her iron will, defiant against the Ebonrock even after years of them trying to break her.

The shadow of Father's voice loomed over me, casting me in darkness.

My reservoirs emptied at once, the power it unleashed spraying in a gout that cleaved the chute in two. The small mountain crumbled, and I kicked off to float above it. Billowing gas flared in my Eye as it tried to swallow me, singeing my skin, and I pushed away from the plume of gas with my power. It was my new binding to carbon that let me affect the pluming gas. I fell to the ground where creeks of magma had appeared in the darkness, hemorrhaging from the broken chute.

I knelt beside the river and plunged my fists in. I braced myself for pain, but the lava was like bathwater. For a moment, Ra'Thuzan and I were one. Where before I had touched a sea of power, now I felt its bottomless depths.

A section of the chute's base broke off in my hands—a piece of land as big as Sanskra. I lifted it, straining, and threw it as hard as I could. It floated through the air, a meteor gliding in slow motion, and collided with the adjacent chute. The ground shook, water trembling. Mountains of rock shattered into millions of pieces.

I DRAGGED MYSELF onto the seat inside the diving bell. "I felt the quakes," Quin said, watching steam rise from my arms.

Krisenth emerged, purring with pleasure while she took her seat. "You did it, you beautiful son of a bitch. Am I ever the foolish one for wondering if it was possible. And so a new realm of the Black Depths is opened to the world."

The horror that had been creeping up on me ever since I'd completed Father's task hit me with full force, the ever-present Word to return to Father safe and sound doing little to buffer it. I'd taken the Ebonrock further than ever before—a cult I'd planned to destroy not a week earlier.

"I'm sorry," I said to Quin.

Krisenth tilted her head to the side. "Sorry? Really?" She *tsk*ed. "And you were doing so well. I'll have to have a talk with Father when we get back."

A somber silence kept us company on the way home. Would Father recycle me once we returned? Krisenth was beside herself enough to pretend it didn't exist, and I was nearly overcome with the need to break Quin and myself away from this place. To find Efadora and Torlo if they were still alive. I was terrified of Father's next command swallowing me, telling me it was time to be recycled, and how the pleasure of obeying His next Word would be so sweet, I would gladly let him annihilate me.

If there was ever a time I could resist, it was now. My hatred for the Ebonrock returned as strong as ever, pushing against Father's Words pushing me to come home, to remain faithful to Krisenth. I was filled with a fire that hadn't been there before, but for all I knew, I'd lose myself as soon as I felt Him squirming inside me again.

His voice rose from within me. It kept rising, louder and louder until it was eating into my brain. When it faded, I realized I had slumped to my side. So had Quin. Father had been calling for help.

The color faded from Krisenth's cheeks. "Father's in trouble."

Quin pushed the bell as hard as she could, but I couldn't wait. I dove into the murk. Krisenth followed, but I quickly left her in the chaos of bubbles behind me. I swam through the depths like a sailfish, buzzing with excitement.

The ecstasy of coming to Father's aid, to be the one to help when no one else could, almost overwhelmed me.

Chapter 49—Efadora

OUR LIGHTS DANCED shadows on Aronidus's back as he dug. It was slow going—he couldn't use his elemental power, and the only reason the dig was possible was due to Geth and me finding a fault line where there was more dirt than rock. We sat around in the cramped space, trying to listen through the wall for any kadiphs, but the wall was still too thick. Before Aronidus had decided to make a custom entrance for us into the Ebonrock compound, we'd heard dozens of kadiphs pounding toward the abandoned sections, away from us, probably to hunt us down. Maybe they thought whoever had killed their friends wouldn't be currently trying to dig into the heart of their compound. As it turned out, stupidity was working in our favor. There couldn't be many kadiphs left in the active part of the compound.

"You're being too hard on Jakar," said a raspy voice.

Anxiety shot up my spine when I heard Sara and realized her words were aimed in my direction, and I considered asking Aronidus to rescind her speaking privileges. "Am I? *I'm* being too hard on him? That's nice."

"He brought you along because he didn't want to lose his power, but so what? What were you to him when you left Augustin?" She rubbed her throat and drank from her waterskin.

Sara could have said the most sensible thing in the world right now and it wouldn't have mattered. I'd stopped caring about her opinion a long time ago, and like Aronidus said, her words were poison.

And so what if they made me think? I just made sure the expression on my face didn't give her the impression I was considering what she'd said. Jakar and I were friends now, but we hadn't been at the start of the trip. Back then, I was just another Adriann who unlocked his elemental power, as well as someone who could enslave him if I ever felt so inclined.

That last part made me pause. *Oh, fhelfire.* She was right. No, no, no, I was never planning on staying mad at him—it certainly wasn't Sara who had changed my mind.

Rock crumbled as Aronidus broke through the other side, and he widened it until he could stick his head through and look around. "It is clear," he said. "We will find the Father now. All of you will be quiet or I will kill you."

I climbed through the hole after him, where we were answered with cool air and the sound of a bubbling stream in some hidden crevice. If anyone had heard us, they would have shown up by now. The tunnels here were similar to the abandoned sections, except better lit with less dust—it was utilitarian in design, with straight, low-ceilinged tunnels of dark volcanic rock streaked with gemstone veins, and glowing red and orange pyremoss growing on the walls. Aronidus pulled out the rhidium blade and picked a direction, seemingly at random, and we set off down it.

This place was a treasure trove of information. Strange decorations, alien-looking glass figurines, and exotic writing etched into the floor. Geth meandered as he examined the opposite walls over and over and peeked inside the antechambers we passed.

We rounded a corner and came face-to-face with a kadiph who had been walking in the opposite direction. The man inhaled, but Aronidus's arm was a blur, his weapon leaving a blue streak in the air as it decapitated the kadiph. The man's head hit the ground like a rock.

The people who had been following the kadiph all froze. They wore simple garments, made to withstand heat and handle rock. The elementals. Dozens of them, walking double-file, presumably to start another passing of work.

The groups faced each other, and for several seconds nobody did or said anything. Aronidus could kill the first few and get away unscathed, but the rest of us were fucked. They didn't attack us, though. Just stared with wide eyes.

Of course they didn't attack. The only kadiph with them was dead and Father didn't know we were here. They had no Word to attack.

The lead elemental, a lithe woman who looked deadly enough to take on Aronidus alone, pointed the opposite way we'd been walking. "That way," she said quietly.

Aronidus nodded. "Peace be to you all. Flee fast. For both our sakes." He turned and motioned us to hurry back the way we'd come.

The elementals broke into a run, disappearing behind a corner. They ran as if their lives depended on it. Their freedom did, at least. As soon as the fighting started, the Father would call out to them and they'd return to rip us to shreds, smiling while they did so.

The halls twisted and turned, and we moved slowly enough to give the elementals time to run while egged on by the possibility of more kadiphs returning from their hunt for us. My heart hammered in my chest. We had taken the plunge, and it was too late to turn back now.

We reached the cavern, the lavafall rumbling nearby, where the Father stood, hunched over by the pool of water where the capsules sat half-submerged. Two kadiphs accompanied the thing.

"I will kill the kadiphs," Aronidus said.

"How do we help?" I asked.

"I'm thinking we stay back and watch," Geth said.

There was approval in Aronidus's eyes. "You have a heart of iron," he said. "Try not to die." He left cover.

Geth and Sara tried to grab me as I left our hiding spot to follow the mountain of a man as he broke into a run, but I was too quick. Hiding like cowards was a surefire way to die—we needed to kill the Father before Jakar showed up. Aronidus closed the hundred-foot distance before I'd made it more than twenty, but it was enough time for the kadiphs and the creature to react. The kadiphs catapulted themselves toward Aronidus, and the Father faced us, eyes and teeth and moist limbs glinting. It showed no interest in attacking or fleeing.

A kadiph scooped up a rock and threw it. Aronidus ducked, and the projectile shattered against the wall, spraying the air with pinpricks of debris. Aronidus met the man and tried to stab at his stomach, but the man slipped to the side and punched the primordia in the jaw, the sound like two boulders colliding. A blade flashed in the kadiph's hand. He tried to stab into Aronidus's side as the second kadiph tried to barrel into Aronidus from the other side, but Aronidus twisted away, slicing the rhidium edge along the kadiph's shoulder. The kadiph gasped and rolled away, and his friend managed to grab onto Aronidus's wrist and hilt, trying to wrench the blade free.

I moved to one knee, sighted down the coil weapon, and took four even breaths while it charged up, the weapon whining in my ear as it sent goosebumps down my arms. "Gotcha," I whispered, and a crack echoed through the cavern. A bright white needle arced through the air, slamming into the kadiph wrestling with Aronidus and sending him to the ground, smoking. Aronidus caught my gaze, wide-eyed, but his fear melted. He stabbed down and put all his weight behind the blade.

The kadiph cried out, the sword piercing his chest. There was a snap of metal and Aronidus collapsed on the man. He rolled away and jumped up to face the remaining kadiph, who held his dagger in one hand while cradling his wounded arm to his chest. The kadiph on the ground screamed while broken, caustic metal pinned him to the rock, and then the sounds died in his throat and he stilled. Aronidus grimaced at the half-length of the meteor blade in his hand, then jumped forward. "Do it now," he tried to yell at us in his small voice.

I led the others toward the Father. It stood by the water as if it were waiting for something, and it shivered. The pool exploded as someone catapulted out of the water. Jakar landed in front of the Father, locks of soaked hair plastered to his face, glowing orange lines covering his arms as they glistened like black granite.

I brandished the coil weapon, trying to aim past Jakar. "No," Jakar cried out, swiping down. Even from thirty feet away, his power slapped down the barrel of the coil weapon hard enough for the metal to slam into my shin. I crumpled, hissing in pain, and tried to raise the weapon again, but it suddenly weighed a hundred pounds.

"Ig, stop!" I screamed. The wound in my shoulder seared like fire—was that what Sara and Father had felt every time they'd given a Word?—and Jakar blanched. Despite the fact I was the one person stopping him from killing us all, it was hard to meet the hurt in his eyes.

He stepped toward us. "Ig, stop," I repeated.

He didn't even flinch. The nervousness and the anxiety that usually filled him when it came to impending punishments wasn't there.

There was the sound of a body hitting the ground, then Aronidus was at our side. "What am I doing wrong?" I asked in a panic.

"Nothing," the primordia said. He studied Jakar and smiled. "His scars are gone. Father transformed him. Took his bindings away. Jakar can only serve him now."

The smile was wiped from his face when Jakar made a sweeping motion and sent the meteor blade flying, and the broken sword splashed into the water with a sizzle. "If Jakar heard Father's call, then so did the others," Aronidus said. "Move fast."

The primordia ran at Jakar and I choked back the urge to cry out. The primordia was going to crush him. Aronidus's fist lashed out, but Jakar caught it with an open hand. The force of the punch didn't even register on Jakar's face.

He couldn't be stopped with a Word, and he had the flesh of a kadiph.

Aronidus rained a flurry of punches on Jakar before grappling with him and taking him to the ground, but Jakar squirmed his way out of Aronidus's grip and flipped away, landing ten feet from the primordia. Aronidus needed his powers to stop Jakar, I realized. Jakar abstained from using his own, and for a moment I wondered if some part of my friend still existed under the Father's word. A part of him strong enough to resist.

Jakar checked the pool, then the tunnel leading into the compound. He wasn't holding back his powers because he was resisting the Father. He was delaying us until the others arrived.

Aronidus launched himself forward, picking Jakar up and throwing him across the cavern. Jakar hit the catwalks leading to the abandoned parts of the compound, sending dust and shards of wood into the air as the structure collapsed. I felt Jakar's hold on the coil weapon loosen, and I pulled it up, slowly, straining to aim it at the Father. Torlo hobbled toward the creature.

As Jakar pulled himself out of the wreckage, Aronidus ran to meet him, but the ground started trembling, almost making me fall. Rock tried to swallow Aronidus's feet, but he obliterated it with a kick. It didn't let up, gobbling up his legs until it reached his waist and rooted him in place. He pounded at the rock with his fists, chipping it away, but it wouldn't let go.

The coil weapon was ripped out of my hands and hit the floor, whining as it prepared to discharge. Torlo was almost to the Father now, but Jakar ran past me and caught up to the boy. He grabbed Torlo's arm, and even from here I could see bone break. Torlo cried out and lost his footing, but Jakar wouldn't let him fall.

"Jakar, stop!" I screamed.

Jakar froze. He looked down at his hand clutching Torlo, the boy crying in agony, and he shuddered. Slowly, Jakar struggled with painstaking slowness to unwrap his fingers, and Torlo fell to the ground, nursing his sooty, red-skinned arm.

Jakar and I stared at each other. There was fear and sadness in his eyes, and a glimpse of the person I knew. It made what happened next almost too difficult to do, but if there was anyone capable of hurting their friends, it was me. I picked up the coil weapon and fired.

The beam of light smashed into his torso, his tunic bursting into flames, embers eating their way outward from the center of his chest. He fell to one knee, then crumpled to the ground, convulsing. "Torlo, go!" I said.

Torlo crawled toward the Father. The creature writhed at us, limbs flexing as though it was angry, and its arms planted themselves into the ground. The Father started to sink. It was trying to get away.

Torlo was too slow to limp to it in time. I had to stall. The coil weapon whined as I aimed it, and I pulled the trigger over and over again, metal tapping on metal. "Fire, please," I said, my teeth clenched, praying to Fheldspra as the creature sank, now halfway through the floor.

Light struck the Father. Its blackened skin rose like a pimple, enlarging until it ruptured and sent flesh exploding out of the wound. Other parts of its body ballooned. Tumors split apart and released more flesh, more limbs, spreading like a cancer. A sour smell filled the air, turning acrid until it burned my nostrils.

Geth ran to my side. "Did you hurt it?" he asked.

The rock around the Father changed from brown to white to black to green until it fractured, sharp cracks filling the air. The space above the Father's skin crackled and sparked with chemical reactions.

"It's growing," I said.

A dozen deformed limbs flailed and lashed out, its torso dwarfing its previous size. The eyes that had been hiding inside the crag in its chest had bulged outward like a lava bubble, and they rolled around in their sockets, twitching. The limbs stilled and the creature calmed. Clusters of eyes focused on Torlo, me, and Geth.

The Father was now three times the size, thanks to me. It was the fuck-up of a lifetime.

Chapter 50—Efadora

ARONIDUS BROKE THROUGH the last of his prison and ripped himself free from the rock, and Sara appeared by my side, dripping with water as she held the rhidium blade. Jakar still hadn't moved. The Father wasn't trying to get away anymore, but was now stuck to the rock, swinging a dozen limbs with enough force to crush anything it touched. We'd have to subdue it some other way before Torlo could try his ritual.

I grabbed Torlo by the scruff of his undershirt and pulled him back with Sara's help. "No, wait!" he said, but was cut off by the sound of a limb slapping where he'd been lying moments before, fracturing the ground. Jakar was still seizing on the floor, ignored by the Father. I had no idea how much longer he'd be comatose. Sara slashed at the Father's limb before it could recover, and the creature recoiled, hitting Sara and sending her rolling away. Geth came to help pull Torlo out of the Father's reach.

"We'll try my pyroglycerin," Geth said. "You can't get close enough to talk to it anymore. Ritual's pointless now, Torlo. We need to kill it."

"It'll absorb the—energy of the pyroglycerin," Torlo said. He held his arm close to his chest. "Like it did with—the coil weapon."

Aronidus came to our side. He pulled the pack off Geth's shoulder, and the cartographer didn't resist. He ran for the tunnel leading into the compound and disappeared.

"What do we do?" I asked Torlo.

"Stick to the—plan," he coughed out. "You have to get me close to it."

"It'll turn you into a stain on the rock," Sara said. "We have to slow it down first."

"Slow it down if—you wish," Torlo said. "Either way, the ritual is the only—thing to stop it."

"You're just going to yell some words at it, and that's all?" I asked.

Torlo nodded. "Words are everything here."

"What if it doesn't hear you? Can you tell us what the words are so we can try in case something happens to you?"

A blast knocked us off our feet and the sound of collapsing rock filled the cavern. Dust shot out of the tunnel leading to the lived-in parts of the compound, and the pool of lava beneath the fall churned violently enough to send sizzling globules onto the ground around it. Aronidus shot out of the tunnel, a dusty wraith, and came to a stop next to us. "The slaves are coming," he said. "I collapsed the tunnel to hold them off, but it won't be for long."

"I'm more concerned about *that*," Geth said, pointing.

A woman stood on the ridge above the ruined catwalks, taking in the chaos below. Unfortunately for her, I'd already picked up the coil weapon again. I fired, and the kadiph fell from the ridge, crashing into wood and rock.

"One down, half a hundred to go," I said as I kept the weapon trained on the tunnel entrance. I almost wanted to cry at the futility of having to face a small army of kadiphs that was probably bearing down on us, not to mention Jakar's tremors, which had almost faded. The Father waved its arsenal of tentacled limbs, a dozen wrecking balls waiting for something to get too close.

"Open your Eye," Geth said.

"What?"

"Just do it."

Quartz glimmered in the floor, walls, and ceiling, but when I focused on the Father, the creature shone as bright as a lava burst.

"You see what I see?" he asked.

"The Father is full of silicon."

"Aye," he said, and in a moment it all clicked.

The algae in Obsidian Lake. The ancient, rotted vegetation scattered throughout the compound. The Father subsisting off the algae of the Black Depths, consuming massive quantities of it so it could get enough nutrients in its body to survive. Living things never contained enough of an element for an elemental to exert force over it, but due to its diet, the Father was filled to the brim with silicon, the one element I was bound to.

"Take this," I said to Sara, shoving the coil weapon toward her, and she offered the rhidium blade to Aronidus so she could take it. "What are you doing?" Geth asked, but I was already running.

I reached the pool of bubbling lava, steeling myself as I got closer, the heat magnifying until I could feel it searing the hairs on my body. Behind me, the coil weapon discharged. Back in Augustin, Jakar would coat his arms in lava because he was bound to most of the elements that made up the stuff, and he could draw heat from those elements to magnify his power. He once told me that silicon was the most abundant element in lava behind oxygen, too. The element of the cartographers. *My* element. I reached for the silicon's heat that churned and bubbled inside the lava, then began to drink it in.

The energy was like a geyser, moving so fast I could feel it writhing under my skin, trying to get out. It made my arms tremble and vibrated my bones. It was intense enough that I almost didn't notice the searing heat at first. It pinched at my left arm as my hand hovered over the lava, my other hand aimed at the Father.

One of the creature's limbs slowed. Then two more. They flailed as if they were underwater, but the rest of the Father thrashed violently. I was pulling at the silicon saturating its body, slowing it down, but my power wasn't enough.

"Gah," I gasped as I felt my skin blister. I pulled away, examining the red skin and pale blisters covering my arm, and the pain intensified until it was all I could think about, making me shudder. It was all I could do not to start sobbing. The pain was almost overwhelming, and a sense of helplessness followed close behind.

"Can you try one more time?" Geth asked. He appeared at my side, cringing at my arm.

"Why?" I asked, my voice wavering. Talking was almost too hard, the pain was so bad.

Geth continued to study my arm, frowning to himself. "We can stop it. We can save Jakar."

I was about to reply, but then he reached out for the lava, turning his face away, and I could feel him start to draw in energy. Putting my hand in again was almost too much to bear. *You can do whatever Jakar can,* I told myself. I could do this. With my other hand close to the fire, I pointed my burned one at the Father.

Most of the Father's limbs struggled now, caught by an invisible web, and Torlo started limping at the creature. The coil weapon discharged again, followed by the sound of a crashing body. Three kadiphs had spilled out of the tunnel and landed on the cavern floor where Aronidus was, and the primordia set himself on them. One managed to clutch his legs into a vice and send him tumbling to the ground while the other two piled on top. Another group of kadiphs appeared on the ridge.

Geth whimpered, his arm shaking while it hovered over the fire. He started screaming, and I watched as blisters bubbled on his skin, but he didn't pull away. His eyes moved erratically while his teeth clenched, and I realized I was screaming, too. Horrible, horrible pain. Dozens of tiny knives carved their way into my skin. "Torlo," I heard myself shriek. I could only slow the Father down for a few more moments.

Torlo moved within the Father's reach. Its limbs tried to smack him away, but he awkwardly dodged them, moving for the bulbous mass in the center still sticking halfway out of the rock. Then he stopped. I almost yelled every curse word I knew to get his ass moving, but then his eyes found mine. He mouthed something. *I'm sorry.*

He touched the creature's torso and his hand sank into its flesh.

"No!" I screamed.

I was pulling away from the lava. Running for the Father. It erupted in a burst of chaos, its limbs striking the floor, the water, the ceiling as loud as an unending pyroglycerin explosion. A pair of hands grabbed onto me, and I found Sara dragging me away. I spotted Torlo in that writhing mass of flesh, half his body already gone, and he turned his head toward me as the Father continued to consume him. He gave me a sad smile.

Torlo had lied to me. The right words were supposed to stop the Father, he'd said, but of course it couldn't be that easy. All rituals required a sacrifice.

And then he was gone.

My elbow met Sara's face and I felt cartilage break. I was running toward the Father again. Someone grabbed onto me once more, and I pushed them off. It was Geth. He fell back, squeezing his eyes shut as he fell on his hands, and I stopped. His face was covered in sweat, his arm a mixture of blisters, white flesh and bright red burns, and he had a horrible look on his face. I realized I was dripping in sweat, too. The pain in my arm hit me in full force—it took only a second for my thoughts of Torlo to be pushed out by the agony.

I pulled Geth up with my good arm and hurried him to the water. We moved past the Father, but it didn't try to reach out to crush us. Its limbs had slowed, moving around like it was unsure of what to do. I brought Geth to the dark pool and knelt down to shove my arm in. I shivered from the bliss of the cold water.

The cavern had gone mostly quiet. A dozen more kadiphs had arrived, and they stood around the destroyed catwalks, watching the Father. Aronidus was being held to the ground, but those restraining him were too distracted by the Father to do more than stop him from escaping. The kadiphs talked to each other, but they were too far away for me to hear. Sara picked up the coil weapon and joined us, moving warily past the Father, blood pouring out of her nose and dripping down her chin. The Father had become docile. Docile like Torlo.

I almost jumped away from the water when a person emerged nearby, wearing kadiph leathers. She climbed to shore and walked out of view until she reached the other side of the creature and stopped in front of Jakar, who was now climbing to his feet. She spoke to him in Sulian, and he rubbed his chest where his tunic was charred.

"Fhelfire," I breathed. "We're done."

The kadiph grabbed Jakar's sleeve and nudged him like she was trying to emphasize her words, like she was trying to tell him what to do. He blinked at her and her voice rose, and he looked at his hands, his fingers curling into fists.

He punched the kadiph in the cheek, sending her flying, just as the Father's limbs relaxed to the ground, splayed out like a wilted flower.

Chapter 51—Jakar

I couldn't hear Him anymore.

Hitting Krisenth had been instinctive—she'd been grabbing onto me, invading my personal space—and it took a second to realize the horror of what I'd done.

But *why* was it horrible?

Because she served Father, and Father was the most important thing in my life. Right? I shook my head and tried to feel His presence, but it wasn't there. Instead, there were holes in my mind. Nausea overcame me, but the feeling quickly passed. I needed Him. I needed a task so I could have purpose in my life. Without him I was directionless. It was as if someone had pulled a knife out of my abdomen, and now all I could do was bleed.

No, my connection to Him had been severed and I was struggling to cope with it. That was all. With each passing moment the revelation of my broken connection sank deeper and deeper.

Krisenth scrambled to her feet but didn't attack. She was studying Father and glancing at the other kadiphs, and she yelled something at the others in her kadiph language. They answered back. "Kill the intruders, all right?" she said to me.

480

"It's what Father wants."

The hole in my chest that Father had left behind narrowed, and when I looked at Efadora, it faded entirely. Shock hit me when I saw Sara standing next to her—her face had lost some of its pallor and she had heavy bags under eyes. She looked awful.

The muted crushing and tearing of dirt and stone overtook the gurgling sounds of the lavafall. It was the other elementals, almost dug through. More kadiphs arrived, jumping from the ridge to land like small meteors on the ground, and the confusion among them only increased. A fight broke out among them—someone rose from the ground to stand over a foot taller than the rest, and he thrashed about trying to get free. Several of them grabbed onto him, quickly overwhelming him, and I sprang into action.

The ground under them shuddered and fractured, and boulders fell from the ceiling, striking the kadiphs. The trickle of debris quickly turned into a torrent, and I had to focus all my attention on the ceiling to keep it from collapsing. Perhaps destabilizing countless tons of rock above and below us wasn't such a great idea. The kadiphs moved out of the way of the falling rock, covering their heads, and their captive shot away, running to Efadora and the others.

"Father's been tainted," Krisenth shouted. "Kill those responsible."

She picked something off the ground, and a moment later a rock struck me in the shoulder hard enough to shatter, leaving my skin reverberating with pain. My body was resilient, but kadiphs were strong. She threw another rock, and I let it slingshot around my body until it blurred into her friends, striking a man in the skull. A dust cloud billowed around his head and he hit the ground. The others took off toward the group by the pool.

The kadiphs slowed when figures emerged from the rubble where the tunnel into the enclave had evidently collapsed. It was the other elementals. The two sides shouted at each other, the cavern turning into a cacophony of echoing commands, but the elementals didn't listen. Instead, they approached the lavafall and reached into the pool. They pulled away, arms dripping with molten rock.

For a moment, nobody moved. The impossibility of the situation, that the elementals were no longer bound to Father or the kadiphs, seemed to make everyone think that any moment now things would return to normal and the flesh bindings' punishment would strike. The kadiphs seemed to believe it as much as the elementals did.

I charged the kadiphs. It broke the elementals' trance, and the first of them followed my footsteps.

My fists seared flesh and left blackened streaks on cheekbones and necks, and I felt hands grab at me, trying to hold me down. The ground and the ceiling shook, and debris was flying through the air, thrown by the elementals and crashing into the kadiphs. I let those nearest me restrain me while I used all my concentration to keep the ceiling from collapsing.

Kadiphs were screaming. It wasn't just debris that the elementals threw—flaring globules of lava struck the kadiphs, hot enough to fuse to their flesh within seconds. Some of them reached the elementals, striking a few hard enough to cave in bone until they were consumed by molten rock.

The elementals were winning.

The pool of water exploded, sending capsules rolling across the ground. The kadiphs loosened their grip enough for me to rip free and break away as water poured into the cavern, and with horror I realized that both gates to the Black Depths had been opened. Krisenth was nowhere to be seen—she must've been the one responsible.

Aronidus picked up Efadora and Geth as the water tried to sweep them away, and he ran for the ridge. The water knocked Sara off her feet, the coil weapon thrown from her hand, and she tried and failed to stop herself from being pulled under. I ran, tracking her as her arms splashed above the surface. I reached her and pulled her up. She yelled in pain as she breached—my hands were burning through her leathers, the material smoking. I moved as fast as I could to the pile of debris where elementals had discarded the rock they had excavated, then deposited her on the slope. Efadora and Geth were on the same pile. Aronidus had left them, hurrying for the Father, who still lay comatose, limbs moving with the current that swirled around it. The water was already a foot deep.

There was disbelief in Sara's eyes as she watched me, which was replaced by fear as I stepped away. She was so innocent, acting completely unlike the sociopath I knew so well. There was no faking that look.

Water swept away elementals and kadiphs alike, and over the roar of water was the sound of hissing steam from the lavafall. Kadiphs struggled from the current, but they wouldn't be crushed from the impending pressure like the elementals would. I had to stop it. I rooted myself in the rock and closed my eyes, drawing heat from the water. My wells of energy had been depleted from destroying part of the Crescent Pyres, and now the energy I drank in from the ocean water rushed in to fill a fraction of that empty space. Water turned to icy slush, pushing against the current toward the pool.

White light flashed across my vision when a fist smashed into my neck. I splashed into the slush, and the torrent of ocean water was renewed. Krisenth was there, pulling me to my feet, and she hit me again. I tried to disable her by pulling in heat from her body—I grabbed onto her wrist, her flesh hissing, but she cracked me in the side of the head with another hit at the same time water crashed into us.

We were rolling, tossed around in muddy, frigid water, scraping against the ground and smacking into rocks and debris. I reached out, grabbing at the ground with one arm while I gripped onto Krisenth with the other. Then I pushed down with the might of my power. We were falling, the ground giving way beneath us like sand. Grinding rock shrieked, drowning out Krisenth's voice, and we fell through heat and stone and dirt and darkness. Water chased after us, filling the gaps as soon as I made them. We fell into Ra'Thuzan, the water filling in the gaps as quickly as I created them, but I didn't let up. Krisenth scrabbled at my body, but she couldn't break my fingers off her wrist. With the crumbling rock scraping at my face, and the building heat and the salt of the ocean, I could barely breathe.

We broke into open air. I smashed into a sharply sloping hill, and I dug my arm into the ground as bright light filled my peripherals. A torrent of sea water washed over us as we came to a halt.

At some point I must have let go of Krisenth, but now she had a hold on my ankle, and her grip tightened in what I realized was panic. I could barely see through the endless jet of water pouring from the ceiling above, but I managed to pick out a field of bright light below us, beyond the steeply sloped ridge I'd dug myself into—we must have fallen into the magma chamber that the lavafall fed into. I kicked her in the face over and over with my other foot, but still she held on.

The weight of the water changed, and then it wasn't trying quite so hard to sweep us away. A figure rode the water out of the hole and hit the slope above us, awkwardly landing on her feet and nearly sliding down the hill, but the water continued to slow behind her, turning to slush.

"Quin!" I yelled. Another figure fell out of the hole after her, falling fast. She dove out of the way, and the kadiph hit the ground and tumbled toward us. Behind him, water turned to ice, and it plugged up the hole, stopping the river of water that flowed over me and Krisenth. The elementals in the chamber above had to be following my lead to stop the Black Depths.

The male kadiph found purchase, but his handhold broke and he started sliding again, then stopped fifteen feet above Krisenth and me. He climbed up the hill after Quin, and at the same time Krisenth let go of my ankle to hold onto the slope. The male kadiph scurried up like a spider, but the murder in Quin's eyes didn't let up. She scooped rocks out of the ground, broke off miniature stalagmites along the slope and threw anything she could get her hands on at the man coming for her. I reached for the ceiling, pulling, and the rock trembled, cracks forming. No, I couldn't. The only one who would get crushed would be Quin. I climbed after the kadiph, but the man had too much of a head start. The anger in Quin's eyes turned to fear. She kicked at a stalagmite twice her size, dislodging it and sending it rolling at us, and the kadiph tripped as he tried jumping over it. I planted my feet in the rock and let the pillar crash into me. It hit me hard enough that it almost broke me out of my perch, but it broke first, its halves flying past. The kadiph was suddenly much closer, and he scrambled to his feet. I jumped after him and grabbed onto his foot.

His other foot cracked me in the face, but I didn't let go. Then another pair of arms were assaulting me from behind—Krisenth, angry and breathing through her nostrils hard enough to sound like a bull—but all the struggling did was make us slide down the slope.

"Fine," she hissed.

She let go and moved past me, her sights set on Quin. I tried to pull from my wells but what little I'd had left I'd poured into my descent with Krisenth. I was still strong enough to break apart some rock, though.

I punched at the ridge again and again and again as I clutched onto the male kadiph's foot with my other hand. The rock trembled, cracks forming, but I didn't let up. Krisenth struggled to keep her balance, but so did Quin. The whole ridge was ready to crumble. I let go of the man, jumped forward to get a hold onto Krisenth by the ankle as she slid down, then managed to regain a grip on the man's arm. They shouted, trying to pry me off, but were careful not to send us all stumbling over the edge.

I couldn't stop both kadiphs. No matter who I focused on, the other one would get the opportunity to kill Quin. It was a stalemate.

Past the edge of the ridge was a lake of fire. Maybe not a complete stalemate.

"No!" Quin screamed as I pulled at both kadiphs, sending us sliding down the ridge.

"I'm sorry," I yelled, but there was no way for her to hear. I'd done what I had come here for. She and the others weren't flesh bound anymore. Father was dead. It would have been nice to see what had waited on the other side of all that, but I was done hoping for a happy ending. Namira had been wrong. I was never meant to get what I wanted.

We were falling through the air again. My vision tumbled between dark rock and the shimmering glow of magma, and then there was nothing but blinding light and heat.

Chapter 52—Efadora

Sara came at me, and I came close to slapping her hand away as she reached for me. "I'm going to help you, all right?" she said, then gave it another go. We were standing on a not-so-steady hill of rocks by the ridge, the sea swirling below us and tossing around fragments of the destroyed catwalks, the water continuing to rise.

"You're going to get me killed," I said. The current barely hindered the kadiphs, who waded shoulder-deep through the half-water, half-slush. The elementals were much worse off. Many clung to the walls with handholds they'd made, getting pummeled by debris and ice, the water pulling some of them under, and others were sucked through the gap they'd created in the collapsed tunnel. One elemental, a Sulian woman, let the current take her toward the miniature whirlpool that had formed in the wake of the hole Jakar had disappeared into, and she dove in headfirst.

"Never," Sara growled in determination. Before I could resist—resisting would've just made us fall off—she wrapped me in a bear hug and jumped. An unseen force jolted me as we flew onto the ridge, and then we were rolling across the rock.

The side of my face stung where I'd landed on it, helping me almost forget the pain in my burned arm. We were safe—at least for the next minute or so. The water was already several feet above the kadiphs' heads and was rising fast. Sara grabbed my hand, pulling me toward the tunnel leading to the abandoned parts of the compound, but I didn't move. "Geth," I said.

The cartographer balanced on top of the debris pile, the water about to swallow him, and he grimaced. He looked disappointed, more at himself than anyone else, though I couldn't imagine why.

"Look," I yelled at him.

The flood was slowing, turning to slush like it had when Jakar tried to freeze the breach. A group of elementals by the lavafall sat on a small island of ice and were drawing heat from the seawater. Ice swept over the kadiphs, their dark bodies beneath struggling as the water froze several feet above their heads. The elementals clinging to the walls managed to climb above the water as the ice reached them, and they jumped onto it, running to the lavafall to help.

Ice grew like a fungus, reaching the side of the cavern where water gushed the hardest. Silence started to replace the sound of gushing water.

I left Sara's side and stood at the edge of the ridge, trembling with weakness. Through my pain, I recognized blurry shapes littering the inside of the ice sheet, still as statues. Other bodies lay on top of the ice, unmoving. I struggled onto the frost and approached one of the elementals, her hands sunk to the elbows, her cheek resting against the frost, eyelids half open. I looked on with morbid fascination at the other dead elementals scattered across the ice, most of them clustered near the lavafall.

Sobs replaced the silence.

It started with shaky words, then the slaves were trying to resuscitate their friends. Nothing worked. The survivors who managed to hold their composure dug at the top half of the collapsed tunnel, likely trying to find those who had been sucked through.

I returned to the ridge, which sat a few feet above the ice and where Geth was waiting next to Sara. He had found a strip of cloth soaked with icy water and wrapped it around his arm. Once again, the pain became all I could think about, and I doubled over, whimpering.

Sara led me to the wall and helped me sit against it. She whistled at one of the elementals, who sat over one of his friends on the ice. "Does your home have anything to treat burns?" she asked, pointing at the tunnel where elementals had managed to burrow through the collapsed rock and ice. "It has to, right?"

"They don't speak Miran," I said, my voice shaky.

She dropped onto the ice and approached the man. She snapped her fingers in front of his face, getting his attention, and the cavern was quiet enough to hear her ask in a stern voice, "Where's your burn medicine? Tell me."

He looked ready to hit Sara, and could do a lot more than that if he was so inclined. "Inside compound," he said. "Third left, down hallway, one right. You find aloe jars."

She gave me a victorious look before stepping carefully over the ice toward the collapsed tunnel. Most of the water near the lavafall had melted, and the ice sheet groaned and creaked, but the kadiphs inside still didn't move.

Geth took a seat beside me. He wore that persistently pissed-off look of someone in constant pain. We sat in silence for over a minute until he said, "I'm sorry about Torlo."

The name needled at my gut. There was no dark figure under the ice where the Father might have frozen to death—it had disappeared, likely having burrowed through the ground to escape the freeze. Wherever it was, it wasn't a threat to anyone anymore. Torlo had changed it somehow. Changed it into something like him?

"He was too good a person to stick around a place like this anyway," I said.

Geth nodded somberly. He took what I said as a gentle way of talking about Torlo's death, but I wasn't sure if I believed it.

Whatever Torlo was now, I didn't think "dead" was the right way to describe it.

"He cared about you," Geth said. "I saw the way he snuck looks at you. Shirallah used to do the same to me, but he was so damn slow that—"

"Stop," I said, and shut my eyes. Keeping my eyes closed should've made it easier not to cry, but the tears kept dripping down my cheeks. There was always an angle. Torlo's angle was that he had been my friend.

The elementals started collecting the dead, depositing them by the ridge in a neat line, arms crossed over their chests. Sara climbed out of the tunnel with a pack over her shoulder. She brought it to us and set about unscrewing the cap of the aloe jar and pulling out a roll of bandages. My arm was pale and shiny, and the pain worsened just by looking at it. I suppressed a groan and shut my eyes. Sara applied the aloe using the lightest touch of her fingers. "Eat this," she said, and handed me a fistful of coal-covered root. It was surprisingly sweet, and I tried to focus on chewing while she applied the gel. "Where's Aronidus?" she asked.

"Last I saw him he was next to the Father," Geth said. "He's probably with the rest of the kadiph."

I didn't feel bad about Aronidus dying, but I didn't feel nothing either. It seemed… unfortunate. Maybe it was because I now knew that he'd suffered in a lot of the same ways Jakar had. "Where's Jakar?"

"Gone," a woman said in a Sulian accent. She limped out of the exit tunnel covered in dust. She was the one who had dived into the hole Jakar had fallen through with one of the kadiphs, the hole which was now buried under the ice.

Sara froze, her hands paused halfway into rewrapping my arm. "Gone?"

"He fell. In the lava. Below." The woman's eyes were glassy, and her gaze roamed the bodies of her friends. Her attention fell on me when I laughed.

"Right," I said. "He's *made* of lava. He's fine."

"Laugh again."

"Laugh again?"

"Yes. See what I will do."

Nobody said anything. I was too tired, in too much pain, wondering if what she'd said really was true. Was Jakar dead? Sara kept her attention on my burns, and tears collected in the corners of her eyes.

"You're not allowed to do that," I said.

"What?" she said, sniffling.

"Just. Don't."

It wasn't fair. Why did I have to lose people like Jakar and Torlo when people like Sara were allowed to live? People like me?

"I know I screwed up in a lot of ways, but please let me have this," Sara said in a low voice. "I spent months thinking I was going to die. That maybe I'd have one more chance to tell you and Jakar I was sorry before the end. That was all I wanted."

"Well, it isn't the end anymore, so lucky you." My voice turned frantic. "And I'm sorry *you* didn't get what you wanted before Jakar died."

"You are Sara Adriann?" the elemental asked, and Sara nodded. "Jakar told me about you."

Sara grimaced, refusing to meet the woman's eye.

I had wondered if the new Sara was either a phase or a ruse to get me to like her again, but Aronidus had drained something from her, the same way she and our father had drained something from Jakar. The world was far from kind, but at least it could be just.

There was a rumble in the ice, followed by a deep crack. The ice vibrated, then it rumbled again. The survivors, on guard, moved toward the source of the noise, and an arm broke through the ice. It pulled out the body it was attached to. White hair and eyes of fury appeared.

The primordia pulled himself to his feet and proceeded to wipe at the slurry of ice coating his body. He saw us and stalked toward the ridge, then jumped and landed ten feet away, the ground vibrating.

"He is gone," he said to me. "Your companion lied to me, said I would be able to speak with the Father."

"We didn't know what Torlo was going to do," I said. "Take it up with him."

"You knew this would happen. I can see the lie in your eyes."

"Well, it's not too late. You can still go after the Father, wherever that thing went."

Aronidus studied me with a grim expression, and Sara moved to stand between us in some pathetic gesture to protect me. I almost laughed. The primordia didn't even notice her, just continued to stare at me. A hint of amusement crossed his face.

The elemental who Jakar seemed to know so well moved to stand beside Sara. Aronidus continued to tower over everyone, someone who I believed could kill me no matter how many elementals stood in his way, but he did nothing. "I *will* find the Father," he said. "And perhaps we will meet again someday, young one." He left the group and headed into the tunnel, the ice groaning from his footsteps.

We watched the dark spot that Aronidus had disappeared inside until Geth asked, "Think he'll find what he's looking for?"

"Let's hope so," Sara said. "He's waited eight hundred years to break his binding to the Sovereign. If he can end his flesh binding, he'll be the first to take the Sovereign down."

"So the Sovereign's been around since way before he founded Mira?" I asked. "What was he doing?"

Sara continued to tie the wrap around my arm, then said to Jakar's friend, "Can you start applying some aloe to the cartographer?"

The elemental pursed her lips, but nodded and moved to kneel next to Geth. "I'm Quin," she said to me. "You must be Efadora."

"I am."

"Jakar's sister."

I didn't have the energy to correct her. I blinked back another tear and settled on watching Sara finish my wrapping.

Chapter 53—Ester

IT TOOK THREE passings to reach Ven Ghulzekch. The Sihraan ruins were remote, serving as a rendezvous point for those fighting the budding guerrilla war, and Ester noticed it was light on the ruins and heavy on the remote. They were deep under Saracosta, where the air was humid and warm and where almost no vegetation grew. A handful of ancient stone buildings lay scattered around a squat cavern along the edge of some cliffs, and past the cliffs just beyond town an abyss loomed, the source of the warm air, which seemed to pulse from the abyss like the breath of a leviathan. Breach had told Ester this place had once served as an outpost to guard against threats that were supposed to come *up* from the chasm. There was no record of it having been attacked, though it made Ester wonder what had made the Sihraans want to build the outpost in the first place.

"There're fewer than I was expecting," Breach said, and coughed into his elbow.

"Maybe some of them aren't back yet," Damek said.

Ester sat up in the cart she'd been resting on. People moved about the ruins tending to their fires and coming in and out of their tents, and many of them were wrapped in crusty bandages or wore splints on their arms or legs. At least she would be at home with the wounded. At a glance, Ester would've guessed about a thousand were in the cavern. At least a fifth of them were hurt in some way.

Breach's mount came to a stop next to a hitching post where ruin folk were clipping the nails of some lizard-like beasts that looked like pack animals. Ester scooted to the edge of the cart and tried to stand, but fell back on her butt. She was still groggy from all the benthic willow she'd been taking. Significantly less groggy than that first passing after the Star Mines, though. It would take weeks for her body to heal—a fact she'd been all right with at first, since the idea of walking around and facing what had happened didn't sound too appealing. But she felt different now. There was work to be done. Breach rushed to her side and helped her up, and the three of them headed to the outpost's biggest building, which was pressed against a half-collapsed watch tower.

Inside, Miyaz was having a heated discussion with the other leaders. He was at the bottom of the authoritative ladder—he'd been left behind at Mulec'Yrathrik with Breach and the others for a reason—but that fact didn't seem to steal any of his thunder. He spoke hard and fast, but he quieted when he noticed the three of them.

"You find what look for?" he asked.

"We did," Ester said. "We killed about a thousand of the Sovereign's best men while we were at it, too."

She regaled them with the events of the last week, sticking to the paraphrased version of what had happened at Stonegate. It hurt to breathe, which meant it hurt to talk, but she had to be the one to tell them what had happened at the Star Mines.

"Appreciate what you've done," one of them said when she finished. "We thought the loyalists would be caught unawares while the Sovereign was gone from Saracosta, but they were quick to respond to our attacks. We did some damage, but it came at a cost."

"There's a reason they say no plan survives contact with the enemy," Breach said.

"Don't have resources to keep this up," one of the leaders said. "Can't even call this a war yet. It'll take time, time we don't have."

"Maybe if you had help from one of the territories, that wouldn't be the case," a voice said.

A woman who had been standing in the corner the whole time, but whom Ester had only just noticed, joined the group. None of the others had noticed her, either. "Who you?" Miyaz asked.

"I'm relaying a message," she said. The woman had streaks of crimson through her black hair and wore the leathers of a climber, not a fighter. "A certain magnate in Manasus has kept her ear to the wall of some of the goings-on among the ruin folk. She's keen to know your plans to make the Sovereign's life harder. She may even be inclined to throw her hat into the ring."

"I recognize you," Ester said. "You left Augustin with Jakar and the Augustin princep. Carina, right?"

Instead of answering, she let out a sharp three-toned whistle, and another woman came to join them, standing next to Carina, looking fierce with the two-handed sword strapped to her back.

"You are no ruin folk," Miyaz said. "You do not belong here."

Ester stepped forward before Miyaz's suspicion could manifest into anything dangerous. "Carina said she's here on behalf of the Manasus magnate. She's not going to map out your secret hiding spot. I can vouch for her, and for her friend, Meike."

Meike frowned at me until recognition glimmered in her eyes. "You should believe Carina," she said. "She's here to help." She set a protective hand on Carina's shoulder, and the cartographer smirked at her partner, nestling a little closer.

Meike's commoner accent seemed to allay a few nerves. Hands dropped from hilts and Miyaz asked, "What Magnate Bardera propose, then?"

* * *

ESTER MOVED THROUGH the clusters of ruin folk, studying them as they went about their tasks. She saw the way they used labor to distract themselves—the same way her brothers and sisters had used Augustin's reconstruction to forget the horrors of the city burning. These people were in over their heads. Magnate Bardera's pledge to provide soldiers and rally the ruin folk living in her territory was sorely needed, but it wasn't enough.

Breach hacked phlegm into his hand. "How're you feeling?" Ester asked.

"Not better, not worse. My vision's been acting funny, though."

"When are you setting out to find a cure?" Breach had spent the trip here studying his symptoms, concluding that his affliction was radiation sickness.

He straightened and cracked his neck. "A journey like that would be counter-productive to what I'm trying to accomplish here."

"Consider it another research project," she said. It was meant to sound playful, but the stress in her voice ruined it.

He took in the look on her face—she couldn't hide her feelings anymore, but she didn't want to, either—and he stepped closer to take her hand. "It'd be a long and difficult chase, and it might end up being pointless, besides. It's not worth giving up what's here."

She couldn't tell if he was talking about the ruin folk or something else. "My exposure was small compared to the pilgrims," he continued. "For all I know I'll be fine. I go looking for a way to extend my life and I'll be like those softheads in Saracosta obsessed with finding the Sovereign's secrets to extending life. I'd rather keep my dignity."

Ester led him down a ragged path threading through the town while she searched for Damek. Not until they reached one of the cliffs did she find her brother kneeling in front of a pedestal of glowing crystal. The pedestal had strange, animalistic designs carved into the rock. He seemed to be praying.

He stood when he noticed them. "I'm going to find Myrilan."

"When?" she asked.

"As soon as possible."

"Wait around a couple passings and I'll go with you. I just need time to find out what the ruin folk plan to do next, now that they have Magnate Bardera's help."

"My priority isn't helping the ruin folk. It's Myrilan."

"Wherever we find Myrilan, I'm betting Bilal won't be far away. The child prince knows Myralin's our brother, and he won't be happy about what we did at the Star Mines."

"Is he coming?" he asked, motioning to Breach.

"If you'll have me," Breach said.

Damek seemed relieved to have Breach along, and Ester realized she now had no hope of convincing Breach to find a cure. She wasn't sure how she felt about that.

As Ester led the two of them back to camp, she contemplated what Myrilan had said to Damek in Stonegate. *I can make you whole again*, Myrilan had promised their brother. They were slimy words, and Ester wasn't sure what they'd meant. She could have asked Damek about it, but considering what had happened to her brothers and sisters in Augustin, she wasn't sure she wanted to know.

Excitement nudged her forward until she was feeling impatient. A few passings was a long time to wait to bring the fight to Bilal again, her injuries be damned. She'd learned a lot about herself since departing Augustin in search of the missing rhidium, such as no longer having qualms about fighting as a member of the Foundry.

But it was more than that. She'd developed a taste for fighting. She liked the idea of beating the Sovereign's best and brightest— it made her feel powerful to beat someone who wanted her dead. But most importantly, it was necessary. The Sovereign and his son Bilal were responsible for a dozen genocides spread across the centuries of the Sovereign's rule, and she knew they would continue unless those two were stopped.

Bilal would be the first to die. Her knuckles popped as she pictured the boy's tiny face stretched in laughter.

Chapter 54—Jakar

JAKAR, A VOICE said. It took a second to realize it hadn't come from the bubbling kiss of fire that cocooned me. It was deeper than that.

I'd been floating in a ball of overwhelming light for who knows how long, the bright magma pressing against my eyelids as I kept it at bay as best I could. Staving off the heat from the elements I was bound to was no problem, but that still left a whole lot of heat from the unbound elements trying to cook me alive. I was miserably warm, dehydrated, and once the wells in my arms finished filling up with the heat I could siphon, the overflowing energy would rip me apart.

The magma was wreaking havoc on the elemental field, rendering my power useless and making it impossible to find the surface. I couldn't even get a proper sense of direction. I was stuck here, floating in a sea of fire, waiting to die.

Jakar, the voice repeated.

"Yes?" I asked, but the chaos drowned me out.

It is your fault.

"What is?" Perhaps hallucinations were part of the dying process.

The door is open. And now they drift.

I tried to locate the source of the voice. It shook me to my bones, cocooning me more thoroughly than the magma, as deep as Father's. "You helped me earlier, didn't you?" I asked. "When Efadora called out my name. You helped me stop myself from killing Torlo, like Father wanted." Overpowering Father's voice should have been impossible, but in that moment, I'd found the strength. "Who are you?" I asked.

Fheldspra.

"*Where* are you?"

We are the same.

It had to be my arms. Ra'Thuzan's blood. The absurdity of it all—that I was floating inside a magma chamber slowly cooking me alive, talking to a god I'd somehow infused with—almost made me laugh. I must have come into contact with Fheldspra when I'd connected with the Crescent Pyres.

"You're in my arms," I said. "Can you stop them from poisoning me?"

Altan is your key. To return your flesh.

"Who's Altan?"

Stop them. Now they drift.

There was a change in pressure and light. I cracked an eye open and found dark rock in the distance—the ceiling. Somehow, I'd floated to the surface. A platform appeared before my eyes, growing on the surface of the magma, an island of rock in a sea of fire. I climbed onto it and collapsed. Fhelfire, I was thirsty and my head pounded.

After a few minutes, I realized my little raft was all the help Fheldspra was going to give me, and that my thirst wasn't going to improve, either. I moved to my feet, wavering, but found myself no worse for wear beyond my entire body looking slightly red. My arms were dark, though, almost black, no longer pulsing with heat and fire despite all the energy I'd absorbed to protect myself.

"You took my wells away, didn't you?" I asked.

Silence.

The cliff the kadiphs and I had fallen off loomed a few dozen feet above my head, and a pillar of ice dripped from the ceiling above it. There was no sign of Quin. The ridge was close enough that I could get there the old-fashioned way—I used the heat of the magma to catapult myself up, flying through the shimmering heat until I landed on the steeply sloped rock. At the top of the slope where it met the wall, there was a dark hole where Quin must have dug herself out.

I climbed through the tunnel and reached one of the corridors in the abandoned parts of the enclave. Finding my way to the primary cavern only took a couple minutes. There, I found a sheet of ice thick enough to almost reach the ridge I stood on, its surface wavy and rippling. The surface was frosty, but under it I could see bodies. The kadiphs, frozen. Dead.

The ice groaned and gurgled from the heat of the lavafall, the only sound in the cavern. Where was everyone? Dirty and bloody footsteps littered the ice, and that's when I noticed all the tracks leading back the way I'd come. The elementals must have fled. Did that mean they'd killed all of the kadiphs?

A figure crawled out of the narrow gap where the tunnel beside the lavafall hadn't filled with ice, its massive body struggling to fit through the hole. Aronidus climbed to his feet and stared at me. It was clear he had no interest in finding the others. He nodded and I nodded back, then I headed for the exit tunnel.

I followed the scuffs in the dirt until I heard voices in the distance. They were chanting, low and calm. I found a chamber with a group of people in a circle, surrounding a pile of bodies wrapped in white cloth awash with flames. The smoke rose and danced over the glowing teal crystals crusting the ceiling. Some of them noticed me, but none of them moved to interrupt the death rites. I wasn't sure which death rites they were, or if they were rites at all. Perhaps just friends burning their dead.

"Jakar!" a voice said in a restrained shout that echoed through the room. Then Efadora was running at me, plowing into me, wrapping her arms around my body. I lifted my arms up, keeping them away. They were still coal black, but no heat seemed to come off them.

Quin came in Efadora's wake, struggling to restrain herself from stealing Efadora's moment. When Efadora pulled back, she was there to replace her. "I should've looked for you," she whispered in my ear. "I'm sorry."

"Don't feel bad. You wouldn't have found me."

She stepped away and touched a finger to my rocky forearm, then wrapped her hand around it, putting her other hand into mine. The rock was as cool as the rest of my body. "I'm too used to losing people," she said, and examined my arms. "This is strange." She smiled, and a tear fell from her eye.

"I can't remember the last time I felt anything *but* strange," I said, then realized that wasn't true when I met Efadora's eyes. Things were normal when I was with her. Things felt like home. Past them, Sara stood next to a pillar watching us—she averted her eyes, and it was hard to see her expression within the shadow of the pillar.

"Hello," I called out. It was probably the worst and the most appropriate thing to sum up how I felt. Sometimes there were no words to match your feelings.

The greeting seemed to give her the courage to join us. "I didn't think I'd see you again."

I shrugged. Things became awkward fast.

"Sara's got the goods on Aronidus and the Sovereign," Efadora said quickly. We shared a look, and I hoped she saw my thanks in there. "She got loads of information from Aronidus—the primordia was a lonely guy, apparently, and shared all sorts with her—but you can decide if you trust it."

"Let's hear it, then," I said.

"ALTAN IS THE Sovereign's true name," Sara said after I told them about my encounter with Fheldspra.

We were sitting in a mausoleum by the looks of it. Crypts with carvings of ancient beasts and monsters, containing elementals of old and the kadiphs who had passed. It seemed this was the only time an elemental had been treated with respect among the Ebonrock.

"That's what Aronidus told you?" I asked. Geth had asked what I would do now that the Ebonrock was defeated, and I'd said I hoped to find the man who could turn me fully back to flesh.

She nodded. "He also said the Sovereign's going to die soon, so you'd better find him fast."

"He's not immortal?" Efadora said.

"He figured out how to extend his life by using his powers on his own body. It doesn't work indefinitely, though. At least that's how Aronidus made it sound. He wasn't allowed to talk about it directly. If the Sovereign got sick, he would operate on himself, and the repeated trauma changed his personality over time. But the body's complex and you can't fix everything, and he became less and less of his original self. That's why he made Bilal as a replacement. A perfect replica."

"...made him?"

"That's how he phrased it. Funny thing is, Aronidus referred to the Sovereign the same way too, that he was made instead of born."

Before, I would've laughed at the idea of a person being made, but that was before I'd visited the nursery. I would never forget the way that place had pulled me apart and put me back together.

"Bilal's as rotten as they come," Sara continued. "Aronidus says the Sovereign screwed up, somehow, when he 'worked' on his son. Could be that he's so old or has gotten so screwed up himself, but Bilal doesn't think like a human. When Aronidus saw Bilal last, he had plans to end the Foundry."

"The Sovereign's always respected the Foundry," I said.

"Bilal has his own ideas for how he wants to run Mira. He's going to kill a lot of people, Aronidus made it sound like. Bilal and the Sovereign are the strongest elementals you'll ever meet, Jakar. They can move flesh the way that Father thing could."

The minerals in my arms would bleed into the rest of my body and kill me eventually, and the Sovereign was the only one who could put my body back to normal. As normal as I wanted it, at least. My flesh bindings were gone, and it would stay that way.

"Then I'm going back to Mira," I said. "I'll stop them." I touched a hand to Quin's arm and squeezed it gently. "Do you want to come?"

She took her time answering. "Krisenth is dead," she said in Sulian. "The Rha'Ghalor are destroyed. Where else would I go but with you?"

The way she said it undercut the joy I felt knowing she'd come along. There was something bothering her, but this wasn't the place to ask. "Good. We might have a chance with two elementals."

"Can I go?" Sara asked.

"Why should I let you?"

"Because you'll need me. And I have nowhere else to go."

I wanted to tell her to jump into a pit, but instead, I blurted out the word "Fine" before I gave myself much time to think about it. She perked up, the start of a smile appearing until something stopped her. I hated that small part of me that wanted her to come, how it saw a hundred small ways in which Sara had changed, causing me to wonder. But I'd have to see it to believe it.

"Ravada's on the way back," Efadora said. "I want to see if Shirallah and the serfs are still safe in the Sihraan ruins, but I don't know what my plan is after that."

"You're not coming home?" I asked.

She gave a single, emphatic shake of the head. "Mira's not my home anymore. There's nothing left for me there except for you, and that's not enough of a reason to go. I'm sorry. But I'm ready to become a cartographer."

I didn't argue. We had from here to Xeriv for me to change her mind.

I watched the other elementals as they continued their death rites. "What about them?" I asked.

Into the Rift

"We'll bring them along," she said. "Let them decide when they want to leave. They'll need direction and help until that point comes."

So it was settled. Despite the danger, I was eager to meet the Sovereign, to stop the man who had enslaved Aronidus and the other primordia. He had saved them from life in the Black Depths, but he was no different from Father and the rest of the Ebonrock. As far as I knew, there was no one else in the world but him still using flesh magic. I would make him change me back to normal, and then I would destroy him by tearing him down to his base elements.

Epilogue

"WRONG, WRONG, WRONG, wrong!" the Sovereign hissed, his fingers plunging into the back of Bilal's skull. Lilianthe watched from a chair, staring at the boy with her usual derision, wondering if the Sovereign would only make things worse again, which seemed to be the trend lately. Bilal's eyes had rolled back until the whites were showing and his muscles twitched and trembled. The Sovereign continued to tweak and pinch at the things that made the boy tick.

"You know, you could just throw him out and start over," she said.

"Replication takes years," the Sovereign said with the corner of his mouth as he concentrated, squinting and pushing. "But I'm sure you wouldn't mind if I passed on with my work unfinished."

In truth, Lilianthe was worried about what would happen if Mira was allowed to continue suffering Bilal, but she would never voice that opinion to the Sovereign. To do so willingly, to do anything willingly, was a gift he didn't deserve.

"It's his pineal gland that needs adjustment," the Sovereign said. "His Eye is lacking in sensitivity. He should have sensed what the pilgrims were doing."

"Maybe he did sense it and just didn't care," Lilianthe said. "He doesn't care about a lot of things, you know."

"And you didn't care enough to help him focus."

The Sovereign still didn't know what she'd done at the Star Mines—it had been her word against Bilal's—and miraculously the Sovereign had sided with her once Bilal had had his temper tantrum and almost killed all three of them.

"The smiths fought back because they found out what you did in Augustin," she said. "You didn't have to listen to Bilal. Remaking the Augustin smiths was a mistake."

"I *know* it was a mistake," the Sovereign hissed, making the sagging skin of his jowls tremble, the words so loud and sharp it made her jump. "But it's too late now."

Whatever kinship the Sovereign felt with the smiths, a kinship he had inherited from his predecessor, would die with Bilal. "Let the master smith go, then," she said. She didn't give two shits if that man Mateo died, but it would deny Bilal the fun of remaking him, and that was enough for her.

"No. We must find out where Aronidus went. Where that Augustin manservant snuck off to."

She could have said the master smith would have told them by now if he knew, but she was already bored of the conversation. Bilal could have him. The silence stretched into the minutes, and Lilianthe passed the time by watching beads of blood trail down the Sovereign's forearms. "What of the gas mines?" he asked. "Have the ruin folk been hunted down?"

"Of course," Lilianthe lied. "The reds took care of it."

"Good," Altan said. "Good. I just want things to be as they were. Peaceful."

"They will be. You'll be leaving the country in peak condition once you die and Bilal takes over."

"Yes. Two centuries of perfect rule, and to have it all fall apart at the end? It is nonsense."

"It won't fall apart. You have nothing to worry about."

The Sovereign brought his attention back to his work, the tip of his tongue poking through his lips while Bilal made animal death noises with his throat. There once was a time when the man assumed anything that came out of his primordias' mouths were lies, but he'd gone soft. Thought his servants had given up on lying. Gotten too fixated on perfecting Bilal and forgotten his paranoia, and now he would pay the ultimate price for it. Lilianthe had heard tales of flesh bound who couldn't lie to their masters—those without the resilience of a primordia's body.

Maybe lying and letting Bilal inherit a ruined Mira was the worst thing she could be doing, but it felt so *good* to manipulate Altan. If people had to die so she could get this last chance at retribution, so be it.

"I have a bad feeling," the Sovereign said, and rose from his chair to wipe his hands on the cloth draped over it. "My hands-on approach was what made Mira. Maybe withering away peacefully isn't the way to go about this. I should go out in a blaze of glory and all that." He moved to the counter and poured himself a glass of ghost wine. His hand shook as he brought the drink to his lips, leaving fingerprints of Bilal's blood on the glass, and for a moment Lilianthe couldn't believe how old the man looked, despite being a quarter her junior. Maybe that's what the invisible parts of her really looked like—decrepit, decayed, half mad.

"I shouldn't be listening to you," he continued. "I shouldn't be listening to anyone. I used to listen, back when I had brothers and sisters, and breaking free from them was what made me a god."

What made Narcael a god, you mean, Lilianthe thought.

"I should be taking a more forceful approach," he said. "The ruin folk have done too much damage to Mira, and now the commoners grow discontent. They expect me to make food appear out of thin air, to find new gas veins and hardwood where there is none? To be in a dozen places at once and stop all these raids on our trade caravans? The commoners are to blame as much as the ruin folk are. They should know to appreciate what I have built for them over the years. If not for me, the merchant kings of old would have destroyed this land and its people long ago." He downed the rest of his wine. "This is all too much. We need to act quickly before the damage becomes irreversible. The commoners of Mira must learn to behave like the nobility. It is time for them to be remade. All of them."

Acknowledgments

To DAD, GRANDMA, and all the incredible people who have showed support for *Flames of Mira*, *Into the Rift*, and beyond. Knowing I have people out there who are there for me unconditionally makes this lonely journey not so lonely after all.

To Joshua Bilmes and JABberwocky. Joshua, you're someone I can always fall back to for support and someone I can always rely on for an honest word or a cookie recommendation. To Amanda Rutter for all the attention you gave to me and my work—I was nervous at the prospect of a new editor, but you exceeded my expectations and then some. Your feedback is excellent and you're an excellent human being to boot. To Larry Rostant and Gemma Sheldrake, respectively, for the incredible cover and bad ass map, and to everyone else at Rebellion who had a hand in this book's manifestation into a real, live thing that can now sit on a bookshelf.

To my friends at Write or Die. These days it's difficult to find an online community where you can just be yourself, and I count myself lucky that I found one with so many genuine and hilarious people. To Tahle for the great feedback and support. To Tony, of course, for being so cool as both a friend and a reader. And to Andrew Watson, who I met through his unbridled enthusiasm for *Flames of Mira*. It still blows my mind that a stranger (at the time) could get that excited about something I wrote. I owe you a beer. Maybe 10.

As always, to Meghan. You have no idea what it means to me to know that no matter what happens, no matter how hard the writing can get, no matter how dark the journey can become, you will always be there to shine a light.

About the Author

CLAY HARMON GREW up outside Yosemite National Park, where he was a long-distance runner and helped lead his high school's military program. While he was falling in love with writing on Star Wars fanfiction sites, he was trying (and failing) to earn his pilot's license before he turned 18. As an adult he worked at Barnes & Noble and received his degree in marketing. He now works for a tech company, and in his off-time lifts weights, loses at video games, and terrorizes his cats. He lives in Utah with his wife. Find Clay on Twitter at @ClayHarmonII or http://www.clayharmonauthor.com.

FIND US ONLINE!

www.rebellionpublishing.com

/solarisbooks   /solarisbks   /solarisbooks

SIGN UP TO OUR NEWSLETTER!

rebellionpublishing.com/newsletter

YOUR REVIEWS MATTER!

Enjoy this book? Got something to say?

Leave a review on Amazon, GoodReads or with your
favourite bookseller and let the world know!